Praise for Lexi Blake and Masters and Mercenaries...

"I can always trust Lexi Blake's Dominants to leave me breathless...and in love. If you want sensual, exciting BDSM wrapped in an awesome love story, then look for a Lexi Blake book."
~Cherise Sinclair USA Today Bestselling author

"Lexi Blake's MASTERS AND MERCENARIES series is beautifully written and deliciously hot. She's got a real way with both action and sex. I also love the way Blake writes her gorgeous Dom heroes--they make me want to do bad, bad things. Her heroines are intelligent and gutsy ladies whose taste for submission definitely does not make them dish rags. Can't wait for the next book!"
~Angela Knight, New York Times Bestselling author

"A Dom is Forever is action packed, both in the bedroom and out. Expect agents, spies, guns, killing and lots of kink as Liam goes after the mysterious Mr. Black and finds his past and his future… The action and espionage keep this story moving along quickly while the sex and kink provides a totally different type of interest. Everything is very well balanced and flows together wonderfully."
~A Night Owl "Top Pick", Terri, Night Owl Erotica

"A Dom Is Forever is everything that is good in erotic romance. The story was fast-paced and suspenseful, the characters were flawed but made me root for them every step of the way, and the hotness factor was off the charts mostly due to a bad boy Dom with a penchant for dirty talk."
~Rho, The Romance Reviews

"A good read that kept me on my toes, guessing until the big reveal, and thinking survival skills should be a must for all men."
~Chris, Night Owl Reviews

"I can't get enough of the Masters and Mercenaries Series! Love and Let Die is Lexi Blake at her best! She writes erotic romantic suspense like no other, and I am always extremely excited when she has something new for us! Intense, heart pounding, and erotically fulfilling, I could not put this book down."

~ Shayna Renee, Shayna Renee's Spicy Reads

"Certain authors and series are on my auto-buy list. Lexi Blake and her Masters & Mercenaries series is at the top of that list... this book offered everything I love about a Masters & Mercenaries book – alpha men, hot sex and sweet loving... As long as Ms. Blake continues to offer such high quality books, I'll be right there, ready to read."

~ Robin, Sizzling Hot Books

"I have absolutely fallen in love with this series. Spies, espionage, and intrigue all packaged up in a hot dominant male package. All the men at McKay-Taggart are smoking hot and the women are amazingly strong sexy submissives."

~Kelley, Smut Book Junkie Book Reviews

Nobody Does It Better

Also From Lexi Blake

ROMANTIC SUSPENSE

Masters and Mercenaries
The Dom Who Loved Me
The Men With The Golden Cuffs
A Dom is Forever
On Her Master's Secret Service
Sanctum: A Masters and Mercenaries Novella
Love and Let Die
Unconditional: A Masters and Mercenaries Novella
Dungeon Royale
Dungeon Games: A Masters and Mercenaries Novella
A View to a Thrill
Cherished: A Masters and Mercenaries Novella
You Only Love Twice
Luscious: Masters and Mercenaries~Topped
Adored: A Masters and Mercenaries Novella
Master No
Just One Taste: Masters and Mercenaries~Topped 2
From Sanctum with Love
Devoted: A Masters and Mercenaries Novella
Dominance Never Dies
Submission is Not Enough
Master Bits and Mercenary Bites~The Secret Recipes of Topped
Perfectly Paired: Masters and Mercenaries~Topped 3
For His Eyes Only
Arranged: A Masters and Mercenaries Novella
Love Another Day
At Your Service: Masters and Mercenaries~Topped 4
Master Bits and Mercenary Bites~Girls Night
Nobody Does It Better
Close Cover
Protected: A Masters and Mercenaries Novella
Enchanted: A Masters and Mercenaries Novella
Charmed: A Masters and Mercenaries Novella
Treasured: A Masters and Mercenaries Novella, Coming June 29, 2021

Smoke and Sin
At the Pleasure of the President

URBAN FANTASY

Thieves
Steal the Light
Steal the Day
Steal the Moon
Steal the Sun
Steal the Night
Ripper
Addict
Sleeper
Outcast
Stealing Summer

LEXI BLAKE WRITING AS SOPHIE OAK

Texas Sirens
Small Town Siren
Siren in the City
Siren Enslaved
Siren Beloved
Siren in Waiting
Siren in Bloom
Siren Unleashed
Siren Reborn

Nights in Bliss, Colorado
Three to Ride
Two to Love
One to Keep
Lost in Bliss
Found in Bliss
Pure Bliss
Chasing Bliss
Once Upon a Time in Bliss
Back in Bliss
Sirens in Bliss
Happily Ever After in Bliss
Far From Bliss, Coming 2021

Nobody Does It Better

Masters and Mercenaries, Book 15

Lexi Blake

Nobody Does It Better
Masters and Mercenaries, Book 15

Published by DLZ Entertainment LLC

Copyright 2018 DLZ Entertainment LLC
Edited by Chloe Vale
ISBN: 978-1-937608-67-5

McKay-Taggart logo design by Charity Hendry

Acknowledgments

It's hard to believe this is the fifteenth main storyline Masters and Mercenaries book. It's also the final book of this particular version of the team. Don't worry. They'll be back. First as a spinoff, and then we'll time jump and see where they are years down the road, but this still feels a little like good-bye. The world is changing, but I'm excited about what's ahead.

So this is a great time to say thank you to some people who have been with me over the years. To my husband who lives and breathes Ian Taggart. You make it easy to write his dialogue. I just wait for you to open your mouth. To my sister from another mister, Kim Guidroz, who was there when I first thought "hey, let's do a sexy James Bond thriller where old JB falls in love for reals." To Shayla Black, without whom the team would look very different. To Liz Berry, champion of authors and never-ending cheerleader. To my kids, who deal every day with the fact that mommy's writing and figure out how to get their own lunch. (But dinner's always on me, kiddos.) Thanks to my team—Danielle at Inkslinger, Jillian Stein, Stormy Pate, Riane Holt, Margarita Coale, and my agent, Kevan Lyon. Special thanks to Kori Smith and Sara Buell who spent days exploring the wilds of Malibu with me.

And thanks to Larissa Ione, Carly Phillips, and J Kenner for creating such amazing bodyguards and letting them hire on at McKay-Taggart! I hope I did Declan, Shane, and Riley justice, my friends.

But this book is dedicated to my mother and father, who taught me to love and to hold on to that love even when it feels like all is lost…

Sign up for Lexi Blake's newsletter
and be entered to win a $25 gift certificate
to the bookseller of your choice.

Join us for news, fun, and exclusive content
including free short stories.

There's a new contest every month!

Go to www.LexiBlake.net to subscribe.

Prologue

Phuket, Thailand

Kayla Summers walked into the gorgeous lobby and tried not to think about how badly her hands were shaking. To her right she could hear the sound of the ocean, most times a deep comfort to her, but today not even that rolling, endless symphony could soothe her.

Of course it wasn't every day she did spy stuff. She'd trained for this day, long hard hours that would leave her wondering why the hell she'd signed up for this gig when she could be playing beer pong and rushing a sorority.

"Hey, it's all right," the man with the slow Southern accent said under his breath. He walked beside her, had been beside her from the moment she'd left DC. "This is nothing at all, Kay. We're walking into the hotel, picking up your sister, and then you'll walk one way with Mr. Bishop and I'll walk the other with Kun. We'll meet up at the extraction point and you'll both be back in the States by this time tomorrow."

"Are you going to arrest her?" She'd been wondering about that, wondering if this whole save-the-twin-I-didn't-know-I-had plan was truly about sending her long-lost sister to Guantanamo Bay. Though with some of the stories she'd heard about MSS, China's version of the CIA, being tortured in Cuba might be a fun vacay for her sis.

Sister. She had a sister. Jiang Kun.

Thank god her fathers had insisted she know something of the culture she'd been born into. One of her dad's taught Mandarin at UC Santa Barbara and she'd grown up speaking it around the house. His Cantonese was excellent as well. Despite the fact that there was not a drop of DNA between them, they always joked that she'd gotten Dad's ear for languages.

If only her sister had been as fortunate.

Tennessee Smith stopped in the middle of the elegant hotel lobby, his long, lean frame looking down on her. "I told you. Once your sister is in the States, she'll be debriefed. That debrief will likely last a good long time, but she's going to be treated as an asset, not an enemy. Jiang Kun was accepted into a program to train MSS operatives when she was sixteen years old. And by accepted, I mean she was selected by the government and there was no way to say no. You know that training you've done over the last few months? That was a tiny taste of what your sister has been through the last several years. And I assure you, the CIA is kinder with our agents than MSS."

After she'd been contacted by the Agency, she'd spent three months in a program meant to give her basic training. What she really thought they'd wanted to do was maintain control over all communications with her sister.

Still, it had been a rough couple of months. Physical training. Firearms training. Learning the ins and outs of procedure, and all for one operation. This one.

The funny thing was, while it had been rough, she'd kind of liked it. She'd liked having purpose. Despite the fact the she was flying through her undergraduate degree at Stanford, she often felt aimless. The last few months had been a revelation. Something had come over her. A sense of true purpose.

What the hell was she going to do when this was over? She'd gotten used to being around Ten and even the super-cold dude. John Bishop. She'd made him smile once. All the other recruits in her class had gotten together and made her a trophy for that because the guy wasn't known for his humor.

Still, he'd taken an interest in her and she would oddly miss him.

"I'm just worried about her." And worried that once Kun was in the US, she wouldn't need Kayla anymore.

Would they even have a relationship? Or would her sister disappear into the Agency while the Agency said "thanks and see ya later" to Kayla?

She thought briefly about the mother who'd given birth to her. How hard had it been? She'd known she was having twins, known given China's one child policy at the time that one of them would be taken or aborted. Everything she'd done had been in secrecy and she'd managed to have Kayla smuggled out of the country. By some grace, she'd wound up in an orphanage that dealt with foreign adoptions, and by the time she was six months old, she was the darling daughter of Fred Summers and Jim Gayle.

According to her sister, their mother had passed away a few months after Kun had gone into training.

Ten put a hand on her shoulder. "Don't be worried about her. She's made a great decision and she's going to be rewarded for it. And honestly, if you want to stay in training to be close to her, I'll approve it."

"Seriously?" She wasn't going to say it, but she'd been upset at the thought of not going back to those classes.

His lips quirked up. "Seriously. I actually think you would make an excellent agent, and Bishop agrees. I think he's got it in his mind that having a set of twin operatives could be interesting. If you choose to stay, you'll work under Bishop, though I'll be around. I've got a new guy I'm handling. Bishop found him but thought I would be better dealing with him. Now I know why. The guy's phenomenal. I've never seen anyone with his skills. Or his damn mouth. If I don't kill Ian Taggart, he'll be a hell of an operative. He's already tangled with your sister once. It should be interesting to see them work together."

She could be working with her sister, too. Working for the Agency. Working for the good of her country. Yeah, that might be cool. "I would love to stay on."

His shoulders straightened. "Then let's get your sister and get this party started."

She walked taller, barely glancing over at the ocean she could see through the open lobby.

Up ahead she saw something she couldn't ignore. John Bishop peeled away from the shadows. While most people felt fairly comfortable with Tennessee Smith, John Bishop was a different proposition. He was cold, calculating. Ten might be as well, but he hid it under that lazy, aw-shucks gorgeous exterior of his. There was a reason they called John Bishop the Ice Man.

Everyone in her class thought she was insane when she told them she could see another man under his chilly exterior. If he ever found the right woman, she knew he would warm up.

Roughly six feet tall, Bishop was blandly handsome, the type of handsome that was hard to describe, and she was certain that worked for him. When she wasn't studying him, her eyes sort of glanced off him like they would almost any person simply walking along the street.

But when she caught his eyes, she saw something stark and eerie there. Bishop was a man who had seen far too much and might never come back from it. He would stand in the shadows because they were his home until the right woman reached her hand out and pulled him into the sun.

She might have been reading too many romance novels.

"Have you talked to our girl?" Bishop asked. He glanced Kayla's way and gave her a nod.

Ten's head shook in the negative. "Not since last night when she checked in. The meetup is through here. This handoff is going down in one of the bungalows. It's off the main property so we should be away from prying eyes. She said she checked it for bugs and it was clean."

"Won't MSS be looking for her?" Kayla asked. This was happening. Her first op.

Bishop turned and frowned her way. "I need you to keep your voice down."

"I'm sorry. We're alone." It wasn't like she hadn't looked around.

"Lesson number one, Kay. We're never alone," Bishop replied. "Never."

"Even if they look for her, she's exactly where she's supposed to be," Ten said quietly as they moved to the path. All around her was lush beauty, but she couldn't seem to enjoy any of it. "She's meeting an informant here at midnight tonight. She's alone and not expected to report back to base for a few days. She'll be halfway to the States by then."

This was their shot. They wouldn't get another one. It could be years before her sister had this much freedom again.

Bishop stopped in the middle of the path, putting his hand to his ear. Though she couldn't see it, she knew Bishop and Ten would both be wearing small devices that would allow them to communicate with base. His jaw went tight, his eyes closing briefly. She felt Ten tense, too.

"Understood," Bishop said, his eyes opening, showing grim reserve there. "According to my contact here in Southeast Asia, we might have some trouble. She picked up a Korean operative who's been on Jiang Kun for years. He flew in on a fake passport, which is why it took her so long to figure it out."

"But the Koreans are our allies." She wasn't sure why they would want to break up an American operation.

Bishop was already moving, shrinking back into those shadows he loved so well, but not before she saw a hint of metal in his hand. He disappeared into the trees that lined the path.

Ten held her there. "The Koreans know nothing about what we're doing. In our business an ally isn't the same as a friend. They're simply people we don't shoot on sight. Not many people inside the Agency know about this operation. It's classified at the highest level. I assure you the Koreans don't. If they think this is a chance to take down a notorious MSS agent, they'll jump on it. Stay behind me."

He started down the path again, but her heart was pounding hard in her chest. She glanced around, expecting at any moment to have someone leap out at her. It was like the entire gorgeous beach setting had turned into one of those haunted houses she'd gone to as a child.

And yet she forced herself to stay behind Ten Smith. She wanted to run, to find a place to hide, but she wasn't going to do that. Her sister was out there. Her sister needed her to remain calm.

It was odd how steady she became, that veil of awareness slipping over her. It was as though the world around her had become more vibrant and clear while it slowed down, allowing her to assess.

To her left she saw a group of tourists. No threat.

A couple holding hands walked by. No threat.

Single man wearing a bathrobe. Her sense heightened as he reached inside but she saw the top of a pack of cigarettes.

No threat.

"Kay, that's the bungalow. Are you sure you want to go inside?" Ten asked.

And that was how she knew something had gone very wrong. She didn't have a small communications device in her ear. She couldn't hear what the woman on the other end of the line was saying, their handler. She couldn't hear what Bishop was saying. Yet there was no need for the words because it was there in Smith's body language. Something had gone wrong.

"I want to continue."

He took her hand and led her inside.

The coppery smell of blood assaulted her as she walked into complete chaos. Furniture had been turned over, vases smashed against the tile, and glass marking the place where someone had smashed in through the big bay window. What should be serene and perfect had been marred with blood and destruction.

So much blood.

"Phoebe, I'm going to need you to pull all the security footage from around the grounds," Ten was saying, his hand on his ear.

John Bishop stepped out of the bedroom. There was blood on his hands, but somehow it looked right on him. As though it belonged there. Ten's brows shot up.

Bishop shook his head. "Not me. I had nothing to do with this. They had a hell of a fight. She managed to gut him, but not before he got his shot in. She's in the bedroom. Had no idea who he was. Says he attacked her roughly ten minutes ago. She's got maybe two minutes left if you want to get something out of her."

Ten stopped, his hand going to his ear again.

"If she's got a bead on him, you go, Tennessee," Bishop ordered.

Ten's eyes went wide, not an expression she normally saw on the man's face. He was surprised. "You want me to take him down?"

Bishop's whole body tensed. "I want the option. If he gets away and reports back, I won't have that option. Take him out. That's an order."

Ten cursed under his breath, but took off out of the bungalow, his long legs eating up the distance between him and his prey.

Kayla started toward the bedroom Bishop had walked out of. What had happened to her sister? The panic was tamped down by the training she'd received. Panic solved nothing and would cost her team so much. Her team. When had she started thinking in those terms? When had she let go of the college girl she'd been and become an operative?

Bishop stood in her way. "I don't know that you should see that."

"Get out of my way," she replied, the words colder than anything she'd ever said before.

His expression didn't change at all, but he stepped aside.

Kayla entered and there was her sister. She was slumped against the bed as though she'd managed to drag herself this far, but couldn't manage another inch. Her cell phone was close, mere inches out of reach. There was a hole in her chest, the white T-shirt she wore a mangled and bloody mess.

So odd. It was surreal to look into her own face. They were dressed exactly alike, wearing black skirts and white T-shirts Smith had bought for them. Everything was the same from the ponytails they wore to the Kate Spade flip-flops on their feet.

Everything was the same except that hole in her sister's chest.

Ten minutes. If they'd been ten minutes faster, this wouldn't have happened.

"Don't," her sister said, eyes fluttering open. Her English was damn near perfect, with barely the hint of an accent. "If you'd been here, he would have changed his plans and likely found a way to kill us all."

"How?" She shook her head. It didn't matter how she'd known what she was thinking.

"I'm your twin," she said with the barest hint of a smile. "Older sister. I know everything. Damn, I wish…"

It didn't take a mind reader to know what her sister wished for. More time. More life. A few moments to get to know the family that had been denied to her.

A world where none of this was necessary and they could have been two college students talking about boys and classes and relying on each other the way sisters did.

"Hey, Kay," Kun said, the words slurring. Her eyes were clouded as though she was on some really nice drugs. Death. Apparently death looked like that, too. "Tell Smith…something bad's coming. There's something deeper moving the pieces around. Heard hints of it, but can't get close. Businesses and power players are changing the game. It's bigger than either of our governments. Hate those fuckers."

Kay reached out to put a hand on her sister's. "We'll call an ambulance."

Bishop stopped her. "I'm sorry. You can't touch her. You can't leave anything to chance if the cops get hold of her body."

There was a barely perceptible shake of her sister's head. "I'm too far gone for help. And don't worry about the cops. I suspect the Americans will clean it all up. Kayla, there's so much I need to tell you. My organization is dangerous. Dangerous to your country." Her words started to come slower and slower, fading with her life. "Dangerous to you…"

The hand dropped to her side and her sister's whole body went still.

Ten showed up at the door, a gun at his side and a chill to his eyes.

"Is it done?" Bishop asked.

"Yes. The body is in a dumpster. We need to move out," Ten said. "Kayla, it's time to go."

She found herself stuck on the floor. Was that really her sister's body? How had things gone so wrong? "Where are we going?"

Ten holstered his weapon, slipping it under the light button-down he hadn't tucked in. "I'm going to get you to the extraction point and you'll be home soon. I'll even let them debrief you on the plane so you can get on with your life. I know we talked about you continuing training, but this should change your mind. It's too dangerous. Let's get you home and you can rethink everything."

Get on with her life? What would that look like? Did they think she could go back to her business classes? That she could study fucking marketing when she knew what the rest of the world didn't? How was she supposed to sell dog food to bored housewives when her sister was dead? When the fuckers who made her life hell were still out there?

What group had her sister been talking about? Bigger than any government?

"There's another way," a silky voice said.

She'd never heard John Bishop speak this low and deep, his voice almost like rich, decadent chocolate. Then again, she'd never heard him play Mephistopheles before, either. Even in her emotional state, she knew that was the role he'd taken on.

"I think I should take her home, John." Ten's tone had gone low and insistent.

Bishop ignored him, putting a hand on her elbow and leading her out of the room. "Kayla, we have a unique opportunity to make something out of this mess. The truth is MSS has no idea your sister is dead and Ten has taken care of her assassin. It's an easy leap of logic that Jiang Kun won the battle and took care of the Korean agent. Nothing has to change in their minds."

Jiang Kun didn't have to be dead. "How would I take her place?"

Ten looked back as though he could see through the wall and into the room that held her sister's body. "You haven't had enough training. A few months isn't going to cut it."

"Kun wasn't expected back for a few days. I can teach her a lot in that time. Besides, as far as we can tell, the Chinese government has no idea she was a twin," Bishop pointed out. "Kayla speaks perfect Mandarin. Hell, we can even use this little brushup as an excuse for any issues that come up. She got knocked out during the fight. She's having some trouble with memory but she was smart enough to follow protocol. We'll clean up. She'll claim the kill, make her contact, and go back to base. She's read the file on her sister."

"That file isn't the same as real knowledge," Smith shot back. "You're going to get her killed."

They continued to argue, but Kay knew what she was going to do. Her mother had sacrificed so both her children could live. Kay was the only one left.

She couldn't sacrifice to save them, but she could avenge them. She could finish her sister's work.

It was the only gift she had to give.

* * * *

California

Joshua Hunt came awake with a start, his hand immediately going for the knife he kept under his pillow. The hilt was always the first thing he felt as he came out of that warm darkness, the first thing that made the nightmare real. When he slept, he was back in a world he understood, a world where his mom was alive, where his dad hadn't been a wretched drunk. A world where someone loved him, took care of him.

It was the real world that was Josh's nightmare.

But he couldn't find the hilt, realized he wasn't on a pillow.

"Hey, it's cool," a feminine voice said. "You're in my car. You're good, kid."

He sat straight up and blinked, the light of the early morning filtering in through the sunroof of her Range Rover. Tina. Tina McArran. She was some kind of do-gooder who'd found him in a convenience store where he was shoplifting a bottle of water and some protein bars. He'd been about to get caught when she'd told the clerk he was with her and she would pay for everything. The clerk had looked unconvinced, but he'd taken her money and let Josh go anyway.

Then Tina had offered him something he hadn't expected—a lift out of Ohio. He'd been in Ohio. For years he hadn't even known how far he'd been from home.

He'd taken it, expecting to give her something in return. It had churned his stomach, and if she'd been a man, he would have turned her down. But he could handle a woman. He could get through that.

She'd merely driven, telling him about how she was moving from New York to LA after her divorce, starting over again. When they'd stopped in Denver, she'd bought him some clothes and gotten him a room for the night, next to hers. She'd sighed as she'd passed him the key.

I hope you don't run because I think we can help each other out. I need clients and with a face like yours, I think I can build a whole industry. I'll make a deal with you. You never have to tell me how you got to be a skinny eighteen-year-old without any identification and I'll make sure everything is legal about the work I can provide for you. I'll be careful with you. I'll be your agent. I'll train you on how to deal with people professionally, teach you how to dress, get you in acting lessons, and you'll have a place to live for as long as you're willing to try to work. And, son, I'll treat you like a son. I don't know what you've been through, but you won't go through it ever again if I have anything to say about it.

He hadn't told her anything about what had happened at the time, but he'd been there in the morning, waiting by the Rover. His stomach oddly had more to say than his brain. His stomach had wanted badly to trust someone, to be full and warm and unworried about being full and warm the next day.

He blinked again as she pulled up to a house with a *For Sale* sign. It also had a metal sign that proclaimed it sold. He could smell something. Something lovely and clean. He breathed it in.

"That's the ocean," she said with a smile.

He stopped and frowned.

"Have you never been to the ocean?" She got out and he followed.

"No. I saw it on TV once." He hadn't seen much of anything, but there had been a TV in most places he'd lived. Not that he'd ever chosen the show or movie that was on. He would sometimes have to hide in order to watch. Sometimes it was turned on as a treat for behaving.

Precisely why *he* hadn't watched much.

"Come on. This will heal your soul like nothing else will." She started toward the door.

Everything was bright, colorful. It was like someone had flipped a switch and his vision had gone from shades of gray to overwhelming color. Flowers wrapped around the perfectly painted fence and vivid green grass was at his feet. Something pounded, the sound close and rhythmic.

He followed her through the door and into the cleanest house he'd ever been in.

"I bought it furnished, so we might have to make some

adjustments," she said as she walked through to what looked like the living room. "There's a loft on the third floor. I was going to turn it into a library, but who am I kidding? I don't have time to read. We're going to hit the ground running. I've got a photographer set up for two days from now. Face up only. We've gotta get some muscle on you before we take body shots. And I have a friend coming out to help with the whole identification thing. Josh?"

He heard her but couldn't make himself respond. The entire back of the house was windows. Pure glass that opened the door to something he'd never seen before.

Tina seemed to understand, and she moved to the sliding glass door that led to the balcony. "Go on. I'll make us some breakfast while you...I would say get used to the view, but I don't think you ever get used to something that beautiful."

The sound was magnified now that there was nothing between him and the ocean except a few feet.

"It's high tide right now. Later on we'll go down and walk on the beach," she continued.

He stepped out on the balcony and wondered why the world had distorted. His vision...he wiped a hand across his eyes, clearing the tears away.

The sun was just over the horizon and the sky was awash with pinks and reds and oranges, giving way to a stunning blue he'd never seen in his life. In the distance, he could see cliffs. Birds flew overhead and the ocean seemed to wash up under the house as though the whole thing was part of the great and grand water.

"Where are we?"

She stepped up but didn't walk out with him, as though she understood he needed space. "It's called Malibu. We're in California and you, my young scamp, you are going to be a star."

He didn't know about that, but as he stared out over the ocean he realized he was the one thing he'd never been before.

He was safe.

Chapter One

Somewhere over America
13 years later

Kayla Summers looked out the private jet's window at the perfect land below. They were flying over farm country and from here the world looked like an ordered place, parcels of land mapped out in squares and defined by the roads around them. From up here it all made sense.

But she knew damn well if someone dropped her in one of those seemingly perfect squares, she would be lost in the thicket.

Perception. It was all about perception and she would do well to remember that. Up here in the air she was a goddess who knew everything, saw everything. Once she hit the ground, she would be just another ant, trying desperately to not get stepped on.

Or tortured. Or any of the terrible things that could happen to a poor little ant.

"Another glass of champagne, miss?"

Kay turned to the flight attendant who'd been gone for quite a while. "Absolutely! Keep it coming. I never turn down champagne."

Ezra Fain shifted in the seat across from her. He was acting as her CIA handler for this particular mission. "Are you sure you should be drinking? We land in a couple of hours."

And he was turning out to be super prissy. She smiled at the flight attendant, who passed her another glass of some truly spectacular champagne. "You know, you are not as fun as I thought you would be."

Fain frowned. "I'm fun. I'm loads of fun."

He was not. He was super serious and had been the whole time. She'd given him some reasonable suggestions and he'd turned them all down. "You know all the subs at Sanctum used to call Tennessee Smith Master No. I'm thinking that title gets dropped on you now. That's all you've said to me this whole trip. No, we can't stop in New York and pick up a few things. No, we don't have time to visit the Rock and Roll Hall of Fame. No, you can't decorate the plane with gummy bears. No, we can't stop in Idaho and have a long talk with one of my favorite authors."

His eyes narrowed. "You were going to Misery that poor woman."

Kay shrugged because she probably was. "Zanetti needs to write faster if she doesn't want to spend some time with me. My point is you're very negative."

Fain sat back in his chair, his handsome lips curling slightly. "And you are way more of a handful than Damon mentioned. I think there's a reason he nearly cackled with glee when I asked to take you off his hands for a few months."

"Is that any way to talk about a lady, Fain?" The second of her two CIA contacts joined them. She wasn't sure where Levi Green had been for the past thirty minutes, but from the flight attendant's slightly mussed hair and flushed skin, she would bet that Green had been vetting the staff. Well, vetting her vagina at least.

Though there had been that one time in Seoul where that counteragent had managed to stuff a small pistol up there, so maybe she should thank Green for making absolutely certain the flight attendant wasn't packing.

The only thing she knew for sure was that Green appeared to be having way more fun than Fain. He sank into the chair beside hers, a glass of Scotch in his hand.

"It's good of you to finally join us." Yep. Fain sounded like an outraged Victorian spinster.

Green tipped his glass Fain's way. "You know I love a good briefing. And don't be hard on our Miss Kay. She's getting into the role. She'll be sipping champagne in Malibu in a few hours."

"If she gets the job," Fain pointed out. "You're both acting like this is a done deal and it's not. She's got to interview for the part. We're not in yet."

"Audition," Green corrected. "Get the lingo right, buddy. She's got to audition for the part, but I have every faith in her that she's going to get that callback. Chill, Ez. We've got this one. It's all cool."

Fain sat up, pointing down at the folder in front of her. "Have you read this?"

She sighed and put down her champagne. All work and no play was going to make Kayla a crabby girl. "I promise I read the file twice. I've seen every single movie Joshua Hunt has ever made, but why don't we go over it one more time? In case I missed something."

Because it was obvious there was some storm banging around Ezra's head. There was more than the Joshua Hunt operation going on here and it was up to her to figure it out. He'd been on edge for days and that wasn't like him. She'd come to rely on Fain being calm and collected. Prissy she could handle, but this anxiety she sensed in him had her worried.

Given that they would be working together for months, possibly, she needed him calm and cool.

"It's a simple op," Green said with a wave of his hand. "You could do it in your sleep."

"There's no such thing as a simple op," Fain replied. "There are nuances to this thing and about a million moving pieces. Hunt himself is a bit of a mystery."

She reached over and flipped the file open. She'd lied to Ezra. She'd gone over this file way more than twice. Joshua Hunt. America's hottest action star. His last film banked over a billion worldwide. He was roughly six foot three, with dark hair and piercing eyes, but what he was truly good at was selling a scene. She believed him when he told a woman he loved her, when he squared his shoulders before some fictional battle, when he put a hand on his heart as he was dying.

He was an excellent actor, even better than the films they put him in, but he was also known for being incredibly private and reclusive.

He was fascinating, and that should scare her on some level. She knew it. She also knew that since she'd felt nothing for so long, feeling anything at all was worth it. Joshua Hunt could be dangerous, but more than likely she would find out he was a douchebag, over-privileged prince of a man and then her job would be a chore.

Because she knew beyond a shadow of a doubt that this job would require sex.

"He doesn't like to talk about his past," she said. "I've spent the last few days going through every interview he's ever given and while he will sometimes talk about little things in his life—who he's dating, what shows he's enjoying—he never talks about the past. Not even his childhood. The one time he got up from an interview and walked out, it was because the reporter kept asking about his father. I take it we know more."

"Daddy was a nasty drunk." Green crossed his long legs, sitting back and getting comfy. "We've got at least five domestic abuse complaints over the years. Joshua Hunt, whose real name is Joshua Stemmons, was born in a small town in Kansas. His mother died of cancer when he was five, but Daddy had a parade of girlfriends he liked to use as punching bags. Senior Stemmons went to jail when Josh was twelve and Josh hit the system."

"He didn't stay long," Fain said. "At least we don't think he did. Records show that Josh's foster care family was paid for at least a year, but the police believe he ran away shortly after he arrived at the house. The parents and social worker were caught cashing checks for kids who were long gone. Josh was one of them. Whether he left on his own or they kicked him out, we have no idea. Those years are a blank. No arrests. No sign of him being in the system at all. He doesn't surface again until he shows up in Los Angeles at the age of eighteen, living with a woman named Tina McArran, who became his first agent. He books his first commercial about six months later and the rest is history."

Fain's fingers tapped along the edge of his chair. He did that when he was thinking things through. Kay liked to know everyone's tells. "As far as we know, this version of Joshua Hunt has stayed out of trouble. He's been working in the film industry for fourteen years. He kept his first agent with him until she died a few years ago. Breast cancer. She left everything she had to him. He stood by her through the end, and by all accounts genuinely cared for her. He's careful with his money. He's never been accused of drug use or sexual indiscretions. He's practically a saint in Hollywood."

"He's never been married, right?" She'd had a lot of Hollywood gossip to catch up on when she'd returned to the Western world. A decade as a double agent, pretending to be her own twin sister, had taken a toll on her pop culture knowledge.

For a second she wished she was back in London, cuddled up on the comfy couch in the media room with Tucker and Jax and Owen watching *Die Hard* and *Star Wars* and *The Godfather*. It was cool because they were experiencing them for the first time and she got to be their tour guide. They would all cuddle up under a big blanket and share a bucket of popcorn or a plate of cookies Penny had baked. Robert and the others would join them from time to time, but Tucker, Jax, and Owen were her boys. Her brothers from another mother. A mother none of the boys could remember because they'd had their minds wiped by an evil scientist, but then she kind of thought that big old mind erase was why they clicked. She'd worked with Owen when he knew who he was and he was way sweeter now.

She already missed the family she'd found in London.

But she hadn't felt a spark with any of them. Her London family were brothers and sisters, and the fact that not a one of them stirred her sexually was cause for concern.

Had that part of her been burned out? She'd been faking normal for years now. Sex was nothing but another part of the job.

"No and he's never announced an engagement, either," Fain replied, bringing her out of her thoughts. "He's dated several actresses publicly, but none for more than a year or so."

"Any idea who put out word that he was into some of the kinkier sexual practices?" She stared down at the picture they had of him. He looked killer in a designer suit that had been tailored to fit his broad, strong body. Mirrored aviators covered his eyes and there was a pretty redhead on his arm. Some other actress. He was rarely seen with the same woman more than once or twice now.

Was he as cold as he looked? Cold and pristinely beautiful, all of his emotion saved for work? Maybe they had too much in common.

"Our intel points to one of his longer-term relationships," Green replied. "Shortly after they started dating, rumors began circulating that Hunt was into D/s. He managed to get the story quashed before the real truth came out and he hasn't seen her since. Neither has a movie or TV screen. She hasn't gotten a job in years. Mr. Hunt has some serious power players backing him up. The new rumor became the actress was lying to get attention for herself."

"But she wasn't lying about Josh, was she?" Otherwise, why would they be bringing her in? If there was one thing Kay had experience in it was the art of Dominance and submission.

"Nope, he's a big old perv," Green said with a charming smile.

The man could be deadly when he wanted to be, but then she'd found there was a certain type of operative the Agency liked to hire. There were always the worker bees, the ones who kept their heads down for years and years, mining for information and never once doing anything to bring attention to themselves. They were like nondescript sedans. Nothing to look at but those suckers were on the road forever. Levi Green was a Maserati. Showy and gorgeous, he would bust down the walls others would quietly and carefully dig under.

She was always wary of the Maseratis of this world. They were stunning and powerful, and sometimes spun out of control when you least expected them to.

Fain was more like a Jeep. Sure, he was hot when he smiled, but he could also put a baseball cap on and no one would notice him. He would take the hard trail around a problem and no one would see him coming.

Gosh, Fain sometimes reminded her of Bishop. It was probably the reason she trusted him the way she did.

"From what we can tell he's a member of a club in Malibu called The Reef," Green explained. "It's super private, but not merely for the wealthy. Membership is closely guarded, but we put a man on the inside four weeks ago. Josh basically works and attends this club, that's about all he does, so this should cover all our bases. Riley Blade has connections in this world and they were happy to hire him on as the Dom in Residence. He hasn't gotten particularly close to Hunt, but then Hunt's only been in twice, and he wasn't with a submissive. He came in, watched a few scenes, and then went to the bar with another actor member, a man named Jared Johns. Our reports show they're quite close friends. Johns was his mentor and trainer when Hunt first joined The Reef."

Riley Blade worked as a bodyguard out of the Dallas McKay-Taggart offices, but Jared Johns had connections there, too. "Johns is Kai Ferguson's brother. Have you thought about bringing him in?"

Fain shook his head. "Absolutely not, and that's why we're being careful about the team. Johns isn't close to his brother, though I know they talk from time to time. Johns was responsible for Hunt being willing to talk to McKay-Taggart about his security issues. He's already hired on Shane Landon and Declan Burke, but I made sure he's never met Blade. Johns is the one who got you the intervie...er, audition, and you should expect to spend some time with him. We need to work this from several different angles."

What Fain really meant was they needed to work Hunt. "And all of this is because some drug dealer in Mexico is his biggest fan?"

Green set his Scotch down and clapped his hands together like a boy eager to play. "*El Comandante*. He runs the single nastiest cartel in Southern Mexico, and that's saying something. The rumors are he used to be in the Mexican military and runs his operation with the same precision he was taught there. He doesn't mind getting his hands dirty. In the last four years, we've attributed over a hundred bodies to what we call the Jalisco Cartel."

"The name comes from the state we know the cartel is based in, though they've now spread out and cover a lot of territory," Fain admitted. "The Commander has become a big-time player, and you know what that means."

She did. "He's got heavy ties to narcoterrorism."

It was always fun when the bad guys got together to create some chaos. And to make a shit ton of cash. "Terrorist groups are working with cartels, sometimes they are the cartel, in order to make money to fund the Jihad. Mexico is one of the biggest recruitment centers for radical Islamic terrorists. That's why the Agency is interested. You think this Commander person can lead you to bigger enemies."

"It's worse, Kay." Fain had gone positively grim. "We're fairly certain the Commander discovered one of our plants. We imbedded a long-term operative in the Jalisco organization four years ago. He's

33

steadily moved up and gotten closer to command. Ten days ago, he failed to make a routine contact. He's been radio silent since and we can't find any trace of him."

Her stomach clenched. Yeah, she knew a little bit about that. She'd been undercover for years, always terrified that any minute someone would figure out who she was and she would wish she were dead. MSS could be terrible to loyal agents. They didn't mind a bit of torture to keep the morale where they wanted it to be. She'd been interrogated more than once. She couldn't imagine what they would have done to her had they found out she wasn't who she said she was.

She would have been alone because the Agency would have denied her very existence. It would have caused an international incident. It was good to know that when it wouldn't cost them too much, they were willing to try to figure out what had happened to an agent. "So the plan is for me to make Joshua Hunt feel comfortable and safe enough that he'll agree to go into a drug lord's house for a party? Because you understand he would have to be insane to do that."

A chill went over Green's face. "Well, then you'll have to drive him a little crazy, won't you?" It was gone in an instant, replaced with another sunny smile. "Hunt doesn't know that the Mexican businessman named Hector Morales who keeps inviting him down for the weekend is a drug lord. He and Hector have met in California several times and it was all cordial. Josh is filming in and around Mexico City in a few weeks. You don't have to convince him to go. He's spending the weekend there. Hector writes big checks to Josh's charities. There's some question as to how close in business the two are. You're simply going to convince him to take you with him."

"And it hasn't occurred to you to sit Hunt down and ask him to go? Tell him what you need him to do and why," Kay offered. "I've found oftentimes men like Hunt want to do the right thing. He's played plenty of military characters. He likely thinks he could handle it. Of course, that's precisely why I would be there. Then we don't have to deal with all this subterfuge."

"You want me to entrust a high-level operation to a Hollywood actor?" Green asked. "First off, I would have to get him clearance, and that's not happening. Second, I'm still not sure our intelligence is correct and that Hunt isn't working with *El Comandante*. That's part of what I need you to figure out."

Fain held up a hand. "Kay, this is the only way this particular op gets done, and the Agency has its reasons. If you can't handle it, I need to know now."

Her first instinct was to tell him to shove his op up his own anus. She wasn't some newbie. She was a decorated field operative, and it was obvious there was more to this mission than met the eye. It would be smart to tell him no.

And then she caught a glimpse of that picture. Joshua Hunt, beautiful and remote. Untouchable, and yet here he was trying to pay someone to touch him.

"I'll get the job done," she promised.

Green held his glass up. "We know you will."

And while she was handling Joshua Hunt, she would figure out what was happening inside the Agency because there was something neither of these men were telling her.

She sat back, sipping her champagne and watching the byplay between the men. Sex and secrets.

Her job never changed.

* * * *

Beverly Hills, CA

"The producer of four of your films was recently accused of tax evasion. Do you have any comment on that, Mr. Hunt?" The brunette in front of him had her phone out. He thought he remembered her from some long ago press junket, but he couldn't quite place the name.

Joshua Hunt bit back a groan. His freaking job never changed. Smile when you don't want to. Keep a civil tongue in your head when all you truly wanted to do was tell someone to fuck off. Never scream the way he wanted to.

Yeah, his life hadn't changed at all when he thought about it. It was just the trappings were all lovely and designer.

"No, I can't comment on that. Please, we're trying to have a quiet lunch. Why don't you send any questions you have to my publicist," he said smoothly, wishing he'd done what his instincts had told him to do. He'd wanted to ask for a private table, but Jared was all about the light.

They'd walked through Spago's classically elegant bar, done in rich masculine colors, and entered the dining room, a stunning indoor conservatory bathed in natural light, and Jared had gone right for the middle of the room. He hadn't waited for the hostess to seat them, merely found his spot in the sun and gave the lady a smile no woman could possibly resist.

Well, except the one Jared actually wanted, hence Josh being indulgent when he should have known there would be some nosy reporter hanging around.

"All right, how about a couple of pictures of the two of you?" The reporter stood over them. It was obvious she'd been here with some friends, but she wasn't about to let the chance go by. "You seem close these days. Anything we should know about?"

"He's an amazing kisser," Jared said with a grin.

Josh rolled his eyes. "Don't encourage her."

He looked toward the bar and finally gave the nod to the man who'd been standing up and waiting for the signal since the moment the woman had approached. He'd hoped they could brush her off without bringing the bodyguards into it.

Shane Landon was there in a heartbeat, putting his body between Josh and the reporter. "Ma'am, I'm going to have to ask you to step away from my client."

She looked up, flustered, and frowned. "This is a public place. You know there is such a thing as freedom of the press, asshole."

"And there is such a thing as getting bounced out of a restaurant and blackballed from all the nice ones," Shane replied with a predatory smile. "This is a private business. I assure you if this comes down to a fight, he's going to win. Now please let the man eat his lunch."

She huffed out of the dining room, Shane following her to the street. It was mere seconds before he'd retaken his seat at the bar and was back to his burger.

How the fuck long had it been since he'd had a damn burger?

Sometimes it felt like he'd been hungry all his fucking life. He'd gone from not having enough money to fill his belly to having to constantly worry about how his abs would look on screen.

"He's working out well," Jared said, pulling the pristine white napkin over his lap. "How's the other guy? Declan, right?"

Because now he required two bodyguards. One for the dayshift and one for the nightshift. Three, really, since he was interviewing for another position this evening, but the third was different. The third would never leave his side. The third would kneel and offer more than mere protection. She would offer him submission.

Fuck, it had been way too long. He had to cool down or he would show up for the interviews with a massive hard-on. What had Jared asked about? Oh, yeah. Burke.

"He's an odd one, but he's good at his job. Hey, he's been on the payroll for two weeks now and I'm still alive, so I would say he's working out."

"Good." Jared took a sip of his iced tea. "I'm glad to hear it's going well. The firm my brother is associated with has an excellent reputation."

That brought a smile to his lips. Jared's brother was a renowned therapist specializing in PTSD in soldiers returning from war. Much of his work was funded by a security company made up of the very people Kai Ferguson helped. McKay-Taggart was one of the premiere security companies in the world. And someone who worked there had married a writer. Josh could have told that dude marrying a writer was a mistake. Writers couldn't help it. All the secrets came out. "On several levels. I've heard *Love After Death* was based on the big guy's life. That was actually a hell of a movie. I was worried about how the romance would be handled, but I ended up liking it. You know you never told me why you backed out of that one. You really would have been perfect for the part."

Jared's smile wavered. "Well, that was around the time I was arrested for killing my assistant."

He held up his hands, trying to let the conversation go. He knew a wall when he hit one. He and Jared had gotten close over the past few years, but there were things they never talked about. What happened in Dallas was one of them. Oh sure, one night Jared had gotten into the vodka and loosened up enough to admit there had been a woman involved, but Josh didn't know much more than her name. Sarah. Stubborn Sarah, as he liked to think of her. "Sorry. Say no more."

Jared's false arrest for murder and the whole shitshow that came with it was one of those subjects they avoided like the plague. Josh was a man who understood that even between friends, some things were private.

Jared amped that smile right back up. "Hey, it's cool, man. I'm good. The show had a great run. Seven years ain't bad, you know. Now we see what happens with the rest of my life."

A precarious place to be. An actor without a job lined up. Jared's long-running show had recently ended and he'd moved to Malibu, buying a house right on the beach, with Josh as a neighbor.

"It's going to be fine. I've already talked to the producer about a new character for *The Quick and the Enraged* franchise. We need a new driver for the next film and I think you would be perfect," he said. "I'm meeting with the screenwriter in a few days. You should come down and we'll start fleshing him out. I'm thinking sarcastic and edgy. Maybe he's a good guy. Maybe not. We can play with that. Keep the audience guessing."

"I appreciate it and I would love to do it, but don't stick your neck out," Jared replied.

Because he was a genuine guy. One of the only genuine human beings Josh had met out here. Or anywhere, for that matter. Naturally the fact that Jared was real with him made him way more willing to actually stick his neck out. "My neck is extra thick thanks to your workouts. And we do need a new character. The series is on its fourth film. We need new blood. Besides, I can't thank you for everything you've done for me. I have no idea where I would be if I hadn't found The Reef."

A lie. He knew where he would have been. The bottom of a bottle. The end of a needle. Wherever junkies went when they'd gone too far. The Reef had taught him discipline. The Reef had given him confidence.

After he'd lost Tina, he'd...well, he'd lost himself for a bit, too. His saving grace had been a movie role he'd taken on at the time. His character had a background in D/s and when Josh had looked for someone to help him understand the world, he'd found Jared. Jared had opened up a lot of doors for him.

"No problem. I was happy to help."

Jared had been his mentor in the world of D/s, and he was still there even after all these years. "So, does that mean you'll come back to the club with me and interview the new girls? You've done all the vetting. You know them better than I do."

An excited gleam hit Jared's eyes. "I was hoping you would ask. I think this is going to be the perfect solution for you. I already like two of them. The New York girl seems to have a lot of experience. Former NYPD. Seems level headed."

And that was important because the last thing he needed was to have his submissive fall in love with him. That was utterly off the table. Good sex? Now that was on it, slathered all over that table he was offering, but the last thing he needed was another obsessed person.

After all, he had three acknowledged stalkers. Two women and a man. Those were merely the ones the police were sure about. There were others who were waiting in the wings, waiting for their piece of him. He got too many nasty emails and threats to worry about every single one.

Yet another reason to not get too close to the woman he would hire. But he needed to be able to connect to her. Connection was important. He wanted to feel for her, but then he didn't have to worry about falling in love. He knew damn well he wasn't capable of that.

"And the blonde bodyguard is stunning," Jared continued as salads were placed in front of them. "She's former Israeli Army. Her credentials are excellent."

He wasn't sure about that one. She had the look of an actress. He would bet she'd come out here looking for fortune and fame and fallen back on what she was good at when she needed money. There was nothing wrong with that scenario, but he didn't want to hire someone who would disappear the minute her agent called with a part.

"Who do you have it narrowed down to?" He'd let Jared run with this. Jared and a couple of the The Reef members he trusted implicitly. They'd done much of the vetting to keep Josh's name out of it. The woman he hired had to have previous bodyguard training, experience with firearms, and knowledge of security processes.

She also had to be a sexual submissive.

That was important to him. He didn't want someone who thought it would be fun to try, who'd seen a couple of movies, read some romance bullshit books and thought it would be sexy.

He wanted someone who needed a top to be sexually complete.

And the fact that she would be an employee under a nondisclosure agreement wasn't bad either.

This time around he would have complete control. He would be her boss, her Dom. He would get what he needed and ensure she was content.

It was probably the best he could ask for. Contentment. Peace.

"You're meeting with five women this afternoon. The best of the best. I think this is going to work out nicely," Jared said. "Honestly, I'm hoping it works out for you because I'm thinking about doing something similar."

That was news. "You breaking the celibacy thing you have going? Because I know a whole bunch of subs who would line up to take care of you."

Before he'd gone to Dallas to visit his brother, Jared had been a bit of a manwhore. He tore through some subs, but since the incident they didn't talk about, he'd been quiet, a bit monk-like.

Jared sighed, his shoulders rolling out. "Well, it's become obvious to me I can't have the woman I want. I've tried calling, sending flowers, texting. She's no longer interested, but then given the last time I saw her my best friend was about to murder her, I guess I can understand."

Yep, there was Stubborn Sarah. She was fucking up Jared's life, and he needed to let go of her. "You know it might be for the best. Civilians…they don't tend to last long in our world."

Any woman who dated one of them would be scrutinized on a level most human beings couldn't accept. Every detail of her body would be up for praise or ridicule—sometimes at the same time. She would be pulled apart, her history laid bare for all to comment on. She would be hated by a large group of "fans" and all because she had the sad fate to fall for a Hollywood star.

Jared nodded, but he seemed to be somewhere else. Likely thinking of her. "Yeah, I know you're right. But just for a minute I thought I'd found the one who could handle it. She's the single most confident woman I've ever met."

Then it would be even worse when they tore her down. He didn't say the words, but he knew Jared was likely thinking the same thing. No one got out of their world whole. There was a hard price to be paid for the glamorous life. He'd started paying it when he was twelve years old.

Hell, maybe he'd started paying it the moment he'd been born.

Jared cleared his throat. "Anyway, like I said, you're the guinea pig. If it seems to work out for you, maybe I'll hire a girlfriend."

He hated how that sounded. "I'm hiring a bodyguard who will also happen to submit to me sexually."

"A warm blow-up doll, my man."

He flipped Jared off. He should have known he wouldn't get out of this without some serious masculine fucking around. "Do you have the contract ready?"

Jared reached down into the backpack he'd carried in for this meeting. "I am always prepared. Well, I'm prepared for other people's shit. Take a look at this and tell me if I've left anything out. You know I could run it by my brother. He's better at contracts than I am."

Josh took the contract that would delineate every aspect of his relationship with the woman he would hire in the next few days. Even holding it in his hands made something in his chest ease. This was going to be a good thing. He would start this relationship with all the cards on the table because the contract between them would be a solid thing. The woman he hired would know everything that was expected of her.

The woman who would live in his home and meet his needs.

Fuck. It really had been too long since he'd fed this part of his soul. He was practically shaking at the thought, and that wouldn't do. He needed to be cool and calm. He needed to keep his distance.

He was the Dom. He was in control, and that was the way it was going to stay.

Chapter Two

Kayla stepped into the cool environs of the club. It was nothing less than stepping from sunlight into shadows, and she rather thought that was part of the theater of the place. Most clubs ran on drama—from the architecture and decorations of each room to the emotion of the scenes that played out. And then, of course, there was the pure human element to it. The Reef would have its share of gossip and it would run on its own rules.

The Reef wasn't The Garden. It wasn't Sanctum, either. It was much more like the dance clubs she'd been to in her younger days. Industrial. Dark. Moody and broody, as she would call it.

It was kind of awesome.

Not that she didn't love The Garden and Sanctum, but there was something raw about The Reef that called to her. There was a devil's head over the comfortable couches that marked the lounge area. The walls had been painted scarlet red and the darkest black, the floor left in its industrial concrete phase. Rock 'n' roll. It looked like a place where an old-school metal band would hang out.

And this was the place where she would play for the next few months.

She'd left Ezra and Levi behind at the apartment that would serve as their base of operations in West Hollywood. She wasn't sure if it was Ezra's or the Agency's, but it was in a nice neighborhood with a dog park across the street. Clean and well kept, it reminded her of the home she'd grown up in, and she'd had to force a well of emotion back down. The only thing it had been missing was two men who slept together, an overactive poodle, and the sound of the ocean.

It was good to be here, good to remind herself that this was an op and nothing more. This club was the last thing that would remind her of her dads.

A couple of guys were hanging out in the big open-space lobby she'd walked into. They were lounging on comfy couches and shooting the shit. One of the men had a length of rope in his hand, working the knots as he talked about the Dodgers.

A man with a neatly kept goatee looked up and sighed. "You here for the position?"

All eyes were on her and it was obvious a couple of these guys did not approve. She didn't take it personally. After all, most of these men took D/s seriously, and they would likely view their actor counterpart attempting to buy a sub as a little out of the ordinary. Or they would view any woman who would sell herself that way as someone to watch. It didn't matter what they thought in the end.

She gave them a brilliant smile, but also lowered her head slightly to show respect. After all, she was a guest in their club. She wasn't going to breeze through like she owned the place.

Years she'd spent perfecting this particular character. "Yes, Sir. My name is Kayla Summers. I'm here for a three o'clock appointment."

"At least one of them knows how to behave," someone grumbled.

That's what she'd been counting on. It had been practically inevitable that some of her competition would overstate their lifestyle experience in order to win a job like this. They would come through thinking showy confidence would get them ahead. Maybe, had this been for a corporate job, but it wouldn't work with these men.

"Thank you, Sir. You have a lovely club," she said with a smile.

The big Dom in front of her held out a hand. "I'm what you would call the coordinator of this club. If there's ever any real boss in a place like this. I was voted in because I was dumb enough to say yes. Angelo DeMaris. It's nice to meet you."

43

"I don't know the complete rules of your club, Sir." Some clubs would have every sub call the men or women with Master rights Master. Some had more lax rules. It was important to honor them. She held out her hand, allowing him to take it. There was no shake. He merely put both large hands over her small one and then the contact was over.

"How about you call me Angelo when we're not on the dungeon floor and Sir when we are," he offered. "If you ever actually play here. Jared and Josh are close friends of mine. Dumbasses, both of them, but they're friends. Anyone they hire will be carefully vetted."

"Of course. I would advise nothing less, though I suspect his bodyguards have already vetted me thoroughly. If the club would like some references from the other clubs I've held memberships in, I can certainly give you names and numbers."

And Damon Knight and Ian Taggart would tell them what they wanted to hear.

Everything was carefully orchestrated to get her this job, to put her in this place. She had every advantage, and she intended to use them all.

"Kayla?" The door to the inner portions of the club came open and a familiar face stood there, clipboard in hand.

She nodded. In this case, she didn't have to pretend. Her cover was that she'd worked for McKay-Taggart for years. She should know Shane Landon. "Hello, Shane." She glanced back at the Doms. "Thank you for having me in your club."

She walked through the doors and into the club proper. The concrete here was painted a shiny black, her heels clicking along the floor. Not that she would make a sound if she didn't want to, but she didn't need to sneak up on anyone. They knew she was coming. And she liked the sound. In the larger spaces, the concrete would make sounds echo, a moan or groan reverberating through the room and making a symphony of BDSM.

Shane nodded toward a small room off the main hall and across from what appeared to be the changing rooms. She followed him in, hoping they would have a chance to talk. Shane had been working for Joshua Hunt for a few weeks now. Anything he could tell her about his demeanor and habits would be helpful. Shane and Declan Burke would attempt to sway Josh in her favor.

But it really was up to her.

Shane closed the door behind her and she found herself in an office. Declan Burke leaned against the desk. Even when the man was relaxing, he looked lean and predatory, coiled and ready to strike. Shane was more of the all-American guy, with a ready smile that belied his dangerous nature.

She was comfortable with these men because she understood them.

"We can talk in here. No bugs," Dec said. "But keep it down. Sound reverberates. If someone comes in, we're doing your initial interview. We've done it with all the candidates."

"She did great with the Doms," Shane said, crossing his arms over his massive chest. "Way better than a couple of the others. It's obvious several of the women have no training whatsoever. I would even say one of them is a top herself. She simply doesn't have enough knowledge to understand her place."

"Any real contenders?"

"Well, the problem is putting the two sides of what he needs together," Dec mused. "He needs someone with extensive bodyguard skills who also happens to have training in the lifestyle and identifies as a bottom."

"And you haven't seen that perfect combo yet?" The trouble was she couldn't force Josh to choose her. If he wasn't into Asian-American chicks with wicked-dark senses of humor, she might be shit out of luck.

"Not that I could tell," Shane replied. "I think if he doesn't pick you, he'll go with the former Israeli Army guard. She's the closest to what he's looking for."

"And what do you think he's looking for?"

Shane glanced over at Declan. "He's kind of hard to read. You get anything off him?"

Dec pushed off the desk and started pacing. "I would say there's a lot of shit going on under his calm demeanor. He's very controlled, but he wasn't always."

"Yeah, I got that, too," Shane agreed. "I would bet a lot that he hasn't always been as clean as he is now. Probably drugs or alcohol since he is careful about what he drinks. One Scotch is all he'll do, and I don't know how much he enjoys it."

"He's pretty cold," Dec continued. "I don't mean that in a bad way. I guess I kind of admire it. Not a lot seems to get to the guy. But I don't know how much of that is front, you know what I mean? He's polite, but cool to everyone around him. We haven't seen him with a sub. I don't think he's had a regular sub for a long time."

"But one of his girlfriends was a member?" Sometimes knowing how another person had fucked up led to the way in.

Shane grimaced. "Yes, and let me tell you these guys don't like it when you try to go public with their business. She was immediately kicked out of the club, and from what I can tell, she left LA because she couldn't find a job. They blackballed her. Not all the members here work in entertainment, but they've got enough power to screw with a person's career."

In an industry like this one, someone always knew someone who could help a brother out.

"Okay, so he enjoys his revenge when the time comes. I can get that. But he's friends with Jared," she began, trying to get a handle on this guy. "Jared is a piece of sunshine according to the subs who met him at Sanctum. Kai tells me his brother is nothing more than walking abs and a smile. Hardly sounds like besties material for Mr. Broody."

"A guy's personality can change when he's actually topping a sub," Dec pointed out. "Again, never seen him top a sub, but I've heard Jared is someone the other Doms look up to. Those hardcore guys out there like the hell out of him. Speaking of, Riley's around somewhere. If you can get a word with him, it could help. We've had to stay away. I don't even want text conversations between us in case the boss decides to do a phone check, and yes, that will be part of your contract. Be careful how you use that phone."

She barely managed to avoid rolling her eyes. She'd tricked China's best operatives for years. She could handle her own cell phone. "I'll try. I'm on a new line but most of my friends from work know how to get in contact with me. Tucker has it. He needs to text me spoilers on films and TV shows that have been out for twenty years. Are you worried Hunt won't like me having contact with other men?"

She couldn't leave Tucker high and dry. He would need to talk about what happened in *The X-Files*. When she'd left him, he'd been binging, and no one else would listen to his crazy theories.

Shane shrugged the anxiety off. "I think Hunt's pretty dark. He could definitely be the possessive type, but he knows you work for McKay-Taggart. You can safely talk to coworkers. Speaking of, Hunt also knows you were raised out here. Have you thought about seeing your parents?"

"No." Now she was the one who sounded a bit cold. She dismissed it all with what she hoped was a sunny smile. "I'm working. The last thing we want is my dads in here. Trust me. I'll call and let them know I'm working. Otherwise...well, one dad will give the man a lecture on all the ways his films spit on science and history and the other will be planning a wedding, if you know what I mean."

Shane held his hand up, obviously letting go of the fight. "I wanted to let you know that if you get some time to see them, you can take it. One of us will be on Hunt at all times. I know it's been a while since you saw them."

Seven months and three days, and they'd had to come out to her. She'd seen her fathers three times in the years since she'd left MSS, and every single time they'd come to find her. Why was she afraid of going home?

"Good to know."

There was a brief knock on the door and Riley Blade strode through. Once a technical consultant here in Hollywood, he now worked for McKay-Taggart. He had a lean frame and a California chic vibe one only got when raised on the West Coast.

He closed the door behind him. "They're ready for you. I'll take you to Mr. Hunt. Kay, he's deeper than he looks. It's easy to see him as a superficial actor, but those still waters might be dangerous. I've been watching him for weeks and I think he's looking for someone who can connect to him. He's a little desperate for it, but he needs to be in control. He needs to think he can handle you. Does that make sense?"

He didn't want to fight her for power. He wanted some peace.

She could do that. Cool. Calm. A motherfucking oasis of peace. That was her.

"And Kay," Riley said, his hand on the door. "I know we're here for the Agency, but this man has real trouble. I've read through some of the incidents that led him to hire round-the-clock bodyguards and these are credible threats."

"How sure are we that the Agency didn't make those incidents happen?" Not that Levi or Ezra would admit to it. It was possible they didn't know. Sometimes the Agency's left hand didn't know who the right hand was stabbing.

"I hate the CIA shit," Dec said with a shake of his head.

"It doesn't matter," Riley replied firmly. "He's got three people following him I would call serious and present threats. I doubt the Agency is playing all three of them. We have to protect this man and that means taking the threats against him seriously. He's trusting us with his life. I know you've got a job to do, but the three of us…we have to take care of our client."

"Because we hate the Agency shit," Dec reiterated. "And Big Tag'll kill us if this turns into a FUBAR situation."

"I won't let anything happen to him." She hated the fact that they didn't trust her implicitly, but she understood why. She was the Agency's tool in this case. She wasn't one of the boys. "I'll do my job, but I can keep him alive at the same time."

"Let us know what you need. Show time." Riley opened the door, his face going bland again. "Through here, Ms. Summers. Mr. Hunt will see you in the dungeon. Let me show you the way."

She followed him out, ready to get to the job.

* * * *

Josh sat back, perfectly unimpressed with the women he'd seen. Yes, they were lovely, with perfect faces and bodies, and not one of them had moved him.

He might need to rethink his plan. He might have gotten to a point where he could no longer be moved.

The last time he'd felt anything at all had been the night he'd lost Tina.

She'd been the only person in his life he'd been able to count on and he'd disappointed her. He'd gotten so involved in being Josh

Hunt that he hadn't seen the signs that she was sick, hadn't forced her to get treatment. Hadn't treated her like the odd mom/boss she'd become to him.

And yet she'd held his hand as she was dying. *Don't let the past screw up your future, my Josh. The past is a burden you can let go of.*

God, he hadn't let go yet. He likely never would. And he'd never told Tina his secrets.

But someone knew.

"She was hot." Jared watched as the door closed and they were left alone again.

The redhead was hot, and yet she somehow left him utterly cold. Then again, Jared thought every woman was hot in her own way. He should have known Jared wouldn't be much help. Despite his recent trouble, the man was endlessly optimistic, and sometimes Josh wondered if Jared could see the darker side at all. "She doesn't have as much experience as she says she does."

Jared frowned. "I don't know. Her form was perfect. She didn't get stuck on the idea of a contract."

"I wasn't talking about her being submissive. I'm sure she's been in the lifestyle, but the vetting notes from McKay-Taggart questioned her job experience. They can prove she was employed by a bodyguard firm, but no one would confirm her field experience. I asked her about a specific weapon and how easy she thought the safety was to use."

"Yeah, I remember that."

"That pistol has no safety," Josh returned. "She doesn't know firearms."

If she didn't know firearms, then she likely hadn't spent much time in the field. She would likely be excellent in bed, but how long would he enjoy her before they all got murdered?

He was going to have to give up his house on the beach. Tina had left it to him. He was going to be forced to move into the canyon, far away from the one fucking place that made him feel like he might make it through another day.

Unfortunately for him, all California beaches were public beaches. He couldn't keep people away. If he had proper security, he could stay. That meant sleeping with a weapon in his house, and he wasn't talking about a Glock.

"Damn." Jared sat back. "That's not fair."

Life wasn't fair, but then he'd figured that out a long time ago. "Maybe we should cancel the whole thing."

How much time did he get to spend here anyway? In a few months he'd be back on a set somewhere working his ass off and living in a trailer. Wasn't hard to guard a trailer no matter how big it was. He would shove his needs down. He didn't want vanilla sex. He could get that anywhere. All he had to do to get a woman in LA to drop her panties for him was to smile her way.

He wanted something more.

Click clack. Click clack. He sighed at the sound. Another one was coming, her heels making that sound on the floor that should get his blood pumping. Should. Didn't.

"Come on." Jared stood up. "We have to try harder. Not everyone lies. I get it. Some of the women weren't as forthcoming as they should have been, but we can still find someone. You know no one ever tells the whole truth."

A lovely woman with pitch black hair stepped through into the room, and Joshua couldn't help but give her his full attention. She was in a black sheath dress that molded to her every curve. He tended to prefer taller women, but she was perfectly formed. Her long raven-black hair came down to her waist, showing shades of navy blue. Everything about her was perfect and pristine, like nothing had ever touched her in a negative fashion.

He was both deeply attracted and utterly revolted. She disturbed him on a basic level.

But that was feeling, too, so he sat up straighter and gave her his full attention.

Her dark eyes met his briefly and then she lowered them in a perfectly submissive fashion that led him to believe she knew something about the lifestyle. "Hello, Sir. If you would prefer another nomenclature, please let me know."

This told him two things. She knew how to greet him before she knew what to call him and she considered herself a submissive who required a name. She'd asked him what to call him and told him what to call her. Not "this one" or "creature" but "me." She played but kept her identity.

50

It was good to know. The rest hadn't been as forward.

"Sir is fine for now. I'll be honest, I prefer Joshua to Master, but there's time enough to go into it." He liked his name. He'd spent far too long without it. There was power in claiming his own name.

"As you wish, Sir," she replied.

She stood in the middle of the dungeon, paying no attention to the chair that had been set up for her. She stood, her body relaxed.

Her body. She was petite, graceful. Her hair was brushed back, falling off her shoulder and revealing the pretty line of her neck. Even her hands were small. He looked at her and the word that came to mind was delicate. Exquisite. Peaceful.

Far too good to be true.

Because there was something simmering under her surface. Something dark and nasty. Maybe it was his imagination, but her stillness didn't feel like peace to him. Her stillness almost felt like that of a predator waiting to attack.

And yeah, that did something for him, too.

"You're a bodyguard?" He wanted to push her. Despite the darkness he sensed, it was still hard to believe that tiny thing could protect anyone. It was definitely hard to believe she could take what he would want to give her.

Her lips curled slightly. "Yes, Sir. I believe I detailed my experience in my résumé, but I'm more than willing to go over it all with you. The last few years I've been employed by McKay-Taggart and Knight in London."

"As a bodyguard," he prompted.

"I handled many aspects of the business for my bosses. Besides working corporate security, I also did close cover work. I was on a long-term detail for Mia Lawless. She's one of my references."

"Yes, the sister of Drew Lawless." He looked down at her résumé. It was impressive. It could also be total fiction. She really looked more like a reporter than a bodyguard. The connection to Mia Lawless worried him. The only Lawless sister *was* a reporter, and wouldn't this make a great story? Undercover—literally. Under his covers. Reporting from close proximity of his penis to tell all the nasty, dirty stories about him everyone had only thought were rumors.

Still, she'd come from the same company as Shane and Declan

and they were working out. He leaned over and whispered to Jared, who immediately nodded and walked out of the dungeon to do his bidding.

She didn't move from her spot.

It was obvious she was waiting for him to offer her a seat, but he rather liked having her stand. A little discomfort was good for the soul.

"Tell me how you got into the lifestyle."

"When I started my job in London, a membership at The Garden was one of the perks of the job. I discovered I liked it and I play a few nights a week. I find it relaxing."

The words rolled smoothly off her tongue and he didn't believe a single one. Either she was lying to him about how she found the lifestyle or about finding it relaxing. He wasn't sure which, but something about the easy way she spoke about it made him uneasy. He knew "dialogue" when he heard it. Well-rehearsed dialogue.

It disappointed him immensely because of all the women he'd seen this afternoon, only this one moved him in any way.

Even if it was mostly his dick moving. Hell, he was happy the thing wanted to play at all, but he wasn't about to let it lead him astray again. Especially when it was likely she was lying about far more than how much she truly enjoyed submitting sexually.

"Before you came on at McKay-Taggart, you claim to have worked with the Central Intelligence Agency."

"Yes, though most of my work there is classified." She didn't react at all to the taunts in his words.

Of course it was. "You're young for an agent. Especially a retired one."

"I'm thirty-two. I became an agent at the age of nineteen by necessity. I didn't have a typical Agency career, and I've found you either get out young or die there. I chose the former. Tennessee Smith is my reference for my CIA work, though again, he can only speak about me in general terms. I had another mentor while I was there, but he wasn't as lucky as me."

How could she sound so charming talking about death? She could be talking about a lovely garden for all the warmth in her tone. Again. It felt like she was playing a part. She was doing it well. If he hadn't spent much of his life trying to figure out who was being true and who was lying, he would buy her story hook, line, and sinker. He was sure Jared would. The minute she walked out, Jared would be all over him, telling him how amazing she was, how good she would be for the job.

Jared was far too much an optimist.

Footsteps fell, warning him that someone was coming. One of the things he liked about the dungeon was the concrete floors and the echoing sounds. No one could sneak up on him. He could hear them coming. Except he only heard one set of footsteps.

And yet three men strode into the dungeon.

Yeah. He needed to get Shane and Dec to teach him how they did that. It might never come up in a movie, but he was a man who liked to learn. It was how he knew about firearms. His brain was a veritable pool of somewhat useless knowledge.

He noticed that Ms. Summers hadn't turned. Merely kept her eyes on him. Most people would instinctively look back, calling it curiosity. Josh knew it was something deeper. It was the lizard part of the brain, always watching its back. Kayla Summers wasn't worried about hers.

"You asked for us, Mr. Hunt?" Shane's deep voice rumbled through the room.

"Yes, I wanted to know if you have any experience with Ms. Summers since you all work for the same company."

"We work in different offices," Shane explained. "I'm in Dallas. She's been in London since she hired on. We've met before, but I haven't worked formally with her. Hey, Kay."

Kayla turned her head and gave Shane and Declan a friendly nod. "It's nice to see you both."

Dec's mouth quirked up in a smirk, though Josh rather thought that was simply how the man smiled. Anything that seemed to amuse the big fucker brought that arrogant smirk out. "I think he's wondering about Kay's experience, Shane. I believe the boss here wants to know if she's padding her résumé with some skills she doesn't have."

Though her face didn't change at all, he practically felt the chill roll off her.

That woman was pissed. Was she pissed because he was about to call her bluff?

Shane's brows rose. "Oh. Shit. Uhm, she's really good at her job, Mr. Hunt. I might not have worked with her, but I've read her file and heard plenty of stories. I would not fuck with her. Not at all."

"She weighs maybe a hundred pounds soaking wet," he pointed out.

Though she had curves in all the right places. Still, he had to know. His life was on the line. Hers, too. He couldn't pick a bodyguard because he wanted her in bed.

Hell, he wasn't going to pick her anyway. Any connection he'd felt had been cut by her answer about how she'd gotten involved in the lifestyle. He wanted, no, required someone who needed to submit. Not for relaxation. Not for kinky fun.

Yet he found himself drawing out the interview, wanting to see how right he was about the calm oasis of a woman in front of him. So self-possessed. Every hair perfectly in place. He wanted to muss her up a bit. The need was there, a nasty kernel rolling around in his gut.

"Ms. Summers, could I have a demonstration of your skills?"

"Of course. Who would you like me to spar with?" She was still holding that Louis Vuitton bag of hers, looking as petite and feminine a woman as he'd ever seen. A good four inches of her height came from those brilliant red Louboutins she would have to take off in order to fight.

Dec put his hands up. "Hard pass. I like my face the way it is."

Shane shook his head. "I'm telling you, man. She is everything she says she is and I don't want to fuck with her. I'm a bodyguard. I was a cop once. She was a CIA agent, and not the kind who didn't get her hands dirty."

But her hands were so fucking perfect.

"Jared?"

Jared stood up, a smile on his face. "Sure thing." He walked up to Kayla Summers. "Don't worry. I'll go easy on…"

Before Jared could get another word out, his air seemed to be cut off. How had she gotten the strap of that Louis Vuitton bag around his throat that fast? How had she gotten it around his thick neck at all? Even in the heels, Jared had a good foot on her. Before Josh could stand up, Jared was on his knees beside her, his handsome face turning a nice shade of purple.

"I don't spar with civilians," Kayla explained quietly. She held the designer garrote in one hand, the rest of her body relaxed as though she took out two-hundred-pound men on a daily basis. "It's dangerous for them. Should I let him go or was this all an elaborate ruse to take out the competition? Are you two up for the same role or something? You can think about it. He's got maybe another thirty seconds before he loses consciousness, and another forty or so after that before he dies. Maybe a little longer. He's in good shape."

For Jared's part, he managed a semi smile, as though being praised was something he liked even as he was fucking dying.

"Let him go."

With a flick of her hand, Jared was free, sucking in air as fast as he could.

"I told you," Shane said under his breath.

Kayla reached out a hand to help Jared up. The dumbass took it and practically hopped up.

"That was awesome," Jared croaked. "Can you teach me that? Although I'll have to start carrying a handbag for it to work. I think I can make it masculine."

Her smile practically lit up the room and he wondered if that wasn't the first real piece of Kayla Summers he'd seen the whole interview. She reached up and brushed back Jared's hair. There was nothing sexual about the gesture. It was almost sisterly, as though she had a bunch of brothers and knew how to comfort them. "We can work something out, I'm sure." She turned back to him, her smile dimming. "That is, if I have the job now that I've proven I'm not some secretary trying to sneak into Joshua Hunt's bed."

Oh, he liked this side of her very much. There was something running under her surface. Something dark and twisted that would fight like hell with that unbelievably sunny smile of hers. Something he would like to explore, but she'd lied to him.

Or she hadn't, and that was even worse.

"I don't think we'll make a good match, Ms. Summers. Thank you for coming by."

The room seemed to still as though everyone in it was shocked the words had come out of his mouth. As though not a one of them believed he would dismiss her because she was obviously perfect.

He didn't trust perfect.

She settled her bag over her shoulder and held a hand out. "Thank you for taking the time, Sir."

He didn't want to touch her, didn't want to know how silky her skin would be or how small her hand would feel in his. Social conventions were a bitch on a guy.

"Thank you for coming in." He shook her hand as briefly as politeness allowed.

She turned and started walking out, her shoes making no sound on the floor this time. Like Shane and Declan. But the first time, she'd clicked and clacked her way in.

"Why did you make all that noise when you walked in?" He was curious.

She stopped, her brows rising over gorgeous dark eyes. "Excuse me?"

"When you walked in the first time, I heard every single step. But it's obvious that's not your nature. You made a choice to be loud when you can walk silently."

"I don't use my gifts against my friends. I consciously made noise so you would know I was coming. Yes, I could have been silent, and then I might have heard something I shouldn't have or caught you in a moment that would have given me the upper hand, but I didn't want to play that way."

He nodded, her explanation making perfect sense to him.

She started to go again, but stopped. She didn't look at him this time. "I said I wanted to play fair, but I lied to you, Sir. I lied about how I got into the lifestyle."

Interesting that she would own up now. He thought briefly about telling her it didn't matter, but he was curious. Or maybe he was simply a bit desperate to keep the conversation with her going. "Gentlemen, would you give us the room?"

Jared sent him a look, but Josh merely nodded, letting him know it was okay. He was sure he was in for a thorough grilling from his friend. He hoped the bodyguards would be cool with his decision, but hey, if they weren't, they were replaceable, too. Everyone was.

No one stayed for long.

When they were alone, he turned back to her. "Why would you lie?"

"So I wouldn't give you an advantage, but now I can see that was wrong of me. D/s is hard. It's supposed to be. I'm not talking about the spanking or play. I'm talking about the emotional part. That part is difficult for me. I don't like being vulnerable."

He stood in front of her, well aware he was too close for social norms. "And yet you say you prefer to submit."

Her eyes came up, catching his and giving him the open honesty he'd been looking for all afternoon. "I don't prefer it. I need it. I was a double agent for most of my adult life. Some of the things I saw...some of the things I did...I can't take them back and I can't pretend they don't play out in my head every single night. When I left the Agency, I was wired, completely incapable of living in a world where I wasn't on guard twenty-four seven. I could smile and joke and laugh, and then I would round a corner and have a knife at my friend's throat because some sound reminded me of a time I nearly died. There were many of those and my hearing is quite acute. And that was when Damon Knight told me I could do one of three things. I could see a therapist, leave the company, or try D/s. I don't like talking about the past and I had nowhere else to go, so I took the class and I hated it."

Now she was giving him some truth. It was there in her eyes and the way her skin flushed, as though she hated admitting any of this. "Did you fool your trainers?"

She nodded slowly. "Again, I'd learned how to read people and I gave the proper responses. I don't know if Damon believed me or if he was merely trying to keep the peace. I'd done the group a large favor and firing me would have been difficult. I decided this was our trade-off."

"He would keep you around and you would pretend D/s helped?"

"Yes. It wasn't that I minded the pain. I can handle pain. It's the questions, the needling a good Dom can do that bugged me. So I found the ones who did it because they thought topping a woman was sexy. Hey, when they got too close to me, I could have some nice, athletic sex and numb out."

Was sex her drug of choice? It wouldn't bother him if it was. Everyone had a drug of choice, whether it was alcohol or cocaine or spending way too much time at the gym. Or taking control. That was his. He'd given up the rest. "When did things turn around?"

"I faked my way through every session until one night a Dom named Clive wouldn't let me play him. He knew I was hiding. He knew Damon was watching and I couldn't walk away. And somehow, he knew what I needed. By the time he was done, I'd cried for the first time in ten years. For the first time in almost as long, I let a man hold me and comfort me, and it was about something other than the job I was working. I got into the lifestyle because I'm fucked up beyond all recognition, but sometimes when I'm playing I remember how far I've come that I can trust another human being with my body. It gives me hope for my soul."

She turned, but he could move quickly, too. He stepped fully into her space, reaching for her hand.

They stood there for a moment as he studied her face, saw the glimmer of tears behind her eyes. She wasn't going to shed them, but they were there—a gift to him that he couldn't help but honor.

"My place tonight. Seven p.m. Bring your things and we'll take a look at the contract. When you show up, you will wear your hair down. I want you in a skirt or a dress, no underwear and no bra. Make sure your grooming routine is taken care of."

"I lasered my kitty a long time ago, Joshua. The grooming routine is quite easy," she said with a smile that kind of kicked him straight in the groin. And the way she said his name—like it was a secret between them. "Are you sure? You didn't seem to want me a minute ago."

"I wanted you. I just changed my mind about letting myself have you." He stepped back. "Don't be late. We have a contract to go over and I would enjoy a session with you if at the end of the night you still want the job."

"I'll want the job."

"We'll see after you've read the contract and you understand what I need from you." He reached out and put a hand on her face, unable to keep himself from touching her. Yes, she was every bit as silky smooth as he'd thought. "I will want sex. Quite a bit of it."

"Good because it's been a long dry spell for me and I'm looking forward to breaking it."

"It doesn't bother you that sex will be contractual between us?" He was used to most women wanting a romantic façade around what was essentially a biological function.

"It's always contractual. Always. Most people merely don't see it," she replied. "I like the idea that it's all on the table. It's one of the things that attracts me to the lifestyle. You should understand that I haven't dated the way other people my age did. I was a studious teen and then I was an operative. My brain doesn't work the same way. I don't need you to pamper me or boost my ego. We can make this work by being honest about what this relationship is."

"And what is it?"

"You're my boss and I protect you, and we fuck like rabbits when the time is right. Oh, you'll probably spank me, too. Other than that, I hope we can find something that resembles friendship."

Friendship. He wasn't sure about that. He had few friends, but he rather thought this was a woman who made them easily. At least on the surface. She would use that guise of friendship to keep the emotional stuff at bay.

He stepped back even though his instinct was to lean over and let his mouth find hers. No. He wasn't going to give in to that instinct. They weren't going to be friends. He wouldn't give her the safety of distance. Master and submissive.

He had a sudden and deep hunger to peel apart her layers and find the woman on the inside. It was a dangerous impulse, but one he couldn't quite deny.

The key was to open her up to him while he held that essential piece of himself apart.

"Again, don't be late," he said solemnly. "You won't like the punishment that will come."

"I won't be, Joshua." She turned and walked out, her feet utterly silent against the concrete.

As though declaring her game. She would feint and hide. He would pursue and find.

For the first time in a long while, he was ready to play.

Chapter Three

Kayla watched as the driver turned off PCH and made his way to Old Malibu Road. The Range Rover made quick work of the turn, a perfect California vehicle. It would be capable of handling the beaches that were to her left as well as the Santa Monica Mountains to her right.

She was surprised though at the turn. She'd expected to go the opposite direction, up into the canyon where the houses were huge and the security was simple. The houses in the canyon were separated by acres of land and high-tech fencing. The canyon and mountains themselves were natural security measures. Above, the view would be stunning and privacy insured.

But Old Malibu Road didn't lead up into the mountains, and here the houses were stacked against each other.

"He lives right on the beach?"

The older man tipped his head. He'd introduced himself as Barry when he'd picked her up, insisting on taking care of her luggage himself. "Yes, ma'am. He lived here with his first agent for a few years and moved back in when she left the house to him after she died. He's got several houses, of course, but those are mostly for show. Investments, I think he would say. This is where he lives. He prefers it down here, and honestly, for the most part it's perfectly quiet. It's only every now and then we get someone disrespectful."

She glanced out, seeing the multimillion-dollar houses that lined this road. They would all have a front row view to the Pacific Ocean.

Like the small house she'd grown up in.

You'll always be able to hear the ocean, Kay. No matter where you go. You'll close your eyes and hear that sound and you'll be home where you're so loved, my darling girl.

Fuck. She was not going there. This was Malibu. Not Santa Barbara. This was a job. Not home.

She wasn't sure she had a home anymore. It was funny because while her fathers had told her she would always be able to hear the ocean and think of home—and she did—it was the moments when their kind voices broke through all the crap in her head that truly sent her into a tailspin.

It was better to concentrate on the job at hand. She'd received a text that she would be picked up at five thirty at her hotel and that she should feel free to check out.

Everything was a go even after how badly she'd bungled things earlier.

"How long have you worked for Mr. Hunt?"

The driver was an older man, likely in his mid-to-late sixties. He glanced up, his eyes meeting hers. "I don't work for him. I'm retired now and sometimes help out the members of the club with odd jobs. He doesn't keep a driver on retainer. He's a bit of a loner, that one."

Cool. She felt more comfortable around a lifestyler. "Dom or sub? Wait. Let me take a stab at it. You bottom for your wife."

He winked at her in the mirror. "For over forty years. Miss her like crazy. I don't play anymore. No need to now that she's gone, but I do like the camaraderie. I like that people remember Mistress Glo. That's for Gloria."

The love in his tone softened her heart. There was something about older couples that always got to her. She supposed they were the goal—to find a love that lasted long after the lust had taken a backseat to reality. Her dads were like that, and one day, they would be separated, too. "I'm sorry to hear that."

He slowed down as the street narrowed. She could glimpse the beach every now and then. The houses were built quite close together.

That had to be giving the bodyguard boys fits. From this side, the houses looked unremarkable, with the exception of the stunning colors that surrounded them. Massive swaths of bougainvillea coated the fences and terraces of the houses like blankets of bright colors. Pinks and purples she'd seen nowhere else in the world brought back other memories of home. Of her papa clipping the vines to try to make them go where he wanted. Then giving up and saying Mother Nature was a stubborn bitch and she would go where she would.

"I was, too," Barry said, accepting her sympathy with kindness of his own. "She liked Joshua. You have to understand he came to The Reef after he hit it big. Jared brought him. He was worth millions and was far more successful than any of the rest of us, but he never once put on airs. He wanted to learn, wanted to train. He takes this seriously, and therefore we take him seriously."

It was obvious that the members of The Reef took care of their own. It was time to start making her way in. This was her true skill as an operative, making a place for herself in a group. "I do, too. And I take my job seriously. I promise he won't get hurt on my watch."

"Good, because what that man goes through..." Barry said with a shake of his head.

"What's it like?"

"I couldn't handle it, but then I never made anything of myself the way he has. I was a character actor for a long time. Bit parts. Had a secondary role on a sitcom during the eighties for a couple of years. I'm the kind of actor no one notices. That might have bothered me early in my career, but when some of my friends hit it big, I realized how terrible the price of fame can be."

"I think most people would say he's living the dream."

"Nightmare is more like it. Now I know I'm the lucky one. I live right down the road from him. I worked steadily in guest parts and secondary roles in films, and somehow it made me rich. Not half a billion rich, but enough that I never have to worry about money. I got the wealth without the fame. Josh can't walk outside without the whole world knowing his name."

"They bug him here at home?" She knew the answer to the question, but was interested in Barry's point of view.

"There are always paparazzi around, though they tend to be a bit thicker when they smell a story or something changes in Josh's lifestyle." He sent her a pointed look through the mirror. "You should expect to be photographed often in the next few weeks. Once they figure out he's got a new woman in his life, they'll be all over you."

That was to be expected, though she intended to be the quietest of Hunt's lovers. And Ezra and Levi would be there to direct the information in whatever way they liked. It would actually be quite difficult to figure out her name unless they had someone on the inside feeding the press information, and then that would give them intel, too.

"I can handle the press. Josh mentioned something about three stalkers. Do you know anything about that? I've read the case files, but sometimes they can be too clinical. Have you ever seen any of those incidents?"

"We keep the pictures up at The Reef in case one of them shows up. They haven't so far, but I know at least two of them have been on the beach watching Josh's house. It's why we'll all feel better knowing he's not alone."

She had to wonder why he didn't move, but she kept that question to herself. Barry was pulling into a driveway. Old Malibu Road was a narrow two laner that sometimes felt more like one and a half lanes. The house she found herself standing in front of was pure white, making a sharp contrast to the vivid green of the grass. Turf, really. It could be difficult to keep grass green in California during a drought, so some had taken to putting in lush turf instead. Josh's small driveway was a checkerboard of pure white and leafy green.

"Wow. It's big for here." And she couldn't see the front part of the house. This kind of beach house was a little like magic. Because the majority was built out and down, the small portion seen from the road would be like walking into a building that was bigger on the inside than the outside. Like the Tardis from *Doctor Who*. Tucker would think it was all incredibly cool.

There were two full garages on either side of a thick metal gate that split the house into two parts. She counted three cameras and a hefty fence that would keep people out of the yard.

Barry had the Rover's backdoor open, pulling her two bags out. "Most of these houses have been split up into two to four units and rented out. There are still people who live here, but a lot of our business is tourism."

"Where is the public access point?" She wanted to know how hard someone would have to work to get to this part of the beach. They'd passed several large swaths of beach where there had been nothing but sand and sun.

"About a mile down the road," Barry said. "And then there's another as we were coming in roughly a mile and a half from here. That's as far as they have to go to get to the beach. Obviously, all they have to do to get to the house is walk up and ring the bell. They park on the street all the time. If it's too bad, we can get the police to come in and force them to move their cars."

It would be simple to not answer the door. This part of the house was all garage and long, dark entryway from the looks of it. She would bet that wasn't true once she was inside. There was no way Josh didn't have a spectacular view of the ocean. And if he had that, all his "friends" needed was to get to the beach to have a spectacular view of Josh.

And perhaps a shot of him with a camera, or something more deadly.

The heavy iron gate opened and Shane Landon motioned her in. "Welcome. You're early, and that's a good thing. I can show you some of the security features. We've been upgrading. Thank you, Barry. Mr. Hunt appreciates you delivering her to him safe and sound."

Barry bowed his head slightly, an almost ritualistic motion that proved there was still a sub deep down in the older man who needed to serve. "Thank him for allowing me to be of service, and tell him I look forward to spending more time with his submissive. Good evening."

Barry got back into his car and drove off.

"Excellent," Shane said with a sigh.

"That was another test, wasn't it?" She should have known. Hunt seemed determined to not take chances.

"Barry is active with the club. If he likes you as a sub, you get to hang with the cool kids," Shane explained. "From what I can tell, they all think he's got great instincts when it comes to people."

"I'm super likable." When she wanted someone to like her, they usually did.

She was fun. She was perky and peppy, and sure she at times got angry at authors who left her hanging, but for the most part she was the very face of patience and peace. No one had to see what happened under her skin.

"You are," Shane said, pulling her bags inside. "Which is why I have to ask why you gave Josh the broody act this afternoon. Have you decided to go through a goth phase? Jeez, what's in this thing?"

"Guns and shoes. The important stuff. And I wasn't trying to be broody. I was trying to figure out how to handle the man. He's different in person. I wasn't sure if my normal sunny self would do it."

"If you ask me, the man needs some sunshine," Shane said, hefting the bags up. "But you should know he's not your type."

Now she was totally interested. "I have a type?"

Shane's mouth flattened, but not in a harsh way. More like those lips were saying *come on, you know what I'm talking about.* "You like overgrown golden retrievers, Kay. You like men who are nothing more than muscular boys looking for a momma. Do you think I didn't see how you treated Jared Johns today? You have to watch that."

She laughed because he completely misunderstood her. "I love the sunny ones, Shane. I love them, but I'm not in love with them. They're like the brothers I never had and yes, I play the big sister. They remind me…"

Shane turned. "Remind you?"

Damn, she hadn't wanted to think about that. She didn't want to think about the big sister she'd lost. The mentor she'd lost. So much loss.

"Hey," Shane said, "I wasn't trying to pry. I was merely giving you some advice about this guy."

Good because she didn't want to go there today. But some of it was funny. She clung to that part. "Does everyone think I'm sleeping with Tucker?"

"I think that is none of my business," Shane replied. "But I know he's a good kid."

And Shane was a good man, giving her space, but still trying to do his job. "Tucker and I are friends. Nothing more. Nothing less. I take friendship seriously, but he needs way more than I could ever give him."

Shane sighed and turned toward her. "Are you really okay with this?"

A good, overprotective man. "Are you asking me if I'm okay sleeping with Joshua Hunt for this assignment? It's just sex and quite frankly, I haven't had any in a while, so I hope it's good sex."

A smile crossed his face. "Okay. I'll back off, but if he hurts you…"

She held up her Louis strap. "Do you need a demo?"

"I do not," he said with a wink. "Just know that Dec and I are here to back you up. I know you're technically on the Agency payroll, but you're our girl and we'll fuck up any of their plans in order to keep you safe."

That was the difference between being a spy and working for McKay-Taggart. Some of them came from the Agency, but they were way more military than spies. They were a team and they didn't leave their teammates behind. "I know, and that's why I'm here."

She started looking around the place, trying to figure out how she would get in if she had to. "How many cameras are on the house?"

"Twelve after Dec was done with it," Shane explained. "We've been revamping the security here for the last couple of weeks. Dec's a paranoid bastard but he gets the job done. There's not an ingress point that doesn't have an eye on it. We've also got two pointed either way down the beach. The locks are all sturdy, but there's a room under the house that's completely open and two sets of stairs that lead down to the beach. I talked Hunt into pulling up the one on the far side of the house. Dec and I took it down. Unless someone can jump really high, we only have to worry about the one set of stairs."

She'd been in many beach houses, had been raised in one. "Is the room underneath where they keep all the toys?"

"There's a place for paddle boards and surfboards and a couple of canoes. There's no door into the house though," he said. "It's super wet down there even though he says high tide doesn't flood the space."

"Consider it the beach version of a basement. And everything gets wet," she explained, walking toward the main house. "He's likely got a hose down there to wash his feet off after walking on the beach. He can also spray out any of the local wildlife that thinks to make his beach basement into their space."

Shane followed. "There's lots of wildlife. I think it's freaking Dec out a little. He's not really into nature, it turns out. The birds are pretty aggressive."

"I'm sure they're used to humans feeding them. Do we know if there are any CCTV cameras at the public access points to the beach?" She walked from the dim light of the hallway into glorious sunlight. The atrium of Josh's home was lit by a large skylight. There the floor went from stone to a pretty white marble. The walls were white. It was stark and minimal.

It made her wonder who had been Josh's designer. Even the paintings were minimalist, done in whites and blacks and shades of gray.

"Uhm, found the CCTVs and already broke into the feeds, thank you very much," a sarcastic voice said. Declan Burke stood in front of a doorway that led to the right side of the house. "I've already got it set up with some sweet facial recognition software that should warn us if one of our peeps shows up. And by *peeps* I mean crazy motherfuckers. And by *should* I mean if they look at the camera."

"That's a big if," she replied.

He shrugged. "One sweet day we'll have tech that flies around and takes pictures of everyone. Until then we'll hope the crazies look up. Most people do. How ya doing, Kay?"

She liked Dec, but then she was the girl who liked to hang with the weirdoes of the world. Declan Burke was a big, gorgeous total freak. He wasn't like Tucker. There wasn't a bit of golden retriever in the man. He was like a Doberman who always had to figure out whether or not he was going to bite.

Still, she was a chick who took chances. She walked up to him, opening her arms, and he grimaced, as she'd known he would.

"Huggers," he said with a sigh, but his arms went around her anyway.

"Huggers are awesome, Dec. You need more hugs." He was so grim and refused to talk much of the time, yet he was loyal and fun to be around.

"I don't think he needs more if he wants to continue to remain employed by me," a chilly voice said.

She felt Dec's hands come up.

"Nothing sexual about it, boss," Dec said. "She's a huggy chick."

She held on for another second before letting him go and turning to face Hunt. Just on principle. It wasn't like she was doing something wrong and he needed to understand that he couldn't make her feel guilty.

Jeez, that man was hot as hell. He was standing there in all black. Black jeans, black T-shirt, black hair that looked like he'd recently come out of a shower. His eyes seemed to have gone black.

She frowned his way. "He's my friend. Like he said, I'm a hugger. I've never slept with him, macked down on him, or played with him. I'm a physical person, Joshua."

"I don't like to share my toys."

See, this was where she knew she should play the part. She should let her eyes go submissively down and agree that she shouldn't upset the man who would be her Master, her Dom. That was the right play, the play Jiang Kun would have made.

"Excellent, because I don't like being referred to as a toy." Shit. She'd been Kayla Summers for too long. Maybe she didn't know how to spy anymore.

He considered her for a moment. "I thought you'd never worked with them."

"That doesn't mean I don't know them," she replied. "We're a small community and we tend to keep up with one another. We also tend to back each other up. If that's going to be a problem, maybe you need a private detective, someone who isn't used to working with a team."

"Challenging me so soon?" One side of his mouth lifted in a wistful smile.

"I have some boundaries, Mr. Hunt. I understand that I'm an employee, but you have to treat me like a human being, too." It was true. She'd totally thought she could go into this job and that she would fall into her old persona.

She couldn't. She'd been out in the real world for too long. She'd been surrounded by people who valued her for who she was, not what she could provide them with. It had changed her yet again.

"All right, then. Let's start over." He held out his hand. "I'm happy you're here, Kayla."

Her heart skipped a beat and she realized how dangerous he could be. She could handle his charm, but there was something underneath it, something that wanted. That was the part of Joshua Hunt that threatened her peace of mind. Still, she placed her hand in his hand and enjoyed the warmth that flowed from his body to hers. "I'm happy to be here, too. Will you show me the house?"

"It would be my pleasure," he assured her. "If you'll come this way, I'll introduce you to my housekeeper. This particular house was built in the late nineties."

She followed him and tried to remember that this was a job and she wasn't here for fun.

* * * *

Josh sat back, a little surprised at how much such a tiny female could put away. She'd eaten her salad, Chilean sea bass with lemon and roasted vegetables, and two helpings of the rice pilaf Josh loved but couldn't have more than a few bites of. He hated wasting it, but Mrs. Glendower insisted on cooking it after she'd found out it was one of his comfort foods.

He didn't have to worry about wasting it tonight. Kay polished that sucker off.

He found he liked having her sitting across from him at the small outdoor dining table on his balcony. He'd chosen to eat al fresco because he'd thought to stun her with his view. The sun was starting to go down, and in the distance the cliffs were lit up with the brilliant pink and red and orange sunset. It was low tide and the beach was marked with people, but they were mostly locals this time of year. A couple passed, holding hands while they walked barefoot in the sand.

It felt good to be here with her.

She stopped, as though sensing he was watching her with amusement. "Sorry. I have a fast metabolism. Always have. It will probably catch up with me one of these days. Did I eat your portion, too?"

He had to laugh. It had been a long time since he'd had dinner with a woman who wasn't counting every single calorie, who actually enjoyed her food. "No. I had my portion."

She frowned, a line appearing on her brow. Yeah, it had been a long time since he'd been around a woman whose forehead moved, too. It was simply accepted in his business that Botox was a must. "That was a single spoonful. That was nothing."

He could see he might have to talk to Mrs. Glendower about changing the menu up a bit. He didn't want this woman to be hangry. It could go poorly for him. "That was a taste and that, my dear, is all the carbs my abs can take."

Her eyes widened. "Oh. Sorry. That sucks. You look healthy. I wouldn't think you have to diet."

"I am healthy right now," he explained. "When I'm not actively shooting a film that requires me to be shirtless, I put on about five to ten pounds. You're catching me at the end of lazy time. I'll shed it in the next few weeks before I have to shoot. That way I'll look perfect on film, but a doctor would likely tell me I'm underweight at that point. Why do you think actresses have to stay so damn thin? The camera really does add pounds. It's not a forgiving thing."

"No dessert, then, huh?"

"I'm afraid Mrs. Glendower isn't used to serving desserts," he admitted. "I'll talk to her about keeping some fun stuff in the house for you."

"Not if it's going to screw up your diet," she replied. "I can survive. Well, I can hoard candy and eat where you can't see it."

"Not at all. I'm quite good at restraint." Denial was something he was very acquainted with. "It won't bother me at all if you have sweets around. As a matter of fact, if you like, you can go over menus with Mrs. Glendower and slip in some comfort food. Make sure I have a decent protein and some greens and then go crazy with the rest. How about one night a week we share some comfort food? It's been a long time since I had lasagna."

She sighed. "My dad makes the best lasagna. Well, he did until my other dad's doctor explained that his cholesterol was that of a walking, talking piece of bacon. Now he makes it with vegan cheese and mushrooms. I totally miss real lasagna."

"How many dads do you have?" He knew a lot about her professional experience, but her personal life had been summed up with a security check that stated she wasn't a threat. He found himself curious about her.

"Just the two."

"Ah, so this isn't a stepdad thing?"

"Nope. Two dads. Happily married since they legally could be but together since they were twenty-two and met at a disco in 1979. Fred was a dancing bartender. Jim was the fly DJ. They swear it was cool at the time. I've seen the pictures. I disagree."

"Where did you grow up?" He knew she'd been adopted and spent her formative years in So Cal, but he couldn't remember quite where.

She stiffened for a moment and he worried he touched some sore spot. She sighed and relaxed again. "I was born in rural China. I was smuggled out of the country with my mother's permission and I found my way into an orphanage. I was adopted shortly thereafter and made my way to Santa Barbara. My dad taught at the UC campus there and my other father was a stay-at-home dad."

"Wow. That must have been interesting back then. Even in the early nineties there couldn't have been too many families like yours."

"I'm sure it would have been hard if we'd been somewhere else," she replied. "I was an Asian girl with gay parents. One white. One black. We were the world, as I liked to say. I'm sure there were people who made fun of me. I never cared. I don't know if that was a function of how well they raised me or simply my personality, but I don't give in to bullying behavior. Oh, I should clarify. I totally give in to it. I tend to beat the shit out of the bully, but I don't let them make me feel bad about me, if that makes sense."

"Everyone cares on some level." He could remember the taunts, the stares, the people who looked through him like he hadn't been there at all. He'd tried to make himself numb, but even now, it hurt. Years later and he could remember those eyes on him.

She shrugged. "I guess I haven't met anyone I thought enough of that their opinion could make me feel bad. Not that I don't have friends. But my friends like me. So far I haven't fucked that up."

"Even with the person you took a knife to?" He was still reeling a little from that revelation. He'd known whoever he would hire would be good with weapons, but he'd thought about guns. Not knives. There was something odd about thinking Kayla might have a couple of weapons on her at all times.

"Owen? Nah, he took it well. He said it didn't bug him at all. Said it happened to him in pubs all the time, and that I believe. He could be obnoxious." Her smiled faltered. "He went to Damon and explained that it was his fault. He tried really hard to get me out of trouble."

"Are you still friends?" Something about the way her expression had shifted made him wonder.

"Yes, but he doesn't remember what happened. It's sad that he doesn't remember all the reasons I care about him." She seemed to shake something off and her smile returned. "He had a work-related accident. Fucked up his memory. But that's not what we're here for. I looked over the contract and there are only a few things I have some questions about. You want me to surrender my phone to you whenever you ask. Is that because you're worried I'll cheat or you're worried I'm working for a newspaper?"

Well, she didn't have problems being forward. He wasn't sure how he felt about that.

Except for his dick. His dick was very sure how it felt. His dick had been hard since the moment she'd turned and told him she didn't like being referred to as a toy.

How did he make her understand the world she was walking into? "Would a hundred thousand dollars help you out?"

She sat back. "I'm sure a hundred K would help almost anyone. Are you saying that's what I could make if I was writing a story on you?"

"One where you could prove the rumors about my sexual proclivities, that would be the basement price. It could go much higher."

"I don't get it. I mean I do," she replied. "You're superhot. People are interested in how you get down and dirty, but I don't see why it's such a biggie."

"In this day and age, a story like that would ruin my career. If the people at The Reef talked, I would be done."

"But BDSM is consensual."

"And Jared Johns didn't kill anyone," he pointed out. "The accusation is all that matters today. He didn't do anything wrong, but that scandal has deeply affected his career. The show got canceled. Oh, it lasted another two seasons, but as popular as it was, it should have gone on for ten years. Now Jared's a free agent and he's struggling to find work, and it's all about the stain on him. Perception is everything, and the truth, well, the truth changes from one person to another until all that matters is opinion."

She thought about it for a moment and seemed to come to some decision. "That's rough, but I understand. I'll write down my phone password. You should feel free to check it whenever you like."

"And what will I find? Anything interesting?" He wasn't going to be a bastard and demand it right then.

"I play a lot of Angry Birds. Way too much. I like to take pictures of food because I always tell myself that someday I'll start a food blog, but I never do. I read a god-awful amount of romance novels. If you make fun of me, we'll have trouble because I sometimes get overly involved and it's almost like they're real people. I text with my friend Tucker all the time. He sends pictures of things he finds fascinating or weird. He finds a lot of things fascinating."

There it was again. A nasty twist hit his gut like it had when he'd walked out and caught her hugging the broody bodyguard. Jealousy. Possessiveness. He told himself it was because he was signing a contract with her, but he hadn't felt this caveman-like in years. It wasn't a pretty look on him.

"He's a friend, Joshua," she said quietly, as though she could read him like a book. "I think of Tucker as a little brother. A real little brother. He's a bit like a toddler, except he wants sex instead of food. Nah. Along with food. He eats a lot. They all do."

"Sounds like an interesting man." The fact that this Tucker wanted sex didn't help. Of course the kid wanted sex. That was probably what all the texting was about. Josh was absolutely certain that Tucker found Kayla fascinating.

God knows he did.

"He doesn't remember either," she explained. "My company was involved in a case a while back. We were tracking a woman, a doctor who developed a drug that erased the memories of soldiers. Once they were free of their pasts, she would retrain them, almost imprinting them on herself. Like ducklings, except with high-powered weaponry."

That was interesting. That would make an excellent movie. He leaned in. "Super soldiers. She was trying to make soldiers free of conscience and loyal only to her. I take it since we haven't been overrun by these guys that she failed?"

"We took her out," she replied. "But we found a whole group of men whose memories she wiped. They had been her experiments, and without her around, well, ducklings need someone to lead them. One of those ducklings was Tucker. We call them the Lost Boys. It's odd how their brains work. They remember things like what a toothbrush is, and a couple of them easily remembered how to drive a car, but they don't know what their names are or whether or not they left someone behind. They don't know if they've ever been in love or what sex feels like. Well, Dante knows because he snuck out one night. It's okay. We had him tested and everything. But that's why I won't stop texting with Tucker. I'm one of the few people he knows."

"You're his anchor." When her brows rose, he shook his head because she'd obviously misunderstood. "I didn't mean that in a bad way. You're a touchstone for him, a landmark. He doesn't understand much, but when he knows you're around, he can handle it."

"I guess so," she agreed. "I like that. I've been a person in need of a landmark once or twice in my life. Anyway, I suppose what I'm trying to say is you can freely read my text conversations with Tucker. And hey, if you want to call him, he's a big fan. He loved that movie with you and the talking baby where you solve crimes."

Josh groaned. *Maybe Baby* and *Maybe Baby 2: Baby B Tripping* were a part of his career he would rather forget. "No. That was not my finest moment. In my defense, I was young and hungry. Like actually hungry." He chuckled as he sat back. "I'll understand you have a family and you like to talk to them. And I'll try to cool the caveman act with Burke. The truth is the guy kind of scares me."

"*Was* it an act?"

"No." That was the hell of the thing. "It was an instinct, but it's not one I have often. I try not to be too possessive of anyone or anything. I happen to know it can all go away tomorrow."

"Yeah," she replied. "I suppose I know that, too."

"Was there something else you were concerned about? I tried to keep the business side to the work contract and the D/s to the personal. You do have days off, but I would like forty-eight hours' notification in order to make plans. You'll receive your schedule on Sundays, and I expect you to follow it as much as possible. You coordinate security with Shane and Declan, but first and foremost, you're with me. You will receive a weekly allowance…"

She held a hand up. "Let's call it a salary."

"This is not part of your salary," he replied flatly. "This is part of your upkeep. You'll receive an allowance for clothes and anything else you need to maintain a flawless appearance when we're out in public."

"And when we're private?"

"When we're private, I'll prefer you with little to no clothes at all," he admitted.

"Then maybe the back of your house shouldn't be made of glass," she pointed out with a grin, referring to the floor-to-ceiling windows that ran all three floors of the house and offered picture-perfect views of the Pacific.

"Luckily, I also have shades that come down with the push of a button," he replied. "Mrs. Glendower only comes in twice a week. She leaves food with instructions on heating, and she cleans on Tuesdays and Thursdays. Otherwise, it's you and me and the bodyguards, who know how to knock before entering."

"All right." She glanced back down at her plate as though she wished it wasn't empty. "I saw in the contract that you already set up appointments for me. Hair. Nails." She picked up a pen and scratched through one section. "I'm not getting Botox, Joshua."

"It was merely an appointment with a dermatologist. Everyone has a dermatologist. I wasn't suggesting you get anything at all done, simply giving you the option."

"I'll do all the mani-pedis and blowouts you like, but don't try to change my face," she said. "I will take the gym membership, although there's such beautiful nature out here I'll probably jog every day."

Damn it. He reached over and put a hand on hers. "I think you're gorgeous."

"But you require perfection."

He pulled her hand in between his. "I don't. Look, I had that contract brought up when you were a nameless, faceless woman. I told the lawyer to draw up language that covered all the bases that could possibly be needed. I'll cancel the dermatologist and change all your appointments over to an exclusive spa I know. Facials and mani-pedis and mimosas."

"I thought I wasn't allowed to drink."

He winced. "Again, written for a nameless, faceless probably alcoholic woman. Kay, I'm not an optimist. I'm kind of the opposite and prepare for the absolute worst. It's not a pretty part of me, but it's who I am. So here…"

He let go of her hand and turned the contract around, quickly slashing through the mandatory self-care section that also stated if her breasts weren't acceptable, that he would pay for the augmentation. Jesus. What had he been thinking? He wrote out to the side.

Party A will be clean and presentable at all public functions.

He initialed. "That's all I need."

"Does that mean I don't get the clothes?"

Finally, something he could give her. He'd been starting to worry that he was going to fumble his way through the entire night. "You can have all the clothes you need. I promise. Your personal shopper will be here in the morning to get you ready for next week. Before we head to the set in Mexico, we'll go out to Rodeo for the day and get anything you need."

"Cool, because my wardrobe is probably not up to snuff red-carpet wise." She glanced down at the beach, the end of day light making the sand shimmer like jewels.

The silence lengthened between them. As did his cock because they were leaving the small-talk portion of the evening. She was lovely and she'd passed his tests. She wasn't running away as fast as she could, so she seemed to have accepted him.

There was no reason to not have her.

The need for his restraint was gone and he could indulge.

"Kayla?"

Her eyes came up, a flash of recognition there. "Yes?"

"Are you going to sign the contract or do you have more questions?"

She picked up the pen sitting on top of the contracts that would bind the two of them together for the next six months. They would reevaluate the relationship at that point in time, but for the next six months, she was his. His bodyguard. His submissive.

Bought and properly paid for. He would take care of her and she would give him what he needed.

She signed with a flourish and sat back, a gleam of curiosity in her eyes.

He was curious, too, and there was zero reason to not satisfy their curiosity. Hard and soft limits had been gone over. They would find their communication style as they went along. But first she should understand that he was in control.

"Come sit on my lap."

She didn't hesitate. She stood and turned, shifting so she could maneuver her way onto his lap.

Her weight came down on him and he wrapped an arm around her waist. Damn but she made him feel big. He'd seen her take out a man twice her size, but sitting here in his lap she felt small and vulnerable, and fuck but that did it for him.

He slid a hand along her knee, letting himself indulge in the silky-smooth feel of her skin against his palm. "Did you do as I asked?"

He was well aware his voice had gone husky, deeper than normal.

"Yes, Joshua." She squirmed the tiniest bit, as though trying to find a comfortable position. It might be difficult for her because she was sitting right on his cock, and it was harder and thicker than he could ever remember it being.

"How can I trust you?" This was all part of the game he loved. Here he could let go and play out the darker of his impulses—to control, to take, to possess.

See. Want. Have.

"You'll have to check," she replied. "Though shouldn't we go inside?"

He reached out and picked up his cell with his free hand, pushing one number and connecting to the security room. He put them on speaker. She needed to understand what she was up against in order for the game to be fair. "Landon?"

"This is Burke," the deep voice replied. "Shane's on patrol. What can I do for you?"

"Burke, I would like to fuck my submissive on the third-floor balcony. Is anyone watching us? Can you see any cameras pointed our way?"

A low, masculine chuckle came across the line. "No, Mr. Hunt. And given the angle relative to the beach, you should enjoy your evening without worry. The only peepers I would worry about would be your next-door neighbor, and Jared is out for the night."

"I wouldn't care if he wasn't. Keep up the good work." He hung up and his hand tightened. "I would prefer when we're playing that you don't question me like that. I know where I want to fuck you. I know when I want to fuck you, and I'm in charge. If I want you in the middle of a crowded freeway, your only response is a yes or a no. Not to question me."

She seemed to relax back against him, as though she was giving up the struggle and choosing to submit. "Yes, Joshua. Yes, I understand, and yes to the sex. Please."

He liked the breathy *please* and loved how she squirmed. Still, he wasn't absolutely sure she'd obeyed him, and he was a man who required proof. He slid his hand up her thigh. "Spread your legs for me."

Her knees fell apart, and he could feel the heat from her core. He slipped a hand up until he made contact with her softest skin. No panties. Nothing but wet heat waiting for him, and it was obvious the play had cranked her up, too. His free hand eased one button on her shirt free, and then another and another until he could move in like a soldier conquering territory. No bra. Her breasts were like the rest of her. Soft and delicate. One nipple rolled against his palm, hardening then and there.

"I can see you've been an obedient sub," he said, his mouth against her ear. "You need to stay that way or there will be punishment. I'm not a sadist, Kayla. I truly don't get off on your pain, but I will give it to you if you need it. I am a disciplinarian. I gain satisfaction from your obedience. In exchange, I'll show you how good it can be to obey me."

He let his fingers slide over her labia, teasing her. She relaxed back against him, completely caged within his arms. He cupped her breast with his free hand while he began gently circling her clitoris.

"Do you like how that feels?" He whispered the question into her ear.

"Yes. God, yes."

He took her nipple in between his thumb and forefinger, pinching. It was quick and hard and would flare through her like a flash fire. Sure enough she whimpered and squirmed, rubbing against his dick. Every movement sent a hardcore thrill through him. "What do you call me?"

"Joshua." Her voice was breathless, the words shaky as they left her lips. "Joshua, yes, I love how it feels."

"Do you want more?"

"Yes, Joshua. I want more. Please, could I have more?"

He started up again, a slow circle of that sweet button of hers. She was slippery and getting wetter by the minute. She certainly hadn't lied about wanting sex, and she wasn't being coy about asking for it. "I like it when you're polite, pet. Something about a sub sweetly asking me to let her come works for me, do you understand?"

"I do." Her hands clutched at his sides, bracing herself against him, while her feet had hooked around his calves, holding her knees wide for him.

"And are you thinking about who might be watching?"

She shook her head. "I don't care."

"You don't care if they're watching you from the beach? I've got your legs spread wide, and that soft pussy of yours is lit by the sunset. Do you think it's all the colors of the sunset? Coral and pink? Your cream like the foam from the waves?"

"You're killing me." Her head nestled against his neck. "And no. I don't care if someone is watching me."

"Shane is going to be walking back up the beach any minute now. He's patrolling the grounds. He could see you like this and I wouldn't care as long as he knows not to touch," he whispered. He rolled her nipple again. "I'm going to enjoy showing you off, letting everyone see how lovely my submissive is, but I won't share you."

"That wasn't in the contract," she pointed out. "You have the right to share me if you like."

He pinched her hard again, the idea repugnant to him. "I don't like. I won't like, so if that's a sweet kink of yours, the dry spell is going to continue."

"I don't need a bunch of lovers. I don't need to be shared. I do desperately need you to put a tiny bit more pressure on me. Please."

"Don't hold back. I want to hear you come. Take it from me. Come all over my hand and let your Master know how much you appreciate him."

He pressed down, his thumb finding her clit and rotating in a way that was bound to please her. Control was the most important thing. Control and restraint. It was his job to send her carefully over the edge and hers to let go and go wild.

Her hips started to pump as though she couldn't help herself, little thrusts against his thumb. A low moan came from her throat, but it wasn't enough. He wanted more from her. Needed it. Very carefully, he licked the shell of her ear before giving it a hard nip.

She screamed out, her whole body tense. Every muscle stiffened and she cried out again. Breath panted from her lips and he felt her heartbeat hammering in her chest. Her arousal coated his fingers.

All in all a perfectly satisfactory experience. She responded beautifully. She was hot as hell.

His cock throbbed and he wanted nothing more than to turn her around, open his slacks, and thrust deep inside her. She would bounce on his cock until she screamed again and he would empty himself into her.

In about ten seconds. No. He was in control. In control of her, and definitely in control of himself. He would come tonight, but his dick would wait until he'd proven his point.

"Excellent, pet." He helped her sit up. "Now I would like for you to stand."

A throaty laugh came from her mouth. Her ass wiggled against his cock, teasing and tempting and damn near sending him over the edge. "Are you sure about that?"

A mistake. Excellent because he'd been almost ready to give in, and he never fucking gave in. He took his hands away, bringing them up and leaving her without balance. It forced her to stand awkwardly.

"Okay, that was my bad," she said, not turning his way. She leaned over the table, her palms down as though she needed a moment. "I promised not to question you."

At least she understood what she'd done wrong. "Go to the dungeon, sweetheart. I need a moment. I want you naked and kneeling to greet me when I come in."

She turned. "I'm sorry, Joshua."

He knew he should be cold, should withhold, but he was sick of the chill. He found himself giving her a small smile. "We'll find our way. Now go and give your poor Master a moment so he can properly discipline you."

She stared down at him. "You're different than I thought you would be. Should I take these plates down?"

He reached for her wrist, dragging her close again. "You are not a maid. I'll handle it. And that was questioning me when I'd given you a clear order. It's not going to go well for you."

He leaned in and brushed his hand over hers, sending a jolt of electricity through his system.

Fuck, she played hell with his discipline. It was because it had been a long time. Yes, it was because she was gorgeous and new and submissive. She flipped his switch in all the right ways, but it would go away eventually.

"Go."

She turned and walked back into the house, not bothering to smooth her skirt back down or to rearrange her shirt so her breast wasn't exposed.

He hadn't told her to therefore she hadn't done it.

His cock practically wept.

Josh took a long breath and stood, looking out over the water. Control. He had to find it before he could touch her again.

The waves pounded in and he took another breath.

Control. He could never lose it again.

Chapter Four

Kayla's hands were shaking as she pulled the last two buttons of her blouse free. Not that she wasn't already hanging out there for all to see, but Joshua wanted her naked and she didn't intend to piss him off further.

It was her job to please the Master. Please the Master. Make the Master value her, crave her. Convince the Master to do her will.

Yeah, she hadn't been thinking about her will when she'd sat in his lap and spread her legs wide. Not thinking about the operation when his fingers had strummed her body like a master guitarist.

What the hell had just happened?

She needed to find some control. The dungeon was nothing more than a second master bedroom that had been redone into a fancy playroom. It was the only room in the house that wasn't white. It was done in shades of scarlet and black. A bit reminiscent of The Reef. He'd briefly shown her the room as they'd walked through the house before dinner. There was a St. Andrew's Cross on the wall, a lushly done spanking bench, a massage table that would likely second as a bed. The ceiling had hard points for suspension play. There was a closet full of toys with all manner of ways to torture a poor sub.

She closed the door and shoved out of her skirt, hanging up her clothes on the hook he'd indicated belonged to her now.

I'm going to enjoy showing you off, letting everyone see how lovely my submissive is, but I won't share you.

His whispered words rang through her head. That whiskey-deep voice of his had been every bit as seductive as his big hands on her body. Every word that came from his throat had rumbled along her skin and shown her that no matter how long she'd spent playing at The Garden, it was utterly and completely different when the Master playing with her belonged to her.

As she sank down to the floor, the chill of the hardwoods beneath her knees was a welcome distraction to the heat still racing through her.

Maybe she didn't have enough experience to handle him since one little orgasm in and she was ready to do anything he wished.

Perhaps because he'd said the one thing guaranteed to make her spine melt.

I don't like. I won't like, so if that's a sweet kink of yours, the dry spell is going to continue.

He wouldn't share her. He wanted her all for himself. It would be stupid to see those words as some sort of declaration of commitment since they'd met earlier today. She'd only signed a contract a few minutes before. Those words only meant what he'd said to her when he'd caught her with Declan. Joshua Hunt was a boy who didn't like sharing his toys.

She would be wise to remember that. She was a toy to him, and one that came with a high price tag, nothing more.

And she was a tool for the Agency. A well-trained, well-paid tool.

Kayla took a deep breath in, settling into the familiar position. There was something meditative about finding the perfect submissive pose. Shoulders straight and proud, spine centered. Hips back and knees splayed wide, allowing cool air to caress her. Palms up in offering. Her body was his for the duration of the session.

Finally, she lowered her head, letting her neck relax even as the rest of her body remained in position, almost a symbol that it was time for the body to rule and the brain to rest.

Breathe in. Breathe out. Kay let her body's rhythms take over so time seemed to flow differently and space became a softer place. Her mind wandered, breathing and heart rate slowing, giving over to the meditative state.

She had no idea how long he left her there, but it was certainly more than a few moments. When she heard the door open, she felt calm and centered again. This was a job. She could do her job. She was good at her job.

His bare feet came into view. Naturally, even his feet were sexy. How the hell were feet sexy?

Just like that, she was off center again.

"You look beautiful like this."

She didn't respond because they were in the dungeon. She wasn't sure of all the protocols he would use. Some Doms preferred their subs remain silent in the dungeon.

A big hand touched her head, palm covering her scalp. "Naturally you have perfect form. Did you learn this at The Garden? I've heard of it, you know. It's so exclusive even I can't get in. I was jealous of Jared when he got a membership to Sanctum. I don't like being left out."

He was an interesting combination of strong Dom and wayward boy. There were major gaps in his history, long periods of time that remained unaccounted for, and that couldn't mean anything good. A good life tended to be documented carefully. What had happened to him between the time he left his foster home and the moment he showed up on Hollywood's radar? What had happened that made him forever need to belong, even if it meant buying his way in?

"You can talk, pet. Unless I give you specific instructions, I never mean to silence your voice."

"If we go to London or Dallas, I can get you into both," she offered. "They're wonderful clubs. Completely different experiences, but both amazing. The Doms in charge are private bastards."

"I belong to a club in Dallas." His hand came off her head and his feet disappeared. "It's very nice."

She knew the one he was talking about. "Well, then if we're in Dallas, you can take me someplace new. I've heard The Club is lovely and that Julian Lodge knows how to treat his clients. It's probably better than Ian Taggart. Ian treats everyone like we're still in the Army and he's the general in charge."

"Lodge is polite, but I still feel like I'm on the outside any place other than The Reef."

She heard the door to the closet open and took a long breath. "It's good to have a place where you belong."

She couldn't see what he was doing. It was part of the glorious mind fuck that got her adrenaline going.

"You seem to belong a lot of places."

"I have a membership to The Garden and Sanctum, but only because of my work status. I feel weird in Sanctum. For a long time I was on the opposite side of Ian Taggart—well, he thought I was on the opposite side. No one was allowed to know my true identity except my handler and his boss. It's the curse of the double agent. Sometimes you feel like no one believes you at all because you've become such a master at lying."

She was surprised that came out as easily as it had. Her former career wasn't something she liked to talk about, but something about being in the dungeon always made her vulnerable. In many ways, the dungeon was the only place she did talk about what had happened to her. It was her confessional, the one place she could be vulnerable because she knew there would be absolution.

"Do you still lie?"

"I try not to. In my daily life, I don't lie at all. I don't care enough to lie. I can be too harsh at times because I gave all my fucks up a long time ago." *Except that I'll lie to you. I'll lie because my job and my friends are all I really care about anymore.*

Yeah, she didn't say that part out loud.

"I like honesty," he said. "No, I require it. I can't stand people blowing sunshine up my ass. I have far too much of that every day. It makes you wonder who to trust. It's why I like Jared. I don't think he's smart enough to lie."

"That feels rough."

"I guess I gave away all my fucks, too. Eyes up."

She brought her eyes to meet his gaze and couldn't help the shiver of desire that went through her body. He'd shed his shirt and every bit of dietary restraint showed in his perfectly cut body. Wearing nothing but a pair of low-slung jeans, he stared down at her. There was no way to miss the bulge in his denims. Joshua Hunt was built on long, lean lines, but that erection was anything but lean. It was a massive beast restrained by denim.

He held a crop in his hand, looking every inch the dark, decadent Dom. He reached out and touched the scar under her right clavicle. His lips quirked up. "Dare I ask where you got this?"

It wasn't her biggest scar but it was probably the most noticeable. She had one on her back, long and close to her spine. A small circular scar above her hipbone from a gun shot. But he was staring at the candy cane shaped one. "That was where I got caught by the bad guys and they started to play around with me. It was a scalpel. Unlucky for them, I had managed to get my hands free. They didn't play for long."

He traced the scar. "Maybe I should call you Little Miss Muffett. It reminds me of a Sheppard's crook."

She wrinkled her nose. "Or you could call me Buffy because it's more like a scythe. We share a last name, you know." She straightened up. "Do the scars make me less attractive to you?"

Oh, he could go cold fast. "You're gorgeous and you know it. Don't ever question that in front of me again and don't pretend like that was anything about me. You can easily tell how much I want you. This is our first session, so I'll go easy on the discipline until I can read your body better. I'll leave your mouth open, but in the future, if you question me while we're playing, you'll find I have a lovely ball gag purchased just for you."

"I doubt it was just for me. You didn't know you were going to hire me until this afternoon."

His jaw tightened and she realized she was totally out of practice. All the Doms she'd bottomed for in the last few years were "play" Doms. She took them on for a night or they served her when she needed a session. They didn't take it as seriously as Josh obviously did.

"Hands and knees."

She shifted position, leaning forward and finding her balance. Her skin hummed with anticipation as he moved around her body. This was part of the play, the uncertainty of what he would do or when he would begin and how hard it would go. "I'm sorry. I shouldn't have been sarcastic."

"You apologize a lot, pet. We're going to have to do something to correct the behavior."

She heard the strike before she felt it. A *whoosh* and then a hard crack as the crop hit her backside. Pain, like a lightning strike, boomed over her. It took everything she had not to lose her position.

If that was easy, it would be very interesting to see what he considered hardcore.

As it always did, the pain flashed through, turning into heat and making her skin come to life.

She knew it didn't work this way for everyone. A person had to be wired a certain way. And it wasn't as though she enjoyed all pain. She'd had plenty that had done nothing for her. Nothing but eat away at her soul. Nothing but show her how futile and useless she could be.

But this, oh, this set her free.

Another hard smack and then she felt the soft leather tip of the crop running down her spine.

"As a matter of fact, I did buy the ball gag specifically for you. I stopped at a discreet toy store before I came home this afternoon. Everything I purchased was with you in mind. I bought the ball gag and some nice nipple clamps."

Her body tightened and that was when he struck again.

She hissed at the sensation. He said he wasn't a sadist? He sure knew how and when to strike.

"Do you like the idea of playing out some heavy scenes with me?"

"Yes, Joshua," she admitted. "I enjoy scenes. I like how a good Dom can make me work for an orgasm."

"You seem to come quite easily."

And wasn't that a revelation? "That was *not* normal for me."

"And what is normal for you?" Joshua asked.

"Being too much in my head to enjoy myself. Struggling to stay focused on my body. I've practiced meditation for years and it all flies out when a man puts hands on me."

"Why do you think that is?"

For good reasons. For bad reasons. "I think I often allow too much time to pass without affection. It's not merely about sex, though the need for sex is in there. It's about all the years I went without a kind hand on my body, without trusting touch. I'm damaged, but I can hold myself together. Sometimes when the right person touches me, I forget I'm damaged at all."

Another hard *thwack* to her ass had her groaning.

"You're very open with me right now. Why were you shut down earlier? Is this some kind of play for you? Are you changing tactics to achieve a desired result?"

"Only if the result I wanted was my ass on fire." She groaned because that brought the crop down again. "I didn't know what you liked. I thought perhaps you were the type of man who required peace in his life. I wanted to seem tranquil. I'm not, Joshua. I'm trouble, and a whole lot of it."

"Now see, I know an honest answer when I hear one." He stepped back. "Let me help you up. You owe me thirty over my lap for the disrespectful questions."

She opened her mouth to ask what the hell he called the last five minutes if not discipline, but carefully closed it again.

"Excellent. We're already learning each other's habits. And that was a warm-up," he said, practically reading her mind. "That was what it took to get you to a place where you could tell me the unadulterated truth. Now I'll tell you some of mine."

His hand came out, helping her to stand. She brushed back her hair, feeling it all over her body. Every strand tickled from the back of her neck down to her aching backside. Sometimes she forgot how much hair she had. But then sometimes she forgot she had a body that needed, craved and wanted.

He sank down onto the spanking bench, patting his lap.

It seemed he liked to talk as he worked. Some Doms never once spoke unless it was to give orders. But Joshua was turning out to be a chatty Dom, the kind who talked more when he found his top space.

He might be the kind who was far easier to manipulate when he was comfortable.

He held his hand out, helping to ease her over his lap. She could feel that big erection and the way his whole body seemed to sigh as he relaxed.

She wasn't relaxed. She was on the edge, but then that was kind of the point. His hand ran over her skin, brushing her hair to the side.

"You're beautiful, Kayla. You have a gorgeous body and a lovely face. I happen to like damaged. Perhaps *like* is the wrong word. I understand damaged. I don't get perfectly happy people. I don't understand nice. Polite is fine, but polite is a construct, learned behavior. I do understand that. I like rules. I like knowing how to behave, and I want to know how my submissive is going to behave."

Like Riley had said, though maybe he'd used the wrong words. "You want peace?"

"I want consistency. I want dependability. Can you give that to me, Kayla?"

"I can try."

"Excellent. That's all I ask. Take care of your job and I'll take care of you. I like having a woman to take care of. I don't think a vanilla relationship would ever work for me. I believe I said thirty."

"You did." Her voice was even but inside she was shaking a bit. This wasn't mere play for him, and that heightened the experience for her.

"You have a safe word."

They had decided on it during their contract negotiations. "I won't need it for thirty, I promise, Joshua."

"I'll remember that, too."

His hand came down and he proved once again that he didn't play. Fire licked along her skin and she held on to his ankles for support. He counted out loud, his strong voice ringing through the room. Over and over he slapped her ass, not stopping to give her time to breathe or to allow the heat to sink in. This was a disciplinary spanking.

This was something to survive. She gritted her teeth against the pain, breathing it in and letting it flow back out. After the first few strokes, she managed to relax her muscles and let herself get loose. The pain couldn't touch her here. Here she could float and the pain became nothing more than a wave that swept her along.

Here the pain shifted and she could feel herself coming alive.

Before she knew it, his hand came down one last time.

He kept her over his lap, his hands smoothing across her heated flesh. "You handled that well. I was worried you might not have as much experience as you claimed, but that was quite lovely."

Her body had tons of experience. Her body could take anything he dished out. The emotional stuff, not so much, but she wasn't about to tell him that.

He shifted her and she found herself on her knees in front of him. Between his knees. It was a deeply submissive position to be in, and she let herself sink further into the place where she didn't have to make decisions or think past her Master's latest command.

Joshua looked down at her, his hands coming out and brushing back her hair. "I don't want you to question my commands or my actions when we're playing. It's perfectly fine for you to stop the play if you find it disturbing. My point isn't to upset you, but I am the Dominant partner and you will obey. Do I make myself clear?"

"Yes, Joshua."

"Excellent. Now carefully open the fly of my jeans." His voice was deeper, tighter than it had been before.

Which was good because she was starting to worry that she was the only one genuinely affected by this scene they were playing out. It was easy to see his body responding, but the tone of his voice proved he wasn't cold to her. His jaw hardened, forming what she liked to think of as a superhero line, as she brought her hands up and eased the button open before gently starting to work the zipper. She had to be damn careful because she didn't want to stop and take another spanking because she'd gotten Master's cock stuck in his zipper. Nope. She wanted to move on from the disciplinary portion of the evening to the part where he made her scream.

Taking her time, she eased the zipper down, revealing the black fabric of his boxers. When she had them down, she smoothed the sides out and sat back because he hadn't commanded her past opening his fly.

"Now the boxers. Pull them down and take my cock in hand."

She prayed she wasn't drooling. Her ass ached and she knew her pussy was soaking wet and ready, and yet the anticipation was heady.

She let her nails skim his cut abs before delving under the waistband of his boxers and easing them over his erection. His cock sprang free, proving he was as perfect as she'd known he would be. Big and thick, his cock barely fit in her hand.

It had been so long since she'd had sex. He was going to be huge and hot inside her. It should have made her wary, but all she could think about was getting that hard cock inside her, riding this massive, perfect male to completion.

"Stroke me. I won't break. You can get rough with me. I'll tell you when to stop." He leaned back, resting against the bench, and his eyes closed.

She gripped him in one hand and stroked, watching his cock lengthen before her eyes. His chest moved with each breath, but he was perfectly calm. She let her thumb swipe over the head of his cock with each stroke and he chuckled.

"Yes, that's what I want. Now suck the head, pet."

She leaned over and let the flat of her tongue find his cock. She licked him before gently taking him into her mouth. He smelled of soap and arousal, the mixture sending her deeper into her submissive state. She kept stroking him with a firm hand, but she sucked lightly, teasing him with little licks and brushes of her lips.

She got lost in the rhythm, in service. Her body warmed, every bit of her energy focused on bringing him pleasure.

"Take more of me."

No questions. No decisions. There was only the sound of his voice, telling her what she should do. Taking more of his cock was a damn fine thing to do. She sucked the head fully into her mouth, whirling her tongue around.

A pulse of pre-come hit her tongue and she lapped it up. More. She wanted more, her tongue worrying the slit on the head of his cock.

A shudder went through his body. "Cup my balls, pet. Roll them in that soft hand of yours."

She brought her hand up and palmed his heavy balls. They were already tight, readying themselves to shoot off, and she couldn't come up with why that would be a bad idea. The thought of sucking him down made her nipples hard.

The rhythm took over, carrying her along with it. His cock pulsed in her hand, pre-come flowing freely now.

"Stop. Turn around. Hands and knees," he ordered.

She wanted to finish, but immediately removed her hands, holding them up as though to show him she was obeying. She turned and saw herself in the mirror there. It was ornate, with a gilded frame surrounding it. It took her a moment to recognize herself. Her eyes were cloudy with desire, her body loose and willing. Her breasts swung gently as she moved into the position he required.

He stood up, rising behind her like a dark, hungry god.

He shoved out of his jeans and boxers, kicking them across the room. He grabbed a condom and slid it on, working his dick with his big hand. He stared down at her while he stroked himself, every muscle of that perfect body of his drawn and taut. She got the sudden feeling that this was what a rabbit felt like right before the tiger struck, but she couldn't move even if she'd wanted to. She was caught by his eyes and she wasn't going anywhere until he'd had her.

He dropped to his knees behind her and gripped her hips. His cock nuzzled her pussy and it took everything she had to not shove back against him.

"Don't move," he growled. "I'm in charge. You can come when you like, but you won't fight me or try to take control. Am I understood?"

"Yes."

He slapped her ass. "Yes?"

"Yes, Joshua." She was close to where she wanted to be, right on the precipice. It wouldn't take much to send her over the edge.

He used his left hand to reach for her hair, fisting it. "Watch us in the mirror. Don't take your eyes off that mirror or your discipline won't be through for the evening."

"Yes, Joshua." That was the last thing she wanted. She watched him in the mirror, taking in his predatory gaze. His eyes held hers as he thrust hard inside.

She couldn't hold back the cry that came from her throat. She was stretched wide. Despite how wet she was, he was still too big, too much, and he wasn't going easy with her.

He thrust in savagely, forcing his way in until she could feel his balls slap against her.

He pulled back out and then used her hair and the grip on her hips to force her to move, impaling her on his cock.

Her scalp lit up, the sensation sizzling down her spine and straight to her pussy. He set a punishing pace, thrusting deep and lighting her up from the inside. He was in control and there wasn't anything she wanted to do to change that. She wanted him in charge, wanted to find this place where nothing mattered but what he was doing to her body. He manhandled her, making her feel tiny and petite and delicate in a way she hadn't for years.

She watched him even as he pushed her higher. He stroked her with his cock, finding that place inside and riding that spot until she couldn't hold out a second longer. The orgasm was a flash fire, burning through her and making her scream out his name. She didn't hold back because he seemed to want her primal, want the deep sensuality she'd always kept under control.

Joshua pounded into her, riding her orgasm even as he controlled every movement of her body.

Another orgasm took her by surprise, this one stronger than the first.

He hissed behind her and let go of her hair, using both hands to hold her body fast against his. He ground against her, his body pumping hard into hers.

One last thrust and he let go, sending her forward without the strength of his hands to hold her up.

He chuckled and stood up, slipping the condom off and disposing of it.

She couldn't find her breath. Every inch of her body felt pleasantly used. Perfectly used. Her blood pounded through her system, pleasure thrumming like a song played at a low level. It was there in the background, still humming along.

"That was a good first session. Let me help you up."

He didn't seem anywhere close to as shaken as she'd been. He held out a hand and she struggled to shove her emotions down. She wasn't supposed to have emotions.

She allowed him to help her to her feet, her body brushing up against his. She tilted her head up. Kissing would help. Kissing would give her a second to center. It would be proof that he was affected, too.

His gorgeous lips quirked up in a smirk. "Okay, now I believe you that it's been a long dry spell. You were quite tight. You'll probably be sore in the morning. There's a soaking tub in the bathroom. Feel free to use it."

He stepped back and reached for his jeans.

She stood there. Yeah, not how she expected to feel. Her body happy. Her brain used.

But she'd signed up for this. If she'd been paying him, she would have happily tipped the man because he knew what he was doing. It was sex. It didn't have to be meaningful. She wasn't some star-struck teenager with a crush.

She was fucking the man so he would do what her CIA handlers needed him to do.

She'd been out of the game for way too long. The Garden had softened her up, made her useless.

"There's a robe behind you if you want it."

She turned and forced herself to put the robe on, her limbs moving in a mechanical fashion. Arm in. Other arm in. Tie the sash. Smile. "Thank you, Joshua. It was a wonderful first session."

He stared at her for a moment like he didn't believe her.

A crack split the air and then the alarm went off, the sound making the walls shake. Kayla didn't think. There was a window to their left. It had a blackout curtain over it, but all someone would need was heat signature goggles to see through that and shoot Joshua.

"Get down," she shouted.

He turned toward the window and she tackled him, forcing him to the floor.

His response was immediate and unexpected.

Josh screamed, louder than the fucking alarm. She was so shocked, she found herself thrown off him. He bucked up and she went flying, knocking into the spanking bench. She groaned, finding herself on her back, looking up at the ceiling.

And then she was looking into Joshua's handsome face. He covered her with his body, chaos all around them. His eyes were glassy and she was sure in that moment that he wasn't seeing her. His hands went around her throat, closing with intent.

Shit. She had a fucked-up PTSD client who she couldn't kill and couldn't let kill her. She started to bring her knee up. He was going to hate her for this.

"Back off, Mr. Hunt." Dec was standing over them, his Colt 1911 pointed straight at Joshua Hunt's head. "Do it. Right fucking now. I will not allow you to strangle her. I will put a bullet through your head before that happens."

Something about the word *her* seemed to get to Josh, and Kay breathed a sigh of relief that she wasn't going to have to knee his balls into his body cavity. His eyes cleared and his hands came up, palms toward the man with the gun.

Josh shook his head. "I…I didn't mean to hurt her."

Kay scrambled out from under him. "You didn't." She got to her feet, nodding to Dec. "He got triggered. I was ready to handle it, but thank you for the save. What's happening? Do we need to get him out of here?"

"I'm not sure." Dec's gun came down, but he didn't relax. "Shane saw someone on the cameras and then the alarms went off. He's already outside trying to chase down the asshole. PD's on its way. I think we should meet them in a room that isn't full of sex toys, and perhaps more clothing would be helpful."

"Mr. Hunt, I need you to get ready to move." She shook her head when she realized her SIG was in her damn purse. Shit. What a fucking rookie move.

Dec reached behind him and pulled his backup out of its holster, handing it to her with a frown. "Don't fucking forget why you're here ever again, Kay."

"Hey, don't you talk to her like that." Josh stepped in front of her.

But Dec was right. She clicked the safety off. She'd briefly forgotten why she was here, what she was doing. It wasn't a mistake she intended to make again. "He has every right. I was up here without any way to protect you. Let's move. We need to get dressed. Mr. Hunt, follow me. Dec, take his six."

She started out into the house, all intimacy gone.

This was a job and it had started now. There was no going back.

Chapter Five

What the fuck had he done? He forced a T-shirt over his head, glancing back at the big guy with the gun standing in the doorway.

Kayla had run across the hall to the room where he'd placed her luggage. She'd seemed surprised that her suitcase wasn't in his room, but then he'd been good at disappointing her tonight.

"Could I get a minute alone?" He needed to close the doors and breathe, to bash his fucking head against the wall until the images left his brain and he was fully in the present again.

The minute she'd put him on his belly, he'd been transported. He'd been fourteen again and utterly helpless. Bile had risen to his throat, but it had been a scream that emerged. He'd screamed like he hadn't been able to back then. He'd screamed and then his hands had been around her delicate throat before he'd even realized where he was.

Declan Burke slowly shook his head, his eyes cold. "Nope. Not until the threat's past. If you want to change, feel free man. It's nothing I haven't seen before."

Well, hadn't everyone seen it? He'd done nudity in a couple of movies, so he figured the bodyguard could be speaking quite literally. He shoved his feet into a pair of Ferragamos. The loafers were easy and he didn't need socks. Between the loafers, his jeans, and a clean T-shirt, he'd be presentable to the police. He glanced in the mirror. He needed a shave, but otherwise he didn't look like a man who'd recently topped, fucked, and then tried to kill his submissive.

At least someone had turned off the alarm so that sound wasn't blaring through his head like a hammer.

He could have killed her. One minute he'd been damn near pulsing with pleasure, and it hadn't merely been about the sex. No. There had been something triumphant about the way she'd responded to him. He'd found himself ready to pull her up into his arms and haul her to his bedroom.

Which was a thing he didn't do. Ever. Not with a submissive. It was best to keep things with clear boundaries. Sex was for playing. His bedroom was for sleeping and privacy.

Sex was a biological function that kept him sane and somewhat happy when done with the proper attention to detail.

One minute he'd found that perfect balance and the next he'd been ready to snap her neck. He could have done it easily. She was small. Delicate, like a doe.

"You know I saved your dick, right?" Dec said, his eyes staring out into the hallway.

"Excuse me?" His hands were on the dresser, but he turned to look at Dec.

The bodyguard's cold eyes were steady. If the man's pulse had gone up a fraction because of the threat, Josh couldn't tell. "You think I saved her when I came into that room, and that's playing through your head right now. You think you had a freak-out moment and almost killed a woman you have some responsibility for, but the truth is you had a freak-out moment and nearly lost your ability to have children."

"I was strangling her. I had my hands around her throat." And he'd been squeezing. He hadn't seen her at all. He'd seen…he could have killed her. He could have snapped her neck, and then where would they be? She would be dead and he would get a one-way ticket to jail because going to jail would be far better than explaining why he'd attacked the woman he'd recently had sex with.

He pushed off the dresser and made his way into the bathroom, realizing that he would have gone to jail rather than pursuing his other option.

Anything was better than telling someone what had happened to him.

"She was three seconds from shoving your balls through your body and out your damn mouth," Dec explained, his voice flat. "You see her and you see something sweet and soft, and don't get me wrong, there's a lot about Kay that's soft and sweet. Her heart, for example. She gives too much of a shit if you ask me. That's probably why she hesitated in the first place. But there's nothing soft about her physically. You're feeling guilty, but she can handle you."

He turned on the hot water in the sink, washing his hands and running it over his face to calm down. "I'm bigger than she is. I know she's more trained, but she froze. She was shocked."

"I explained that. She's a softie at heart. Or she was worried that you would fire her if she was the reason you could no longer reproduce." Dec glanced down at his phone, easily maneuvering it with the hand not holding the massive gun. "Shane's got the guy and the cops are here. He says it's a new crazy. He's going to take a picture, see if you recognize him."

"I'll go out and see if I can ID him." He wasn't afraid of some asshole who'd tried to throw a rock through his windows. He also wasn't stupid. Those windows were hurricane proof, even though they didn't get storms like that on the West Coast. They were bulletproof. A rock was only going to cause the alarm to go off. Nothing more.

"Absolutely not." Kayla strode in, looking nothing like the sweet submissive she'd been fifteen minutes before. She'd changed into slacks, a light sweater, and a scarf that would be perfect for a relatively breezy night on the beach. Of course, he knew why she'd added the scarf and it wasn't about the slight chill. "You are not going out there."

He wanted to be back in the playroom, locked in and cozy.

She'd been fucking gorgeous, naked and waiting for his attention. She'd taken the spanking like a champ, like she'd needed it, and the connection that flowed between them had sparked something inside him. He'd wanted her like nothing he'd wanted in a long time, which was precisely why he'd forced her to her knees and made her take him from behind where he could control the encounter.

Where he didn't have to look into her eyes and truly feel her. The connection had been too much, overwhelming.

"I think I'll make the decision about whether or not I leave the house, Kayla." He was well aware his voice had gone positively arctic.

He wanted to walk over and drag her back into his arms and apologize. He wanted to make sure she was all right. He could call in a doctor to take a look at her throat.

Did she even want him to touch her now? Or had he ruined the nice place they'd found?

It was the very fear of the answer to those questions that sent his voice dark and cold.

If it bothered her, she didn't show it. She merely glanced his way over the glow of her telephone. "Not when there's a man out there who wants to hurt you. That's when I get to step in as the voice of common sense. I know. Boring part to play, and yet you pay me to play it. Have you ever seen this man before?"

She turned her screen toward him as the front bell chimed.

"I'll go let the cops in." Dec nodded his way before disappearing down the hallway.

"I don't like being told what to do." Josh stared at her instead of the picture.

"You also don't like being put on your belly," she replied, her tone completely bland. "Do you react the same way on your back?"

He took the phone and stared at the screen, unwilling to go any further down that road with her. He'd revealed enough of himself for one night. There was a man on the ground, his face up toward the camera, but it was obvious the impromptu photo session hadn't been his idea. Brown hair, glasses, thin lips. There was nothing at all remarkable about the guy, but something stuck in his memory. "He looks vaguely familiar. I might have seen him on a set." The memory hit him squarely. "Shit. That's a screenwriter. I don't remember his name. Allen something. He sent me his script, but I don't read things that my agent doesn't send directly."

"He said something about you stealing his script, according to Shane," she said.

"Can't steal something I've never read." This was what he dealt with constantly. Everyone wanted a favor. Everyone wanted a leg up, and when he couldn't come through they turned on him. He was the monster who kept them down. He was the asshole who'd taken everything but gave nothing back. He'd fucking heard it all.

"Let's go down and talk to the police," she said. "Do you want to press charges?"

He felt his jaw tighten. Pressing charges meant he would have to show up in court. Not pressing charges meant the jerk would go on his merry way. "I don't know. Let's see what all he did. He's not the first asshole to throw something at my house. I can't imagine he'll be the last."

She nodded and started to move. He reached out and it hit him suddenly that he was about to go talk to a bunch of cops and all she would have to do is take off the scarf she'd draped around her neck and he would be the one they were taking in.

"I didn't mean to hurt you."

She stopped. "I didn't say you did."

"No, but I suspect I should pay for it. How much to keep you from explaining the situation to the cops?"

Confusion clouded her expression. "What?"

"Let's call it a bonus for putting up with my poor behavior. I'll write you a check. Ten thousand? Fifteen?"

Her face softened and she moved into his space. It took quite a bit for him not to step back. She seemed to understand that he needed space because she suddenly moved to the door. "It wasn't poor behavior, Joshua. I scarcely think you end sessions with breath play. Besides, that was one thing you were uninterested in."

Because he didn't want to hurt anyone that way. "Still, that is how I ended it."

"Don't be so dramatic. I triggered you when I put you on the floor. I didn't know. I reacted because I wasn't sure what I heard and I always think gunshots, not rocks. I'm sorry. Is it any time you find yourself restrained or only when you're facing down?"

He didn't want to talk about this, but her voice was soft, as though she understood. And really, she deserved an explanation. He'd fucked her silly and then tried to kill her. It wasn't how he'd seen the night going. "I'm okay on my back. I don't like not being able to see what's coming at me."

She nodded. "Okay. I promise I'll remember that in the future. And don't insult me like that again. I get that everyone wants a piece of you, but I merely want to do my job and do it well, and that means not allowing you to be killed. It also means not killing you myself. I'll have to think about it if you can't stop accusing me of betraying you before I even have a chance to put in a solid day's work. Can we agree on that?"

He found himself nodding. "Yes."

"And Josh, I enjoyed myself before then." Her lips curled up briefly before she was back to business.

Had she? He knew she'd enjoyed the sex, but there had been that moment right before all hell had broken loose when he'd sensed her pulling away from him.

It didn't matter because she was accepting him for now. He followed her downstairs, willing to try again.

* * * *

Kayla stepped on the stairs, calling out before she turned down the flight that led to the main floor. "Officers, I'm bringing Mr. Hunt with me. I am armed."

"Come on down," a deep male voice said. "Mr. Burke explained the situation. Mr. Hunt's staff already sent over copies of the security teams' concealed carry licenses. You're all up to date paperwork wise."

She stepped down, fairly secure they weren't going to shoot her. "He's very organized since I just got in this afternoon. Thank you for coming out, Officers."

They introduced themselves as Officer Hernandez and Officer Keller, two big, fit men who obviously had a couple of years' worth of experience under their belts.

"No problem," Hernandez said. "Mr. Hunt is a valued member of our community. He's also the most likely member of our community to get harassed. We've been telling him to bring in private security for years. Looks like it already paid off. You okay, Josh?"

101

Josh moved from behind her, gesturing to the big living room. "I'm fine. Please come in. It's nothing more than another crazy. I'm sorry you had to come out to deal with it."

"Nah, it's cool," Keller said. "We go off shift after this. You want us to take him in? I'm a little worried about this one. When we came in, he was spouting some crazy shit, and you know the press will be all over it. I might be able to put him on a psych hold. No press allowed there. I happen to know all the beds are full here, so we can ship him downtown."

She glanced over to see what Josh would do. A seventy-two-hour hold would make anyone think, especially when it wouldn't be somewhere nice and high-end. It would be nasty and dark. It could be a nice punishment for a man interested in such things.

"I would like to talk to him first," Josh said, his face grim. "Let's see if we can settle this without wrecking his life."

The officers shook their heads like they'd known what was going to happen, and then Hernandez nodded toward Declan. "Bring him in."

Kayla sat down on the couch beside him. "Do you think talking to him is a good idea? If he's a stalker, then you're rewarding his behavior. You're giving him attention, and that's what he wants."

"I know the psychology behind a stalker," he replied. He'd relaxed, but she would bet it was all an act for the cops' sakes. So calm and peaceful when only moments before she would have sworn he'd been on the edge.

"Yeah, you did that film," Hernandez said, slapping his buddy's arm. "What was it? The one you liked so much?"

"*Deep Midnight*," Keller replied with a nod her way. "Josh there played a psychologist who specialized in serial killers. His character was working with the local PD on a series of murders, but it turns out he actually had a split personality and he was responsible for all the killings himself."

"Hey, spoilers," Josh said with a grin.

She waved it off. "I saw that one. I still don't see how that makes you an expert in stalking."

"I took three months and sank myself into the profiling world," he explained. "I actually have enough classroom time to qualify for a

BA in psych, if I wanted one. I learn everything I can about a role. It's important for me to get as much as I can right."

"He's a fucking Renaissance man," Keller said. "I swear, he knows more about police procedure than I do."

"That's 'cause you're lazy as fuck," Hernandez replied. "But seriously, Josh is a genius."

And it looked like he wasn't as much of a recluse as she'd pegged him for. The officers seemed friendly with him.

"I still don't see how that makes you an expert," she pointed out as she heard the door open.

"I have been stalked over the years by numerous people, some amateur, but a couple of real pros. This guy...he's not stalking me. He's pissed at me and I would like to know what set him off." Josh relaxed back as though this was an everyday occurrence.

Perhaps it was and that was why she was here.

Shane and Dec came into the house. Shane still had the man by the elbow, but his gun was back in its holster. The man he'd caught shuffled along. The bottom half of his slacks were wet, as though he'd been in the surf, which he likely had at this time of night.

The man's head came up and he practically snarled Josh's way. "You fucking cheating bastard."

And there was the stench of vodka and regret. Or maybe it was whiskey. She wasn't close enough to tell, but the regret was certainly going to be in there tomorrow. Their suspect was definitely over the legal limit.

"Allen. It's Allen, right?" Josh stood up, his whole demeanor calm and patient.

That seemed to catch the guy off guard, but he straightened up, his face flushing with anger. "Yeah, I'm Allen. You know exactly who I am. Allen Houston. I'm the man who's going to sue you. If you think for a second I'll let you get away with this, you don't know who you're dealing with." He turned his eyes up to the officer to his right. "He's the thief. I want you to arrest him."

"Sure, buddy," Keller said. "What exactly did he steal? Your sobriety?"

That got Hernandez to chuckle.

Allen's hands made fists at his sides and Kay prepared to take him down if she had to. "My story. He stole my story. I was at a bar earlier tonight in LA and I overheard this guy talking about Joshua Hunt's brand-new movie. Did you think I wouldn't find out? I'm going to sue you, you ass. You can't get away with this. I can't let you."

Josh gave Allen his full attention. "Which movie are you talking about? I have three in various stages of pre-production."

"You know which one I'm talking about because I gave you the script," Allen ground out. He started to pace, but Shane got in his way and he was forced to stand, fairly vibrating with rage. "I was stupid and handed it over to you. I should have known someone like you would steal it and put his own name on it."

Josh shook his head. "There's not a single movie I'm working on where I take script credit."

The writer waved him off as though he'd expected an excuse like that. "So you gave it to one of your buddies."

"Please tell me what the movie's about," Josh requested quietly. "I don't know because I never read your script. I don't read scripts my agent doesn't put in my hand. I certainly don't read unsolicited scripts."

"Then what do you do with them?"

"I would have thrown it out," Josh said, not unkindly. "I can't take the chance that I would read it and have any piece of it show up in something I do down the line and have you come back to sue me. That's how I've worked for a long time. So you'll have to tell me which of the films I'm working is similar."

Allen stared at Josh intently. "You're a liar. I talked to someone who knows you."

She would hand it to Josh. He could handle scrutiny. She knew a lot of people who would have put some distance between them by this point, but Josh was cool and calm.

"A lot of people claim to know me," he replied.

Allen pointed his way. "He said you were working on a film about a dad and his son who ride the rails during the Great Depression. That was my film. My film about my father and grandfather."

There was some actor in the writer. At least some definite

dramatic tendencies. He was playing out the scene with theatrical flair while Josh kept everything quiet.

Josh shook his head. "Allen, I don't have anything historical in the works. I've got a big-budget sci-fi thriller, a romantic comedy, and the sequel to *The Quick and the Enraged*. I have no plans to work on anything like what you've described. I haven't heard anything about a project like that and I know pretty much what's happening everywhere. Whomever you were talking to lied to you."

Allen stopped, seeming to deflate all at once. "But why? Why would he lie?"

"He was probably a troll. A real-life troll," Josh replied. "I bet you were halfway drunk and mentioned something about it to him and he took the pass and played it until you were ready to hurt someone. Hell, maybe he knows me. Maybe he hates me and thought he could use you to hurt me. I don't know. Did you get his name?"

Allen put a hand on his head like he was trying to wipe away some memory or invisible pain. "Yeah. Bob Black. That's what he called himself. He bought me a beer. Three really. He said he worked with you."

"I don't recall the name," Josh replied. "But then on a film set I can work with hundreds of people."

But Kay knew the name. She looked up and Shane was frowning while Dec discreetly rolled his eyes. Was it a coincidence? Black was the name almost all CIA assholes used when they were undercover. The question was which of her CIA assholes had sent a bomb into her midst on her very first night on the job.

Of course if she asked, they would likely lie. The good news was she had skills, and figuring out if her CIA guys were already messing with her would be fairly easy.

"What bar were you at?" Kay asked.

Allen seemed to realize he wasn't alone with the cops and Josh. He cleared his throat and his eyes wouldn't meet hers. "I was in Santa Monica. It's a place called Dirk's close to my apartment. I go there a couple times a week. I sometimes like to write there." He looked back at Josh. "You're really not making my movie?"

There was a tinge of perverse sorrow to the question that Josh seemed to respond to. "I'm not. But you should send the script to my agent. It sounds interesting and I'm always looking for something fresh. If she reads it and thinks it's good, she'll either send it on to me or to someone who can give you some tips. I'll let her know to look for it."

Tears rolled down the guy's flushed cheeks. "Why would you do that for me?"

"Because I know what it means to be desperate, too. Because I know how it feels to be used against someone else," Josh replied.

"Because he's way too soft," Keller said with a sigh. "Come on. We'll get you back to your apartment. You're so fucking lucky. Pitt would have had your ass thrown in jail."

"Did this Bob Black person drive you out here?" Kayla asked as the cops were turning the man back toward the door.

Allen nodded, seeming to sober a bit. "Yeah. I didn't drive myself. That was lucky, I guess. He dropped me off at the public access. Didn't get out of the car, but he pointed the way. Didn't tell me how high the tide was already. Asshole."

"It's okay, Allen. We've all been there." Joshua held a hand out.

Allen shook it. "You're an amazing man, Mr. Hunt. I'm sorry I said otherwise."

"All right, let's get this show going," Keller said. "Hernandez, do we have guests?"

Hernandez was already at the front door. "You know the bastards listen in on the radio. I count two news trucks and three indie vultures. Let's get this over with. What do you want me to say, Josh?"

"There's press out there?" How had they gotten here so fast?

Josh was staring at the door as though imagining what was behind it. "They're always close by, always waiting. The word *vulture* is suitable since they circle overhead constantly."

Dec sighed. "I'll take door duty."

"Say it was all an accident," Josh told the cops. "Mr. Houston was walking on the beach and didn't understand the tide was coming in. When he tried to avoid it, he tripped my alarm. Everything is fine and you're giving him a ride home."

She saw flashes as the door opened and there were at least ten people standing in the tiny front yard. The cops pushed their way through.

"Hey, move those trucks," Hernandez yelled. "Move them or I'll have them moved for you."

"He's so nice," Allen was saying to one of the reporters. "Joshua Hunt is a great guy."

Shane sighed as the door closed. "Well, that was smart as hell. The man won't say a word against you now and the reporters won't have a story beyond Joshua Hunt helps out lost man."

Josh stared at the door for a second longer before sighing. "Yeah, I know how to handle the press at least. I've learned that being a nice guy makes for a shitty story. Why were you so concerned about who riled that man up, Kay?"

She looked over at him. Now that the doors had closed, a tension had crept back into his stance. She wasn't about to crank him up more. It also wasn't like she could blurt out *hey, I wonder if the CIA is involved in tonight's clusterfuck.* "I'm curious about who would send him your way."

He shook his head. "Like I said, some real-life troll. Or a reporter. He was very likely standing outside waiting to see if he could get some exclusive photos. Calling me a liar and a thief always sells papers. I didn't recognize the name. I'm not going to worry about it. I have lots of other things to worry about. Shane, we're going to bed. Thank you for your work this evening."

"Dec is taking the night shift. He'll be up and monitoring the security system. I'll see you two in the morning when I take over," Shane said as he turned to go back to the east wing of the house where the men were sharing a room. "Kay, ping me if you need anything."

Silence descended as Shane walked away, leaving them alone.

She stared at him for a moment and wondered if he'd really done it to manipulate the press. Nothing about how he'd acted in the last half hour told her he'd been lying to Allen Houston. "That was enlightening, Joshua."

"In what way?"

"I think you were telling that man the truth. I think you let him go because you know what it means to be desperate. It was a very nice thing to do."

His face went blank. "Was it? Don't think I'm some sort of nice guy. I do know what desperation feels like. I won't ever go back there again, and don't think for a second I wouldn't squash that man like a bug if he truly threatened me. He's nothing to me, but I'm smart enough to know that it's better for me if he shuts down the trouble himself rather than gets filmed being hauled off my property kicking and screaming. Now take it off and let me see it."

There was no pretending she misunderstood what he wanted. He'd been fixated on her neck since the moment she'd walked back in wearing the scarf. He wanted to see it, she would let him. She unwound the scarf and let her head fall to one side.

He moved in, his fingertips brushing the places where he'd lightly bruised her skin. He stepped back and seemed to have lost a lot of his coloring. His skin was a pasty white in the low light. "It should heal in a day or two. It'll be worse tomorrow."

"It's not a big deal." She could wear the scarf for a day or two if she had to, but she'd looked at it herself and didn't think it would bruise badly. After all, this wasn't her first rodeo. She knew what her skin looked like when someone brutalized her, and this wasn't it.

"Yes, it is. I think you should go to your room now."

She didn't want to leave him alone. She wanted to get at least partially back to the intimacy of earlier. They'd been working toward something. "You know what would make me feel better?"

His eyes fastened on her. "What? Ice cream? I don't have any, but I can send someone. I should have thought about that. Or hot tea? I do have that. I can make you some tea and there's organic honey somewhere. I've heard that can soothe a sore throat."

She shook her head. "I don't need that. How about a kiss? We've had sex, but you haven't kissed me. How about you kiss me until I can't think any more and we'll call it even?"

It was one thing she'd missed during their scene. He hadn't kissed her, hadn't pressed those magnificent lips against hers and stroked his tongue into her mouth. The truth was she'd been thinking about kissing him since the moment she'd agreed to take this job.

He was quiet for a moment. "You're under a mistaken impression. That's not going to happen. Not ever. I don't kiss, Kayla."

"What?"

"I don't kiss. I haven't kissed anyone in years, not unless it's in the script, and I'm not going to start now. If you were looking forward to teenaged make-out sessions, you're out of luck. I'm not going to sleep with you either."

She'd meant to talk to him about that. "I thought the whole point was to have me close so I could protect you."

"No, I hired you so I didn't have to find a woman who would get hurt because she was close to me. You're convenient. You possess the skills to protect me and you don't mind me using your body. At least, that was supposed to be our bargain. I assure you, you'll hear me scream and come running if something happens, but I was never going to share a bed with you. Did you read the contract? Have I made a mistake?"

Wow. That hurt. That was an actual kick in the gut, and if she hadn't felt used before, she sure as hell did now. She put a hand up to stop his questions. "I read it. I assumed since we were having sexual intercourse that I would be sleeping with you and that you would kiss me from time to time. I get it now. Only penises and vaginas involved."

An arrogant smirk marked his face and he crossed his hands over his chest. "See, this is why I told Jared it couldn't work. No woman can accept sex on a base level. You always want more."

That was where he was wrong. He'd very effectively killed any fantasy she still held about him. "I spent years and years of my life accepting exactly that. Thank you. I'm going to be honest, you're very good at what you do. You made me feel a connection to you that didn't exist from your end. I'll kill it from mine and we'll both be free to enjoy the physical aspects of our contract. Am I allowed to find my bed now?"

His whole body seemed to sigh. "I don't kiss anyone. It's not...it's not about you. Kissing...it means something to me. It's intimate and I can't do it."

But on screen he kissed like a god. Kissed like a god and made everyone in the audience believe he was a real live boy.

It was all part of his gorgeous façade, and she forgot that at her peril.

He was a job and it wasn't her place to fix whatever was broken inside him. She thought she was damaged? Well, maybe she wasn't as far gone as she believed. At least she was willing to try. She wouldn't be trying with him, but there was no reason for anger. Anger was utterly irrational in this case. He hadn't promised her anything. He'd given her pleasure, and it was obvious there was a whole war fought inside that beautiful body of his.

It wasn't her war. After all, she had a job to do and he'd made it easier because she wasn't going to become emotionally attached to a man as cold as this one.

She looked up at him, banishing all those stupid thoughts that had played around in her head. "It's okay, Joshua. I haven't kissed anyone in a long time and I was looking forward to it, but you're right. It should be meaningful. It should mean more than some contractual obligation. I'll save my kisses for outside the job."

He blocked her when she tried for the hallway. "What is that supposed to mean?"

She sighed inwardly, so sick of sulky boys who pretended to be men. The truth was he'd been honest with her all along. He'd shown her exactly who he was and what he thought of her. She was a toy, and while he didn't want to play with certain pieces of her, he wouldn't allow anyone else to either. "I wasn't saying I'm going to look for a date. This is a job. It will end at some point in time and then I'll find someone to mack down on."

"Back in England?"

She shook her head. "I'm not doing this with you. You can't have it both ways. I've sworn I'll honor the contract. You can't tell me in one sentence that I'm nothing to you and then be a jealous ass two seconds later."

His face clouded as though he hadn't thought about it. His shoulders came down and red stained his cheeks. "I'm sorry. You're right."

At least he could be reasonable. "Good. I'll see you in the morning. Do you want me to join you for your run or Shane?"

He stared down at her for a moment. "You're not planning on sulking?"

"I am totally sulk free."

"Because it won't get you anything from me."

Jeez, who did he deal with on a regular basis? She couldn't help but laugh. "I think I can forego the sulking. Can you do the same with this broody thing you have going on? I won't try to kiss you or climb into your bed for cuddles if you promise to do this weird thing with your face I want you to try."

One brow rose. "And that would be?"

She gave him her biggest grin. "Smile, Mr. Hunt. Just smile a couple of times a day and we'll get along. I'll let Shane run with you. I think I'll make muffins in the morning and watch the ocean. Good night. Scream if someone's trying to kill you."

"Kayla," he began.

But she was done for the night. Well, with him. She had another couple of men she needed to yell at before she went to bed. "Good night, Joshua."

He was silent as she started upstairs and found her room. She closed the door and took a long breath. The room was as colorless and clean as the rest of the place. A designer paradise with nothing of the owner in it.

Joshua Hunt was very much like this place. Beautifully designed and vacant of real humanity.

She had to remember that always.

Chapter Six

Kay came awake to the knock on her door. Without thinking about it, she reached for the SIG she'd placed on the nightstand and eased out of bed. Sunlight crept in through the blinds, but it was only a hint at this point, the gray of predawn giving way to a stream of pinks and oranges.

She glanced down at her phone, but there was nothing there. No texts or calls. Dec or Shane would have contacted her first on her phone. So that meant this was likely Josh.

Still, she wasn't putting the gun down until she had confirmation.

She glanced at the clock. Six twenty-two. He was an early riser. Damn CIA jobs. She could be all warm and cozy in her flat at The Garden, but no, she had to go back into the spy shit. They'd tempted her with patriotism and sex with a Hollywood hottie. When this was over she would have a long talk with her libido about toning it down and accepting that her true soul mate came with batteries and a detachable head.

Belting her robe around her naked body, she moved to the door as another, more insistent knock came.

She opened the door, her SIG still in her right hand. "Is there a problem?"

He was big and muscular, and there was that vulnerable thing in his eyes again that seemed to kick the shit out of her good sense. He stood in her doorway, a delicious piece of man meat, and all she could think about was the look in his eyes. Hungry. Wary. Unsure of his welcome. God, she was a sucker for that look.

He wasn't dressed for a jog. He was still in a pair of cotton pajama bottoms and nothing else. Those wretchedly hot abs were on full display and yep, her libido was starting to groove about real-man loving. Her libido had very little common sense.

"Are you still mad at me?" Joshua asked, his voice husky with sleep.

Seriously? There was only one reason he would ask that question. He wanted some exercise that wasn't a run. If they'd been trying a real relationship, she would have slammed the door in his face and told him to fuck himself.

But they weren't. This was what she'd come here to do. She'd come here to gain some kind of power over him, and she wasn't going to be able to do that by playing the outraged lover. Distance wasn't going to solve her problem. Hell, she had to know if she *could* solve her problem.

Besides, the mere sight of the man did things to her pink parts. She wasn't stupid. Her body already craved his. The trick was to keep her soul out of the bargain. He'd made himself plain the night before. It had been a kind of gift. She hadn't gone to sleep dreaming about being in his arms or some shit.

"Did you want me in the dungeon?" She pulled at the tie of her robe and it fell open, giving him a glimpse of her naked body.

Let the games begin.

That was how she would view it. They were playing a game and she intended to win.

His eyes went straight to her breasts. "Just like that?"

"You're the Master, Joshua. That's how this works." She strode back into her room and placed the SIG on the nightstand table. She eased out of the robe because she'd promised him nudity. Vulnerability. "If you want me, you tell me. I'm in no physical discomfort where I wouldn't enjoy a session, so I'll comply. We settled things last night. This is about sex and it's about you and not me. I'm here to please you and to protect you."

His jaw tightened but he didn't look away from her. "And in return?"

Why was he pushing this? "I get a paycheck. A rather large one."

She could see easily that her reply displeased him and yet it was exactly what he'd asked for.

He stepped into the room, blocking her access to the door. "Then I suppose you should earn it."

She put her hands on her hips. "What is the problem now? I asked you to kiss me and yes, it disappointed me that you wouldn't. But I'm not sulking. You didn't want to sleep with me. I came in here. Again with the not sulking or making demands. You knock on my door and ask for sex. I offer to meet you in the dungeon. So far, I've done everything you've asked me to do and none of it has pleased you. I think it might be time to cut our losses."

If she had no control or influence over him, she was useless, and humiliating herself wasn't something she did for fun.

They would have to find someone else or another way to get to him because it didn't look like seduction was going to work.

"You're the only person in my life who fucking does that," he said with a rueful shake of his head.

"Does what?"

"Tells me when I'm being an ass."

Probably because he got rid of all the ones who did. Or was it possible no one ever stood up to him because they were scared of getting thrown off the gravy train? "You're definitely being an ass. What do you want from me, Joshua? I'm not going to be your doormat. There's not enough money in the world for that."

He moved in, his eyes still on her body, his hands coming up to cup her shoulders. He stared down at her for a moment, his thumb tracing the scar under her clavicle. He seemed fascinated by it. After a moment, he looked her in the eyes. "I felt bad about last night. That's not it. I *feel* bad about last night. I can't seem to let it go. You asked for one thing and I didn't give it to you."

This was about his trigger episode. "I told you; it's all right. I'm not even sore today."

He shook his head. "It's not all right and I want to make it up to you. You asked me what I want. I don't know. I haven't had this kind of relationship before and I thought it would be simple. I guess I thought it wouldn't be a real relationship, but it kind of feels that way already. I didn't like the thought of you being upset. I definitely didn't like being the reason for it. I'm on shaky ground here and I don't deal well with that. I like being in control, and I'm not entirely right now. I don't want to kiss you because of things that had happened in my past. Can you accept that?"

Kissing was a bad idea. She got that now. "Yes."

"I don't want to sleep with you because I have terrible dreams and I'm worried I'll wake up with my hands around your throat again."

"Then I would set you on your ass." She shook her head because that wasn't what he needed. He needed smooth and easy compliance. "It's okay. I can hear you if something happens. I'm fine in this room."

"But I sat up most of the night and I thought about something you said." His hands moved down her shoulders and onto her arms, smoothing the skin there. "I can adapt. Come here. I don't want it to be cold between us. I don't. I get enough cold. I need something in my life that's warm."

His arms went around her awkwardly, as though it had been a long time since he'd initiated a hug. Who the hell was this man? He was going to kill her because she was softening up again when she'd promised not to.

She let her arms drift up and around his chest, reveling in the way his skin felt against hers. Warm and secure. This was what she'd missed last night. The sex itself had been spectacular, the work of a true master, but they'd lacked any kind of deeper intimacy, anything that went beyond the contract between Dom and submissive.

She'd thought sex was all she needed, but he was proving her wrong. It was easy to lean into his hard strength and let him wrap his arms around her. After the initial awkward moment, he seemed to clutch at her as though afraid of letting her go.

"This isn't so bad." His forehead came down, nestling against hers, and he breathed her in. "Did you sleep naked?"

"I did. It's a habit, but I keep a robe close." She let her hands wander over the strong muscles of his back because he seemed to enjoy the sensation. It made her wonder how long it had been since he'd had anything but straight up D/s sex. It reminded her that even something as intimate as sex could be made cold. Even kinky sex. "I promise I won't run out to save you with my hootchie on display."

His hands roamed over her back and the curve of her ass. "I think it would be an effective way to distract whoever was coming for me. You're so fucking gorgeous. I thought about you all last night. I wanted to come in here."

He wanted to have sex, but she was way more okay with the thought than she'd been before. Her body was heating up quite nicely, and she could feel his erection against her belly.

It would be a nice way to wake up. It would also be a nice way to bind him to her. "Do you want to go to the dungeon?"

His forehead moved against hers, shaking in the negative. "I want you to lie down on the bed and I'll…adapt."

Adapt because he didn't have sex outside the dungeon? She had to admit it would be nice to do it in a bed every now and then. Of course, if she wanted to get to the dungeon, the way to do that was to question him. He'd told her what he wanted so she moved away from him, walking to the bed she'd spent the night in. It was a lovely queen with soft sheets and the sound of the ocean there to lull her to sleep. She climbed on it and laid back, wondering if she would find herself flipped over and the discipline beginning.

Instead, he gripped her ankles and pulled her down the bed until her backside was on the edge.

He dropped to his knees. "I can make up for the lack of kissing. I can still give you my mouth and tongue."

Before she could take a deep breath, his mouth was on her. Right on her. His lips covered her pussy, tongue immediately licking out and exploring.

Heat blasted through her body, a tsunami that threatened to drown her in an instant. "Joshua…"

His hands were on her thighs, pushing them apart. "Don't fight me. Let me have you. This isn't play. This is for you. This is for me. It doesn't have to always be in the dungeon or at the club. It can be for comfort, too, right?"

She was really comfortable. So freaking comfortable. "Please don't stop."

She glanced down her body to where he was working her over. He looked up, his lips glistening with the evidence of her arousal, and gave her the most sweetly salacious grin she'd ever seen.

"Of course, just because we're not in the dungeon doesn't mean I'm not in charge," he said. "Don't move. I want to enjoy how good you taste. Come all over my tongue. Let me feel it. This is how I'll kiss you. So good and so deep."

He covered her again and she felt his tongue on her clit.

Kayla bit back a groan, and it took everything she had to not shift her pelvis up and ride his tongue. She forced herself to be still, her hands fisting in the sheets she'd slept in the night before.

"I stayed up most of the night thinking about doing this," he murmured against her flesh. Every word rumbled along her skin, lifting her higher and higher.

She'd spent the night trying desperately not to think about this. When he'd said he wouldn't kiss her, she'd thought he'd meant anywhere. She'd imagined him sucking her nipples perhaps, biting her flesh during some kinky games, but this was so intimate. And soft. And only for her.

Fucker kept finding a way to pull her back in.

He ate her pussy like it was the finest of delicacies, spearing her with his tongue and then suckling on her clit. He knew exactly how to use his tongue and mouth to take her straight to the edge and then pull her back so she didn't fly over. He managed to keep her right on the edge. Edge of the bed. Edge of orgasm. Edge of screaming out how he was making her crazy.

He kept her there for what felt like forever, as though he enjoyed how fast and far he could push her. This was where he found some of his power.

"Master, please." She couldn't stop the words from rolling out of her mouth. Her body was taut, aching, needy. If he didn't send her over the edge soon, she wasn't sure what she would do. "Joshua, please."

"This pleases Joshua quite a bit," he said, dragging his tongue over her labia. "Much more than I would have thought. Do you have any idea how long it's been since I went down on someone?"

Through the haze she heard him, but she was way past caring. "Please. I can't stand it. I need to come. Do you have any idea how long it's been since I begged?"

She didn't beg, but she would for this. It was too overwhelming. She needed there to be closure.

His head came up and his eyes focused on hers. "You don't have to beg. I thought a lot about this last night. I want to take the contract seriously. You don't have to beg me. I want to give this to you. I want you to ask and I'll give. You protect me, I take care of you. Let me show you what I mean."

His hand moved and suddenly she felt his fingers invade, entering and stretching her. He curled those big fingers deep inside her as he leaned over and sucked her clitoris into his mouth.

The orgasm slammed into her, stealing her breath and a good portion of her will. He kept it up for a few moments, licking and nuzzling her as the aftershocks hit.

"Kay?"

She opened her eyes, the world a bit hazy, and he was staring up at her with desperate expectation in his eyes.

He was asking? She'd given him permission, but he seemed to need more today.

"Yes. Yes, please."

He didn't need to be told twice. He was up on his feet, shoving his pajama bottoms down and rolling a condom on his massive erection. He'd come prepared. She had to wonder how long he'd stood outside the door before he'd knocked. How long had he sat up the night before thinking about what had gone wrong and how he could fix it? He was a mystery, but it didn't matter because all she cared about in that moment was feeling him inside her again.

She waited for him to roll her over, but he was all about the unexpected this morning. He stepped between her legs and positioned his cock, rubbing it all around and getting it good and wet before entering her in one long, hard thrust. He kept nothing back, didn't give her a moment to get used to the feel. He simply started fucking her. This was his time. He'd given to her and now it was his time to take, and she was all for that.

The man could fuck like a god. Two thrusts in and she was lifting up to meet him, wanting so desperately to find that place that only he could seem to take her to. Since she'd come back to the civilian world there hadn't been a ton of sex, and what she'd had proved frustrating at best, disappointing at worst. But this…this was transcendent.

He took her out of herself and lifted her to a place where all that mattered was the next sensation, where her body was more than a tool to be used. It was an instrument of pleasure and connection.

It was a gift.

He stared down at her as he thrust in and pulled out. She was entirely at his mercy. If he moved away from her, she would likely fall off the bed. He was the only thing holding her up and keeping her safe.

"Tell me you like this," he demanded, his voice as hoarse as sandpaper.

"I love this, Joshua," she replied. "Your cock, that is. Your cock is the best I've ever had, and I wouldn't lie about that. Please keep fucking me."

He held her hips and her legs wound around him as he drove into her, making the bed move. If it bothered him, he didn't show it. He simply moved with the bed until it hit the wall on the other side and couldn't move any further. "Your wish…"

He picked up the pace and sent her over the edge again, a bomb going off inside her body. She clutched him, his strong arms the only thing real and solid in the world.

"I'm going to have to break that whole *your wish* thing now," he said with a smile that was so boyishly handsome it damn near made her heart break. "Can't keep fucking you. Feels too good. Damn, it feels so good. Hasn't felt this good in forever."

She was fairly certain that she'd never once felt this good about her body. She'd craved sex, needed it, but that had been a bodily function. This was luxury. The difference between flying coach and a personal luxury jet with all the amenities.

His hips flexed, sending sparks through her again, but this was his time and she watched as his body stiffened, every muscle defined. He was a freaking work of art, from his carved muscles to the silky dark hair on top of his head, to his cut-from-granite superhero jawline.

That gorgeous face of his contorted as he held himself hard against her. His chest sawed in and out, breathing heavily, and then his head fell forward. He withdrew and kicked out of his pajama pants.

"Hold on," he said after a long moment.

"What?"

He picked her up, wrapping one strong arm around her waist and lifting. She tightened her legs around him and wound her arms around his neck.

"What are you doing?" Were they going to the dungeon now? She wasn't sure she had the energy for a session.

"Have to deal with something." He stepped into the small bathroom in her room and grimaced as he reached under her with his free hand. "Don't want to make a mess of your bed."

Ah, he was getting rid of the condom. "And carrying me around?"

One side of his mouth lifted in the sexiest grin. "I did that because I didn't want to let go. Also to prove how strong I am. Are you impressed?"

Charming Josh was deadly. She found herself smiling back and wishing he would kiss her. All it would take was a few inches and his lips would cover hers.

"I'm absolutely impressed with your strength, Joshua," she replied, keeping her distance. Not that their bodies had a bit of distance between them. Nope. She was practically sliding all over him.

Both hands free now, he gripped her ass and strode back over to the bed. "I needed that. I think I need this, too."

He fell on the bed, taking her with him and wrapping her around him. He laid back and yawned.

Her head found his chest, resting down and listening to his still-racing heart. It was slowing, having done its exercise for now.

"I thought you weren't the cuddly type." It felt nice and warm being so close to him.

"I'm not, but I think you are. I think you need this to feel close to me. I can't give you some of the other things you need, but I have to admit that this is kind of nice. I haven't done this in a long time," he said with another yawn. His hand played idly in her hair and his eyes started to close.

"Do you want to sleep for a while?"

His arm tightened. "I should go to my own bed."

He'd bent for her. She could do the same. "How about I stay right here until you fall asleep, and then I'm going to get up and take a shower. After that I'll have some coffee and make breakfast. In an hour or two, I'll wake you up, okay?"

"You said you'd make muffins." He pulled the covers over them both.

She didn't mention that he was supposed to be avoiding carbs. He could stand some comfort food. "Muffins it is."

"And eggs and bacon and some orange juice."

He should be glad she knew how to cook. "All those things." She sighed and listened to his heartbeat. It was strong and steady, a reassuring sound. "You get some sleep."

Slowly his breathing evened out and his arm relaxed.

And still she laid there, watching him sleep and wondering what the hell she was going to do about him.

* * * *

An hour later, Kay stepped down the stairs and into the main house. Someone had already made coffee, the scent leading her toward the kitchen.

"Morning," a deep voice said. Shane was standing in the kitchen dressed in sweat pants and a T-shirt, a mug of coffee in his hand. "I take it my morning jog has been put off for the time being?"

It was a damn good thing she didn't embarrass easily. "He's out for at least another hour."

"He paced all night," Shane replied, his eyes going to the stairs. "At least that's what Dec told me before he went to bed. The bedroom he's using is right under Hunt's. You didn't stay in his room?"

"He doesn't want to sleep with me," she admitted. "He's got a lot of baggage and he doesn't like to share it."

"He gets his hands around your throat again and I'll share some of mine with him," Shane replied, his tone dark.

She moved to the coffee pot, smelling the rich aroma. "I can handle myself. He's got some issues. You have to let me deal with them. I think he's going to be very territorial when it comes to me, and while I appreciate your help, it's going to hurt my relationship

121

with him if you step in."

He leaned against the counter. "You can't expect me to let him hurt you."

"I don't, but he's not trying to hurt me. I triggered him last night. In more ways than one. I know better and we handled it this morning. We're back on a good footing and I don't want to waste it. Please tell me he has some actual sugar around here?"

Shane chuckled. "The king of abs? I doubt it. Luckily I know Dec and how nasty he can be if he doesn't get his fix. I brought along a box of sugar packets, and there's some cream hidden behind the almond milk. Dec would never think to bring it himself, but I've been around him long enough to know how to deal with the beast."

Thank god. She poured a cup and loaded it up with sugar and cream. Heavenly perfection. It was good Josh was sleeping because she had some questions. "Did Dec get my message?"

Again, his eyes wandered over to the stairs. "Let's enjoy the morning out on the balcony."

Shit. She'd known it. She took her coffee and followed him outside. It was high tide and she couldn't see the beach at all, the waves going under the balcony and making the whole place look like it was actually on the water. It was magical, but more importantly, it was loud. It was so loud that no one would be able to hear what she and Shane were discussing. Not unless they literally walked out onto the balcony and sat down with them.

Shane shut the heavy door behind them and joined her at the bistro table. "Dec managed to get a plate off the car that dropped off the screenwriter at the public access point. It was a midsized American-made sedan, rented from a Santa Monica store by Robert Black."

Despite what Bond films would have, the Agency didn't open up their wallets for Ferraris. "Which one am I dealing with—Ezra or Levi?"

"He said he couldn't get a face off the CCTV," Shane replied. "Dec said there was one person in the driver's seat, with Allen Houston in the passenger seat, but he couldn't see if anyone was in the back. How do you know you're not dealing with both?"

"Honestly, I don't, though I think Houston would have

mentioned a second man. Still, if I had to bet, this is Levi. Ezra would have warned me."

"Ezra Fain is CIA, Kay. He wouldn't warn you if he thought it could possibly compromise the operation. Perhaps he wanted you to look surprised."

She let her jaw drop, her eyes widening as she stared in the distance. "Oh, my god."

Shane nearly knocked over his coffee, twisting and turning to get to the threat she'd "seen." His gun was out and pointing while she sighed and sat back.

"I give excellent surprise face, Shane, and Ezra knows that. There's zero reason for him to leave me out." She sat back and thoughtfully sipped her coffee. No. There was something else going on here. "It must have been Levi. He hasn't seen how good my surprise face is."

Shane frowned as he sat back down. "Damn it, Kay. You nearly gave me a heart attack."

She shrugged. "Now you've seen it for yourself. This face goes where I want it to go and Ezra knows it. I probably could have been an actress if I hadn't figured out I like hurting people so much. Do you ever wonder about that? All the things you could have been if you'd managed to suppress your violent side? The problem is now I know if I had an office job I would be the one who murdered the obnoxious people. Every office has one of those, right? Back at MSS it was totally a dude named Hai. Secretary screwed up, you did not see her again."

"I fear for the office bully if you're around." He stared at her for a moment. "Sometimes you scare me, Kay. So why do you think Ezra is different from every other Agency asshole you've worked with? I'll admit I've spent very little time with the guy, but he seems pretty routine when it comes to operatives."

That was because he didn't know Ezra like she did. "He's different because he knows what it means to lose someone. Ezra lost his brother during a mission a long time ago. He thinks about something other than the op. He values lives."

"Then he won't be working for the Agency for long."

She did worry about that. "From what I understand, he's already on thin ice. The only reason he's working this op is his close ties to Chelsea Weston. He was her handler for a couple of years and he became involved with the mission to find Theo Taggart. He ingratiated himself to Ian Taggart, and I think that's why they keep him around."

"Really? What does a grateful Big Tag look like?"

She shrugged again. "Mostly the same, but the sarcasm has a friendlier feel to it. Ezra has been instrumental in keeping the Lost Boys off the Agency's radar. I think without him, one or more of my boys might have found himself being experimented on, and not in a fun, sexual way."

Shane's brows rose as he considered that. "All right, so if Ezra's here to watch over you and handle the relationship with McKay-Taggart, why's Levi Green riding shotgun? Agents don't normally come in twos. They tend to be known as lone wolves."

"Levi is the expert on the Commander. That's the code name for the drug dealer Josh is connected to. Levi's been working in that part of the world for a couple of years now. He took over that territory after my old boss died in the line of duty." It was hard to think that it had been years since she'd heard the news that John Bishop was gone. The Agency had simply handed over the reins of her op to Tennessee Smith and moved on like John Bishop had never existed, but she'd missed him. Even as cold as he'd been, he'd managed to take care of her. Bishop's death had opened up a spot for Levi Green, and now they were all here and working together.

She remembered thinking if they'd taken out Bishop, she likely didn't have long. Bishop had been cold and calculating, the best of the best. If he'd made a mistake it was only a matter of time before she did, too. In the moment, she'd kind of welcomed it. Not Bishop's death, but the inevitability of her own.

She hated thinking about losing Bishop.

"Why not go at this straight?" Shane sat back with a groan. "Why all this subterfuge? Why not simply tell Hunt what's going on and why we need you in there? He's not a bad dude. Weird and a little on the twisted side, but not bad."

"Do you think I didn't try to go that route?" Of course, then she wouldn't have had the most amazing orgasm of her life. Damn. She needed Penny. Or Ariel. Ari and Pen were her girls. Someone should know she was making time with a superhottie. "Ezra shut me down. I don't think he trusts Josh."

"I don't feel right playing a civilian this way," Shane said with a shake of his head.

"Because you've always gotten to be Captain America, and some of us have to play Batman and go undercover and do nasty things to get the criminals. You were a cop. You got to be one of the good guys. I was Agency. I was literally one of the bad guys for years. I get that sometimes you have to be willing to get your hands dirty in order to do right. Besides, this is about taking down a man who's killed more than one agent, and now Levi thinks he's holding another operative."

Actually, when she thought about it, she kind of owed the Commander and his friends. Maybe she would give the man a gift on her way out. The gift of peace and rest. The eternal kind. But not until she'd given him the gift of lots and lots of pain.

She could see how that conversation would go. *Hey, Joshua. I need to put you in actual serious danger with a drug dealer who's holding a CIA agent hostage, and then when we get that dude out— and he will likely be twelve kinds of fucked up—but on the way out, I'm going to do some assassinating. Then we can totally go for an ice cream and maybe have some sex.*

Yeah, she probably should play this Levi's way.

"If they have one of our operatives, then we're working on a clock," Shane mused. "Another reason to get this thing done fast."

"Which I suppose is why Levi is likely trying to push Josh to the breaking point." When she thought about it, it made sense. Put Josh in many situations that would lead him to make poor choices. Shove the mark in a pressure cooker and turn up the heat until he would do anything to get out of the kitchen. She would have appreciated a heads-up though.

Shane sat back. "Well, I think we should expect something to happen and fairly quickly."

She sat back, too, a comfortable silence coming over them.

It wasn't fair. She was the sexual plaything of an actual Hollywood megastar and her squad wasn't here to talk about it. Of course, sometimes her squad could be all adult and rational. Pen would worry that she was being used and that she might feel dirty afterward. She totally felt dirty, but in a hot way that made her want to get dirty again. Ariel would likely think she needed a therapy session. She would go all intellectual on the subject. She needed Teresa or Nick's new wife, Hayley. They wouldn't mind talking about her suddenly hot sex life. Hell, even Tucker would listen to her. He would grab some popcorn and ask all kinds of super-invasive questions, but he would listen to her. Damn it. She needed to talk and Shane was the only one here.

"He won't kiss me. I'm kind of offended by that. I have nice lips, right?"

Shane went still, no movement at all. One moment went by and then another.

She rolled her eyes. Asshole. "I'm not a dinosaur. I can still see you." She smiled brightly. He was a dude, but he would get used to listening to her. After all, he was her backup for this op. That meant he totally had to have her back on everything from watching her six when they were in danger to talking her through her very serious love issues. "You would mack down on this if you were so inclined, right?"

His eyes went wide. Like super wide. The way a mans did when he was facing down something that scared the shit out of him. "No. Absolutely not."

"Way to shut a girl down. That was harsh."

He leaned in. "I wasn't talking about your mouth. It's a nice mouth and if I was the guy sleeping with you, I would kiss you. It's weird to not kiss your partner, but it fits into the fact that dude is a walking-talking cash machine for some lucky shrink. No. I was talking about the fact that you are not going to turn me into your girlfriend. There will be no talking about your physical relationship with the client. Or emotional relationship with the client. Which I should point out is not something that you should have."

"But Shane, I don't have anyone else. A girl needs to talk. I have a lot of feelings. Mostly they're in my vagina, but I'll admit he touches me some other places, too." Okay, now she was kind of teasing him, but she did want to talk.

Shane's handsome face twisted into a horrified mask. He pointed at her. "That. That is what I am trying to avoid. Find a chick to talk to about your vagina. Call Kai. He likes listening, but it won't be me. You want to talk about the op? I'm here for you. You want to shoot the shit about anything from politics to history to the Dodgers, I'm your boy. But I will not turn into Big Tag. Big Tag is a gossipy old lady. He can pretend all he likes that he vomits when someone says the word 'love' around him, but he's practically a fairy godmother to half the couples he knows."

"And that's bad, how?"

"Because it's not very masculine," he replied with a shake of his head. "No vagina talk. Shut it down."

"He's really good with my nipples, too."

Shane got up and backed away. "No private parts of any kind, Kay. None."

"Okay. Come back. I want to talk about the op."

"Do you?"

"Not really. I want to talk about how good the sex was."

He practically ran into the house, slamming the door behind him.

Sucked to be the only female bodyguard. She was going to make some serious complaints about the lack of sexual diversity at the office. All boys and Erin. Erin was practically a guy. She would have run away, too. The next hires better be super-deadly girly girls. No one wanted to talk about relationships or guys or sex. Work. Work. Work. Baseball. Beer. Boring stuff.

Oooo, a dolphin. There was a dolphin. And another. A pretty pair.

She bet they did the dolphin equivalent of making out.

Kay sighed and thought about her dads. Not that she would talk about sex with them. Ewww. But she could talk about some of the other stuff. Except then they would want to know more.

She could call Pen or Ariel, but it was dinner time there.

"Hi, dolphins," she said as they continued their slow swim by. "I had really great sex today."

They didn't say anything but she knew they heard her.

She sat out on the balcony for the longest time, the sounds of the ocean soothing her soul.

Chapter Seven

Two weeks later, the sun shone down through the sunroof of the limo, a brilliant Southern California day, but nothing seemed as bright as her smile.

God, had he just thought that? What the fuck was wrong with him? He sounded like Jared did when he talked about that chick in Dallas. The last thing he wanted to do was turn into Jared, who couldn't even sleep with a sub because he was staying true to a woman who wouldn't return his calls.

Kayla returned his calls. She answered immediately, and there was always warmth in her voice, like she'd been wanting to talk to him. Like she'd waited all day to tell him that she'd bought some cheese and wine at Ralph's or walked the beach and found some seashell. Stupid shit. He'd spent his days making high-powered deals that would be worth millions and millions and all he wanted to do was hear about what her adopted dolphin pod had gotten up to. She made up the craziest gossip and it always had him laughing.

He was getting way too comfortable, but he didn't want to stop.

"Josh?" Kayla looked at him and he got the feeling it wasn't the first time she'd tried to get his attention. "Are you there? Or did you take a nap on me?"

He was wearing mirrored aviators. All the better to hide the fact that he'd spent the entire drive from Malibu to Beverly Hills staring at her. She wouldn't know if he was looking out the window or napping.

It gave him the chance to simply watch her, watch how her eyes widened when they passed some restaurant that apparently was the focus of a reality show, watch her as she couldn't take her eyes off the beach as Declan drove them down PCH, watch her as she frowned at her cell phone when she got into some kind of weird emoji war with her not-brother, Tucker.

She was the single most fascinating woman he'd ever met. And it wasn't simply about her quirks, though there were many of them.

"Nope, just thinking," he said and sat up. "Lots to do in the next week."

Because they were going to Mexico in a few days and he would go back to work. For the first time in his adult life he wasn't looking forward to work. He usually hated his downtime and longed for the rigors of filming. For weeks and weeks he wouldn't be able to think about anything but the character he was playing, from early morning call until he fell into bed exhausted and had to do it all again the next day. He would be able to live and breathe a whole other life.

Where would Kay fit in? He suddenly realized he liked those other lives because his was quite empty. How would he concentrate when he knew Kayla was waiting on the sidelines or back in the trailer? Typically he didn't have sex when he was working.

No fucking way that happened this time.

"I've been thinking about that," she replied. "How many days are we spending at your friend's place? It's not on the ocean, right?"

"No, it's in the interior but it's lovely. Hector's place is in the jungle, but not like a scary jungle. And you'll still need a bathing suit. This is no shack. It's a mansion in the middle of a lot of green and nature. I'm excited to show you."

"What's your friend like? And how did you meet some guy who lives in the jungle?"

He chuckled because she still sounded a little uncertain about the accommodations. She'd asked a ton of questions about the compound. He thought it was funny that a woman who'd been in as many crazy situations as his spy chick was nervous about the jungle. "He's a huge donor to the children's charity. When you write a million-dollar check, you end up getting invited to a lot of galas. A couple of years back, Hector came to our annual ball in Palm Springs and we kind of

129

hit it off. He's a bit older than me, but he's self-made. He came up on the streets of Mexico City and built his business. I respect the hell out of him. I think you'll like him, too. And don't worry about the jungle. I've spent some time training. If we get lost, I promise I can find our way out."

"What role was that for? Don't tell me." She snapped her fingers. *"The Explorer."*

He'd played an English explorer who charted the Amazon. It had been one of the harder shoots of his life. "Yeah, I spent a couple of weeks getting used to the terrain. I had a guide teach me what I needed to know. I don't like to pretend. I like to know and then show. Well, about the things I can. Never shot anyone, but I've done it a lot on screen."

"Sometimes it's fun. Sometimes it's just messy and sad. It really depends on the victim. It's like having a co-star. They affect the scene so much. You want someone you have some chemistry with."

And then there were times she scared him. Oddly those times did something for him, too. Even when she casually talked about assassinating people, his cock perked up. How much time did they have before they got to the store?"

"But I totally think you should stick with research that doesn't get you thrown in jail." Her eyes narrowed. "Did you spend time in jail for *Proven Innocent?*"

There was only so far he would go in the name of research. Besides, he already knew what it meant to be in a cage. "I talked to some convicts, toured a couple of max-security places. But I did learn how to get out of a pair of handcuffs. All the stuff about the prison break, I did the stunts. It was cool. They don't let me do the dangerous stuff anymore. Insurance."

Stupid insurance. He liked the car stunts especially. He was basically an expert after all the time he'd clocked on *The Quick and the Enraged.* He could drive just about anything, knew how to break into any car, get through any security system, and he was a master at hot wiring.

"So what all do you have to learn for this film?" She sat back, those petite but athletic legs of hers crossing as she got comfortable.

God, she was pretty. "It's a film about a DEA agent who gets in too deep with a Mexican drug cartel. We've got a couple of weeks shooting in the jungle and Mexico City and then we head back home to shoot on the lots. I know most of this stuff, but I've got a former DEA guy who's going to answer my questions and make sure I've got all the training right. The lingo is always hard. Every damn branch has its own, but I like to be spot on. I know it's an action flick, but I give it a shot. Especially because if we get something wrong, I will hear about it. I get hate mail all the time about historical inaccuracies, continuity errors—anything that's not perfect gets picked apart on the Internet. I want to at least be able to say I tried."

"Yikes," she said with a grimace. "I hadn't thought of it that way. Now I feel bad for being wicked hard on a couple of romance writers out there."

"Come here." He didn't like her sitting over there. He couldn't touch her. Now that they were in the city proper, the traffic was slowing them down and he didn't worry as much about an accident. Declan was driving carefully.

She slid across the long seat without hesitation and didn't struggle when he lifted her onto his lap.

"That's better." He wasn't going to fuck her. They didn't have the time and the last thing he wanted was Declan to park, open the door, and have some paparazzi catch them mid-bang. But he found he didn't like not touching her. The minute she wiggled a bit, his dick responded, but he was okay with the discomfort. "I need to do a spy film so I can use all your stories. You can be my consultant. I bet you're way prettier than Tyler Williams."

He slid the strap of her sundress down and let his nose brush along her neck. He loved the way she smelled. Citrus and sunshine and ocean. He definitely loved that she didn't seem to mind that he took great pleasure in smelling her skin and hair. Some women would view it as kinky, but Kayla just giggled when it got too tickly, as she would say.

She was the single most tolerant lover he'd ever had.

"So are you spending time with this guy? The DEA guy? Is he coming out to the house?"

Because she would cook for him. She would want to plan a dinner party and play the gracious hostess. She seemed forever obsessed with feeding the people around her. He let his hand cup her breast through the thin material of her dress. No bra. She wasn't allowed one, but then she didn't really need one. Her nipple peaked against his hand.

"I know he'll be in Mexico. I'm hoping to catch him before we all head down," he murmured. "He's sent me a bunch of reading material and I talked to him on the phone. The man I was supposed to consult with decided he couldn't take the time to come down to the set. This guy is a last-minute replacement, but he seems smart enough. I wish I had more time with him, but I've played FBI agents and at least four different cops. I know the basics. This guy will make sure I don't miss the complexities."

She was complex. It was what he obsessed over with her. Smart and funny and deadly all wrapped up in an erotic package that made him crazy.

Maybe they could skip the store and drive around LA fucking in the back of a limo.

The barrier between the front and back dropped down and Declan looked at them through the rearview mirror. "I'll drop you two here and then find a place to park. Unless you want me to check it out first."

Damn it. It was a reminder that things would change and soon. He had a job to do and part of that job was making sure she was ready to do hers. He couldn't take her down there without a proper wardrobe. No one would believe she was his girlfriend if she wasn't dripping in designer crap.

Regretfully Josh shook his head and eased her off his lap. "I think we're fairly safe. I can't remember the last time a person got shot at Chanel. Park and take a break. We'll call you when we're ready. I think it'll take more than one store to get what we need. After all, variety is the spice of life, or so someone said. If she shows up wearing exclusively Chanel they'll think I signed a deal."

"Is it wrong that I'm super excited about this?" Kay asked, her hand on the door. Her dress had been righted and she didn't look like a woman who'd been manhandled.

He reached out and stopped her. "Don't be so excited you forget my manners."

She was the kind of woman who bounded out of a car when it stopped, but he liked being the gentleman. So much of his life had been about brutality that he enjoyed the ease of social niceties, even when a lot of people considered them outdated. That's why he called them his manners. Of course, what they really amounted to was protocol. They were finding their way with that. She was to allow him to give her every courtesy. He wasn't allowed to call her property or be insanely jealous when she talked to another man.

Well, he wasn't allowed to act on it.

He opened his side of the car and found Declan had already gotten out. The big man towered over him.

"You have to stay with her," he said.

His bodyguards were pushy and all too often forgot who the boss was. "We'll be fine. It should be a few hours. Take a nap or something."

The big bodyguard's eyes were also hidden behind sunglasses, and Josh was happy for that. Something about the man unnerved him at times. Shane was the all-American type, but there was something almost otherworldly about this dude. "I'll be around if you need me. If you text, I'll be there."

Josh nodded and moved around the limo. He'd wanted to take the Porsche out, but apparently that went against bodyguard rules. Those rules that were meant to keep him safe were beginning to chafe. He needed his alone time, but that wasn't happening anytime soon. He'd had some more threatening letters, these sent to his agent and publicist.

It was all crap. *I love you. I want to kill you. I know your secrets.*

Yeah, he didn't buy that one because the person who knew his secrets didn't send him letters through representatives. No. That bitch knew exactly how to get hold of him.

He was getting antsy. It was almost time. Almost time again.

He opened the door and held out a hand. Already someone walking down the street was turning, sunglasses coming off as though she couldn't quite believe what she was seeing. Josh ignored the gawker, preferring greatly to concentrate on the one good thing to have come from all the bodyguard crap.

Kayla slid her hand in his, allowing him to help her up, though they both knew she didn't need any help from him physically. She was strong and steady. She could run in those mile-high heels and not break an ankle or a sweat.

And yet her eyes were wide as saucers as she looked up at the store. That almost childlike joy kicked him in the gut every time because he was the one providing the experience for her. This was a woman who wouldn't get jaded or cynical. Who wouldn't take for granted the little things in life. Hell, she talked to dolphins.

"You ready to have some fun?"

"Are you sure you want to come with me?" she asked, her eyes on the storefront. "I know you've got stuff to prep. I can handle this if you have work to do. I'll call in a stylist to make sure I don't pick up something embarrassing."

"I can read the new pages while you try stuff on," he assured her. "I've got my tablet and I can jot down questions for Tyler Williams. He's already sent me a list of mandatory training my character would go through and some interesting case files that can serve as backstory. Besides, I like your style. If we bring someone in, she'll try to put you in as many trends as possible. You tend to like soft, feminine stuff. I like that, too. On you."

The limo drove away and they were left alone on the street. It was nice to be alone with her. He could pretend they were just another couple. He was the Dom, indulging his lovely submissive in a free-for-all shopping experience that would likely cost him six figures. Okay, maybe they would never be normal, but he liked it when they didn't have an entourage around them.

"Are you sure you're not protecting your wealth?" She grinned up at him.

He put a hand on his wallet. "Should I?"

"Oh, yeah. I can do some damage," she promised. "And seriously, it's been years since I shopped this way. Well, the Santa Barbara mall version of this."

"I would have thought the life of a spy was filled with designer wear."

"See, that's where Hollywood gets it wrong. We mostly try to fit in, not stand out. Though there was this one time when I infiltrated the king of Loa Mali's…oh, let's call it a harem, for lack of a better word.

There was designer wear then, but mostly bikinis and lingerie. We were on this unbelievable yacht. There wasn't a lot of evening wear."

He stopped, his brain working overtime. "The king of Loa Mali? The one who got married recently? What do you mean by harem? And how would you work in a bikini?"

She started toward the store. "Oh, I can work in a bikini. It makes hiding weapons a lot harder, but it forces one to be more creative. I killed this dude with a straw from one of those coconut drinks once. I had to. That string bikini was useless when it came to hiding a gun. And yes, it was that king, and maybe I shouldn't tell you these stories."

"Because they're classified?"

She shook her head. "Nope. Because you look a little crazy pants right now."

Because he was jealous. Didn't matter that she told him he couldn't be. He fucking was. He loved her stories. She'd started telling him crazy spy stories and he would sit and listen, soaking them in without ever quite believing them. But he could see her in a harem. He might not be able to truly visualize her assassinating the heads of the five top Yakuza syndicates at a conference with an ice pick and not getting blood on her catering uniform, but he could damn straight see a kinky king picking her out of a crowd for some dirty sex. Yeah, he could see that all too well. "I don't like thinking about you using your body like that."

Her brows rose. "Are you serious?"

He shook his head. "It's different."

She stopped and the joking left her face. "How is it different, Josh?"

Shit. Was it? He reached out to the only thing he could. "Well, for one you're not lying to me. All our cards are on the table. We know this is an exchange, but then it always is. This is an honest exchange. I bet you didn't tell the kinky old king who you were and why you were there."

"No, and just for the record, he wasn't that old. He's only a couple of years older than me."

Awesome. "Also, we're involved in a D/s relationship. Did the king give you what you needed?"

She frowned. "He was way too gentle. And see, you call him kinky, but he wasn't. He called me his delicate flower. I actually hated that part. Kash is a good guy, but he was a little fucked in the head in those days. And I did eventually tell him. I had to because a man working for The Collective showed up, blew up Kash's lab where he'd been building an engine that ran on water, and tried to kill us all. I managed to get the king off the boat with scuba gear and the last of his research intact. And *that's* totally classified."

He stopped, frowning because he'd heard that story before. "That sounds like that movie. *Love After Death.* Hey, did someone drown after she managed to switch a bomb to the bad guy's boat, and then the hero pulled her out and made everyone leave because he didn't know what she'd done. And then he brought her back to life?"

That brilliant grin was back. "I have no idea how they haven't arrested Serena yet. Probably because no one would believe it."

He followed her inside. "Holy shit. You were the crazy CIA double who saved Pierce Craig."

"I like to call him Big Tag," she admitted and then sighed. "It smells like joy in here."

The well-manicured attendants were already circling like sharks, but he drew her close anyway. "Sometimes I think you're too good to be true."

"Only sometimes?"

"The other times I think you're too crazy to be true."

She went up on her toes and met his eyes. "Maybe I'm both. Good and crazy, but I promise you, Josh. I am true. And you're right. This is different."

When she got close to him like this it was almost impossible to not lean down and brush his lips against hers. She was right there and she would welcome his kiss. He could be normal for a moment.

It didn't do him any good to think like that. "If I stopped paying you would you stay with me?"

Her stare turned serious. "Yes."

Why was he going down this road? He couldn't seem to stop himself. "If I didn't have money, would you still sleep with me?"

"I would pay money to sleep with you, Josh."

A chill went through him and he stepped back.

"Josh?" She reached out and put her hand in his. "Do you want to go somewhere and get some lunch? I don't need clothes. I'm actually pretty stylish all on my own. We have the afternoon. Let's go do something fun for you. I think the Dodgers are playing."

She killed him. This was how she fucking killed him. He knew how much she wanted those damn clothes. He'd watched her talk about designers and shit with his agent's wife at a party they'd gone to a couple of nights before, but unlike the other women he knew, she would give up her shopping day to please him. This. This was why he said it was different with her, why the D/s part was different. In D/s, each partner had a role to play, but at the heart they were the same role—to please the other.

She pleased him. He'd probably never had a woman in his life who pleased him the way Kayla did.

He let go of the little ache that had come with words she hadn't meant to wound. He brought her hand to his lips. "I want to see you in pretty clothes." He leaned over. "Although you look best naked. Now spend some cash, baby."

She moved in, brushing her body against his, her head tilting up. He loved how small she was compared to him, though he knew damn well no matter what his muscles said, she was the deadly one. "Are you sure? Because I would love to make you happy. I don't know what I said…"

It took everything he had not to kiss her. He wondered if that was inevitable. Of course then he remembered where his lips had been and it was easier to back away. "You say all the right things. Ladies, this is the most beautiful woman in the world. Do you think your clothes are worthy of her?"

"Mr. Hunt, she's going to look beautiful in the new collection," one of the circling salesladies said.

"I think the colors this season will highlight her hair," another said.

"I don't know. She's gorgeous. I think she'll make our clothes look good." The one male salesperson stood back, eyeing her with a totally non-sexual gaze.

"You"—he pointed to the man—"anything she wants, she gets. Now, I'm going to need a spring water and a quiet place to read. Can

137

you do that for me?"

As always in his life these days, the answer was yes.

* * * *

Three hours later, he sat in Carolina Herrera's North Rodeo boutique as Kayla fluttered about, three saleswomen working overtime to find her things to try on. He planted himself in one of the chairs between the bookshelves that lined the walls of this part of the store.

Three hours. Five stores. God only knew how much money he'd spent, but he liked this particular role. Indulgent Dom. That's what he would call it. His submissive was being treated like a queen, and even then she'd found the time to pick out a new tie for him at Louis Vuitton. She'd claimed the blue reminded her of his eyes, and she'd insisted on paying for it.

Eight-hundred dollars versus the tens of thousands he'd spent on her wouldn't be fair in some people's eyes, but Josh understood the difference. He had eighty million socked away and it grew every single month. Kayla was not in the same position. Eight hundred meant something to her, so in a way, it was far more precious than what he was giving her. He had a hundred ties like it, but this one would be special to him.

Shit. When was the last time anyone had bought him a gift?

He pulled his phone out, the screen gleaming in the low light. It was peaceful in here. He could make some notes on the script changes. Notes like who the hell wrote this? And why hasn't he been fired yet? His DEA agent shouldn't sound like a just-out-of-college dipshit. The dialogue was peppered with youthful slang when this was a man who'd gone through the military and was pushing forty.

It all had to be changed and fast.

"Mr. Hunt?"

He looked up, expecting to see one of the saleswomen. It was their job to take care of not only Kay, but him, and he'd known at some point they would ask after his welfare. Saleswomen and men in Beverly Hills were the best trained in the world. They knew when to offer and when to step back.

And these were no different, every single one of them paying attention to Kayla as he'd asked. If he'd taken every glass of champagne he'd been offered today, he would be drunk. Unlike his girl over there. He glanced her way, but she was staring at a cocktail dress. She'd had way too much champagne and there she was, steady as a rock. His girl could handle her liquor. He would give that to her. He glanced up and the woman wasn't wearing a name tag, but sometimes managers didn't. "I'm fine, but you might see if Kayla wants a glass of champagne."

If he got her tipsy, maybe they could play a game in the limo on the way back. She could be the naughty wife who'd bought way too many clothes and would be forced to pay her hubby back the only way she could…

"I'm not an employee, Mr. Hunt." She was a tall blonde, maybe in her mid-thirties. Utterly perfect, and that made him wary. Everything about her was flawless, from her honey-colored hair to a body she probably worked on a few hours every day. He glanced down and sure enough there was a ridiculously large diamond on her left ring finger.

"All right, then. What can I do for you?"

If she asked for an autograph, he would force himself to smile and do it. Kay was mere feet away and she'd talked about how important it was to put a smiley face on in public. He preferred to shove people away, but this was her day.

The woman in front of him smoothed down her dress, making sure she cupped her ample breasts. "I'm your biggest fan, Joshua. You should know that. I'm also a regular here. I know every inch of this place. I thought you might like to take a tour of the dressing rooms. They're very private. Very quiet."

He frowned, his body going cold. "What would you like me to see there?"

She leaned over, giving him a view of her assets. "You could see anything you liked."

Again he caught sight of the ring on her finger. He glanced up and it was apparent she wasn't alone. A woman was watching her, frowning all the way, as though she couldn't quite believe what was happening.

"I don't like anything you have to offer. In fact, I'm insulted you would think I would take you anywhere at all."

She seemed to fumble, going from seductive to a little horrified in an instant. "I was just…it's more private in case you want to work."

Sure. "I'm fine right here, and before you attempt to give me another private viewing of what you have to offer, try to remember that I came in here with a woman. Does she look like my sister? Hell, even if she was my sister, what kind of brother would I be if I left her alone to screw some random chick in a dressing room? You have a wedding ring on. I suspect that's a present from the man who's paying for this outing. Perhaps I should talk to him. I suspect the sales associates know who you are. Would your husband enjoy talking to me?"

She pulled back. "You're an asshole."

"A faithful one." He didn't cheat. He didn't play around and he no longer sold himself. "An asshole who won't mind calling out a faithless wife. Go away. Don't come back or I'll do something worse. I'll ask my girlfriend what she thinks. You won't like what she thinks."

The woman practically ran the other way.

One of the salesladies stepped in. She wore a black sheath dress, her face pinched in consternation. "Are you all right, Mr. Hunt? Did that woman bother you? I'm sorry."

At least he was getting stellar service. He forced his expression to clear as the woman and her friend—who was probably a nanny because she was pushing a baby stroller—fled the store. He didn't want to put anyone on edge when they were being professional. "She asked a question I couldn't give her an answer to, that's all. Make sure my girl tries on the blue jumper. I think it would look wonderful on her."

The saleslady grinned. "She's wonderful. So funny and kind."

That was his girl.

His cell buzzed in his pocket and he glanced down at the number. Fuck. *Unknown*. It was either honestly unknown and someone wanted to attempt to get him to vote one way or another or…it was time.

His gut was in a knot. "Is there someplace private I could take this?"

She pointed to the back of the store. "There's an alley behind us. Follow me." She led him past Kayla, who was slipping into a dressing room. She didn't notice him. "We take smoke breaks back here. The door is going to lock, but the alley leads around to the front of the store. I could prop it open if you like."

And risk anyone overhearing him? Not a chance. Actually, this was one of the reasons he'd decided to take Kayla out today. He had a long lunch planned for tomorrow and a meeting the next day, all so he could easily slip away from her and take this particular call.

He didn't like hiding things from her. That was a surprise since most of his life consisted of hiding his past. He was used to it. Didn't give it a second thought, but the fact that he was manipulating things in order to make certain she wouldn't overhear a phone conversation bothered him.

When had he lost the upper hand?

He slid his thumb across the screen to accept the call as he made his way to the back. "This is Hunt."

He pushed through the door going from the cool darkness of the back room into the heat of day.

Her voice rasped as though going through some kind of filter. It was always like this. "Tomorrow night. Solstice Canyon, eleven p.m. Leave the package at the foot of the statue of the Virgin Mary. As usual, come alone or we'll have to believe you're all right with everyone knowing your secret."

"I know the spot." Shit. They were supposed to go to The Reef tomorrow night. There was a party after the play session that he would be expected to attend. He would have to sneak away.

Fuck. He would have to sneak away from his bodyguards. That was easier said than done. Though they tended to think he was safe in the club. Likely he could convince Dec and Shane to merely do drop-off duty since Kayla would be with him all night.

"Don't be late."

There were other problems with his blackmailer's plans. "And if there are hikers? You know night hiking is kind of a thing around here."

"Then I suspect you'll find a way," she replied. "And watch out for the local wildlife. I've heard they get hungry at night. Don't bring that new girlfriend of yours or she might get eaten right up."

A chill went down his spine. "Leave her out of this."

"I can't. You brought her in. I find it curious that there's little information about her out there. Oh, don't get me wrong. I can find a bunch of well-crafted documents meant to throw off the casual investigator. I'm not casual, Mr. Hunt. I'm concerned that you've suddenly hired one of the premiere security firms in the world to do your security."

Thank god it wasn't about Kayla in particular. Although it really worried him that this woman knew so much about his business. Had he been fooling himself all this time thinking she was merely concerned with their business dealings and nothing else about his life? Was she always out there watching him? The thought irritated him, made him less cautious than he normally was. "Yeah, well there are more threats out there than some nasty bitch who knows about my past."

Her voice deepened, whatever tech she used to disguise it making her sound the slightest bit demonic, and wasn't that fitting? She was his personal demon made flesh. "Don't think that opening up old wounds is all I can do to you. I can give you some spectacular new ones. If I find out McKay-Taggart is trying to find me, you'll have some new scars that will make the old ones look minor."

She hadn't talked like this in years. Not since the one time he'd rebelled. "What's changed?"

He probably shouldn't question her. He should get off the line and get back inside and try to figure out how he was going to slip away from the club tomorrow night, but he found the curiosity overwhelming. And a bit terrifying if her answer came close to the one in his head.

Only one thing had changed.

"I told you. I don't like you hiring investigators."

"They're not investigating anything except some of the crazies who've attached themselves to me. They know nothing about you at all and I intend to keep it that way. I haven't done this for years to let this shit come out now." It would ruin him in a way the actual crimes against him hadn't. Letting everyone know how weak he'd been, how he'd been used and treated like trash.

"I'm not one of your crazies?"

This was the longest conversation he'd had with her in years. She typically got on, told him a location, and hung up. Something was wrong. Something had truly worried his always calm and cool blackmailer. "Not at all. Those people have mental illnesses. You're evil."

A throaty laugh came over the line. "Well, I should expect such drama from an actor. Evil? I'm a businesswoman and you're an excellent source of income. Do you ever wonder how I came about my information?"

He stilled, not even the late afternoon sun warming him. A pit had opened in his stomach. He'd never been asked the question before, though he'd always, always known the answer. "I assume you know it all firsthand. Over the years I have wondered who you are, which house you worked in."

A cold laugh came over the line. "You think I'm one of your pimps, Joshua? One of those sweet mommas who beat the shit out of you when you were bad and then tried to cover up the bruises so you would look good for the night? Or perhaps you think I was one of the women who purchased you, though I assume it was mostly men. No. It would surprise you to know that I'm younger than you."

His heart constricted. Of all the scenarios he'd gone through, he hadn't come up with this one. "Then you were…"

"No," she said with a sigh. "I wasn't one of the kids. Though I do know what it means to be in a prison not of my own making. You would be surprised how much we have in common. I found a way out, but it didn't pay well. Not in cash. A smart person figures out how to turn assets into cash. You're an asset, Joshua."

"Who the hell are you?" He didn't like the way his heart was pounding, his vision not as acute as it should be. A mist seemed to come over his eyes, the world tilting and turning.

Out of control. His control was nothing but an illusion. He fought so hard for it and it could be blown away with the slightest of winds.

"Isn't that the question? The problem is if you find out, I'll have to kill you, and that wouldn't do either one of us any good," she replied. "Make the drop. And I'm magnanimous. I get it. There are crazies out there. You need bodyguards, but not tomorrow night.

143

Keep them out of our business and everything can go on the way it always has. But the second I find out someone's sniffing around me or mine, I'll do what I have to. You and yours should watch out. You know what I can do."

The line went dead.

He stood there for a moment, utterly unable to move. Somehow he'd convinced himself that the blackmail was nothing more than the price of doing business. Everyone had secrets. God, in his business it really was everyone. No one wanted it to get out that they had a coke problem or weird sex fetish. Producers hid the fact that they fucked every starlet who wanted to be in their films, and actors pretended they hadn't spent a little time on the casting couch, too.

Somehow it had become normal. Anything could be normal if you let it.

She watched him all the time. She knew his every move and she could take it all away.

His wealth, his success, it was all built on sand, and that woman was the tide who could wash it all away.

He hated her. Hated her with a violent rage he'd never felt before, and that was saying something since he'd killed a man when he was seventeen—his escape. He could still feel the man's throat in his hands, see the way his eyes nearly popped out of his head. He'd known in that moment that if he didn't get out, he would do this again and again and again. He would trade one horrible cage for a prison eventually.

He would love to kill that woman. To make it slow and painful.

"Josh, come on, man, give me a good shot."

He barely heard the words through the haze of red floating in front of his eyes. He glanced over and there was a man walking into the alley from his left, his expensive camera pointed Josh's way.

Fuck. Two minutes. He'd needed two fucking minutes alone. He needed to get back inside and then he could calm down. He would see if they had something stronger than champagne and he could get back into his role.

Indulgent Dom. That's who he was right now.

Even though he was thinking about taking on the role of psychotic killer who needs to get his freak on.

"Please go away, man," he said, his voice as bland as he could make it. "I need a little time."

He tried the door, but it was locked. Damn it. He'd told the sales staff he would walk back around to the front of the store because he hadn't wanted anyone to be able to listen in. He glanced to his right. There was a throng of people walking down the street, following someone who was speaking. They stopped at the edge of the alley, though they hadn't looked down it yet. Some kind of tour. He didn't need that.

"Give us a smile, Josh," the man insisted. "Come on. One little smile. You always look sad. What do you have to be sad about? One smile and we can be done."

Sure they would. No one would stop until they had their fill, got their strip of his hide. Everyone wanted something from him and they never, ever left until they were fucking satisfied. He might as well smile and get it over with. Grin and bear it. It'll all be over with soon.

Except it never fucking ended.

Somehow he ended up turning and reaching for the man's camera. It was in his hand before he actually understood what he was doing.

"What the fuck?" The man behind the camera was probably in his mid-fifties, his body showing signs of too much junk food and not a lot of exercise. His face went a florid red. "That's mine."

Josh tossed it against the side of the building. The camera came apart with a satisfying bang, its parts shattering and landing on the ground in pieces that would never fit back together again. That felt so fucking good. How much better would it feel to take the guy apart? He could see it plainly. He'd trained for this now that he thought about it. He'd trained in everything from Krav Maga to jujutsu to going through actual BUD/S training with a group of Navy SEALs. He could take a man apart without breathing heavy.

Take him apart. Bathe in his blood. Show that fucker a real smile. Yeah, he would be smiling at the end, and wasn't that the best part? Everyone got what they wanted.

"Step back, Mr. Hunt."

Declan Burke put his big body between him and his target.

"Get out of my way."

Burke looked back at the photographer. "You need to run and fucking now."

"But my camera," the asshole complained.

"You're about to look a whole lot like it," Burke shot back. "Get the fuck out and next time I see you, I'll let my boss here take you apart. Hell, next time I might help him." He turned to Josh. "Calm the fuck down now. That tour group hasn't noticed yet, but they will."

"I don't care." He watched as the paparazzo ran out toward the street. Getting away.

Declan's big body blocked the sight. "You think I don't know that look? I know that look, man. I know it because I see it in the fucking mirror when I wake up."

Maybe they would be well matched then. "You don't know a fucking thing."

"I know you feel out of control and deep down there's this instinct inside you telling you how to get it back. It's the alpha dog that lives in our guts. That alpha dog knows how to handle shit. He shows every single fucking yappy POS who the boss is. He bares his teeth and takes his hunk of flesh, and they either fall in line or they don't get the fuck up again. Alpha dog doesn't care. But man, the police do. Take a deep breath or better yet, do the other thing that will help."

His hands were shaking but Burke made sense.

"Go inside that store and find Kay."

His breath hitched. Kayla, who was sweet and submissive during sex and who was absolutely the alpha female. "I'm on the edge."

"And she can bring you back." Burke seemed to relax a bit. "At least that's what she tells me. I think she cares about you and wouldn't want you to hurt someone else."

"And if I hurt her?"

"You won't if you're the Dom you say you are." Burke took a step back. "Or we can go get a drink, but first off I'm going to get rid of that camera. When the cops show up, you can decide how to handle it, but they won't have any evidence against you."

"Keep them out of the dressing rooms until I'm done." He heard the words come out of his mouth but his mind was already on her.

Yes, she was exactly what he fucking needed.

Chapter Eight

Kayla looked at herself in the gorgeous lace-pleated chiffon evening gown. An elegant velvet belt cinched her waist in, the deep V of the bodice showing off her golden skin. The color was what drew her to the floor-length gown. It was a lovely ocean blue. The long skirt of the gown and slightly lighter lace panels made her think of waves as she moved.

"It's stunning," one of the saleswomen said, shaking her head as though she'd never quite seen anything like it.

"So beautiful. That is from our fall line. Straight off the runway," another commented. "Everyone will be talking about this gown. It's perfect for red-carpet events."

Or private formal events. Josh had told her his friend liked to dress for dinner and she would need several formal gowns. She'd found a couple, but nothing that suited her the way this one did. This was the one. This was the one she would be wearing on the night she completed her operation. There would be a big party to celebrate Josh and she would sneak away, find the Commander's office and get the intelligence she needed, and look perfectly stylish while she did it.

"We need a private dressing room."

Her whole body went still because she knew that voice. Deep, dark, with the edge of a growl. Predatory.

Her Dom was in the house.

Around her, the saleswomen were fluttering as though they suddenly found themselves sharing tight space with a hungry tiger.

Kayla caught his stare in the three-paneled mirror she stood in front of. His eyes were dark, his jaw tight. And was that a bit of blood on his fist? Her first thought was to run to him, see where he was hurt, try to baby him.

That was not what he needed. Not even close.

A thrill went through her system. A totally selfish thrill. Josh was on edge and this was one of the ways he brought himself back. Something had happened and he likely wouldn't talk about it. At least he wouldn't until he'd regained control. If she refused him, he would probably walk away, find a gym and punish his body until he passed out.

Or he could punish hers. Punishing her body ended in her screaming out his name when she came, so she knew which path she was voting for.

Either way, she was going to let him make the decision, let him take control. This was the time when he needed her submission the most. He didn't need it in the real world. He needed a partner there, and she rather thought he'd been surprised by how well they worked together. He asked her opinion, followed it most of the time, allowed her to take the lead when it came to security.

But when he got that look in his eyes, she knew the time had come to give him the other piece of herself—the part that submitted to the right Master.

Her body was still, but she could feel a ripple of pure arousal start to flow. He stared at her in the mirror, their eyes locking in understanding.

He needed what only she could give him.

Yep, that did it for her.

"Private?" one of the salespeople asked, as though she'd forgotten the definition of the word.

Josh's eyes never left hers, holding still as though neither would move again until they were alone and could find their proper roles. "Kayla, have you decided on that gown?"

She shook her head. "I think I need a couple of minutes to decide, but they could start preparing the rest of the order. It should take them a while because I'm going to want it all."

A little gasp left the sales staff as though they'd collectively realized what that meant. Money. Lots of commission. Enough that they could let go of any prudish ideas rattling around in their heads.

The lead saleswoman was suddenly all solicitous concern. "This whole section of the store can be made private. For bridal and formal wear, of course. You need a lot of space for gowns like these. I'll pull these curtains down, tie them together, and you'll have your own private space. Please take all the time you need to decide. We'll handle everything else."

One of the younger women's eyes widened. "But I think he means to…"

The lead put her perfectly manicured hand up. "Appreciate how beautiful this dress is and very likely decide to purchase it along with all the others? Yes, I think that's what he's going to do, too. Chrissy, why don't you go and turn up the music? It's far too low. We don't want it to sound like a tomb in here after all."

That was an experienced salesperson.

The heavy velvet curtains dropped and she found herself alone with him. The question was which Josh was she about to get? He liked to play roles. She'd watched him do it. There was the private Josh and the one who showed up a party, the all-business Josh and the one who built walls faster than anyone she'd seen before.

But this one? Hungry Dom.

Was Hungry Dom also Hurt Dom?

"Josh? What happened?"

He shook his head. "Take off the dress if you want to keep it. I don't care either way."

He would pay for it even if he left it in tatters on the floor, but he was going to have her naked one way or another. She got that message loud and clear. Luckily it was a fairly easy dress to get out of. Flowy was always easier than tight. She turned to watch him as she undid the belt at her waist and then eased the bodice down. No bra. No way she could hide the fact that her nipples were tightly peaked and he hadn't put a hand on her yet.

"I'm serious, Kayla. Get rid of the dress. This is a dungeon now.

I told you when you signed that contract that I would have you when I wanted and where I wanted. When I wanted and how I wanted."

Yes, his want was perfectly clear to her. His want was need, and that made everything different. She shoved the dress down and laid it over one of the chairs left behind in the space. She pushed the thong she wore over her hips, placed it with the dress, and then turned back to him. He hadn't mentioned the shoes and likely wouldn't, so she crossed the space between them, her sky-high Yves Saint Laurents making no sound on the carpet before she sank down in front of him. Knees wide, palms up, head bowed.

"How can I serve you, Joshua?"

He was silent for a moment and she watched his boots. They didn't make a move. He was tightly coiled and she waited for him to go off. "Just like that?"

"Yes. No questions asked. No need to talk unless you want to. You need my submission and it's yours."

A hand touched her head and then she felt his fingers sink in, twisting lightly at first. "I wonder if you mean that."

"I do."

He kept twisting and pain flared along her scalp. A bite, nothing more, and then he was petting her again. Then another, longer twist, a harder bite that had her gasping and biting back a moan. "Will you mean it when I'm rougher than I've ever been? Will you mean it when you realize everyone in this store is listening to what I do to you?"

"Haven't you figured out that I don't care what other people think? Not about this. Not about much. I find people who care about me no matter what and I try to stick close to them. Are you going to hurt me?"

"Yes."

"Thank god." Her body relaxed and then tensed again as he forced her head back.

"I hope you mean that." He leaned over. So close she could almost feel his lips on hers, knew she was about to get what she wanted.

And then moved away. Yeah, that part sucked. The spankings and canings and that part where he pinched her nipples right before

150

licking them was awesome, but the no kissing was starting to rankle.

One more wall she couldn't climb.

He stopped and his hand fell away. "I'm on the edge. I went out to take a call and a fucking photographer showed up."

She could handle that. "Do you want me to kill him? I have a really slender knife with me. One good poke through the right ribs and up into his heart and he won't even bleed too much. I can leave him in a nice alley and it could be days before someone thinks he's not just sleeping it off."

He stopped for a moment and he had that look on his face—the one lots of people got when she talked. It was that "what did you say?" look. "You're not joking. Sometimes I have to remind myself that you're not joking."

Sometimes she was. This time she wasn't. "No. If he's out there, I'll take care of it."

Something seemed to ease inside him, his shoulders coming down the barest notch. "Take care of me instead. Stand up and go over to the chair. I want you to bend over. This discipline isn't about anything you've done wrong. It's not to correct a behavior or to instill a lesson. This discipline is about me. I need to spank your ass until it's red and know you like it. I need to put a mark on you and know you accept it. If you don't want that or it scares you, I'll find another way."

She couldn't help it. Her eyes rolled. She'd loved to say they kind of did that on their own, but the idea that a spanking scared her made her bratty side come out.

"What did you just do?" That hand was back in her hair, twisting viciously this time, forcing her to look him in the eyes. This time, the pain sizzled along her scalp, lighting it up. "Did you roll your eyes at me when I was kindly explaining what the parameters of the scene were?"

Put that way, it might not have been the most polite thing to do. "I wasn't rolling them at you. I was rolling them because of you. I've been tortured by professionals."

"Then I'll have to up my game, won't I? I'll have to try harder so I don't bore you." He leaned over, his mouth against her ear. "You should feel lucky that I'm not equipped to properly discipline you. If I had a tube of ginger lube right now, I would show you what I do to brats who roll their eyes at me. I suspect that by the time we're done here, the impulse will have passed, but you should know it would not go well for you right now."

The threat sent a delicious shiver down her spine. This was what she'd been missing with the Doms at The Garden. They were all about the play, and not one of them would have seriously punished her. The relationship wasn't intimate enough.

"Since I don't have a handy tube of lube," he began, "go and bend over that chair. Your legs better be fucking wide and your back straight. Go. Go right fucking now or I'll start this here and you won't like it."

Like? She loved how rough his voice was. He *was* on the edge, but she trusted him not to fall over it. This was how he was trying to keep himself sane. She moved as quickly as she could, crossing the space between her and that chair, getting into position so he wouldn't have any other reason to punish her. When she turned her head, she could see him in the mirror.

His jeans had tented, the long line of his erection plain against the denim. How long would it be before he ditched the jeans and stroked that big dick in his hand? She loved watching him as he stroked himself and stalked her. He was staring at her now, his eyes on her form.

He moved to the place where she'd draped the pretty blue dress over the chair closest to the velvet curtains. "I like this, Kay. It looks beautiful on you. We'll get this for you. After we get back from Mexico, awards season starts. You can wear this to the Oscars and I'll find a place to fuck you backstage. You'll do that, right? You'll let me fuck you backstage? You'll spread your legs and welcome my cock while they announce best picture and everyone's clapping. They'll really be clapping because of how well and thoroughly I'll have you that night."

"Yes, Joshua." She couldn't tell him she probably wouldn't be around then. God, she didn't want to think about it. Why should she? He would still want a McKay-Taggart team around him. Dec and Shane would rotate out eventually, but she didn't have to. She would be done with the CIA job, but Josh didn't have to know she'd ever done it. She could still be his close cover expert. Why shouldn't she?

He didn't have to know they'd started with a lie.

He picked up her thong. "I don't like this."

"I was trying on clothes. They tend to like you to have undies on," she explained.

"I don't care. You're mine. You're not theirs. I make the rules when it comes to you."

There was that overly possessive caveman she'd come to count on. He seemed to not bond to many, but when he did, it was quick and fierce and he held on tight. "Yes, Joshua. I won't wear them again."

He palmed her ass, his hands so big he could almost cup both cheeks in one. "I'm probably going to have to talk to the police in a bit."

"What?" She started to come up.

His hand moved in a stinging arc, striking her left cheek with ruthless intent. One and two and three until she'd settled back into the position he'd put her in.

"Are you okay?" Kayla asked on a shaky breath. She was damn glad the chair had wooden arms because she needed them to stay upright. "Do we need to call a lawyer?"

Another nasty slap. "You need to concentrate on this. I was telling you because I don't want you to be surprised if there are cops on the other side of that curtain when I'm done with you. Or if they rush in and catch us. I don't care at this point. At this point, they could storm the place and I'll answer all their questions while I'm inside you."

He moved his hand over her ass as though tracing the marks he'd already made.

"What happened?" She braced herself.

He smacked her again, but this one was almost idle, and then his hand moved between her legs, brushing her core. "I went outside to take a phone call and I got into it with a fucking photographer. I'll likely have to pay for his camera, though perhaps not. Burke said he would take care of it and then sent me in here to you."

Smart man. "He's getting rid of the evidence." She gasped as he skimmed along her clitoris. "Oh, Josh."

That was when he pinched her. Hard. It made her squirm and

squeal and gave him the excuse to spank her more. Over and over, he brought his hand down on her backside, fire licking along her flesh.

She squeezed her eyes shut, holding in the tears that threatened. Tears were good. They were cleansing and she often needed a scene like this one to release the stress and have a good cry. Somewhere along the way, she'd forgotten how to do that. Oh, she knew it had happened sometime during her MSS years. She'd been forced to go cold, forced to shut down entire sections of her personality so she could slip into her sister's shoes and live out a nightmare that wasn't supposed to be hers. Only D/s had ever given her a safe place to cry, but she couldn't do it now. Now wasn't for her. Now was for Josh, and she couldn't have the police storming in here because they thought he was hurting her.

So she bit her bottom lip as he executed another volley of stinging slaps.

"You'll wear a plug tomorrow. You're going to get that sweet ass plugged up in front of the entire club. They'll watch as I work that plug inside. How is it going to feel knowing everyone will be watching you? Everyone is going to know what a bad sub you've been that you deserve your Master's plug stretching that tiny asshole all night long. Depending on how gracious you are between now and then, I will decide what kind of lubricant to use. But before I work the plug in, I'm going to play. I'm going to stretch your cheeks wide and show off what belongs to me. I'll let everyone look and all the Doms will have to shift around because they'll be hard at the thought of that tiny hole squeezing their cocks. Thinking is all they'll get to do because it's fucking mine. That pretty hole belongs to me and I'm going to take it. First with a finger diving in, opening you up and fucking deep inside, and then later with my cock. You're going to feel the burn, my luscious little sub."

She could practically feel it now. He was so good with the dirty talk that sometimes she thought she might come simply listening to his voice.

"I wish I had more time," he said. "I suppose I'll do what I must. Don't you let go of that chair."

She took a deep breath and felt him move in behind her. What happened next was fast and furious, his cock thrusting in hard, penetrating her in an instant.

She bit back a cry. He held on to her hips and fucked deep inside her.

"Tell me you're mine."

"I'm yours."

"Tell me I get to do whatever I want to you."

"Anything, Josh. Anything you want." She was worried that she was starting to mean every single one of those words. This man seemed to own her soul for some reason, and she didn't want him to give it back.

There was something deep and primal to the rhythm he set, a ruthless pounding that found its crescendo all too soon.

The orgasm swamped her senses, making the rest of the room fade away until all that mattered was the pleasure coursing through her veins. Josh's hands tightened and he forced himself in as far as he could go. He held her tight, spilling himself deep inside.

Then she felt him step back, heard him moving.

"Get dressed, pet." His voice was calmer, perfectly steady now. "I'm going to dispose of this condom and I believe our friends are here."

"Mr. Hunt, this is Beverly Hills, PD," a deep voice said. "I'm going to need you to step out now. There's been a complaint made against you."

Kayla reached for her jeans, picking up the thong Josh had tossed back over her street clothes.

"I'll be out in a moment, sir," Josh replied calmly. "After I stop my girlfriend from making a horrible mistake. I said no underwear."

Holy shit. "Josh, the police are out there."

"And the police understand the necessity for rules. You do, don't you, Officer? Rules are important to a society and they're important in a relationship. They set the boundaries and foundations on which trust can be built."

"Uh, I came out because someone accused you of beating a photographer," the voice came back.

"Naturally," Josh conceded, tucking his shirt back in. He shoved the thong in his front pocket and didn't seem to care that it was kind of sticking out. "I didn't beat the man. I did, however, give my lady in

155

here a proper schooling on the role of underwear in her life. I'm glad you're here. Perhaps you can scare her straight. When I said no underwear, I meant absolutely none. I understand this thong might not qualify as clothing at all, but it's the thought that matters."

She stared at him, wide-eyed.

He shrugged. "I'm feeling better. Burke was right."

"Ma'am, is he hurting you in any way?" the officer asked.

She finished dressing and faced Josh. Two could play at this game. "Not in any way that didn't lead to a screaming orgasm, Officer. And I learned my lesson. No more panties for me."

She threw open the curtains and was faced with a bunch of people who seemed a bit on the disconcerted side. Except Declan. He was leaning against the jewelry countertop, yawning.

"I told you my boss was doing something way more interesting than beating up on some out-of-shape photog," Declan said.

Kayla picked up on his plans. "I'm very sorry, Officer. I'm afraid he was doing me. I bought a lot of clothes today. Gotta work that off somehow."

Then the officers were chuckling as if they'd seen this a thousand times before and at least the poor schmo whose credit cards were getting a workout was getting something out of this, too.

As the police began to sort things out, she had to wonder what had come over Josh. He was incredibly private and yet in that moment, it seemed he hadn't cared at all that everyone might know about his sex life.

What had changed? And did she dare to hope the change was her?

Chapter Nine

The next morning, Kayla sank down into the chair outside the Starbucks, the smell of coffee making her sigh. Not that she was here for a vanilla latte. That sweet treat was merely a by-product of her current occupation. Still, she would take her comfort where she could. Breathing in the sweet smell rising from her cup, she looked out over the small shopping center that contained a drug store, a couple of boutiques, a Ralph's she spent way too much time at, and this Starbucks. Because it was Southern California, she sat outside, despite the fact that the rest of the world was fighting the encroaching chill of the fall.

In England she would have pulled out the sweaters, but here she was still in shorts and a tank top. And it was easier to have a classified conversation in the beautiful outside where she could see pretty much everyone and all around her people were making noises of their own.

She was starting to get paranoid, but then that was kind of the lifestyle she was leading now.

Was that a photographer? Nope. Tourist. Or he was a paparazzi specializing in PCH photography. Still, she pulled her hat a little lower.

How did Josh live like this every day?

Where the hell was Ezra?

Her cell phone trilled and she grimaced, glancing down. Her dad.

Damn it. She touched the screen to decline the call. Two weeks into her current assignment and things were coming to a head on the family front. She was going to have to call them and soon or they would be all over Damon.

It wasn't like they weren't used to her being out of touch for long periods of time. She used to go six months to a year without talking to them. She would say she was in rural Asia teaching kids English or some shit. The Agency would send out the occasional postcard for her and her dads would be appeased for a while.

She'd read the postcards later on and had been surprised how close they'd gotten the handwriting to her own. She'd talked about the kids she was teaching and how much she missed home. Later she found out her dads had sent her care package after care package— none of which she'd actually received because MSS might have been suspicious about their deadliest agent getting boxes of M&Ms and orange Fanta from the US.

Maybe a postcard would placate them now.

Dear Dads, On assignment in the wilds of Malibu. It's been two weeks and I'm all Pretty Woman'd up, except the clerks in Bev Hills were nice to me. Guess they learned. Recently had sex in a dressing room with a feral movie star. He won't kiss me and it's making me crazy. Send condoms because the dude is insatiable.

Yep, that would make them feel better. Not that they would buy it now. They knew about her work for the Agency. Not the true extent of it, but enough to worry about her every minute of the day.

Damon would deal with them. And when this was over with, she would go back to Santa Barbara for a nice long visit. Hell, she would invite Tucker over. He had some nicely faked paperwork to keep him safe when he went out of the house. Her dads would love him and it would do him good to spend some time outside The Garden.

She stopped, her hand on the coffee cup. Someone was watching her. It was an instinct, an icy finger going up her spine. Slowly, she glanced around looking for anything, anyone out of the ordinary. Nothing. The Pepperdine kids were talking basketball at the next table. Two women were discussing plans for someone's birthday and who the best caterers were. A lone man sat at a table in the shade, his baseball hat low on his head as he sipped his coffee and stared down at a newspaper.

Nothing out of the ordinary, but still she could feel eyes on her.

"Is this seat taken?"

She looked up and Ezra stared down at her, his eyes steady. If she told him she was waiting for a friend, he would know she couldn't talk right now. Should she send him away or was that feeling of being watched just more Josh Hunt induced paranoia? "Please join me."

Ezra slid into the seat next to her and she was sure they looked for all the world like a couple simply enjoying the gorgeous So Cal weather. "He's been damn good about keeping you out of the papers, but he slipped up."

He slid a magazine her way. It was a celebrity rag with full glossy pictures, the kind you could find at any grocery store checkout aisle. She glanced down at the photo. Josh was wearing what she liked to call his casual chic. Jeans, motorcycle boots, a button-down shirt he didn't tuck in. He was walking into a building. Yes, she recognized it. They'd been going to see his agent to talk about the shoot coming up next week. She'd sat with him listening to an outrageous amount of demands she'd been told were all perfectly standard. His trailer was to be kept at a certain temperature. He drank only bottled water and needed it available to him at all times. The bedroom of his trailer was to be stocked with one-thousand thread count sheets. Yadda, yadda.

Diva. He was a diva, or rather his agent was since Josh had mostly sighed and rolled his eyes. He'd had other concerns. He had demanded that the studio hire a former DEA agent to tutor him in the role. He'd demanded time at the gun range.

She was in the shot, too, walking a few feet behind him wearing a yellow sundress that cost more than her entire wardrobe at home. It was an Elie Saab straight off the runway, and she would wear it until she was eight-hundred years old. Josh appeared to be holding the door open for her, her body in profile.

Not too bad. The girls looked good. The Louboutin stilettos made her legs look way longer than they were.

The caption read *Josh Hunt's New Girl?*

She slid it back Ezra's way. "It was inevitable. I'm actually surprised it took a whole two weeks. They're always on him. Josh has drones fly by. Freaking drones. I took one out this morning. Pretty sure it got a couple of shots of me, but not with Josh. They'll reach the proper conclusions no matter what we do. Is my cover good?"

The tightening of his jaw let her know he was worried.

"Ezra?"

He sighed and sat back. "Your cover is solid, but I'm worried the Agency is preoccupied right now."

"What does that mean?"

"It means a couple of things have happened recently that's thrown normally solid teams into chaos."

"And naturally it's classified," she surmised.

"Naturally, but I'm going to tell you anyway because it concerns you on several fronts."

"Is Josh at risk?" She was surprised at how worried she was about the answer to that question. She was taking him into something perilous and he didn't even understand the danger he would be going into.

"I don't know," Ezra admitted. "Two things have happened, and while I believe they're coincidental, I can't be sure. Three weeks ago, the Agency received proof that John Bishop wasn't killed in the line of duty and is, in fact, alive and well."

Her stomach took a deep dive and despite the heat of the day, a shiver raced along her skin. The Ice Man was alive? There was only one reason she could think of that a man like Bishop would fake his death. How could that have happened? She'd believed in him. God, of all the people she'd met in her time in the Agency, Bishop had been the stalwart one, the one who would make the hard decisions, but they would always, always be in the best interest of his country. "He turned? Who's he working for?"

"That's what we're trying to assess."

"Where did they find him?" She never thought she'd go back to the Agency. After Ten had brought her home, she'd quit and vowed to never do the deep dive again, but if Bishop was in trouble or…if Bishop had turned and become the enemy…well, he'd been her mentor. She would have to save him or be the one to put him down. Maybe she was looking at this wrong. Maybe he was in trouble and he'd turned against his will. That could happen.

"Colorado," Ezra replied. "A tiny town in the mountains called Bliss."

Of all the places he could have told her Bishop had been hiding, small-town Colorado wasn't one of them. If he'd turned, he should have been in a big city. "Is there a high-value target in the town? Like a nuclear plant?"

Ezra snorted. "There's barely a grocery store. Although it does have an oddly high murder rate for such a tiny town. But all of those are easily explained by police reports. I don't see how Bishop could have used any of those incidents, though I'm fairly certain he was responsible for a few of those bodies. He had a very specific technique he liked to use."

John Bishop had been the one to teach her how to internally decapitate a person. Quiet. Easy. No blood. No muss. No fuss. "I think I know what you're talking about. Is he killing people?"

A long sigh issued forth. "From what I can tell any killing he's done has been in defense of others. At some point in time, the cartel he'd been investigating when he 'died' found out he was alive. I don't know how, but they went after him and the operative who's now working on them found out and told the Agency."

"Levi," she said, the word flat on her tongue. Levi, who probably would never have told her despite the fact that he knew her connections to Bishop. Complex, complicated connections.

"Yes, which is why I'm here early. He should be along in a few minutes and I would appreciate it if you don't mention to him that I let you and Tennessee know," he requested.

"Of course not." She still had some questions. "Do we have any intel on what his cover has been?"

"Bishop has been living in Bliss for five years under the name Henry Flanders. As far as I can tell his only contact from his previous life there was a man named Bill Hartman. Bishop served under him in the military. We're looking into him and his contacts as well to see if he's the one who drew Bishop in." Ezra looked down at his tablet, turning the pages of the report. "Bishop married a woman named Nell Finn. She's a part of the problem. She's an activist. Save the everythings. We're looking into her to see if she's got ties to left-winged terror groups."

Somehow she couldn't see Bishop going all communist or anarchist. He'd been a true believer, a real protector of his country.

"What has he been doing all these years?" She took the tablet out of his hands and stared down at the photos there. John Bishop. His face was the same but not. The eyes were the same, but they looked warm in the photo, his normally tense body relaxed as he smiled and wrapped his arms around a petite woman with brown hair and shining eyes. A couple. They were a real couple who leaned into each other.

John Bishop looked…happy.

Once you go into this, you'll be your sister, possibly for life. Get in. Do your job. Get as much intel as you can. If you ever see even the glimpse of an off-ramp, take it. Take it as fast as you can and don't look back. And Kay? I hope one day you can forgive me.

His last words to her before she'd gone into the belly of the beast.

"As far as we can tell, he's been in deep cover, a possible sleeper agent. He's lived and worked in Bliss, Colorado. He and his 'wife' sell products at traveling fairs. Things like handmade crafts and vegan bread or some shit. He takes his cover seriously. The dude's wearing Birkenstocks and according to our operative, he's living a vegan lifestyle."

She flipped through some of the other photos, her eyes clouding over with tears as she realized what had happened. She didn't try to hide these tears. They were good tears. She'd left out one scenario to explain Bishop faking his death. The best scenario. There was only one reason a man like Bishop ever left. He'd been cold, ruthless in his protection of his country. He'd finally found some warmth. "It's not cover. He fell in love with her. He found his off-ramp and he took it. Holy shit. John Bishop in love. That must be something to see."

The Ice Man had fallen. He'd melted for a woman and now he couldn't even eat a burger. If he could find a life outside, if Ten could find his Faith…what did that mean for her? Could she do it, too? She'd taken her off-ramp, but trusting someone enough to hand over her heart still seemed so far away.

If only he would kiss her…

"Kay, you can't know that," Ezra admonished, taking the tablet back. "His reasons are his own. You can't start prescribing some random romantic crap to them."

"What did Ten say when you told him?"

There was a moment of quiet. "That if John Bishop walked away he did it because he found something he loved even more than his country."

"Has anyone talked to him? Can I call him?" She wanted to suddenly. It had been a long time and she'd missed him. She wanted to hear his story, find out what the hell had happened to put that smile on a face that had so rarely smiled before. She wanted his advice. No one knew the job like Bishop did. He'd sent her in. Maybe he could help her truly find her way out.

"Absolutely not." Ezra stared at her. "You're involved in your own op and you're nothing more than a contractor now. I could get in trouble for telling you any of this. I'm sorry. I mentioned it because I know you worked for him. I thought you should know he could be arrested, and I didn't want you to hear it through back channels. I don't know what's going to happen with him. Right now the Agency is deciding how to handle the situation."

Arrested wasn't the term. Renditioned. Dropped into prison with no thoughts to his human rights. Those were the kinds of things that happened to an agent who did what Bishop had. Would his wife mourn him? Would he be happy he'd had those five years with her?

What could she do to ensure that he had more? Fuck it all. She liked a damn happily ever after.

"And what's the second issue?" Kayla began because she was fairly certain this was one of those lines of questioning Ezra would shut down and quick. She would have to ponder it alone. Or perhaps talk to Big Tag. Big Tag had worked with Bishop, too. She'd heard Bishop was one of the only men in the world Big Tag shut the sarcasm down for.

Maybe the team would take a little ski vacay in Colorado.

Ezra tensed, his shoulders going straight. Without turning, he clicked off the tablet. "Nice of you to join us, Levi."

She glanced behind Ezra and sure enough Levi Green was walking up. He was dressed in So Cal chic—skinny jeans and a V-necked T-shirt, a pork pie hat on his head and loafers on his feet. Unlike Ezra's masculine slacks and plain black T and sneakers without a single designer name on anything. It seemed to her like one was playing a role and the other merely wanted to blend into the background, his clothes another function of his daily life and nothing more. She would bet Ezra had a whole closet of basic, while there would be some flamingo in Green's. He could stand out like a preening peacock when he wanted to.

"Well, since I'm here on time, I have to suspect you and Ms. Summers wanted some time to yourselves." Green smiled, but the words came out like an accusation.

She merely sat back and let her face find the sun. "I arrived a little early. It's too gorgeous a day to waste it inside. It's the first time I've been alone in weeks. And Ezra's already yelled at me for the tabloid fuck up. You want to yell, too?"

Anything to make him not wonder about what they truly had been discussing. The last thing she wanted was to get Ezra in the doghouse when he was trying to help her out.

"Absolutely not." Levi winked her way. "You looked stunning in that dress. I take it Hunt hooked you up? Because the Agency didn't pay for that."

"We did the *Pretty Woman* thing up and down Rodeo." She had a closet full of designer wear that per her contract was all hers. Dresses and shoes and lingerie and jewelry. All of it bought by Josh and heading home with her when their contract was voided.

"So he dressed you like a pretty doll?" Levi asked. "Or did he toss you to a glam squad?"

"A what?" Ezra proved he wasn't up on all the hip lingo.

"Oddly enough, no," she replied, ignoring Ezra. "I kind of thought he would drop me off or hand me over to a stylist, but he went with me the whole day. Not that he was up in my business or anything. He let me buy what I liked, but he was sweet about it. He wanted to see it and give me his opinion."

And he'd fucked her in the dressing room about halfway through the day. He'd fucked her hard, his hunger so evident she hadn't even had a moment's qualm about accepting him.

But apparently she wasn't supposed to talk about that. If her CIA handlers were anything like Shane they would get all prissy and prudish. Maybe it was time to move on. "You two called me here to ask about my new clothes? Because I can talk about that all day. I bought the most gorgeous Prada sheath."

Levi sat forward, his elbows on the little table. "Did anything odd happen yesterday? Did he get any phone calls or talk to anyone you noticed?"

"He's always on his phone." Though lately he'd started turning it off when they were together physically. He claimed he wouldn't let anyone interrupt their play time.

It was starting to feel like something more than play. He'd stopped knocking on her door. He slid into bed beside her each day, the early morning light barely kissing the room as he put his hands on her and brought her to life.

"So there was nothing that seemed off to you?" Ezra stared at her like he was waiting for something.

"He disappeared for about twenty minutes, but Declan had an eye on him. He walked out of the shop, took a phone call, got into it with a photog, and then came back in."

And that was when he'd come into her dressing room, filled with demands, a rough edge to his voice and that "won't take no for an answer" gleam in his eyes. The paparazzi must have been unpleasant, to say the least. The police, however, had been quite pleasant.

Levi's eyes narrowed as though he was sizing her up. "According to records, at two thirty-three p.m. yesterday your boy got a call from a phone number that had recently been activated and had never been used."

"So someone called him from a burner," she prompted.

"That number is now out of service," Levi continued.

The man was good at stating the obvious. "Hence me calling it a burner."

Levi frowned her way as if she was taking all his fun away. "We can't trace who bought the phone. It was paid for with cash and there were no cameras close, but we do know the date and time of the call. Every year on this date at close to two thirty, Joshua Hunt receives a phone call. A day later, Hunt transfers funds from his own account to an offshore one, and that's where we lose track. This happens four times a year. Like clockwork."

What was Josh hiding? He hadn't mentioned what the phone call had been about and now that she thought about it, she should have been surprised that he'd gotten violent with a photographer. Still, she'd gotten to know the man. "You honestly believe that Josh is…doing what? Funding a cartel? I've lived with the man for weeks. I can promise you he's not doing drugs himself, so he's not buying. He's the single healthiest man I've ever met. He's certainly not selling. Shane and Dec vet absolutely everyone who stops by. They're all Hollywood types or his housekeeper or people from the club, and Riley has vetted those."

"Then where is all that money going?" Levi asked. "We're talking millions over the last few years. I know you like the guy, but you can't be naïve about this. He's spent time with the Commander. He's met the Commander several times over the years and he's planning on staying at his house while he's in Mexico."

"Wouldn't that be a better time to make a transaction? Look, as far as I can tell, Josh honestly believes this guy is a businessman and a philanthropist," she replied. "He's donated generously to Josh's children's charity. That's kind of the way things work out here. You pay and Josh entertains. I don't think it's more than that. I think Josh would be horrified if he found out who his 'friend' really is."

Levi slid Ezra a look. It was subtle but she caught it. Ezra's lips flattened out and she knew she was in trouble.

They thought she was getting too close. This was something they'd obviously talked about, worried about. If she pushed it too hard, they might even have backup plans. That was how these men worked.

She sat back, letting her expression go bland. "I'm playing devil's advocate, guys. We have to look at this from every angle, and one of those angles is that Josh is innocent in all of this."

"I've got twenty million dollars wired to accounts in the Caymans and Switzerland that tell me otherwise." Levi sat back.

"And we have reason to believe that his next drop is coming up some time this week. We'd like to be there to see who picks it up," Ezra explained.

"I'm scheduled to meet with Mr. Blade next," Levi said. "I'll take it from there. We need Hunt's schedule for the next few days and we would like to put listening devices in the house and his car."

She wanted to argue. God, she wanted to quit and tell them to leave her Josh alone. This was a man who had so little privacy and they were invading the last of it. All that would do is get her ass canned from both jobs and they would still get their way. And Josh wouldn't have anyone on his side when the time came.

Was she really thinking about sides? Because she was supposed to be firmly planted on one and she was wavering. Two weeks of gauzy Malibu mornings and late nights in his playroom had her rethinking her whole damn life.

"Of course." She had a job to do and if she was right, Josh likely would never know the Agency had been listening to him, watching his every move. If she was wrong, then Josh Hunt was in way worse trouble than losing his precious privacy.

"Excellent." Levi's deep voice held a wealth of satisfaction. "I'm glad you agree since it's being done as we speak."

"What?"

Ezra sighed. "We've got eyes on Hunt. Shane's his shadow today. Declan stayed behind so we have access to the house. Hunt was driven into LA, and that means we also have access to his vehicles. I thought it would be better to have a team do it than you."

"He thought it would be easier," Levi corrected. "The truth is we're both concerned about your level of…friendliness with the target."

"You knew I was going to sleep with him. I believe that was exactly why you picked me." Although who the hell else were they going to get? If they wanted a McKay-Taggart operative, there was a dearth of single females. Since Des died, she was the only female agent on the London team, and the Dallas team had a bunch of married women. She doubted Theo Taggart would have allowed his wife to sacrifice her body for her country.

Not that it was a sacrifice.

"I'm not stupid, Kay. I see the way you look at the guy. I get it. If I swung that way, I'd probably be all over his bad boy hot ass, too," Levi admitted.

A brow climbed over Ezra's eyes. "I wouldn't put it like that, but the man obviously is attractive and has some charm. The bodyguards might have mentioned something about you getting hurt."

Damn the boys. "It was nothing. Josh has some issues with

167

PTSD. Not sure what the incident was about, but he's got some triggers. I can handle them. I was about to handle them. Unfortunately, Dec walked in while we were having a little altercation."

"Shane mentioned something about you talking about how good Hunt is in bed," Ezra mentioned.

Tattletale. "I'm a talker, Ezra. You know that. I talk about everything. It doesn't mean I'm ready to throw my career to the wind over a couple of nice orgasms. They were spectacular. He does this thing with his tongue."

Ezra blanched. "Stop. I don't need to hear that."

Levi grinned lasciviously. "I don't know. Sounds like an interesting story. What exactly does he do with his tongue?"

"No. We're not going there." Ezra leaned forward. "All we're saying is try to keep some professional distance. I know how hard this is. I've worked some intimate operations and it's tough on a person who has any kind of soul. If you find yourself getting in trouble, call me and I'll pull you out."

Levi's eyes narrowed. "Not your call, man. This is my op."

"And she's *my* operative, so we'll have to agree to disagree. I promised I would watch out for her. I promised Knight and I promised Big Tag. I assure you, I will pull her if I think she's in trouble," Ezra vowed.

That was a whole lot of testosterone flying around. She needed some popcorn to go with all the boy drama. If she was lucky, they might throw down right here in front of the Starbucks.

Her money was on Ezra in a physical fight, though she was certain Levi would be sneaky.

Levi chuckled, a humorless sound. "Wow. I thought the rumors about you were all jealousy and gossip. Turns out they're true. You are on thin ice, my man. The Agency likes its employees to be loyal to the Agency. Not some security firm whose leader couldn't hack it. There's a reason you're playing second team. One more bad move and you know what's going to happen."

"I don't need advice from you on what a bad move would do to me." The words came out of Ezra's mouth, low and dangerous. "I've been doing this job a lot longer than you."

Levi's eyes rolled. "Yeah, a whole four years."

"In the field," Ezra shot back. "I'm a field agent. You're a glorified paper pusher. You've never had to do the job she's doing. You sit back in your cushy office and make decisions that affect the rest of her life and you've never even done the job."

"Just because I work with my brains and not my hands doesn't mean there's not blood on them, brother. Remember that." Levi stretched as he stood up, his big body moving with ease. "I'm only trying to watch out for you, buddy. You know the brass can get an itchy trigger finger when it comes to burning an agent. Your friend knows all about that."

Ezra was completely still, not a muscle moving except his jaw as he spoke. He was a tightly coiled cobra and Kayla wondered if he was about to strike. "Funny, I think Ten Smith is pretty happy now."

Levi was as loose as Ezra was tight, as though he deeply enjoyed the tension. "Don't let your name get too close to Smith's right now. With everything going on, you don't want to be associated with Smith's crew. You'll be painted with the same brush and it won't go well for you. I hope Big Tag is as loyal to you as you're being to him because I'm worried you're going to need a job one of these days."

It was time to pop the testosterone balloon. Kayla leaned forward, speaking to Levi in low tones. "No one is going to need to pull me out so stop threatening him."

"Oh, sweetheart this is about far more than you." Levi glared at her. "Has he told you?"

"Told me what?" She wasn't about to give the dude up. Ezra was the only one she could trust on that side of the op.

Levi looked between them like he couldn't quite trust either of them. "Were you aware that we believe someone is interested in continuing Hope McDonald's work?"

It didn't surprise her at all. The fact that it had taken this long for the Agency to identify someone was the surprising part. "Interested? I would assume that's pretty much every military in the world. They would never admit it, but the idea of creating super soldiers with no loyalties except to the teams they work with would be intriguing."

"See, now you are being naïve," Levi replied. "And you're not thinking outside a narrow box. Her work is about more than soldiers.

The time dilation portion of her work alone could be worth billions. Think about how it could be used. We would no longer need prisons. A prisoner could serve years in the blink of an eye. Minutes would pass in the real world, but with the right drugs and computer simulation, fifteen years complete with all the memories of confinement would live with the prisoner forever. He would come out the same age he went in, but with the wisdom of all those years."

"It sounds like torture to me." She didn't like the almost admiration in Levi's voice.

"Then you're not listening closely enough," Levi complained. "What about the twenty-five-year-old who gets a disease we can't cure? He can live a life with that technology. He can have a whole life, memories that no disease can take from him. This technology can give us the one thing in the world there's never enough of. Time. A doctor working on a cure for cancer can have more time to research, to push the boundaries of his mind. Think about what we could do."

"We could torture our enemies without laying a hand on them," she replied. Did he honestly think this wasn't something that kept her up at night? She lived with the men McDonald's drugs and therapies had damaged. She knew how ruined they were. Not that he knew that little fact of life, and she didn't want him to. "We could throw out the justice system and put a potential criminal under the influence to find out anything we wanted."

"And that's wrong?" Levi asked with a sigh.

"It's a slippery slope."

Levi huffed, a sound that let her know he thought she was foolish. "Almost all technology is and yet I would bet you wouldn't get rid of the Internet or your car."

"Why are you telling me this? It has to be classified." She would completely understand if Ezra had told her, and she was fairly certain this was the second piece of intel he'd meant to give her, but Levi tended to toe the company line. If a piece of information was classified, even if it could help one of his field agents, Levi Green would keep that shit tight. Why was he opening up now?

"Because if those underground fuckers get to this tech first it could hurt our country," Levi said, fire in his voice.

She was well aware that Ezra was now the spectator, his eyes shifting between the two of them. "Again, not understanding why you're telling me."

"Tell me you don't know where those boys are." He stared at her like he could see through to her soul. "Ezra was allowed to talk to a few of them a couple of months ago. He claims he's not sure where he was taken, but I have my ideas."

Yes, this was the second thing Ezra had wanted to tell her. The Agency was getting angsty about the Lost Boys. She'd known the CIA and several other intelligence groups—not to mention countless big pharmas—wanted a crack at testing her boys, but up until now they'd been fairly quiet about it. She'd known at some point that would change. Apparently they'd reached the tipping point.

"Boys? Are you talking about the men McDonald experimented on?" She gave him her best dumb girl look. "I've met a couple. Why would I know where they are? I hope they're back with their families. That's a partial lie. I do know where Theo Taggart is, but then so do you."

Levi sighed and a look of disappointment crossed his face. "Yes, I thought you would say that. I know why Taggart wants to protect those men, but eventually someone will come for them. I think he would want it to be his own country. Those men hold the key to breaking open everything McDonald was working for."

"Slavery? Loss of home and family?" Ezra finally spoke.

"It doesn't have to be that way." Levi pushed his chair back. "But it might be if it falls into the wrong hands, and whether Taggart likes it or not, he can't hide those boys forever. Someone will find them, and then the blood that spills will be on everyone who hid them from the Agency. It's time to pick a side. War's coming and it won't be pretty. I hope you two don't choose poorly. I'm going to meet with Riley. Kayla, think about what I said. I know you have influence. Ezra, I have to go. Can I trust you to bring her up to speed on how we want her to handle Hunt, or are you going to hold her hand and commiserate on how rotten a boss I am?"

Ezra didn't look up at him. "I think I can handle it."

Levi sighed and sent her a sad smile. "I'm sorry, Kay. I know I'm being a dick, but this is important. And someday, you'll tell me about that tongue thing. This dude's a total prude. See you soon and take care of yourself."

He walked off in the direction of the parking lot.

"Being a dick is that guy's natural state," Ezra said under his breath.

So much of this crazy op fell into place. "You're here because you're worried Levi is going to use this op to get me to talk. I won't. You know how I feel about those boys."

She loved Tucker and Owen. Cared about all of them. They'd started out as strays who needed shelter, but they were part of the team now. And she didn't let her team down.

"Watch out for him. Don't underestimate Levi Green. He wants to move up and he knows if he can bring in one of McDonald's victims, it will help. The Agency wants that tech and they'll do a lot to get it. The only thing that's saved Theo Taggart is his last name."

"Big Tag would burn it all down if they took his brother, and he wouldn't believe that there was an accident or that Theo walked away," she warned.

"They know it. Believe me, I've explained all of that. Theo Taggart is safe, but the rest of them aren't. Owen Shaw is safe because he's known to the British government. We can't take a known British citizen in for experimentation without causing an international incident, and MI6 can't because they won't piss off Knight. But that leaves a bunch of boys with no protection beyond what McKay-Taggart gives them. At some point, Knight has to think of his own team. It won't be merely the Agency or MI6 or even MSS who comes after them. When rogue elements get involved, all bets are off, and The Garden won't be as safe as you think it is."

The Garden was filling up with happy couples. Damon and Penny, Nick and Hayley, Brody and Steph. There were two kids living there now. Oliver and Nate. She could imagine Nick and Hayley wouldn't be far behind in the procreation game.

Would those kids be in the line of fire? Could she live with herself if one of those babies got hurt?

"Hey—" Ezra leaned over, his expression softening. "I'm not going to let it get there. I know I'm barely hanging on to this job and that my connection with Taggart and Ten Smith doesn't help, but I still have some influence. I have people on the inside who I believe when they tell me they'll give me a heads-up. I promise I'll do everything I can."

"Does Damon know? Big Tag?"

"Ten Smith knows. I can't get too close to Dallas right now," he explained.

But if Ten knew then the rest did, and if Big Tag thought someone was coming after his family, well, she hoped the Agency or whoever it was went quickly and without too much pain. "I would hate to be here if I was needed in London."

Ezra shook his head. "I think the fact that you're here and McKay-Taggart is helping out is the bridge we need. Right now everyone's playing nice and I want to keep it that way. I'm working on pinning down the rogue group that's taken up McDonald's cause. I'll find them and take them out, and then we're all back to players with too much to lose. That's the way I like it."

The Agency would be predictable, as would the other intelligence groups. It was the rogue nations, the anarchist groups, the criminals who wouldn't care that they could destabilize the fragile peace they lived in that she feared.

So she would do her job. The wavering had to stop. Her London family was at stake, too. She had to do her job so Ezra could do his and keep Levi Green in line.

"What do you need from me?" She shoved aside all those dumbass girlie feelings about Josh. She couldn't be his girl. It was time to be Knight and Taggart's operative again.

Ezra sat back and went over the plan.

* * * *

"So how's it going with Kayla?" Jared asked, looking out over the dungeon floor. "It's been two weeks and you seem to smile more. It kind of scares me. Are you doing that because it's good between the two of you or because you're thinking up ways to murder me for talking you into this crazy plan?"

Josh chuckled at the thought of finding somewhere to bury Jared. It would have to be a decent-sized hole because the man was jacked. He was taking his workout routine to the limit. Josh hoped that was

173

all about the upcoming movie they were set to film and not about the new woman in their lives. More than once, he'd found Jared working out on his balcony while talking to Kay as she sat on theirs. Suspicions. He hated them. "It's good, man. We're getting along okay."

Okay might be putting it mildly, but he wasn't one to overshare.

The truth was it was going so well, he kept waiting for the rug to get pulled out from under him, and that was where all those nasty suspicions came in. He glanced over at the hallway that led from the dressing rooms to the dungeon floor. She would walk out here any minute wearing her corset and tiny thong, her feet in ridiculous heels that he'd had wound around his neck far too often in the last two weeks. He fucked her in the morning, going straight from his room to hers the minute he woke up. If he'd slept too long, he had to go find her, always sitting on the balcony, watching the ocean as high tide brought the sea to their doorstep. He would drag her back to her room like a caveman. He fucked her every night, taking her hand after dinner or when they came in from whatever event they'd attended and leading her up to either the playroom or her room, or when he couldn't stand another minute, he'd picked her up in the front hall, pressed her against the wall, and shoved his dick inside.

He was drunk on sex and her submission and her weirdness. Yeah, she was weird as fuck, and damn but that did something for him.

"I like her. I think she's awesome. The way she took out that drone with a baseball was amazing," Jared said with a chuckle over the low thud of industrial music.

"Yeah, that made the news. Fuckers managed to get just enough footage to see her face," he admitted. The footage had come out right before they'd left for the club. One of the big tabloids had posted it on their website. The photographer was suing, yadda yadda. He didn't give a shit, but it was going to put her squarely in the spotlight and he didn't like that. "And they got your face, too. Did I thank you for providing the baseball?"

Jared grinned, either not hearing the edge to his tone or completely ignoring it. With him, it could be either. "You're welcome. I thought about doing it myself, but I kind of wanted to see what she could do. Your girl is solid, man. That was a fastball for the ages."

And one that put Kayla squarely on the press's radar. For two weeks, she'd managed to stay in the background, walking into restaurants with Shane or Dec, who would deliver her to a private room. There were plenty of photos of him meeting superproducer Sullivan Roarke at Nobu, but not a single one of her. He'd considered it a real accomplishment. "You know they caught you tossing that to her from across the balcony. How often do you meet her out there in the mornings?"

Jared's brows rose. "I work out in the mornings, Josh. You know that. You used to come over and work out with me until you started needing a ton of beauty sleep. I talk to her because it would be rude not to. She's out on your balcony. I'm on mine. Am I supposed to ignore her?"

He hated this feeling. Yeah, this was the shoe that would eventually drop, his gut-churning possessiveness. It was why he tried hard not to get this way about people. Still, he didn't seem to have control of his mouth tonight. "Is that really the reason you spend so much time with her? You're trying to be polite?"

"I like her. She's crazy. She talks to the dolphins and she's got this seal she's decided is her friend," Jared said with a long sigh. "How am I supposed to ignore that? I find her highly entertaining and she's given me some good tips. Do you know what we talk about?"

He could only guess. Jared would be "talking" with his shirt off. He never wore a fucking shirt when he worked out. "Your abs?"

"Sarah. We talk about Sarah and the fact that she's never going to forgive me," Jared explained.

"That doesn't sound like Kay," he murmured, feeling like shit. This was what his inner caveman did. He fought when he didn't have to. He was constantly looking for the battle, for the next person who would try to take his stuff and leave him with nothing.

Inner caveman? Fuck. That was his inner street kid.

"Oh, Kay thinks I can get her back, but she's optimistic about a lot of things," Jared replied, seeming to settle, as though he knew the danger had passed. "She thinks I should throw it all away for love."

"What?"

"She thinks I should walk away from the Hollywood thing and move to Dallas and spend all my time trying to win back a woman I haven't even slept with," Jared admitted. "It's funny but talking to Kay made me realize I'm never going to get that woman. She saw me at my worst, and that's all she'll ever see. She'll see my best friend trying to kill her and me begging and pleading. She's not going to see me as a man again."

"That is absolutely not what Kayla would have told you." Because Jared was right. She was incredibly optimistic. She was a weird combination of Disney princess and superhot assassin chick. There was a small part of him that wanted to see what she would do and say if he walked her down a red carpet full of reporters. Would she simply smile and wave and act the part? And how would she answer the age-old question every woman got on that carpet?

Who are you wearing tonight, Ms. Summers? Ryan Seacrest would ask, shoving a microphone in her face.

Well, Ryan, tonight I'm wearing something I got in Beverly Hills, a shit ton of diamonds, two SIG Sauers, a couple of blades, and a butt plug my Master gave me for being a brat. Thanks for asking.

Yeah, he wasn't sure Hollywood was ready for his girl yet.

Jared waved him off. "Nah, she says shit about how I can bring her around. But the last time I managed to get Sarah to talk to me she told me the only shot I had with her was if I happened to be the last man on earth, and then and only then would she consider seeing me again, and only because she was a very social person and would be lonely. So, I think that sums it up. It's time for me to move on. Time to forget about her. Hey, there are lots of fish in the sea."

A sub walked up, tray in her hand. He couldn't remember her name, only knew she was a fairly recent addition to the club. There was a collar around her throat, but no charm or mark of possession that told him who she belonged to. So she was working. "Can I get you anything, Sirs? Water or sodas? Or perhaps you would like a scene partner for the evening? I am available."

He bet she was. "I'm taken for the evening, but thank you for the offer. This guy here has nothing to do. What do you say, Jared?"

Jared's eyes widened in what could only be described as pure horror as he took in the petite blonde with her perfect tits and an ass to

176

die for. Yeah, he was totally ready to go girl fishing. He was looking at the sub like she was a snake about to bite.

"Christine, I think Master Jared would prefer to be alone for a bit," a deep voice said.

He turned and a large man stood to the side, his leathers clinging to muscled hips. He had on a leather vest and a frown that would have sent any sub scampering off.

"Yes, Master Riley." And Christine did exactly that. She practically ran back to the break room, her heels *click clacking* across the floor.

Master Riley. The new Dom in Residence. He was basically The Reef's hired gun. He was the one who would vet new members, open and close the club, oversee the subs who worked here, and generally keep everyone in line. He'd been hired by the board. Normally Josh would have had a vote, but he'd been on set during a particularly grueling shoot and had allowed Jared to vote for him.

Josh didn't like the new guy. Not that Riley had done anything, but there was something about him. Riley watched him in a way he didn't the others. Maybe that was simply the price of fame and shit, but he wasn't sure.

And given what he was going to have to do tonight, the last thing he wanted was someone watching him with suspicious eyes.

He had to get away from his bodyguards, and that included Kayla. He had to do it all so he could pay off his blackmailer. One million dollars four times a year. Winter. Spring. Summer. Fall. Just like clockwork, he paid for the privilege of keeping his past firmly in the past.

"Did I misread the situation?" Riley asked, looking between the two of them. "I can call her back. I assure you she'll overlook a little embarrassment to bottom for either one of you, though I worry about what your sub might do if you try to take on another one, Master Josh."

"Kayla knows the rules of the club. She's not going to misbehave, and she's certainly not going to question me if I decide to bring in a secondary play partner." He was well aware he'd gone into arrogant-asshole mode, but he couldn't help it. He didn't want to become the laughingstock of the club. He wasn't about to become *that* Dom, the one who couldn't control his submissive.

Sometimes he was absolutely certain this was the *only* place he was in control.

Still, he wasn't about to tell the man that the thought of taking on a second submissive—even if only for a scene—hadn't occurred to him once. She was more than enough woman for him to handle.

And it would hurt her, something he couldn't do.

"Of course, you know her far better than I do," Riley said, inclining his head politely.

But there it was. It wasn't the same tell every time, but it felt like Riley Blade knew something he didn't. Something important. It was probably paranoia. He got that way when the payment was due. He let it go, but he couldn't help but think that the Dom in Residence wasn't quite what he said he was. "I do. Is our scene set up? I want to have plenty of time before the party."

It was the monthly birthday party for the members. Silly thing, but he tried not to miss it. These people were his family and friends. His only family and friends. It was also the perfect time to sneak away. Everyone changed into street clothes for cake and ice cream, wine and beer. He could slip out the back, hop on Jared's Ducati, and make it to the trail he'd been directed to. He would have to haul ass to find the statue of the Virgin Mary, leave the package there, and get back before the bodyguards knew what was happening.

And hopefully he didn't step into a nest of rattlesnakes or get torn apart by a mountain lion.

It wasn't even like he had a million in cash. He was delivering a small box that contained an electronic key. The key would allow his asshole blackmailer to access the account he'd dumped the million in. It changed every time and at no time in the past five years since the blackmail had begun had the jerk allowed him to simply transfer the funds himself. Nope, the fucker liked to make things rough on him. Always somewhere dark. Always alone. Always dangerous.

Like a reminder that no matter how far he'd come, there was someplace dirty and rotten for him to fall back to.

No matter how often he fucked his sub, no matter how good she felt and how well he seemed to sleep after she'd given him everything she had, she was still bought and paid for. She wouldn't writhe under him, holding him close, if he didn't keep the payments up.

When he thought about it like that, his whole life was one big blackmail scam.

"Everything has been prepared for you," Riley said with another nod. "The red room is closed until you and your lovely sub are ready for play. I was surprised. You typically like to play in the larger dungeon."

The red room was all about intimacy. It was the smallest of the play rooms, and even if he'd wanted a crowd, he wouldn't have been able to fit more than two or three extra people in.

He wanted her to himself. Even when they were here. It was odd and wrong. She was a woman who enjoyed being watched. He'd never had a single problem showing his submissives off. He would parade them around, allowing the rest of the club to enjoy their naked beauty.

He didn't like the way they looked at Kayla. She was a bright light and everyone in that dungeon could see it. When she walked in, every head turned, and not simply because she was lovely. They were all attracted to her because she put them at ease with her smile, her bright eyes, her infectious laugh. If she were an actress, she would be the star of every film, the strong center around which the story turned, the lead female every male wanted and every female wanted to be.

"Tonight we're playing in the red room. Do you have a problem with that, Master Riley?"

The Dom held his hands up in obvious defeat, or perhaps as a way to say he chose not to play at all. "No problem. I'm sorry if I gave offense. I'll go and check twice, make sure everything is in working order."

He turned and walked away.

"Dude, what do you have against that guy?" Jared asked.

"Nothing."

"That is not what it looked like." Jared watched the man stride toward the back of the club. "I don't think I've ever seen you so...shit, it's tonight, isn't it? When were you going to tell me?"

He felt every muscle in his body tense. "I wasn't. I was going to lift your keys from your locker, take your bike, and hope you didn't notice it was gone."

"My locker is kept locked. You don't know the combo."

"It's Sarah's birthday. I'm not stupid."

Jared sighed. "I'm going to change that."

He wouldn't but Josh wasn't about to point that out now. Jared would be pissed enough as it was. "I didn't want to bring you into it."

"Except for stealing my bike. You could have gone out there and gotten yourself killed and I wouldn't have known anything was wrong until I went out looking for my bike," Jared replied, bitterness in his tone. "Does Kayla know?"

He didn't want anyone to know, wished Jared didn't know as much as he did. "No."

"How is she supposed to guard you if she doesn't know what's going on? I thought the whole point of hiring all these people is to keep you safe. She can't keep you safe if she's not with you."

That was where Jared simply didn't understand. "I hired them to keep me safe from stalkers, not to follow me around, figure out my secrets, and use them against me."

"You think she would do that?"

He didn't *want* to think it. Not for a minute. He wanted her to be exactly what she looked like—loyal, sweet, kind, moral. "I can't take the chance."

Besides, she was basically a mercenary. There wasn't anything wrong with it. It simply meant she would watch out for herself first, and wasn't that what everyone did? He had one friend he trusted—to a point. Jared knew he was being blackmailed but didn't know why. Jared thought it was about some kind of a sex tape. He'd tried to convince Josh that everyone made a sex tape at some point in time.

Those people had made them to have fun or to spark controversy that might help their careers. They hadn't done it to eat. They hadn't done it because they didn't know how to do anything else.

What they'd done was playful and fun, and the trouble those celebs would get into if their tapes got out was nothing more than a few days of ridicule. What he would get out of it if *he* didn't pay up was something altogether different, something sick and insidious, something he would never be able to outrun.

He would pay up again and again. Anything to keep the world from knowing his secret.

Jared leaned in. "Give me the package and let me make the drop."

It wasn't that he didn't like the guy. It was that sometimes trouble followed him. Like always. And then there was the fact that Jared was easily distractible. One shiny thing and he would forget where he was stashing the very important blackmail payment. But he wasn't going to hurt Jared. "I can't. It has to be me and me alone or the deal is blown."

"You need to bring the bodyguards into this," Jared said, his voice tight. "They're trained for this kind of work. They can protect you."

"I don't need to be protected," he shot back. "Do you honestly think she wants to kill me? And have all that money dry up?"

Jared stopped and Josh realized he'd made a horrible mistake. "She?"

"Or he." Why had he fucking said that? He was careful. Always careful.

Jared pointed his way. "But you said she. You know who this is."

"No," he replied. "But I did catch a glimpse of her once. Just a second, and I only saw her back. She had long dark hair. She picked up the package and she was gone before I could follow her. She's not alone, though. She's got muscle behind her and they're very attentive. That same night I got the shit kicked out of me because they knew I had stayed behind to watch. He came out of nowhere. I was at a gas station and he pulled me into the shadows and beat me like I've never been beaten before. I thought for sure I was a dead man."

And that was saying something. His life had been about beatings at one point before he'd broken.

"When the hell did that happen?"

"Five years ago. It was the second time I paid." The memory was crisp in his head, the way a breeze had come off the ocean, the feel of his body being not his own. Again. The smell of blood and fear and failure.

He wasn't going there again. And he wasn't exposing Kayla to that side of his life. Or Jared, for that matter. They were shiny and happy and they would stay that way if he had anything at all to do with it.

"All right." It was obvious from the slump of Jared's shoulders that he wasn't happy about giving in. "But be careful. I worry about you, man."

It was good to have someone who worried and someone who watched his back. He wished he could trust that it would last. "You know you can do something for me."

Jared's eyes lit up. "What's that?"

"Find out everything you can on Riley Blade. Something about him makes me nervous." Or maybe he should get Declan and Shane on that.

"There's no need to. If you tell the others you want him gone, they'll find someone else," Jared assured him. "You're important to this club. Hell, you're the reason we have a place of our own at all."

"You paid for part of it," he pointed out.

"Only because you called me. I didn't know we were in trouble. I was shooting in Vancouver. If it hadn't been for you buying this property, we would likely have broken up and found other clubs. If you don't like Riley, he's gone."

"I'm probably being paranoid." He didn't want to cost a guy his job if there was nothing there. "The other guys seem to like the hell out of him."

"I'll keep my eyes open," Jared replied.

Maybe it would help distract Jared while Josh did what he had to do.

He looked over to the hallway and Kayla walked in, arm in arm with another sub. She was talking and laughing and generally making all the people around her smile. Infectious. She was utterly infectious, and he was doing the right thing.

Yes, Kayla was smart and deadly, but the truth was she needed someone to care about her, to protect her, to want her safety and satisfaction more than his own.

He couldn't take his eyes off her as she turned and found him. She was dressed for play, but he was caught on her eyes. Shit. He was caught period.

He was falling for a woman for the first time in his life and he was going to make it work.

And that meant keeping her as far from his past as possible.

Chapter Ten

Two hours and one fairly hardcore scene that had her ass aching later, Kayla stared at the computer in front of her, the email she was writing open and half finished. She felt a little half finished. Oh, the scene had gone all right. There had been bondage and spanking and pinching and rubbing, finished off with a giant Hollywood cock giving her an orgasm, but it had been different. Josh hadn't been with her. Not fully. Something was distracting her Master and she had no idea what it was because Levi wasn't returning her calls and she hadn't had a chance to talk to Riley. She'd meant to, but she'd found Josh's eyes on her every time she tried to get away for a few moments.

He'd kissed the top of her forehead—way too far away from her damn lonely mouth—and told her she had thirty minutes to get ready for the party and maybe she should spend that on her new project.

He was on the edge, and it bugged the crap out of her that she had no clue what was going on in that gorgeous head of his.

It was making her cranky when she needed to be penitent. After everything she'd seen with Josh and Jared and the others, she'd wondered if some apologies should be made. She'd talked to Josh about it and he'd decided she needed some email therapy.

Dear JR Ward,
Please forgive me for my last email. You should write as quickly

or slowly as your muse leads you, and you probably know your characters better than I do. So forget that small threat about Butch and V. I didn't really mean it. You know who best they should be mated with, not me. No one's coming for you in the middle of the night and while I do know your address, I promise to respect boundaries.

That was good, right? Nothing creepy about that.

"Writing some emails?" Barry asked as he entered the lounge.

Most everyone had changed into street clothes in anticipation of the party. Everyone except Subby Sue, who claimed street clothes gave her the hives. The closest anyone could get her to wear was leather short shorts and a bikini top. Her Dom had to force shoes on her feet when they went "formal," as they called it.

Funny, Josh hadn't come back out yet. He'd set her up, given her instructions that she was to write apology letters to at least three of the authors on her list, and went to take a shower.

"I like to call it my grand apology tour," she replied with a smile. "Apparently I've been hard on some people."

Barry sat down beside her. "Hard on them? Sometimes tough love is the best kind."

"I might have sent many emails with suggestions on how some of my favorite authors could…change things."

"Things?"

How to explain? "Like plot things that maybe didn't feel right to me. You know—constructive criticism. I also might have given them examples of things that could help to boost their efforts and productivity."

Barry took a sip of the coffee he was drinking. "Do I want to know what these examples are?"

"Just simple motivational stuff." Like *hey, I could show up on your doorstep and help out. No problem. I know all about floggers and pain as motivation.*

When she thought about it, she should have been more positive. More cheerleader like. *Go author, go!* That would probably be better. Looking back, she could maybe see how someone could construe her innocent comments as vaguely threatening.

If she was super sweet in her apology email, maybe Kristen Ashley would rescind that whole restraining-order thing.

"You must really like this lady's books," he said. "Have you thought that maybe you get too involved?"

"Oh, all the time, but honestly, when I was a double agent for the CIA and they had me posted in China, I was bored out of my mind. Turns out the Chinese government isn't hot on erotic romance and the books that do get through there are mostly political treatises on how the government should serve the people and vice versa. Yeah, total fiction but boring, too. No sex. No romance. When I got back, I might have binged like crazy. After you read fourteen books in someone's world, you kind of find yourself forgetting it's not real. You start talking like the characters, talking to the characters. Yeah, I'm lucky Damon didn't lock me up. I spent a lot of time in conferences explaining to him what I thought Wrath would do."

Barry frowned, but didn't ask. "Well, I just wanted to come and tell you that I think it's wonderful you and Josh are getting along. It's about time that young man found some peace."

"We're getting along quite well." Too well. After he'd made love to her the night before, she'd sat up forever, her soul torn between doing what was right for Josh and her family in London.

"But? I hear a but in there somewhere."

She flipped the laptop closed. "He still doesn't talk to me about his past. He knows a ton about mine. He knows some classified shit that could get us all in trouble. You know, I really wasn't cut out to be an operative. I like to talk too much. It was okay when I was embedded with MSS. They were all kind of dicks there."

It was surprising her sister had turned out so well. The kind of training and torture the Chinese put their agents through didn't typically kick out loving, kind individuals. Of course, she herself hadn't gotten the full Agency training either.

"I don't think Josh talks too much to anyone about his past," Barry said. "Sometimes not about his present either. He's known for being quite silent on both subjects. I think he talked a bit to the one submissive he brought to the club, and that didn't turn out well."

"Because she went to the press."

Barry sighed. "I don't know everything that went on between

those two. I know they had some things in common. They had both been raised in foster care. They seemed to click and then one day I overheard her talking to another sub about how much money she was going to make off him. She had contacted a reporter with a tabloid and was planning on doing an exposé on the whole club. They were going to give her millions."

"You told Josh."

"I told my Glo and she handled things from there," Barry explained. "She had been quite close to Josh's agent at one point. Tina wasn't in the lifestyle, but she was certainly part of the acting community. My wife was a casting agent. She made sure that woman was never cast again."

It was good someone had been looking out for Josh. Still, he'd had a girlfriend. A submissive he'd selected for their compatibility and not her skill with knives and guns. "Can you tell me something, Barry?"

"I don't know. I have to protect him, too."

"It's okay if you don't answer. I wanted to know if he kissed her. The other girl, that is. Did he kiss her during scenes?"

He froze for a moment, as though processing her words, and then a look of sympathy hit his face.

She held out a hand. "It's okay. That's all I need to know. I'm going to pack this laptop up before the party gets started. It looks like they're bringing in the keg now."

Barry put a hand on her arm. "Give him time. I see the way he looks at you. I don't think he'll be able to hold out forever."

She wasn't as sure. He was damaged, and maybe beyond repair. One couldn't fix what was never acknowledged. If he held that pain close to him forever, he would be stuck. The pain would be his mistress, holding if not his affections then most of his attentions.

She couldn't compete with the past.

"I'll be back in a minute." She would check her makeup, ensure the last few minutes of emotional talk didn't show up on her face. Josh would want to know what was wrong, and she was too tired to make shit up.

Time was spinning and before she knew it her time with him would be up and she would have a serious decision to make. She would have to decide to stay with him and see what happened or go back to London and get on with her life.

The thought of leaving Malibu made her heart ache.

She was turning the corner to head to the locker room when Riley stepped out of the shadows. His eyes traced right and then left before he took her by the elbow.

"Your boy's on the move."

"What?"

"Damn it. Deal with that and then find me outside. Hurry." His whole expression changed. "See you at the party, then."

Jared had stepped out of the locker room, now dressed in jeans and a *Dart* T-shirt. With his own face on it. He was a lovable douchebag, but right now he was trouble on two muscular legs.

She gave Riley a smile she didn't feel in any way. "Absolutely, Master Riley. I'll be there in a moment."

Riley disappeared into the front room, mingling with the others.

Jared frowned at her. "I think you should probably stay away from that guy. Josh doesn't like him."

That was news to her. How much time did they have? She didn't want to lose Josh. If he was on the move, something was happening. He wouldn't leave her without an explanation. But maybe that's why Jared was here. Maybe Josh had needed something and ran to get it. Condoms. They went through a ton of those.

Why would he leave without his bodyguards? Without telling her?

"Why doesn't Josh like Riley?"

Jared shrugged. "I don't know, but I think it's important that you not spend a lot of time with the dude. Look, Josh can be weird about some things. He gets feelings about people and he tends to follow his instincts. He thinks Master Riley is hiding something. Give him a wide berth. Don't give Josh a reason to get suspicious."

"Of me?" She didn't like the implications.

"He's not used to being in a relationship and he needs time before he can trust anyone implicitly."

"I think I should talk to him about it," she offered.

And that was when Jared wilted like a hothouse flower. His face flushed. "Josh?"

So Jared was in on whatever this was. "Who else would I talk to?"

"Oh, that's…he's… He's in the locker room. He could be in there for a while. Something he had for dinner didn't sit well on his stomach." Jared shook his head as though finally picking the story he was going to stick to. "You do not want to go in there, if you know what I mean."

Nice. He was going with the old irritable bowel syndrome fake out. "That's terrible. Maybe I should go get something to help him with that."

Jared shook his head. "Nah, he's good. He'll be out in a bit. Wouldn't want to miss the ice cream."

Yeah, Jared needed to rethink his story, but she didn't have time to needle him. Something was happening and it wasn't innocent. Luckily for her, she wasn't as terrible a liar as Jared was. She was quite good. "All right, then. I'll go put my computer up. I need to call my dad, but that shouldn't take long. I'll see you at the party."

He practically sighed in relief. "Awesome. And don't worry about Josh. Happens all the time."

She heard him curse under his breath as she walked into the locker room.

As quickly as she could, she slammed the laptop into her backpack, checking to make sure she had everything she needed. SIG, check. Cell phone, check. Nasty knives, check.

Lucky for her she was already in street clothes, but then it was lucky for Josh, too.

He'd planned this. What was he doing? Why had he brought Jared in on it?

God, if Levi was right she would never live it down. Hell, if Levi was right…she didn't want to think about a world where Joshua Hunt was involved with drug dealers and aiding a man who took out US operatives as fast as he could.

She took a deep breath and slung her backpack over her shoulder. She was taking a chance. She needed to follow Josh and get back here without him knowing she'd been gone. Fuck. Jared would be waiting for her.

She quickly dialed the one number she could think of that might help.

"This is Ferguson," a deep voice said.

"Kai, it's Kayla. I need you to call your brother," she said quickly.

"Fuck. You know I don't like to get involved in the business side of this crap, Kay," he replied. "He just started talking to me again. We keep it light. I don't want to risk him blowing me off."

She didn't have time for his family issues. "A CIA operative's life is at stake and if your brother is involved in this, he's going to get in trouble. I need you to distract him so I can figure out what we're dealing with. Please, Kai. He'll answer your call. I'm running out of time."

"I'll do it. Damn it." He hung up.

She glanced from behind the curtains. Sure enough, Jared's phone went off and a smile came over his face. He brushed a finger across the screen.

"Hey, Kai. What's going on?" he said as he walked back into the men's locker room.

Jared liked to pace while he talked on the phone. He would also do numerous squats and lunges. No moment wasted for that boy.

Kayla ran out the back, taking advantage of the quiet. She eased out the door. At least she was going with someone who could get her back in. If she could have sent Declan or Shane...

She had to be honest. She wouldn't have. Josh was hers. Her lover. Her Master. Her target.

Wheels crunched against the pavement as Riley's Jeep pulled up. "Get in. We need to go."

She hauled herself up, closing the door behind her. Riley took off, turning out of the private drive. "How far ahead is he?"

"Five minutes, but I know where he's going. If Levi asks you saw me leaving and jumped in."

Damn it. "He wanted to cut me out?"

"He pretty much ordered me to, but I think he's a dick and I take orders from Big Tag. Big Tag thought you might like to come along."

Thank god for Big Tag. "In that case, yes, I jumped in the back of the Jeep and you couldn't get rid of me. What the fuck game is Levi playing? And how do you know where Josh is going? Never mind.

You have the phone I duped from his. You're listening to his calls. Is there a reason you haven't given me an update? And where exactly are we going?"

He turned on PCH. "You know why. I can't exactly call you. The house is wired so Levi would know I was talking to you. You can't call me when you're outside the house because Josh is already suspicious. I was hoping to talk to you before the play tonight but he never gave you a second alone. I'm worried about him. I think he could be dangerous."

"So you've been listening in. How'd you like the phone sex?"

"I thought it was quite inventive." He didn't look at her, keeping his eyes on the road. "I did *not* put that into my report. Does he really do stuff to your feet?"

Finally she gets a dude who wants to talk and she was too mad at him to do it. Life sucked. And damn it, she wasn't mad at Riley. She was mad at Josh. He was hiding something, probably something terrible. "What's he doing out here, Riley?"

"I think he's making a dead drop."

Shit. Her stomach threatened to plummet. "To the Commander?"

"I don't think so, but I can't be sure. He's involved in something nasty. The woman he talked to, she implied that this has been going on for a long time. Levi thinks this has something to do with his ties to the drug dealer, but I think it's pure blackmail."

That didn't mean this wasn't about the Commander and what Josh knew about him. It could be he was being blackmailed because of those ties. "It was a woman?"

"Yes, though she was using voice alteration. I still think the voice was female. She threatened you, Kay. Josh got extremely upset about that. You should know how he talks about you when you're not around."

"Hit me." It would be good to know.

"He talks about you like you're the sun in the sky. Like he didn't understand what sunshine was until you walked in. When his publicist told him you might think about getting a little lift in the chest area…well, there's a reason he's getting a new publicist."

Her heart softened. "He didn't mention that to me."

"But he's volatile. He's a powder keg waiting to go off, and I'm worried you're going to be too close when he explodes. I know you're capable of handling yourself, but it's different when you care about the person. Emotions get in the way and there's nothing you can do about it."

"What am I supposed to do? Pretend I don't care about him? I can do that around Levi, but I can't around you guys. You're my team and you have to know everything. I do care about Josh."

Riley nodded. "Just remember that when the shit hits the fan, and it will. Remember that you're compromised when it comes to him and you might want to listen to people you trust. Or follow your instincts. Here's our turnoff. Reach in the back and grab the boots I brought for you."

She reached around. "Hiking boots?"

"You can't go running all over Solstice Canyon in those heels. I swear I breathed a massive sigh of relief when you walked in wearing jeans. Tuck them into the socks I brought along. There are lots of snakes where we're going."

"Snakes?" The socks were super thick and long. She pulled them up over her jeans. "I hate snakes."

"Yeah, I don't think they like us much either, Dr. Jones," Riley said with a sigh. "But I'll be happy if snakes are the only predators we have to deal with tonight."

* * * *

Josh turned the Ducati into the parking lot, lights off because despite what he'd told his blackmailer about night hiking, there wasn't a lot of activity here in Solstice Canyon. Those adventurous hikers would be looking for city views.

What they would get out here would be a whole lot of nocturnal predators and potential places where a hiker could fall to his very adventurous death.

Of course, that was likely her point. She enjoyed forcing him into nasty situations. Once he had to make the drop in the middle of a tent village in Skid Row. He'd been given specific instructions for that one. He was to leave his vehicle at the outer edges of the "city," parking it close to the mural proclaiming the city limits and population—Too Many. He had to walk the streets at midnight.

He was sure she'd watched him from some high ground, playing the god who liked to teach the piddling human a lesson.

He'd ghosted in and out of that place without ever bumping into one of the desperate, sometimes violent residents. Did she think he didn't remember how to go unnoticed? He'd had a lifetime of disappearing into the shadows. Sometimes his life had depended on how well he could hide. Those lessons from his childhood had never left him.

But fuck he hated snakes.

She might have finally found something that really freaked him out. He could handle the dark, deal with being alone and vulnerable and watched. This was something different.

He parked the bike at the far edge of the lot and thanked the universe for Jared's choice of the color black. The bike blended in well and unless someone was looking for it, would likely go unnoticed. He left the helmet on the seat and checked that the laces on the shit kickers he was wearing were well tied. Not his normal loafers, but they were made of thick leather and he could move in them. Leather gloves on his hands and a leather jacket and jeans completed his look for the evening. He liked to call it "dude who didn't want to get bitten by snakes or covered in poison ivy."

Fuck. He needed to do this fast. He pulled out a small flashlight. His phone would throw the light far too wide and bright. He needed to be subtle because he didn't want to attract some curious park ranger.

As quietly as he could, he moved to the north end of the lot where the trail choices were offered. One a nice paved trail. Yeah, that wasn't his. He got the stairs that led to the dirt path.

The road less traveled.

Thank you, Robert Frost. The road less traveled might have made all the difference to that old poet, but it likely meant rattlesnake bites to him.

How much time had already passed? He'd left the minute he could, throwing on some clothes and hauling ass out. Kay would want a shower. That would take her a while. His boots thudded along the stairs. Off to his right, he could see the Pacific in the distance, illuminated by the full moon. Somewhere down there was his house, the one he shared with Kayla now, the only place in the world he'd ever felt halfway safe.

He turned away and jogged down the trail. Fast. He had to get there, stash the key and get back. Jared was handling Kay. If she came out before he got back, Jared would explain that he was in the locker room taking an important call about the film. Those could last for a nice long time, and Kay understood the rules of the club. She wouldn't go in there to check on him.

Jared would keep an eye on her and everything would be okay.

Something flashed up ahead of him, twin lights on a face that immediately disappeared into the shadows. He caught the merest glimpse of a big body lumbering along the canyon and back into the trees.

Cougar. That was a fucking cougar.

He crossed the paved road and then turned right. Rising Sun Trail. He could use some sun right about now. He started the climb, the trail cresting and diving, following the lines of the canyon.

The trail began a descent, but Josh stopped, instincts kicking in. He wasn't alone.

He clicked the flashlight off. There wasn't a lot to shield him where he was and now he cursed the bright light of the moon.

Was that a person coming up behind him? Or had the fucking cougar decided he was hungry and Josh looked like a halfway decent meal?

He stood for roughly thirty seconds, listening to the sounds around him. Crickets hummed, the underscore to this particular soundtrack. Something crunched through the shrubs to his left, but it was small, likely a prey animal. Everything was silent. Eerie, creepy silence.

Fucking hold on to this feeling. He could use it if he ever did a horror movie.

He clicked his flashlight on again, following the trail down.

Up ahead he could hear a stream flowing. Close. He was getting close. He stayed on the east bank of the stream, jogging now, looking for the steps.

Bingo.

He had no idea why someone had built a shrine to the Virgin

Mary out in the middle of the Santa Monica Mountains, but there it was, just to the north of the trail. He breathed a deep sigh of relief.

Almost there.

Almost there.

He hit something in the trail and slipped. Fuck. Pain flared in his right ankle before he fell on his ass.

And that was when he heard it.

Rattle Rattle Rattle.

Shit.

Josh went still. The flashlight had fallen to his side, but it managed to illuminate enough of the path to see a big-ass rattlesnake coiled not four feet in front of him.

His breath stopped in his chest. The thing looked like he was ready to strike at any moment, its diamond-shaped head up and alert while that rattle on its tail kept its tune.

Keep calm. Assess the threat. Some of that military training he'd taken for various roles started playing through his head. Nothing was done until his heart stopped.

He had to stay still. As long as he was still, that thing seemed happy to remain in pending strike mode. The good news, the first thing he thought the snake would hit was his left shit kicker. That leg was closest to the incredibly large snake. If it struck, it might hit the rubber sole of his boot or the metal tip, both good places for him.

The bad? His ankle hurt like a motherfucker. And his time was definitely running out.

"Don't move, Josh."

He tensed but managed to stay where he was. "Kay?"

"Don't move. I don't want to hit you."

He stayed as still as he could. Even when he wanted to look back, to make sure that really was his submissive somewhere behind him and not a park ranger. *Please let it be a park ranger with a super-sexy voice.* He could deal with that. He could bribe a park ranger. Kay would want her bribe in the form of answers, and he had none for her.

"Get out of here, Kayla. That's an order." He wasn't lucky enough for that to be anyone but the one person he'd been trying to avoid.

"You want me to leave you with the snake?"

"Yes." He meant it.

A ping sounded through the air and that fucking snake's head exploded. It was a phenomenal shot, one in a million. Maybe less if you had as much training as she'd had.

Now a different panic threatened to take over. Someone would be out there watching him. Having Kayla even close by meant he was breaking the rules, and his blackmailer didn't like it when he broke the rules.

"I mean it, Kay. Go away. You're fired. Get the fuck out of here."

She knelt down beside him, the scent of her citrusy soap hitting his nose and reminding him of how good she smelled. He would likely never get that scent out of his head. Citrus and sex. Soft and tangy with a bite. "I think I need to get you the fuck out of here. You can fire me later, but I'm doing my job now."

"Kayla, I don't think we're alone out here. We need to move. We've got no cover," a deep voice said from behind him.

"Who the fuck is that?" Had the whole damn club come out to witness his humiliation?

She started to put an arm under his. "It's Riley. I would have taken Dec or Shane with me, but you gave them the night off. I wonder why. You thought I would be easier to get away from? I saw you sneaking out and Riley was the only one close. He wouldn't let me take his Jeep alone and you took the keys to the car. Though I noted you didn't take the car. I suspect Jared's in on this. Whatever this is."

This was about to become a clusterfuck of a situation. Not only was she out here in the middle of the fucking night, but she'd brought Riley Blade with her?

"Leave right now," he commanded. "Go back the way you came and maybe I'll think about not firing you and everyone from your firm. I'll think about not calling your boss and telling him he'll never get another job in this town again."

"You do that. I would love to see you take on Big Tag," she insisted as she managed to get him to his feet. "And he would fire me for letting my client get killed by a rattlesnake. Want to explain why we're hiking this super-scary canyon at night?"

"If you want a little night hike, might I suggest the trail that leads to Griffith Observatory," Riley supplied helpfully. "How's that ankle? You took that fall hard."

He hated the fact the other man had watched him go down. Hated even more that he'd been the one to bring Kay out. "I'd like to know what you're doing with my sub."

"If I hadn't given her a ride, she would have found another way," Riley explained. "Did you want her up here alone?"

He got a good look at the other Dom. Riley Blade looked long and lean against the moonlight. Dangerous, and he looked mighty comfy with that big.40 in his hand. "I didn't want her to come at all. Now get her out of here."

Kayla stood at his side. "I'm not going anywhere, Josh. You're hurt. You can barely walk."

"I'll manage. Now get the fuck out of here and take your boyfriend with you."

A low groan split the silence. "Don't go sulky child on me now, Josh. I told you why he's with me. If anyone should be pissed it's me. You have a girlfriend out here? You meeting her for a quickie?"

"Of course not. I wouldn't..." Fuck. This was not the time for a goddamn relationship discussion. It was certainly not the time to realize he was an asshole for being jealous when she'd never once given him a reason to be. Maybe he was handling this wrong. He was being aggressive and Kay responded to something else. He put his hands on her shoulders. "Baby, I need you to let me do this. Please. Let Riley take you back to the parking lot and I'll meet you there. It's important to me."

She looked up and was about to speak when another sound split the air.

Gunfire. His time had just run out.

* * * *

Kayla heard the sound and pushed Josh down, rolling his big body to her left where the trail slid down. God, she hoped they weren't rolling into the canyon to their deaths, but she had to take the chance. Her back bumped into the trunk of a tree after they'd rolled through some truly thorny bushes. Pain flashed through her as Josh's full weight landed against her.

"Are you okay?" Josh's voice was a whisper.

They were in the wrong position. "Yeah, but I need to get in front of you."

"Absolutely fucking not. She's shooting at you. She doesn't want to kill me."

"She? Who's out there?" And where had Riley gotten off to? She'd seen him moving before she'd jumped on Josh. "What does she want?"

Instead of the answers she wanted, a cell phone trilled and Josh cursed.

He shoved his hand into his pocket and brought the phone to his ear. "I did not invite her along."

Though the phone was to his ear, she was close enough she could hear an eerie robotic voice over the line. "You know what happens when you disobey, Joshua."

A chill went through her. This wasn't something Josh wanted. This wasn't some business he was trying to hide from the press. He was in trouble, the kind that had him doing near suicidal stuff like jogging through the canyon at midnight.

"I wasn't trying to. I was doing exactly what you asked and I got waylaid by a fucking rattlesnake," Josh growled into the phone. "If Kay hadn't come along, I would have died and then where would you get your cash? Because I assure you there's no way you're named in my will."

There was silence for a moment. "I would have handled it. I'm not a bad shot myself. Get rid of your friends and complete the transaction or I'll take them out one by one and you'll still give me what I want."

"I won't," he replied quickly. "You hurt her and I swear you won't see another dime out of me. You hurt her and you better kill me because I won't care about anything else. I'll spend every dime I've got tracking you down and making your life even more miserable than you've made mine. Or you can let me make the drop and get the fuck out of here."

"Send the girl."

Oh, the *girl* was so ready to be sent. The *girl* was ready to meet whoever this bitch was and show her exactly how the *girl* handled threats to her man.

"No." Josh's tone had gone completely flat.

"Let me go," Kay said.

His eyes found hers and she shivered at the anger she saw there. She'd known he would be pissed. When she'd seen him fall, heard that damn snake rattle, she'd known the game was up and she would have to scramble to save her job. She hadn't hesitated. There had been no mental list of pros and cons, not a thought in her head about the mission. All she'd cared about was saving Josh.

That voice came over the line again. How many times had Josh heard it? How many of these "missions" had she sent him on?

"Send the girl, Joshua," the voice over the phone said. "Give her the key and send her. You won't make it. She can. And if you don't do it quickly, I'll kill the man first. You don't care about him, right? I've got a nice line of sight and I can take him out with a headshot, no problem. I'll do it simply because I'm irritated."

Riley? Where was he? She tried to look around, but Josh had her pinned and in this case, her experience was nothing compared to his sheer weight and strength.

She needed to make him understand. She couldn't let Riley get killed. "Please, Josh. Let me do it. I don't think you can make it down that path. Your ankle might not be too bad, but that's uneven ground. What happens if you roll it again? You won't be able to make it back up. Tell me what to do and I'll do it."

Those eyes of his were black in the dark, as black as the night, with only the whites of his eyes holding any color at all. He wasn't her lover in that moment. He wasn't her client or even her friend. He was her Dom and he was pissed.

He was in a corner, and she got the feeling it wasn't going to go well for her when he found his way out.

He forced himself to sit up, the phone still at his ear. "You hurt her and you heard what I said."

Kayla winced at the pain in her back. Now she couldn't hear what was said from the other side. He'd moved, obviously unconcerned about whoever was out there. She glanced down and was happy for the tree she'd nearly broken her back on. If it hadn't been there, they would have kept rolling and rolling, right down to the bottom.

"Then shoot me fucking now because I'm done with you. Do your worst," Josh was saying.

She was silent, allowing him to deal as much as he could. It was apparent to her what the outcome was going to be. He winced every time he tried to move that right foot. He might be able to make it back to the parking lot, but it wouldn't be without help. There was zero chance he could maneuver further into the canyon. Not on his own.

He needed her. He might not want to. It might enrage him, but he needed her.

After a moment Josh sighed and hung up. He reached into his pocket again and pulled out a small box. "You will take this down the trail. Stay on the east bank of the stream and you'll come to some ruins. Go up the steps and turn north. There's a shrine there. Put this box in the offering dish."

That sounded super freaky. She took the box and got to her feet. "Okay. I'll be quick."

His hand closed around her wrist. "Do not look for her. She will kill you if she gets the chance. You have to leave the gun behind."

"I don't need a gun to take care of her." She wanted to get whoever the hell was on the other end of that line in some hand to hand. She would make it last and that bitch would go down slow.

"Don't you dare," he said. "Do everything she tells you. I know you don't give a shit that I'm the boss, but if you don't do this and do it right, my career will be in the toilet. I will lose everything if you don't give her what she wants."

She hated the slight tremble in his voice, loathed how he struggled to stand. He was always strong, stalwart, and this weakness killed her. She tried to help him up, but he pushed her hand away.

"Don't touch me right now." His voice was low. He was a wounded animal, and those were the most dangerous kind. "You wanted to follow me and find out what I'm doing. Here's your chance. That's my whole future in your hands."

But she had to wonder if it wasn't really his past in her hands. This felt like blackmail, his desperation familiar to her. He had a secret. She understood what it meant to have a secret that could ruin not only her future, but end her life. What had Josh done or been through that could possibly be bad enough he was willing to pay blackmail?

She'd been so sure of him. Was he working for a drug dealer? That would do the trick. If someone had found that connection, it could ruin his career.

She couldn't think about that now. Later, she would take out the information and carefully consider it, like a box to open and explore. For now, she had a mission. "I'm going. I'll be right back and we'll get you out of here. And Josh, I was only trying to do my job."

"Your job is to do what I tell you to do," he replied, the chill in his voice nearly making her shiver. "Don't think this fight is done just because I give in on one front."

She nodded and turned, catching sight of Riley. "You watch after him."

"I don't need a babysitter." Josh's gaze found Riley and she knew there would be trouble on that front as well.

Another problem for another day. She needed to get the job done and figure out a way to deal with Josh.

She couldn't get kicked out. Not now. They were close to getting where they needed to go, and tonight had merely proven that Josh was in way over his head. Hell, he didn't even know what kind of waters he was swimming in, much less that there were sharks circling. He thought this was his real problem.

Kay moved over the uneven ground, her natural grace allowing her to go quickly down the path. She found the stream, banking to the east. Certainly during the day, this was a kind of haven, but as she moved through at night, her flashlight picking up the flare of eyes watching her from scrub and bush, she couldn't help but think that this wasn't a place for her kind. Humans. At night this was a foreign world and she was the interloper. Something howled in the distance and she hurried the fuck up. There they were, the stairs she'd been told to find. They rose from the ground, a piece of humanity that had zero place out here.

Moonlight cast shadows around the small shrine. Built of roughhewn rocks, the semicircular shrine looked oddly at home in the canyon. In the deep gloom, she could see the statue of the Virgin Mary on her pedestal. The white rock she was sculpted from shone against the moonlight, giving the place an eerie glow. There was a smaller, kneeling statuary to her left, and a circular offering bowl that looked to be filled with pinecones.

At least it wasn't something bloodier. With a long breath, she approached the shrine.

Yep, she'd feel better with a gun in her hand. And a couple of grenades. Maybe a flamethrower. Damn, but she missed flamethrowers. She was really more of an urban spy. She hated the fact that everything made sounds out here. Her boots crunched across the path despite the fact that she was trying to walk as quietly as possible. Wasn't happening out here.

"It puts the lotion in the basket," an electronically modified voice said.

Good to know someone had a sense of humor. And a working knowledge of pop culture. Kayla placed the packet Josh had given to her on the bed of pinecones. "Okay, Lecter, your move. You going to shoot me or let me get my boy out of here?"

"Your boy? That's a little arrogant of you, don't you think?"

Where was it coming from? The voice was low, but it seemed to come at her from every direction, the sound bouncing around and confusing her senses. "I'm the one taking care of him."

"You've known him for a whole ten minutes. And by know I mean that in the biblical sense. You've spread your legs for him but you have no idea who he is. You have no idea the things he's done."

"I don't care. I'm his bodyguard and yeah, I sleep with him because he's really good at it, but that's the extent of our relationship. So make your decision. Do I go or do you want to throw down right here?" She closed her eyes. It wasn't like she could see much anyway.

"You're a violent thing, aren't you?" that voice asked. "You think you can solve everything with a bullet, but I'm more subtle than that. Smarter. I think I'll forego the fight today, but don't think this is over. If you stay with him for any amount of time, you'll deal with me."

"And you are? I would love a formal introduction."

"I bet you would." The voice sounded eerily amused. "Again, I believe I'll forego that. The question now is how do I ensure you leave? I think you might enjoy staying here and trying to catch a glimpse of me."

"Nope. I'm ready to head out. Not for nature." Kay still couldn't figure out where that voice was coming from, what direction to defend.

"I think you might hang around, or that friend of yours might. He looks a bit dangerous, like he's had some training that goes beyond Hollywood. No, I think it's good that I brought some friends along, too. Get out of here or I'll have one of my snipers blow Josh's head off. If you're not in the parking lot in ten minutes, Josh is dead," the voice pronounced.

"Why would…"

"Your time starts now," the voice insisted.

Kayla took off, her boots pounding along the path. Sure enough, when she made it back to Josh, there was a laser painted on his chest. And another had a bead on Riley. Josh stared down at the red dot and she saw the moment Riley got the picture, too.

"She's got at least two shooters on us," Kay shouted. "Riley, pick him up. We've got ten minutes or they fire."

Josh grunted as Riley tossed him over his shoulder.

Kay started to reach for her gun.

The dirt two inches from her hand exploded.

So whoever was out there was damn good and wanted her unarmed. Fuck. "Let's move. I'll take the front and light the way. We can't stop so if we come up against momma mountain lion, expect a fight."

"Lead the way," Riley said.

She started back up the path, praying all along that Josh was worth more to that bitch alive than he was dead. Because if he wasn't, she feared they were all in trouble.

They jogged along, Josh arguing quietly that he could walk and she and Riley ignoring him entirely. She breathed a bit when they reached a patch of trees. She glanced back and those red lasers that had been following them were gone.

"She's not going to kill me," Josh said. "She wanted to get you away from the drop site. That's all. She's long gone now."

"I'm not taking the chance. We're not stopping until we get back to the club. Then we're getting in the car and we're going home. When we're at home, you can decide if you want to fire me or give me a heads-up the next time you decide to try to kill yourself." The minute the words were out of her mouth, she knew that wasn't the way to handle Josh, but she couldn't seem to help herself.

He'd almost died. If that damn snake had gotten him, he could have died out there. He wouldn't have been able to walk, and even if he'd been smart enough to call her, she might not have made it in time. She would have raced out and found his big body growing cold on the trail.

Anger flared now but she tamped it down as they made it to the steps that led back to the parking lot. She put a hand out, stopping Riley. If someone was going to jump them, this would be the place to do it. The lot was dark and they could come at her from all sides.

And she'd lost her fucking favorite SIG. Agnes. She and Agnes had been together for a long time, and now she was likely getting a rubdown from a rattlesnake. Some asshole would find it on the trail and she would have questions to answer because that sucker was registered.

"Are you still carrying?" She moved to the side of the steps as Riley came down, showing no sign that he was bothered by Josh's weight. Big Tag kept his men in shape.

"Reach into my right boot. There's a semi in there." He stopped, allowing her to pull the small gun free.

"You keep a gun in your boot?" Josh was squirming, trying to look around. "There are no weapons allowed in The Reef."

"I keep it in my Jeep. I actually do quite a bit of hiking. And it's all legal. I can show you my license to carry," Riley replied.

Shit, she might have blown his cover, too.

There was a beeping sound as Riley unlocked the Jeep and then tossed her the keys. "I'll get him in the back. You start up the Jeep and get us out of here."

"I have to get the motorcycle. Jared's motorcycle," Josh insisted.

"He can get it later." She wasn't going to split them up. Besides, Jared should understand there was a price when he lied to her.

She moved around the edge of the lot, ensuring the way was

clear. She winced when she walked by Jared's bike. It had been pushed over and she could see where someone had viciously slashed the tires. "They got to the bike. Let's hope they left us a way out."

Riley groaned. "Fuck. That's going to cost me a pretty penny."

The Jeep's tires had been treated to the same amount of love.

How had she worked so fast? How many people had been out here, watching them, waiting for Josh to make a mistake?

Riley propped Josh against the Jeep. "I think it's safe to say they don't want to chance us following them."

She pulled out her cell phone and pressed the button to dial Shane. When he answered, she got straight to the point. "We need a pickup at the Solstice Canyon parking lot, and bring Declan because we've got to move two vehicles, and someone's got to go back up that trail to find Agnes. Also bring an ice pack. Our client had a night to remember."

Before he could ask the obvious questions, she hung up, unable to debrief anyone right now.

She was too angry. Too confused. Too scared for him.

"Kay?"

She looked up at Josh. Riley had moved away, as though giving them plenty of room. "Yeah?"

He should thank her, but that wasn't what she expected.

"Nice boots. Those new?"

Yeah, she had some explaining to do.

Chapter Eleven

"I told you they weren't my boots." Kayla enunciated every word because Josh didn't seem capable of understanding English. She turned the Porsche onto PCH.

"You're stripping the gears," he complained. The only way she'd been able to keep him from driving was pointing out the fact that if his ankle didn't heal quickly, his movie would be put on hold. "And I'm supposed to believe Riley Blade's girlfriend just happens to be your size and she left her hiking boots in his car? That's awfully convenient."

Oh, she had such good fucking news for him on that front. "Not my size, buddy. They were too small. Do you want to check and see how bad the blisters on my feet are? The backs of my feet are completely trashed."

It was clear Riley thought she had a ten-year-old's feet. She hadn't noticed how bad it was when the adrenaline had been pumping through her body. It was only later when she had to peel those suckers off that she realized how tight they'd been.

She glanced down at the clock. How could it only be one thirty? It felt like they'd been in that canyon for hours. Her phone went off. She didn't even look down at it. Her dad had called earlier and anyone else who was calling this late could leave a damn message. It was probably Tucker, who always seemed to forget that there was a time difference.

Josh sulked in the seat beside her like a big, gorgeous, made-bad-decisions man boy. After wrapping his ankle, he was moving quite well. One of the members of The Reef happened to be a doctor. They had told the doc a complete bullshit lie about Josh falling in the parking lot. The doc had looked him over and found nothing was broken and Josh only had a mild strain of the muscle.

"When we get back to the house, you'll pack your things," he said, staring out at the road ahead.

Shane had dropped the two of them off at the club while Riley had stayed behind to help with the vehicles. She didn't like to think about one of them having to go back on that trail after Agnes, but she couldn't afford to have the cops show up asking why her SIG Sauer had been found in the canyon. There would be far too many questions.

"So you're firing me? For doing my job?"

"No, I'm firing you for bringing that asshole with you. Tell me something, Kay, you playing around with him? Having some fun when I'm not here? That's the only way to explain why you would hop into his car without a second thought, putting my privacy on the line. Maybe this is what the two of you planned all along."

Such an ass. These were the times she could easily walk away from him. "Yeah, there's no other explanation. I'm just a whore."

"Well, give me a better explanation," he shot back and then shifted in his seat. "And I didn't use that word."

"You used that tone. Every woman in the world knows that tone. And my reason? I panicked. I freaked out. I lost my shit when I realized you were out there with absolutely no protection. You didn't even have a gun."

He shoved a hand through his hair, sweeping it back. "I wasn't allowed to take a fucking gun. And guess what, I wasn't allowed to take a bodyguard either. I'm going to pay for that."

"You lied to me. What was I supposed to do? Sit back and hope everything worked out? You didn't tell me anything. You didn't explain anything. How was I supposed to know you were even leaving of your own volition?"

"Because you were supposed to do what I asked you to do." He still hadn't looked at her. The whole time they'd gone back to the club, gotten his things, seen the doctor—who apparently was used to not asking a lot of questions—that whole time he hadn't looked at her once.

"I did exactly what you told me to do. I got presentable for the party. I'm sorry if I stepped outside to get some fresh air and happened to see you hopping on Jared's bike." Yes, this part was a lie, but she didn't feel bad about that anymore. He'd nearly gotten himself killed. He couldn't handle the truth.

He went silent.

She squeezed the steering wheel, frustration welling inside her. "You can't honestly think I was out there to…do what? Meet with Master Riley? Was I making out with him? Did I need more sex after the four orgasms you gave me in the red room? I'm not just a whore. I'm a crazed nymphomaniac."

"Stop it. I didn't fucking say those words," he said. "This is a stupid argument. There's zero point to it. It doesn't matter now."

"Because I'm fired."

He went silent again.

She was not going to panic. Logic. She needed to bring down the emotional charge and present him with sweet logic. "Are we all fired? Because I assure you Shane or Dec would have done what I did. They wouldn't have allowed you to run off into the night. Not even if it meant their jobs. They would have been running after you, flagging down anyone they could because the one thing we cannot live with is losing a client."

He stared stubbornly ahead.

Okay, logic wasn't going to work. Maybe emotion was the way to get to him, but not anger. He needed warmth. Softness. Vulnerability.

Fuck it. She would give him the truth. As much of it as she could.

"Do you have any idea how it felt to see you facing down that damn snake?" When he didn't answer, she continued. Even if he kicked her ass to the street, he would hear the truth. "I thought I was going to lose my damn mind. I don't know that I've ever been that scared."

"Couldn't tell. That was a hell of a shot."

That was bothering him? "Josh, my hand was almost shaking too much for me to take it."

"Like I said, couldn't tell. You're cool under pressure."

"You say that like it's a bad thing. This is my job. But it didn't feel like a job when I was out there. I wasn't some super-agent. I was a freaked-out sub watching her Master try to kill himself."

"I wanted you to stay out of it." His tone had softened, a bit of the stubborn will seeming to ease out.

"What is *it*? What is so important you would pull a stunt like this? And who the hell is that woman? She's obviously got something on you. How much did she take you for?"

And then it was right back. He straightened up, his shoulders broadening, hands in tight fists. "It doesn't matter. It doesn't fucking matter now. Maybe if it had been you I could deal with it. But Riley? Do you think that guy is going to let this go? You think he's not going to try to figure out what's going on and use it against me? You might have simply been doing your job, but he wasn't. He's like everyone else—looking to make a big play, and guess what? Josh Hunt is a huge play. He can use this. He can manipulate me to get him a job, to get him a foot in the door, or he'll use it to take from me exactly the way that bitch in the shadows does."

God, what must his life be like that he thought everyone in the world was out to use him? "He's the Dom in Residence. He signed a nondisclosure. It covers everything that goes on with members in and out of the club. If you like, I'll have your lawyer send over one that specifically covers the events of tonight."

"Why would he sign that?"

"Because he's not a massive ass." Sometimes Josh was exhausting. "Not everyone in the world is out to get you. There are people in the world who are good and who do good things without thinking about how much they can cash in at the end."

"I only really knew one of those," he said quietly. "And even then she got something out of me."

"Tina?"

He nodded. "Yeah. I sometimes wonder if she would have bothered to help me out if I hadn't had this face. This face has been my curse. My blessing. I often wonder what my life would have been like without it."

"We can't change the past, Josh. We can only face it and accept all the good and the bad it did and move on. Believe me. I understand that."

Josh's head shook. "You can't possibly understand what I went through."

"I can't understand the minutiae of it. The details would be different for me, but don't think for an instant that I don't know what pain is. That I don't know how it feels to be locked in a cage with no way out. To be used even by the people who cared about me."

He went silent again, but some of the tension was gone.

"How long has this been going on?" Kayla asked.

"Almost five years."

She kept her eyes on the road, finding the turnoff to Old Malibu. "You don't have to tell me what you're hiding."

"I don't have to tell you anything at all."

"Except that I'm fired."

He went silent again.

"I was scared. Does that mean anything to you?"

"Of course it does," he replied with a sigh. "Do you think I don't feel something for you? Fuck, you're all I think about, but that can't matter now."

This didn't feel like she was working a target. Her heart ached. This wasn't some conversation meant to manipulate her way back into the job. She felt like a girlfriend desperate to fix what was wrong between them. "Why? Why can't it matter?"

"I…I have to let you go," he said haltingly. "It's not about what I want anymore. She could hurt you. She could kill you. You think you were scared? God, Kay, I couldn't breathe until you showed back up on that trail. I sat there waiting to hear a gunshot, waiting to listen to her kill you."

Finally, they were getting somewhere. "I don't think she intends to kill me. I think she wanted to show me my place."

"What makes you think that? Spy intuition?"

"She had the chance tonight and she didn't take it."

He shook his head as though there was no way he was buying

209

that line. "Only because she wasn't prepared, Kay."

Oh, but she knew something he didn't. "I think she's always prepared. Why else would she have at least two snipers with her? She's got a team. You might have thought she was there alone, but I doubt she's ever alone. I bet she's got muscle around her every time she pulls one of these jobs. Think about that. Two snipers when she thought there would only be one of you. Look, when I was at that shrine thing, she had an easy bead on me. She was there when I made the drop. She had probably hidden there the whole time, waiting to watch you like some icky creeper. I couldn't see her, but she spoke directly to me. She couldn't have been more than a few yards away. I was perfectly helpless. All she had to do was pull the trigger and I would have gone down."

He turned, his face stark white. "She was there with you?"

"In person. And that thing she uses to modify her voice is definitely portable," she replied. The road was narrow and curved. She slowed down because she wasn't entirely sure he wouldn't kick her out of the house the minute they got home. If they got home before Shane and Declan did, Josh might lock them all out. It was important to keep him talking because he was starting to calm down. "She was waiting for me, which means she was waiting for you. She quoted *Silence of the Lambs*, letting me know I was not Clarice in her opinion. I got the whole 'you're nothing but a whore' speech—it's the theme of the night—and then she promised to blow your head off if I didn't get you out of that canyon in way less time than it really took us. She wanted her money. I assume it's money. I guess it could be information of some kind."

"It's money. Only money," he insisted. "I wouldn't put anyone else at risk. Not ever."

That was the first honest thing he'd said in hours. "She's blackmailing you."

"Yeah. I guess that's obvious."

At least she had that much to work with. "Okay. You know the best and easiest solution is to put it out there yourself. Whatever she's got on you. We can get you a lawyer and a crisis management PR firm. I can have them here within twenty-four hours. The only way to deal with a blackmailer is to take out the threat."

"How much would it cost to take out the threat?" Josh sounded numb.

She was going to have to get on the phone with Big Tag. She was fairly certain he would know how to start. His personal lawyer, Mitch Bradford, used to practice in this part of California. He would definitely know how to help. "I don't know. Probably less than you've paid already. It depends on what the threat is and how much work the publicity team will have to do. Do we need a criminal lawyer, too?"

For him, that is. Perhaps he did something in his youth that was coming back to haunt him. She didn't want to think about it, didn't want to think Josh was capable of doing anything truly awful.

"You don't understand what I'm asking," he replied quietly. "I meant how much would it take for you to kill her?"

Oddly enough, that wasn't something awful. That was something that needed to happen. Years spent working in the gray areas of morality had definitely had an effect on her. "I would do that for free. I would do that for fun, Josh. Give me the information I need to find her and I'll make sure she never calls you again."

He sighed and leaned against the window. "Sorry, I wouldn't ask you to do that. You've been through too much and I don't want you back in that world. I don't want you involved in any of this. I wanted to keep you out. I wanted to protect you. I wanted…who the hell is that?"

He sat up straight and Kay turned to see what he was talking about.

Someone was standing in their driveway. Two someones. The light hit them and she gasped. Two men. One black, one white. Both dressed like they were going on a cruise in white pants and casual loose cotton shirts. One held a poodle.

"Reporters?" Josh asked.

"So much worse." She stopped in the middle of the road. She'd thought the night was as bad as it could get. Nope. "Those are my dads."

* * * *

211

The night had been so horrible. He'd known the minute she'd caught up to him on that trail that this night would count as one of the worst of his life because this was going to be the night he lost Kay. One way or another. Earlier he'd been worried sick he would lose her to a bullet and then to the need to keep her safe and away from his trouble. He'd known this would be one of his darkest nights.

But somehow that look on her face—utter horror from a woman who'd looked into the heart of darkness and tried to tickle it—brought him out of his morose brood. He'd been having a brood, as she called it, and now he couldn't help but feel something lift at that look in her eyes. All this time, she'd been the strong one, the stalwart, never-say-die ex-spy. She'd assassinated world leaders without blinking an eye, but those elderly men and that dog scared the shit out of her.

"Are you going to drive by them?" Somehow her complete and total shutdown stopped his own. One of them had to be functional, right? They were…they were partners. He hadn't had a partner he could truly count on in years, one who picked up the slack when he couldn't. One who needed him to do the same when her two dads showed up on their doorstep.

It was a perfect sitcom moment, and he didn't want it ruined by that bitch.

"Baby, I think they know it's you," he pointed out. "We could run, but they might get in that…is that a Prius? I think the Porsche could take it but not the way you drive."

She frowned and turned his way. "I drive fine. I'm a magnificent driver. I once got away from a Russian operative driving a hundred and ten miles an hour down an icy Siberian highway."

"You didn't do it in this Porsche." Somehow even through his misery, he'd been sad about how hard she'd been on his other baby. If she'd been anyone else in the world, he would have kicked her out and called in a driver.

When had she become more important than his things? Materialism had been safe for so long, but he hadn't done much more than bitch a little about her stripping his gears. He hadn't forced her to comply with his wishes.

Because her feelings, her will, had somehow become more important than his own.

He was in way too deep. He had a drama playing out on his yard and he wasn't freaked out about it.

"Why are my dads here?" She asked the question with a vulnerability he'd never heard from her before. Not once.

And yet he knew she cared about them. This wasn't fear. Not fear that they would hurt her. She was a teenaged girl who got caught with a boy. It was enough to throw him off.

"Why don't we ask them instead of staring at them in the middle of the road at one thirty in the morning? It's weird and someone's going to notice," he pointed out, but with none of the panic he would have thought he would have. Normally he would want any drama at all in his life hidden away from reporters.

What would they say this time? *Joshua Hunt Meets the Parents?* He kind of didn't hate that headline. That headline felt nice and normal and good.

He did want to meet her parents.

The taller of the two men leaned over, putting a hand over his eyes as though trying to see into the car. It was obvious they were arguing over whether or not the sports car stopped in the middle of the road contained their wayward daughter.

The one carrying the poodle used his free hand to pull out his cell phone.

Kay's phone trilled. She sat as though completely incapable of getting unstuck. She simply stared out the window as though they might go away if she thought about it long enough.

Yeah, he'd had his silent time. It looked like it was Kay's time to win the quiet game. He grabbed the phone. "Hello?"

Kay turned to him, reaching out. "Hey, that's mine."

She'd taken over his blackmail drop. He could take over dealing with her dads.

What was wrong with him? He needed to move. He needed to kick them all out and decide on how to deal with his blackmailer. Why the fuck was he sitting in a car with her, eager to meet a couple of men who shouldn't matter at all to him?

Why couldn't he tell her that seeing her tonight had been all he'd wanted? That when he thought he was going to die, all he'd wanted was another couple of minutes with her. A couple of minutes where he stopped fucking pretending she wasn't everything he wanted—everything he never knew he wanted.

"Young man, I am trying to get in touch with my daughter," a cultured voice said over the line. "This is her telephone and if you've done something terrible to her, you will pay the price."

There was zero missing that judgmental tone. He pulled the phone away from his ear and hung it up. "It's definitely your dads."

"I know that, damn it." She lowered her head until it touched the steering wheel.

Her tactical reasoning skills were obviously shot. He needed to point out a few truths to her. "Did you realize that if we don't get them off the lawn soon, Shane or Dec is going to come back? Do they know your dads by sight? Or will they tackle them, suspecting they represent elderly stalkers who love canines?"

"Shit." She put the car in first and totally stripped the fucking gears.

She was going to owe him a new engine. He winced but at least they were moving again.

He was moving again. How long had he been still? Since that first moment he'd gotten the call? He'd been stuck in some never-ending purgatory of a second act, the one where the hero finds himself in trouble and falling back on all his old ways. After Tina died, he'd closed down. He'd done some destructive shit, but nothing was more destructive than never moving or changing or opening himself up to the possibilities of the world.

Tonight had been a turning point. The question was which way did he turn? Funny that his life always seemed to turn because of a woman. First, Tina had asked him not to run and despite his instincts, he'd stayed with her.

Now he could choose to protect Kay…no. What the fuck was he thinking? He didn't need to protect Kayla Summers. She was a badass who could take him down in a heartbeat. He wasn't going to lie to himself. He was the one he was trying to protect. He could protect himself from potential heartache or he could take a chance with her. He could hope and pray that the universe gave him just one more good thing.

Was he actually considering talking to Kayla about the whys of his blackmailer? Was he considering discussing the situation with her? He was pinging back and forth between utter fear and anger and a desperate need to not be alone again. It would be worse this time around.

Alone meaning losing her because he was fairly certain no one on earth could take her place. Before he'd been fairly content. He'd had his work and that was enough. He wasn't sure anything could fill the void she would leave in his life.

She turned the Porsche into the drive and managed to put it in park without stalling the engine. That was one miracle.

Now he had to find a way to get her out of the car or they would sit out here all night, staring at each other. "I'll go first. You come out when you feel like it." His hand was on the door. "I kind of thought you liked your dads."

"I love them."

He knew. She talked about them a lot and always with great affection. "So why the total terror?"

"Josh, have you ever met a pair of overly protective, slightly pretentious father knows bests? Who know you're probably sleeping with their precious daughter? Do you have any idea the questions they're going to have? I'm scared for you."

He called bullshit. This was abso-fucking-lutely about the questions they would have for her. Well, they'd both introduced each other to the troublesome parts of their lives. She'd met his blackmailer. He had to deal with her dads. All in all, he probably got the better end of that stick.

"I'm good with parents." He'd played the romantic lead many times. *This* he could handle. Maybe that's where he was going wrong. He was being far too controlling and trying to take on all the roles. But they had been perfectly cast for this day and age. He should handle charming the parents and she would murder the blackmailers. They should play to their strengths. "Watch this."

He left her phone behind and got out of the car.

She scrambled behind him as he limped across the lawn, hand held out.

"Hello, sir, I'm Joshua Hunt. It's good to finally meet you. Kayla has told me so much about you," he said with his best leading-man,

215

don't-worry-about-your-daughter-at-all smile.

The man with the poodle frowned, not taking his hand at all. "Well, I'm glad she mentioned us since she hasn't bothered to mention you. This whole thing is a complete surprise. One would think that when one's daughter is going to be dating a celebrity, she would call and give her fathers a heads-up. We had to hear about it from that obnoxious Marty Dixon at the potluck. First he brings that horrible tuna casserole that the seventies spat out and then he announces to all our friends that our sweet daughter is dating…"—the man shivered as though this was something truly distasteful—"…an action star."

The poodle barked, as though adding its two cents to the discussion.

"Now, Fred, give the kid a chance," the taller of the two men said. He reached out a hand, shaking Josh's. "I'm Jim and this is my husband Fred." He put a hand on his husband's shoulder, glancing down at him. "You know our Kayla likes to keep her secrets. I blame the CIA. What that institution needs is more transparency. Perhaps a civilian oversight committee."

"Yeah, dad, that would go over well with clandestine ops. I'm sure voting on what actions to take wouldn't cause trouble at all." Kay finally moved up beside him. "Sorry I didn't call back. Do you know it's one thirty in the morning?"

Jim was a tall, elegant-looking black man. His close-cropped hair was graying, but in a way that lent dignity to his handsome, intelligent face. "I am, in fact, well aware that it's one thirty in the morning, young lady. We left Santa Barbara at six. We got stuck in terrible traffic."

"There's a fire north of here." Fred was at least six inches shorter than his husband. "They closed down the highway for over three hours because fire likes to jump around like a kid on a pogo stick. I thought we were going to be squatters. Luckily I had packed a care package and had a couple of lawn chairs. We met this lovely couple driving down from San Francisco and had a nice supper. Well, as much of a supper as one can make from goat cheese and crackers and wine. Thank god, I'm prepared for anything."

"By the time we got here, it was after midnight and every hotel in town is full," Jim explained. "So we're here. Now could someone explain why my daughter is sleeping with a man who thinks King Arthur listened to rap music?"

Damn, naturally that one came up first. He'd thought that Arthur as a rock 'n' roll kind of superhero would be a cool, modern take on the legend. No one outside the cast and crew had agreed. A definite misstep.

"No, sir, that was an artistic choice by the director. I'm well aware that Arthur wasn't into Jay-Z. He was likely more of a pan flute kind of guy." Everyone was a critic.

"I'm not sleeping with him," Kayla said, keeping her distance. "I'm his bodyguard. I told you I was working. This is the job. I'm sorry about the rumors."

Did she think she was getting away with that? Hells to the no. If he was going to have to defend his movies to her erudite father and deal with that poodle who looked like trouble, she was going down with him. "She's totally sleeping with me. We're exclusive. Though she *is* my bodyguard." He slid an arm around her. "And my submissive, but we can go over what that means later. Should we get your luggage inside? Kay, baby, do you want to see if we've got some leftovers to feed your dads?"

"I think I would rather murder you," she said under her breath. "What are you doing?"

He was making his decision. He was making his stand.

"I'm sorry, what did he call you?" Fred asked, holding the poodle up, showing dual expressions of complete horror on their faces. "You had better be talking about a sandwich or a submersible vehicle, though neither of those explanations fit my sweet baby girl, either."

Another car pulled in behind them and Jared was out of the passenger seat like a shot, Shane following behind him. It looked like Declan had been the one to draw Riley babysitting duty.

Jared was all over him. "Dude, are you okay? Is the bike okay? Forget about the bike. The bike doesn't matter. I can get a new one. I'm sure. You're the important thing here. Did you almost get killed by a rattlesnake? And I'm sorry I screwed up. I forgot the whole you taking a call excuse and I fell back on explosive diarrhea. I'm such a fuck-up."

Josh groaned. He should have known better than to give Jared Johns the high-pressure job of informing Kayla he was indisposed. "Hey, new friends, buddy. Let's can the bodily functions."

"Is everything all right?" Shane asked, hanging back as though ready to strike at the first possible opportunity.

"Kayla's fathers have come to visit," Josh explained.

Shane sighed. "I told her to call."

Jared immediately turned and gave the newbies his best smile. "Kayla's dads. Wow. Hello, I'm Jared Johns." He turned to the poodle, obviously amping up the charm. "And who is this? Well, hello, pretty girl."

The dog growled, eyes kind of bugging out. It was cool because he'd never seen a creature great or small who didn't love Jared Johns. The man was like a walking, talking magnet. He pulled them all in, young and old, straight or gay, human or puppy.

"He's a boy," Fred said, dismissing Jared entirely. "And what is this about a rattlesnake?"

"Are you that actor from the TV show about the darts?" Jim asked.

Jared's smile widened. The fucker practically glowed any time he got attention. "I am indeed. Hey, can I sign anything for you? Anything for a fan."

"Yes, you can sign a document stating that you completely ignored both history and physics when making that ridiculous show. Did the writers attend school in any way?" The professor was in the house and it didn't matter that it was late. He was obviously going to school them all. "Because it doesn't appear so. A dart is far too small to transverse a human body, much less three. Also, when dealing with three human beings, their hearts wouldn't all be in the exact same place, therefore making it impossible for the aforementioned too small dart to pierce each heart if it was on a fixed course."

Jared's eyes went wide. "Huh?"

The professor wasn't done. "And no, the dart was not a weapon invented by cavemen."

Jared shook his head and glanced over at Josh as though someone should save him. "No, the weaponized dart was given to the first Dart, who happened to be a caveman. See, ancient aliens knew that

218

someone had to save humanity from darkness, thus the Dart was born. I was merely the contemporary man who was chosen by fate to protect earth."

Jim stared at him for a moment and then shook his head, turning back to Josh. "Tell me you have more sense than he does."

Oh, he was going to be fun to deal with. "Absolutely. I carefully research every role despite the fact that the screenwriters and directors often get the historical facts wrong in favor of drama. The key is to know what you're fictionalizing and then figure out how to still find the character's truth."

"And who is the new guy?" Jim asked, staring at Shane.

"I'm the bodyguard," Shane replied.

"I thought Kayla was the bodyguard. And something else. What did he call our daughter? Is the new body person also the other thing?" Fred was caught on that one little word.

"Bodyguard. I'm his bodyguard." Kay was still trying, but he could have told her that ship had sailed away. "Shane's also his bodyguard, but I'm his main guard."

"What's the other thing?" Shane asked, having missed that amazing exchange.

"She's also my sub," Josh reiterated.

Shane backed away as though the word itself could hurt him. "Nope. Just guarding the dude's body. I'm here to take the bullets and nothing else. Nope. No penetration except for the bullets. Jeez. Why did I take this assignment?"

He needed to let that dude get to bed. "Come on in. I'll get you both a drink and we can discuss my and Kayla's serious relationship. We have a contract and everything. I'm surprised she hadn't told you about me. She likes to talk a lot. It was inevitable, darling. You were going to show up on my arm at some point in time."

"Hey, isn't the sub stuff supposed to be like secret?" Jared asked.

"Yes. Yes, it is," Kayla insisted, her eyes narrowing on him.

"Well, no one on the face of this earth respects my secrets. Why bother to keep them? Isn't that what you told me to do? Tell the truth and shame the devil." There was something a little freeing about saying it out loud. Kayla was his sub. There was nothing wrong with that. They were adults. They consented. Hell, they consented so much they had a contract to prove it.

Fuck. He was going to tell her. He was going to tell someone what happened to him, and it was going to be Kayla. That was why he'd finally relaxed. It was also why he was drawing out this scene.

Because she could hear about what happened to him and be disgusted, be shocked that she'd slept with someone as dirty as he was.

He had to tell her. He supposed he'd known as he'd sat on the trail watching her run toward the drop. He'd known the evening would end one of two ways, with him telling her everything and giving them a real shot, or he would play it safe and kick her out.

He couldn't play it safe anymore. He needed her too badly. The little boy inside him was shaking and rattling the cage, begging him to protect them, but the man needed something more than safety. The man he'd become needed her.

She turned her head up slightly. "This is punishment, then?"

He turned and did something he promised he would never do. He should wait. He knew that. It was right there on his conscience to wait, tell her everything and then give her the option of accepting what he was about to do. He leaned over and kissed her anyway, brushing his lips across hers in a way that set his world right again. "No punishment. This is complete and utter surrender."

She went still for a moment and then her hands came up, cupping his face like she couldn't quite believe he was standing there. She went up on her toes and tentatively kissed him. He let her, his hands finding her waist.

And then she was back on her feet, her arm hugging him close as she looked at her dads. For as dark as she'd been since the moment they'd met on the trail, now she was all about the light. She practically glowed. "Dads, this is Josh and I'm totally his submissive, and I mean that in a sexual fashion. It's a beautiful thing."

Shane winced and shook his head. "And I'm out of here. I have something to monitor I'm sure." He stared at Kayla's fathers. "I don't know what you intended to do for her, but she's way too open about that shit. You needed to shame her way more than you did."

Finally something that seemed to stun the couple. They stood there, and even the dog seemed a little shocked.

"Shall we take this inside? I've had a long night and I personally would like to go to bed at some point."

Kayla tilted her head up. "Where are we going to put them?"

Because she was in the guest room. Shit. In for a penny... "The guest room, of course. I'll hurry up there and make sure everything's ready for your dads while you...explain stuff."

"Yeah, thanks for that," she replied but that smile on her face...damn, that was everything.

He'd put that smile on her face. He'd done that. Somehow even with all his accomplishments, it was making her smile that made it all seem worthwhile. "We still have things to talk about."

She went up on her toes again. "We're going to be okay, you and me. I promise, Josh. Whatever the fallout is from tonight, we can get through it."

He was awkward when he leaned over and kissed her. He was out of practice and too emotional to make up some character in his head. He was nothing more than a man kissing the woman of his dreams and hoping he could be enough for her.

She looked up at him like he'd done something amazing. "It's going to be okay." She turned to her dads and finally ran up to them, hugging both men. "I'm sorry I'm being weird. I'm happy you're here. I can tell you all about Josh. And I can show you all the clothes, Papa. You always said you loved me in yellow. Come inside."

He watched her start to show her dads around.

"Seriously, are you okay?" Jared asked.

He'd fallen for the one woman in the world who could handle his current issue, who he didn't have to protect because she was far deadlier than he could ever think of being.

"I think I am."

She could handle his now, and he wanted her to be his future.

If only she could accept his past.

Chapter Twelve

Kayla stood in front of the door to Josh's bedroom almost two hours later. She wasn't surprised that the lights were out and all was quiet. He'd sat beside her for an hour or so and then kissed her cheek and said he wanted to give her some time alone with her dads.

She kind of thought he'd retreated.

After the day they'd had, she didn't blame him. It felt like the last few weeks had been spent in a perfect snow globe, the types tourists took home to their kids, showing them how gorgeous the world was. They'd been in the bubble, their days and nights moving in perfect tandem, making her forget all that was wrong between them.

Someone had upended their globe today, and she wasn't entirely sure where they'd all landed.

Damn but she wanted to wake him up and figure out what the hell he was doing. After that first strangely awkward and entirely thrilling kiss, she'd settled a bit, trying to tamp down the desperate and sudden need to get her hands on a *Brides* magazine. Before she said yes to the dress, she needed to understand if this was nothing more than Josh's way of chilling her dads out.

Then they would need to go over the definition of chilling out because her papa had been twelve kinds of freaked upon finding out she was involved in some fairly kinky things. Josh's new truth resolution had cost her a very awkward conversation with a man who liked to pretend she was still a virgin, even though he knew she'd lived over a BDSM club. Her dads were great believers in hearing only what they wanted to hear.

"Hey, are you okay?"

She turned and Dad had come out of the bedroom that had been hers until tonight. He closed the door and spoke quietly, as though trying not to wake Papa.

"Yeah. I'm good." Dad was easier to talk to than her papa, perhaps because Dad had been the one who went to work while Papa had stayed home to raise her. Dad seemed more capable of reason when it came to her.

"Are you sure because I know Papa was hard on you," Dad said, adjusting his glasses. He'd changed out of his traveling clothes and into his pajamas and robe. Still, he managed to make it all look very professorial. Forty years in academia had left their mark. "I might have talked to him about what people have historically considered deviant lifestyles. He wasn't trying to be hypocritical."

She blushed. "It's all consensual."

"Oh, baby, I know that. What you do with your partner is all up to the two of you. As long as that man is treating you right, I've got no problem with him. You've got to forgive Papa. I think in some ways he never wanted you to settle down. I think deep down he kept waiting for you to come home and be a proper millennial. He longs for a freeloading child. I told him maybe our grandchildren will need a place to crash someday, and until then he can take away the dog's dignity."

She frowned. "Puddles looks good in a sweater. There's no indignity there."

"That is in the eye of the beholder, my daughter." He glanced over at the door she'd been standing in front of. "How much does he know about your past?"

"Enough to probably get me severely reprimanded," she admitted.

"Does he know about your sister?"

She stopped. "She's classified, Dad. Her life is literally classified."

Her life, her death. Jiang Kun was a ghost lost in the machine. Even MSS believed she was dead, killed in a plane crash.

"A lot about your life back then is classified, but you still talk. I don't blame you. You can't keep secrets and be happy in life."

Her gut tightened because she was keeping a lot of secrets. "I don't know about that. What if you know something that will hurt the person you love, but telling him won't change anything—except to hurt him."

He sighed. "Is this spy stuff?"

"Maybe."

"I rather thought there was more to this than a basic bodyguard job. You're too smart to follow some actor around twenty-four seven. Is the CIA involved?"

There was only so far she could push the classified talking. "Maybe."

"Do you love this man?"

That was the million-dollar question, but she couldn't lie. Not to her dad. "Yeah. He's frustrating and complex and he can go from sulky boy to incredibly kind man. He's complicated."

"I don't know. He sounds pretty human to me," her father said.

That was one of the best compliments her father could give him. Her dad believed in humanity. Why had she thought it was a bad idea to talk to them? She'd thought she would get weak if she opened herself up in that way a daughter only could for her father, but she'd forgotten how much strength she found in the connection. There wasn't an ounce of blood between them, but this man and the one sleeping in the bedroom had created the path of her life, had taught her everything she needed to know about love and living. "He's got something nasty in his past. Something that's still haunting him."

"Again, that sounds awfully human. The man who gets to his age and tells you he isn't damaged either hasn't lived at all or is lying. We're all walking wounded if we've lived at all. I know you are." He reached out and brushed his hand along her cheek, a sweet gesture she remembered from her childhood. "And I know I haven't seen you smile the way you did tonight since that man took you away from us."

"He didn't take me away." They tended to disagree on John Bishop. "I was going to go back to the Agency no matter what

224

happened. I'd already talked to Tennessee Smith about it and he'd agreed to let me join the class."

"Joining the class is not the same as sending a young girl who had barely begun her life into a snake pit."

"There's a lot I haven't told you, but I hope you understand that I did good in there," she said. "Bishop did what he did for this country, this country that took me in. This country that saved me, that let my dads love each other."

His eyes narrowed. "Not for years, and don't start in on the jingoistic anthem, Kayla. This country has a lot of problems."

"Yes, and one of them isn't a full out trade war with China. One of them isn't biological warfare. And yes, I was a part of stopping both of those things. I know we have our problems, but that doesn't mean that we don't do our part. We're struggling right now, but that doesn't make me less of a patriot than I was before. It doesn't make my sacrifice less. It makes it more."

He sighed and leaned over, kissing her on the forehead as he had all those years ago. "I'm an old academic, my baby girl. I never once thought I would raise a warrior. I'll follow your lead when it comes to warfare. So why don't you follow mine when it comes to having a long-lasting and loving relationship? Whatever you're hiding from Josh, tell him before it comes out."

The thought scared her more than she could say. "What if it never comes out? What if he doesn't have to know? What if I can do both?"

He shook his head. "It always comes out in the end. Always. Go get some sleep. Tomorrow we'll take you two out for brunch. You know how your papa loves him some brunch. We'll get out of your hair, Kayla, but don't expect us to stay away for long. If you're living here in California, you better get used to seeing your parents."

For the first time, the thought made her smile. Maybe they weren't hard to talk to about this stuff. Maybe they did understand that she wasn't the same girl she'd been. "I think I can handle that. And thanks for going easy on Josh."

He stepped back. "Oh, that's only because it's late. Tomorrow we're going to have a long talk about historical accuracy in films. And if you want to invite that puppy who lives next door along, don't tell him, but Papa actually does have a little crush on him." He sighed.

225

"I just wish his brains were as developed as his abs."

He turned and disappeared behind the door.

What was she going to do about Josh? She was stuck. If she told him and he walked away, she was risking another agent's life. She'd been that agent. For years she'd been the one who had to rely on others' silence for her continued existence. Was it fair to risk someone's life so she could clear things up with her boyfriend?

It had to wait. If it was strictly about her, she could throw the truth down in a heartbeat. If it was her own life, she could risk that. She would put her faith in Josh.

Did she have the right to risk someone else's?

She eased in the door, trying not to wake him.

"Hey, did everything go okay with your dads?" In the low light from the window above them, she could see him lying on the bed, an arm above his head. He was wearing boxer shorts and nothing else.

"Yeah. It was good." She sat down on the edge of his big bed and started to reach for the lamp on the nightstand.

"Don't turn it on," he said quickly. He took an audible breath. "I would rather do this with the lights off, please."

She felt her whole body stiffen at the words and what she thought they might mean. "Do what? If that was your way of keeping me calm in front of the guests so you could fire me in private, I swear we're going to have trouble, Joshua. You kissed me. You can't kiss me and fire me."

His hand found her arm, tugging her down to the mattress. "No, baby. I'm not going to fire you. I know I should. I know that would be the selfless way to go, but I'm not selfless when it comes to you. I'm a selfish bastard and I can't send you away. Not even for your own sake. That means I have to tell you the truth and give you a chance to leave of your own volition."

She lay down beside him, facing him, their legs brushing against each other. "Will you kiss me first?"

Even in the low light she could see those gorgeous lips curling up in a self-satisfied smile. "You are obsessed with kissing."

"I'm obsessed with you kissing me."

His hand came out, smoothing back her hair. "I'm not good at it. Oh, I'm great on screen, but that's someone else. I have to figure out how I kiss."

"All this time and no personal kissing? How did you learn to do it on screen? And what's the difference?"

"I was nineteen when I made my first movie," he started. "I was supposed to kiss this actress. She was my age and gorgeous. I got sick at the thought of kissing her."

"That must have done a number on her ego."

"Oddly not. Even then Alicia was pretty cool."

"Alicia Kingman?" She was one of the hottest actresses working in Hollywood. "I guess I haven't seen that one."

"It was a small indie film. Anyway, Alicia is a sweetheart as long as you're not involved with her. Great to her friends, a horrible romantic partner, but she asked me if it was girls I was opposed to as a whole or just her. I told her I'd never kissed anyone. At all. And she taught me how to kiss for the screen. It's different. You have to be aware of what it's going to look like. I don't think it's that way when you really kiss someone. I want to put my tongue in your mouth, and I won't give a shit that it doesn't look delicate and romantic. I want to eat you up with no thought past getting inside you and taking you hard so you remember who you belong to."

He said all the right things. "I think you have the principles down pat. Now you simply need to put them into use. You know what they say. Practice makes perfect."

He was quiet for a moment. "You might not want to kiss me after I tell you my story."

She wasn't stupid. She reached out for him in the darkness. "I know someone hurt you when you were young. Maybe more than one person. And I would bet it was sexual abuse, but it doesn't matter. Josh, I will still kiss you. I will kiss you because I'll be grateful you survived. I'll kiss you because I'll want to take away the pain even though I know I can't. I'll kiss you because I think we belong together, you and I."

"Who the fuck are you?" He whispered the question, but there was awe in each word. "Sometimes I'm absolutely sure you're too good to be true."

Before she could answer, his lips were on hers, tentative at first, and then moving with more confidence. She submitted utterly, letting

227

him take his time. He explored her lips, brushing against them over and over until she finally felt his tongue drag along her lower lip. He tasted her slowly, as though trying to find his way. He sucked her bottom lip gently between his teeth, nipping her and sending sparks through her body.

His hands tightened and she was suddenly flush against his body as his dominant nature seemed to take over. One big palm found its way to the back of her head, holding her still as he feasted on her lips. His tongue surged into her mouth, taking over and making her shiver with pure desire.

And then he was done, breaking off the kiss but holding her close to his body.

"I'm not going to tell you everything. I don't want to relive it. I know this sounds weird because I was against sleeping with you, but I want this to be our bed, and it's sacred. I want it to be a place where it's only the two of us and no one else gets in."

A sanctuary. She was already getting emotional. "No one else. Josh, I'm not going to leave you. No matter what words come out of your mouth. You're not in this alone. Not anymore."

He lay back, taking a deep breath before he began.

"I had a fairly decent childhood in the beginning. Then my mom died and my dad dove deep into a bottle. He wasn't the same after. He was so mad. He took it out on his girlfriends. When I was older, he took it out on me. After he went to prison, I went into the system. Some of those homes are quite nice and the people are good. Well, they have good intentions. Life screws things up. I got moved around a couple of times because I was angry and not an easy child even when I wasn't angry."

She reached up in the darkness and smoothed back his hair, hoping touch and affection would make it easier for him to talk. She remained silent because this was his story and he would tell as much or as little as he wanted.

"Then I found myself in the home of a family who lived in a rural part of the county. The social worker told me he thought fresh air would do me some good. They had me and three girls in the house. Except the girls claimed that there had been two more of them at one point and they didn't know where the girls had gone. I didn't think much of it. Kids came and went all the time. I was scrawny and they fed me. Good food. Anything I wanted. The mom always talked about my face and how my face was going to be worth millions one day."

A shiver went through her and she cuddled closer to him. She wished he didn't have to say it, but they needed the words between them. He needed to speak them and she needed to let him know they didn't matter. His past didn't matter.

He sighed as though he'd needed her to breach that small distance. His arm tightened around her. "Then one night a man came. They woke me up and I was told I was supposed to go with him. I remember how late it was, how dark the night was. They told me I had to be quiet because they didn't want to wake the other kids. He was huge. It's funny but I remember him as more of a shadow than an actual man. It wasn't until I got to the car that I realized I wasn't alone. He took me and Hannah Lovell, a girl with long blonde hair. She was quiet and shy. I think she was seven at the time. Maybe eight. They put us in a car and we thought we were going to another foster home. We didn't know we'd been sold."

She put her head on his chest. Every word that came out of his mouth was precise and measured, but his heart was thundering in his chest. "I would like to know the names of everyone involved."

His breath hitched. "I bet you would, baby. I bet that would be a hell of a meeting."

"So it was a human trafficking ring?" She needed to name it, to put that horrible label on what had happened to him.

"They specialized in children," he explained. "They took us out of foster homes. I suspect they said we'd run away. They were careful about who they took. They wouldn't have taken a temporary."

"Temporary?"

"Uhm, like if Mom went to jail and no one else could watch the kid. That kid wouldn't have been a candidate because Mom still gave a shit and could still cause trouble. They wanted true orphans, kids who had no one in the world who wanted them. My dad had signed away his right to me. I had no one. Neither did Hannah."

How terrible it must have been to realize he was alone at such a young age. Not one moment of her life had she known that feeling. She'd been loved from the second she was born. Her mother had loved her so much she'd given her up so she could live. Her fathers had poured their love into her.

Even when she'd been in MSS, she'd known they were there, loving her, wishing she would come home. She'd had Bishop, who'd watched over her while he could, and then Ten. Josh had been a child with no one in the world to love him.

"I fought and got hurt pretty bad. That was when they decided there were people out there who liked a little fight and my life got worse. I learned to submit."

How hard had that been? He was such a dominant male, quiet, but always in control. Had the seeds been planted in the crimes against his younger self, or had his own nature made it worse?

"Josh, this changes nothing. It makes me think no less of you. It makes me think more."

"When I was seventeen, I killed a man. Killing him was the only way I could escape."

"Good. Now I can kill the rest of them." She would make a hobby of it. There could be a list and she would study each of them and torture them in psychologically significant ways before she killed them.

He shifted, rolling on top of her. "I killed someone, Kayla."

He seemed to forget who he was talking to. "I've killed lots of people, Joshua."

"Yeah, well this wasn't sanctioned by the US government."

"It was sanctioned by right, by self-defense," she argued. "Was the man you killed planning on using you in a nonconsensual way?"

"Yes."

She reached up, cupping his face, that gorgeous face that was both heaven and hell for Joshua Hunt. "Then fuck him. Fuck all of them."

"I don't even know where I was held most of the time. When I escaped I was in Ohio. I was so far from home and I didn't know anything. I should have gone to the police, but the man I killed was, well, he was wearing a suit and looked clean, and I wasn't. They always told me if I ever talked to the police, no one would believe me. I would be one more piece of trash trying to find a meal ticket. I ran and hid and prayed they didn't find me. By that time they'd taken

Hannah out of the place I was being held. We were held together for years. They pretended we were siblings. She was the blonde angel and I was the dark-haired devil. She became a lot like a sister to me, but she got badly addicted. I worried she would overdose. I hated not being with her. Heroin was one of the ways they kept us all calm and quiet. I didn't have anyone left to protect so I did what I did. I was utterly lost and that was when Tina found me."

"I'm glad she did." She'd been right. Not a word out of his mouth changed a thing. "This is why you have the children's charity."

"I have to help in some way." He dropped his forehead to hers. "I'm glad you're not running."

She had to smile at that because he was pretty much lying on top of her. She couldn't run if she wanted to, and that was likely somewhere in the back of his head. He caged her, but this was one cage she didn't want to be free of. As long as he stayed in it with her. "I told you I never run away from a good thing."

"You need to know that I am rapidly falling in love with you, so you better mean that," he whispered right above her lips.

"And you remember what I told you," she replied. "You are not alone in this. I'm right there with you."

He kissed her again, this time sweet and brief, and then he rolled off her, cradling her close. "Get undressed and get into bed with me. I want to hold you. I'm tired."

And he'd just talked about the worst moment in his life. He needed pure affection, not sex. She chucked her clothes off and settled in beside him. His body was big and warm.

Thank god for her dads. There was zero chance the evening would have ended like this if they hadn't shown up. She wasn't sure if Josh would have gone through with his threats, but she definitely wouldn't be climbing into bed with him. This wasn't a change for the night. They'd crossed a bridge and there was no going back.

He pulled the covers over them and laid down, his tension palpable. "I've never slept with anyone. Not in years and years. If I have a bad dream…"

"I'll wake you up and we'll deal with it." She laid her head on his chest and breathed him in. He'd taken a shower at some point and smelled clean and fresh and masculine.

"And if I try to hurt you?"

"I'll put you on your ass. Now do you want to know what you get when you sleep with me?" She had the feeling it would be difficult for him to close his eyes, his mind still back in the past.

He chuckled, his lips finding her head. "Besides getting put on my ass?"

"You get a bedtime story." She would give him something else to think about. He had a spectacular imagination. She'd seen some of his ideas for films. If she told him a story, he would see it in his head like a film being exhibited just for him.

He rolled to his side and curled against her. "Excellent. Tell me a story."

"So I was in Singapore," she began. "And my handler was supposed to meet me there."

"Good," he whispered against her ear. "I love the John Bishop stories. He's a badass."

She could feel him relax as she began her tale. "He was indeed. So Bishop was late and I started to worry that I was being watched…"

Before she could even get to the good part—the super-bloody part—he was snoring lightly beside her. She cuddled against him and let herself find some sleep.

Chapter Thirteen

"You're different than I thought you would be," his companion said.

Josh looked up, smiling at the man sitting across from him in a suite at the Chateau Marmont. It was lunchtime and he was meeting with his new consultant, a lovely table of room service between them.

Tyler Williams was a blandly handsome man somewhere in his mid-forties. He was the kind of man who would blend in depending on the clothes he wore. Put him in a suit and he was a cog in the corporate wheel. Give him jeans and a button-down and Josh could see him in front of a computer coding some new software. He could be everyman, someone's dad, someone's happy husband. It was weird to think of this quiet-spoken man as a hardened DEA agent.

Until he started talking, and then the dude knew his shit. It was a little like listening to his Kayla.

His Kayla. Who was back in Malibu, probably showing her dads around town. They were somewhere having brunch together, and damn but he wished he'd been able to go with them. Duty had called. Tyler Williams had made it into town and been willing to meet before he headed to Mexico tomorrow to spend some time with the director. Until Josh got down there next week, this was the only face time he would get with the man.

This was typically the kind of thing Josh lived for. He loved meeting people like Williams and getting under their skin, finding little tics and mannerisms he could use in his characterizations. Sometimes he loved this part of the job as much as the actual acting.

So he should pay attention to Williams instead of thinking of all the dirty things he'd done with his girl this morning.

"I'm not what you expected?" Josh asked. "How so? I've found most people have an opinion of me and it can be hard to counteract that. People tend to see what they want to see."

"Yes, I've found that, too," Williams agreed. "It's human nature to not look much past the surface of what's going on around us. In some ways it's a defense mechanism. If you don't understand what's going on, you don't have to feel bad about not stopping it."

Like a sullen boy being dragged from a car into the house. From the outside, it would have looked like nothing more than a harried parent trying to deal with his demon spawn of a child.

No one wanted to see what had happened to him. How would they handle the mere fact that it *had* happened to him? Should he show his true self or let the world believe he was nothing more than blessed with a pretty face and the right ties to the business? "So what's under my surface?"

Williams sat back, an iced tea in his hand. "You smile more than I thought you would. I've done some research on you in the last couple of weeks. You're a very serious man. You don't tend to come off as this friendly in interviews."

He winced. He was going to have to work on his reputation. "I might have some issues with reporters. It's hard to be open around them when they can use anything you say against you. Though I have to admit you're not who I thought you would be either. Tough as nails DEA agents don't typically order tofu burgers."

A brilliant smile crossed the man's face. "Oh, they would if they had my cholesterol. And my wife's love for all things with a face."

"That's a lot to do for love." Thank god Kay was a carnivore.

"I'd rather face down a mountain of tofu than a single reporter," Williams admitted. "I've always been very private. It would bug me."

"Oh, it bugs me. It bugs me every day, all the time. It's why I don't talk about myself a lot, and it's probably why I don't smile. Not that I'm some happy-go-lucky guy. Never have been. My girlfriend would say I'm a brooder. I can be a little paranoid, but I'm in a good relationship right now. It kind of changes the way you look at things. I guess it's kind of my first good relationship."

It was absolutely the first time in his life he trusted a woman he was sleeping with. He'd trusted Tina, but that had been a different kind of relationship. This was full-on, musical-worthy romance. And he was the dipshit almost ready to break into song. Of course, the song would be about blackmail and human trafficking, so it would be on the dark side, but Kay could handle it.

The man seated across from him smiled, showing even white teeth and a single dimple in his left cheek. "There's nothing a good woman can't fix. I've learned that myself. Well, nothing inside a man she can't fix. There's plenty of stuff we fuck up ourselves that need fixing."

"Amen, brother." He still had to deal with the blackmail, but he had some time. His lady blackmailer would back off for a while. He had three months before he had to make a decision. Three months to talk it all over with Kay and decide what to do. When they got back from Mexico they would sit down with a crisis management publicist and a lawyer and talk everything out. "My girl might not be able to fix everything, but she makes it seem possible, if you know what I mean. Things that before were impossible problems seem a little simpler to solve."

"I do indeed," Williams replied. "I married a lovely woman. She fixed a lot of my problems simply by loving me, but things from the past creep up. Especially in my business. You make some tough calls out in the field and you have to live with them."

They'd gone over a few of Williams's issues with the script, some procedural flubs the screenwriter had made and some language Williams thought the fictional DEA agent would use. Williams had been open about all aspects of working for the government—some good and some bad. He was an easy man to talk to. "You have many of those regrets?"

For a moment Williams's eyes seemed to darken, and that was the moment where Josh could see the agent he'd been. Dark. Ruthless. Capable of getting the job done. "Oh, yes. I made a lot of calls in the field. I stand by most of them. I made them for the right reasons at the time. When you're out in the field you have to go with a combination of the intelligence you have in front of you and what you feel in your gut. Sometimes your gut is far more important and then sometimes you ignore your gut because the setup in front of you is too perfect to pass up. That's the worst thing you can do."

He was completely fascinated by this man. He didn't even fully understand why, but there was a rich character arc flowing through Tyler Williams's seemingly normal veins. Josh could see how interesting it would be to dive into the man's psyche. "At the time? Are you saying you wouldn't do the same thing now?"

"I'm saying I'm a different person now," Williams corrected. "The person I am today does not make the same calls, but I understand his reasoning. And honestly, I don't know that the person I am now would be better at his job than the person I was. It's the difference between youth and wisdom, though sometimes wisdom never comes to some. As I've aged and seen the world from a different light, my priorities have changed. But for the purposes of this script, I can explain things from my old self's point of view."

"How did you get into the DEA?"

"I went into the military straight out of high school," Williams explained. "It was the only way I could get into college. No money. No family. I was good at being a soldier. I enjoyed the discipline of the lifestyle. After, I found myself recruited by the government. I worked for them for a good decade and then left to pursue other opportunities. It's funny but when I joined up, it seemed like an inevitable thing. I had a brutal childhood and I went into a rather brutal business. It was what I knew. Sometimes we take the road we know simply because we don't think to look for off-ramps. We have blinders on, and even a violent world can seem normal and comfortable while you're inside it. Being able to see through another's eyes, to understand that there are other worlds out there, that's the true mark of maturity."

"Are you sure you're not a shrink?"

Williams chuckled. "Just a guy who's seen a lot. I'm worried about you."

That was a surprise. "About me? Why?"

Williams's face went grave. "I'm not going to beat around the bush, Joshua, and I hope you'll do me the courtesy of being open and honest with me. There's a reason I wanted to meet with you before we get on set. I'm no longer in law enforcement so your answer to this question is merely for my own intelligence and will not leave this room."

Shit. What the hell was going on? He'd been a little surprised the guy had insisted on meeting in his hotel room when Josh had offered to take him out to lunch. Had the ex-agent brought him here because he'd found out about Josh's previous use? He found himself tightening up for the first time that day. Damn. He hadn't realized how much of his life was spent tense and waiting for the other shoe to fall. "All right. Ask away."

A sad smile crossed Williams's face. "I mean what I say. I don't care how you answer this question. I simply need to get a lay of the land. And if you're in trouble, you might talk to me about it."

"Trouble?"

"Joshua, are you planning on seeing Hector Morales while you're filming in Mexico?"

"Of course. He's a friend of mine." That was overstating things. "Friend is probably not the right word. He's an acquaintance who's been extremely good to my charity over the years. I've spent some time at his place before."

Williams's sharp eyes narrowed on him and Josh was reminded of a hawk looking for dinner. "You've been to the compound?"

"I would call it a mansion. Compound has a weird connotation." A working connotation. A compound was where cults lived and militaries trained. It wasn't a good name for Hector's gorgeous manor house.

"Are you aware that Hector Morales goes by another name? Have ever heard the name *El Comandante*?"

He suddenly felt like he was being interrogated. Which was ridiculous. He glanced around the room. Was this some kind of setup? Were there cameras on him? "If this is a joke, I don't think it's a terrifically funny one."

Williams stood up and went to his small laptop bag. He pulled out a folder and came back to the table. "Hector Morales runs one of the largest drug cartels in the world. You wouldn't know that unless he told you and you're a part of his inner circle or you're a member of elite law enforcement or intelligence. The file I'm about to show you is highly classified."

Definitely a joke. "Okay, now it's kind of funny. This is Kay's doing. She knows I love the classified stuff."

Williams looked grim as he placed the folder in front of him. "Is that your woman? Kay is a nice name. You should be careful about taking her into dangerous places."

He opened the folder and it took everything Josh had not to jump back. Blood. That was Hector, but not the way he'd seen him before. Not a smiling businessman in tailored suits. This was a snarling animal, watching over a group of bloody men.

"The men with the guns to their heads were two of his lieutenants. Unfortunately, they had large shipments confiscated by the DEA shortly after they were smuggled over the border. You don't get a second chance with the Jalisco Cartel."

"Are they dead?" A stupid question.

"Oh, yes. In my estimation, Morales has had over two hundred people murdered or assassinated. He's killed members of his cartel, civilians who threatened him, several members of US intelligence, and I won't go into how many Mexican law enforcement officers he's had murdered because they were trying to do their jobs. He specializes in opioids. By some reports he's responsible for about half of the illegal opioids smuggled into the US in the last five years. We believe he took on some new partners who have aided in his business, people who helped him get around the DEA and local law enforcement. One of those partners…well, do you remember when I told you I'd made mistakes? She's one of my mistakes."

"Why are you telling me all of this?" He closed the folder. He didn't need to see anything more. This man was a DEA agent. He would know who the drug dealers were.

"I'm telling you because I think you should cancel your trip out to his place. Over the years, I've learned to trust my instincts, and something isn't right. I wish you could stay out of Mexico entirely, but I get that you're filming. Are you supposed to visit him at the end or beginning of the shoot?"

His head was reeling. How could he have not seen what that man was capable of? He prided himself on being able to see through the masks people wore, but Hector had fooled him entirely.

Was that why Hector always insisted on staying out of the spotlight? Josh had thought it was refreshing to have a person who wasn't interested in being in the tabloids, who didn't want to take pictures with the Hollywood actor. For Josh, that meant Hector was real, authentic.

Hector was a criminal who was somehow using him. But how? Why start up a friendship with him and lie about everything?

"Josh? I know this is hard," Williams was saying.

He shook his head. "I don't understand why he would lie."

"I'd like to find that out, too," Williams explained. "I've been out of the game for a few years, but I have some worries that this isn't about you, though you're being used."

"Used to what purpose?"

Williams's mouth closed.

"What? It's classified?" Now the man clammed up on him?

Williams sighed. "It's better we leave it here. The truth is I'm not sure what's going on and who's involved. Some of these people could be very dangerous and it's best you don't get in too deep. In this case, the less you know the better off you'll be. I'll be down there with you and I'll take a look around, talk to some old contacts. When I can, I'll let you know what's going on. And until then, I definitely think if you care about that woman you talked about, keep her far away from that place."

He took a deep breath. This was good. It was good that he knew what his "friend" was capable of. And yes, it was good that he now knew not to take Kayla into that compound. No matter how badass she was, she was still human, and she would be outnumbered and outgunned and moving into a situation neither one of them understood. Hell, just the fact that she used to be CIA could get her killed at that compound.

"I might leave her here altogether." He could take Shane and Declan with him. "I'm scheduled to go out to Hector's place at the beginning of the shoot, but things can go awry with a shoot like this. It will be fairly easy to tell him I can't come until later and then fly out early. I can keep the set closed and if he shows up, I'll act like nothing's out of the ordinary."

"You think you can handle that?"

"I know I can. I'm actually quite good at my job." It would be convincing Kay that it was best she stay behind that would be the real task at hand. He wouldn't be good at that, but he had to make it work.

Her life depended on it.

* * * *

Kayla walked along the beach, her feet sinking in the sand. The tide rushed in, covering her ankles with Pacific Ocean water. The water was a chilly tickle to her skin in direct contrast to the heat of the sun on the rest of her body. Oh, this was her home. This was where she felt healthy and whole, and she'd avoided it for so long because… Well, she was certain Ariel would tell her she hadn't felt worthy of being healthy and whole.

Maybe she was finally coming out of it, finally processing that she was here in the real world and she'd done her duty. She was ready to move on and find a real life.

With Josh.

She glanced down the beach and the one thing that could trip her up was striding her way.

"You know you're dressed for the part of the beachcombing tourist, but no one will buy it because your shoulders are around your ears. What's going on, Ezra?"

She'd watched him as he walked up the beach. He was in a pair of board shorts and a T-shirt, showing off toned arms and his muscular body. A pair of aviators completed the laid-back look, but unlike all the people around him who were enjoying a low-tide stroll, there was nothing at all relaxed about Ezra Fain. He'd walked onto the beach with one purpose, and it wasn't looking for seashells.

"We need to talk."

"Yes, I rather thought you covered that with your text. You know according to the contract I signed, Josh has the right to check my phone. I don't know how much he's going to like some random number sending me gibberish."

"I don't care. I want to know what happened last night," Fain demanded.

She sighed. She should have expected this. "I'm sorry I haven't sent a report in. It's been crazy around here. My dads showed up and they do not take no for an answer when it comes to brunch. I had to do some fast talking to get them to go home. As it is, I promised we would visit when we get back from Mexico. Let's walk a little bit. I've got a serious food baby going on, and if the press gets a pic, then all the real baby rumors will start up."

"You know you're falling way too deep into this role. We? You mean you and Josh, right? Your op is over when you leave Mexico."

"It doesn't have to be." She knew he wasn't going to be on board with her plan, but he should probably know what she intended to do. "I've been thinking about it and it kind of makes sense for me to stay on for a while. It would look weird if I up and quit right after a shoot. He still needs protection and McKay-Taggart can provide it. I'll simply shift from the Agency's priorities to my company's."

"God, Levi is right. You're in love with him."

"My feelings for Josh will not compromise this op. I promise you that. I know how important this is."

"You think I'm only worried about the op?" He put his hands on his hips and did an excellent impersonation of an annoyed older brother. "Did you or did you not nearly get murdered last night? What the hell was that about? Because according to Riley, you did. Not only did you nearly get killed, but he was worried about sending you off alone with the man. He said Josh had shown no signs at all of any fear or emotion other than anger at the two of you."

"Riley doesn't know him very well." She glanced up and Shane was standing on the balcony.

Shane cupped his hands and shouted down. "You've only got about fifteen minutes. Dec says they're on their way back now and Josh wants to talk to you."

She gave him a thumbs-up to let him know she'd heard him and then started down the beach toward the rocks in the distance.

Ezra strode along beside her. "All right. Tell me what happened from your point of view."

A lot had happened. "Josh tried to go rogue. Riley and I followed him. Lucky for us Levi told Riley when and where the thing was going down or Josh would have lost us. He wasn't playing around. He knew how to ensure we couldn't follow him. Not that he knows his plan worked."

And that fact started the guilt building up in her gut.

He'd told her his truth and she was lying. She was lying for a good reason, but she was still lying.

"Yes, but from what Levi told me we're no closer than we were before to figuring out if that drop was to Hector Morales. All Riley could tell us was they were well armed and ready for the two of you when you went in after the target. He said the three of you got separated."

"Josh twisted his ankle."

"He's moving around fine today," Ezra pointed out.

"No, he just looks that way. Josh is good at hiding the pain. He's sore, but he's able to walk because he got off of it pretty fast. And like I said, Riley can't read him the way I can."

"You haven't answered my question," Ezra insisted.

"Yes and no. Yes, I did find myself in a cozy situation with his blackmailer last night. No, she didn't nearly kill me."

He stopped. "Blackmail?"

Shit. She'd known she was going to have to give the Agency something. There was no way anyone believed she hadn't discovered at least some of the facts. "Yes, he's being blackmailed."

"Over?"

She was silent for a moment. "I don't know."

He gently gripped her elbow, pulling her around so he could look at her. "You're lying. He told you. I need to know."

She shook her head. "You don't. It has nothing to do with Hector Morales. It's not the Agency's business."

"And if I told you I thought you were wrong?"

"I would want an explanation."

He let go of her and started to pace, his bare feet moving over the sand. "When did the blackmail start?"

"About five years ago."

He pointed her way as though she'd made some point. "Yes, about five years ago, and that's also when the Jalisco Cartel started to come into its own. Up until five years ago, they were a subsidiary of a Colombian cartel, think of it as the Mexican arm of a company. And they specialized in something other than drugs. After that cartel's head was literally cut off, Morales rose up and took over their drug distribution. He filled the void, but he also took over a lot of the old head's men. Five years was also the first time Hector Morales sent a contribution to Hunt's charity."

She was getting this history lesson why? They were going in to see what happened to their operative. How did Joshua's problems fit in? "What does any of this have to do with the blackmail?"

"Everything started happening at roughly the same time. I don't like it."

"You can not like it and it can still be coincidence. Things happened and they're not always some grand conspiracy." She wasn't seeing how the facts lined up. "Josh was already a big star then."

"Yes, that's my point. Why had this blackmailer waited? Unless you tell me this is about something he's done recently and this is not about those lost years of his youth."

"I can't tell you that." She wouldn't break Josh's trust, but she also wasn't going to blatantly lie to Ezra. He would know if she was lying. But there was something about the way he was talking that made her wonder if he hadn't already figured it out.

"All right, if this is some secret that's been out there for a long time, why not come forward five years ago?"

"There could be any number of reasons," she replied. "She could have been in prison and unable to reach him. She could have waited until he had the money to give her a big payday. Now that I think about it, it makes more sense that they waited until Josh had something to lose. She wouldn't have wanted the information to come out before he had the assets to give her what she wanted."

"You keep calling her a she. Are you sure?" Ezra asked.

"I can't possibly be sure that the woman who met with me last night is the mastermind behind the blackmail scheme. She could be working for someone else, but Josh thinks it's been the same woman all along. She hides her voice, but I do think whoever was around me last night was female."

Ezra stopped and let his head fall back for a moment. Frustration was evident in every muscle of his body. "This is all wrong. I feel it. I want to pull you out now."

There was no way she let that happen. "You can't because I'll quit. I'll quit and I'll stay with Josh. You might as well allow me to do the job you hired me for because I'm not leaving him."

He pulled his sunglasses off his face, his blue eyes fierce with intensity. "You damn straight will if I tell Dec and Shane to fucking carry you out of here."

She stared at the agent, well aware that he was simply worried about her. Still, there was the alpha female part of her that wasn't about to take that shit from anyone. "No. I won't. I'll just make Dec and Shane wish they hadn't been born male."

"I can call Big Tag and Knight and explain to them that you're in over your head and you're going to get hurt," he continued. "They'll see things my way."

"And I'll quit and stay here with Josh and have no one to watch my back." She had him in check and she knew it. He knew it.

He was quiet for a moment and she could practically see every wheel in that big brain of his working.

She needed to calm him down and see reason. "Tell me what you're really worried about. It's not me dealing with Morales. You know I can handle him."

"Don't underestimate Morales. He's a killer."

"And I've dealt with men like him," she assured the agent. "Many men like him over my years of service. It's the joy of being a five-foot-three-inch chick. They underestimate me. Always. They see a piece of arm candy and don't bother to look past the surface."

"I don't know. I'm worried that *we're* not seeing past the surface. I'm worried we're seeing exactly what they want us to see and that's going to get you killed," he replied.

"All right. You obviously have a theory. Let's hear it."

"What else happened five years ago, Kayla? It's all in the history. That's what I think. Before five years ago, the Jalisco Cartel was small. They ran some drugs, but mostly they did the bidding of a Colombian cartel, one of the biggest. Then something happened and shortly thereafter, Morales's cartel took over and started getting damn lucky with the DEA. They started getting lucky by avoiding raids on their properties both in Mexico and the States. Did you know that years before, when Morales's father ran the organization, I heard about a case involving human trafficking and drug cartels? One of the cartels was involved in a slavery ring that ran from South America up to Canada and all through the Midwestern US."

A chill went over her skin. "The Jalisco Cartel was responsible for that?"

"Yes. Before they took over the Colombian drug routes, that was what Morales was suspected of running. Prostitutes. And he didn't care about age. They talked about it in the Agency because all the files went missing. This all went down shortly after the operative working on the case was blown up in his car. Kayla…"

She shook her head, utterly denying every word that came out of his mouth. "It wasn't John Bishop. It wasn't. You didn't know him. Call Big Tag. Call Ten. They'll tell you that John Bishop wasn't capable of doing the things you're accusing him of."

"John Bishop was known as the Ice Man, and he didn't get that reputation by being warm and fuzzy. It was Bishop's faking his own death that started all of this. I know it. That was the trigger that led to the Jalisco Cartel taking off and putting Morales into the position he's in now."

"No. Okay, maybe, but it can't mean what you think. Maybe John Bishop leaving the case led to that, but Bishop didn't leave so he could help Morales build the cartel. No way. According to your own records, he's been in Colorado."

Ezra's head nodded tightly, as though her very words proved his point. "Yes, and I've studied that town. Did you know there are two ex-DEA agents who live in town? I find that highly suspicious. They would have contacts with their former coworkers. It would be easy for them to feed Bishop information about where and when their buddies were going to raid. They could all be in on this. It all fits."

"But it doesn't," she argued. "I know you're looking at this puzzle and seeing how the pieces fit, but you don't understand how the most important piece works. John Bishop would never hurt his country. He's capable of some deeply ruthless shit. You want to tell me he's sent an agent into situations he knew the agent could die in, I'll believe that. I was that agent. He did it because I was his asset and he was the spy master. I signed on knowing that could happen, and I knew damn well Bishop might have to make a call that ended with me getting hurt or dying. It's part of the risk we take when we take the job. You've done it, too."

"Not the way that bastard did," Ezra shot back. "Don't you put me in the same folder as him. I would never have sent a college student into fucking MSS. I've read his files, well, the ones that aren't redacted. He's beyond ruthless."

"But he wasn't a criminal. And you know what, he never let me down while I was on the inside. I knew what I was doing. If he hadn't offered me the job, I would have found a way to make my sister's death meaningful. I would have gone after someone, and it likely wouldn't have ended well. I know he saw that fire in me that night."

"He left you inside when he ditched the Agency."

"No, he handed me off to Ten, who took care of me, too." She took a deep breath. "Look, this is easy. Let's get him on the phone. I can talk to him."

"He's gone. Disappeared a couple of days ago," Ezra explained. "Well, we think he's disappeared. His so-called wife says he's out on something called a nature walk, and she doesn't expect him back until he's rethought his life choices. No one in town will say anything else. I don't believe her. He's not out on some fucking nature hike. I think he's on the run. I wouldn't be surprised if he's in Mexico right now."

She couldn't help but think about the smile on his face in that picture. No. If he was in the wind, he had a reason for it. "I can't believe that John Bishop has spent the last five years as the mastermind behind a cartel."

"Someone is," Ezra said. "Someone is working with Morales, and I don't like the connection between Morales and Joshua Hunt. And I'm starting to worry that we're being led down a path we don't want to go down. I don't like this. Any of it. I don't like Levi. I think he's in on this with Bishop."

A chill went down her spine. "That's a hefty accusation, Ezra. Do you have any evidence to back it up?"

"Nothing but the feeling that this is a trap of some kind. Someone is working against me back in DC. The files I request go missing or the exact information I need has been redacted. I'm being blocked.

And it's not just in DC. You know that nasty feeling you get in your gut when you know someone's watching?"

She'd felt it. God, she'd felt it over the last couple of days several times, but she couldn't be sure if that wasn't about the fact that the press stalked Josh like an animal. "I do, but we've got an op to run and we don't get to cancel it because we feel like something's off. We have to figure it out. If Levi is working some angle, it's up to us to find out and take him down."

"And if that angle leads to Bishop?"

She couldn't quite bring herself to even contemplate that path. "Do we even know if they ever met? Levi hasn't been around as long as the rest of us."

"He's been around long enough, and I know Morales and Bishop have to have a partner on the outside. Perhaps several."

There was a whole bunch that didn't make sense to her. "But what would be the purpose of this op? Why would he want the two of us in a particular place at this particular time? Why bring us into this at all? I would think it would make more sense for them to want to keep us as far away as possible. Do you think he made up an agent in trouble? Or was that a mistake?"

"No, not even he could make up some phantom operative. Our plant *is* gone. Unless, of course, he's in on it, too."

She put her hands on his shoulders. "Ezra, when this is over, I need you to take a vacation and think about getting the fuck out. You sound paranoid. It's not good for you."

"It's not paranoia if everyone really is out to get you," he said quietly. "I can't talk you out of going?"

She shook her head. "No. I can't let Josh walk into this alone, and I do not for a second believe that he's involved in any criminal way. Josh is innocent. And if Bishop *is* involved, well, I probably know him better than anyone but Ian and Ten. Certainly better than anyone on this particular team."

His shoulders slumped, obviously giving up the fight. "All right. I'm supposed to head back to DC in the morning and coordinate from there. Levi is your contact while in Mexico, but I'm going to shadow you. I won't be far behind. I promise."

"I don't think that's a good idea." There was no question in her mind that it was time for Ezra Fain to look for different opportunities. Maybe he could join McKay-Taggart since they were definitely in a hiring phase after losing several experienced agents to a new firm started up by Adam Miles and Chelsea Weston, but she was worried with how he would go out. "Levi said something about you being on thin ice. Do you want to get burned?"

"Chelsea can cover my tracks," he assured her.

"And if you get caught?" It was a dangerous game to go directly against orders.

"I don't know that I care anymore." He stared off into the distance. "I don't think I care about much of anything anymore. None of it matters, you know what I mean?"

She would have to disagree since he'd been arguing with her over her safety for the last twenty minutes. "Let's get through this and then when we get back, we'll talk about your options. You've done your time, Ez. Maybe it's time to take the off-ramp. I know you don't like him, but that's what Bishop always told me. He said if I saw a way out, I should take it."

He sighed, a weary sound. "And take what road, Kay? This has been my life for years. My entire adult life has been about the Agency. I don't know much else, and I fear I'm not doing any good here now. When I was in the field, taking out terrorists or gathering intel on potential attacks, that was pure. What I do now…well, let's just say there's a lot of gray in what I do now. This job is my whole life. My brother's gone. He was my only family. I've only ever truly cared about one woman and she's a Taggart now."

Mia Lawless Taggart. Her heart ached for him, but she couldn't believe there wasn't someone else out there who could ease his soul. She'd found hers. "I didn't think I would ever feel about anyone the way I feel about Josh. You can't give up on the rest of your life. You're in your thirties. You've got a lot ahead of you."

"Yeah, that's what scares me. All that time and nothing good to fill it." He turned away from her. "If I can contact you once you get to Mexico, I will. Be careful, Kayla. Watch your back. I wouldn't trust anyone except your boys, and I don't include Josh in that. You don't know enough about him. I would hate to see an operative like you go down over a guy."

He walked away without looking back, and Kayla was left with a chill despite the hot California sun.

She stared out over the ocean, praying she was right and Ezra was wrong.

Her cell buzzed and when she looked down it was Josh.

Come home, beach babe. We need to talk.

There was a heart emoji after the message.

She smiled. She had to be right because this feeling was everything.

She would fight to the end for it.

Chapter Fourteen

Josh stood on the balcony, watching her. He could see her standing and staring out at the ocean. A man was walking down the beach, but Josh hadn't seen if he'd stopped to talk to Kayla. Not that he would blame the dude. He would hit on her, too, if she wasn't already his.

Oddly, the idea of men hitting on her didn't bother him the way it probably should. Not as long as they were respectful and took her *no* with politeness.

Because she would tell them all no. She was his. His girlfriend. His sub. He got that now.

She didn't watch the man as he walked away from her. Her eyes were out on the ocean. She loved it here as much as he did.

They could build a life here if he was brave enough to. She'd heard his story. She wasn't leaving him.

All the things Tyler Williams had said came back and made his stomach churn. He couldn't risk her. Oh, he knew damn well he was in for a fight, but he couldn't make the choice to put her in danger. He pulled his phone out and texted her. Complete with a heart emoji. Jeez, he was turning soft. Going all kinds of soft for a girl.

It was kind of cool.

He watched as she pulled her phone out and that smile on her face was fucking everything. She didn't wait. She turned immediately and started coming home.

Because she wanted to be here with him. Because him asking her to come home was meaningful to her.

He smiled as she picked up the pace.

"Her dads are awesome, man," a familiar voice said. "I hate that you missed brunch this morning. How did it go with your expert?"

He glanced over and Jared was lying on a lounger on his balcony, soaking up some sun. "He was a smart man. You know I like to listen to the experts." Kay was still a couple of minutes away. She would have to wash off her feet at the base of the house. "I kind of got the feeling the dads didn't approve of actors."

He couldn't necessarily blame them. If he had a daughter as smart and funny and capable as Kayla, he wouldn't want some dumbass actor who showed off his abs to the world coming and whisking his baby girl away.

What would Kay's daughter look like? Would she come out of the womb with ninja skills?

Why didn't the idea of potentially, someday in the future, maybe having a kid with her scare the holy crap out of him? Why did it kind of make him happy?

Because he was going so fucking soft.

"They totally warmed up to me," Jared replied with a grin. "Papa Fred was absolutely impressed with how many pull-ups I can do."

Yeah, Josh bet he was. He was going to have to make a better impression on those two men if he wanted his family life to run properly. It would be weird to have parents around—even if they weren't his own. He hadn't really known his own. Nothing except his father's fists. "Well, I expect they'll be around a lot."

"Do you think the other dude will be around, too? Is he like an adoptive brother or something?"

"What? Who are you talking about?"

Jared stood up and waved a hand down the beach. "The dude who talks to Kay a lot. I've seen her with him probably three times over the last couple of weeks. At first I thought he was hitting on her, but they seem friendly. Not like friendly friendly, but like family friendly. She rolls her eyes at him the same way my brother does with me. You know, the dumbass look."

"Who are you talking about?"

Jared pointed. "The guy who just walked by. Like I said, at first I thought he was a new neighbor or something, but according to a realtor I know, no one's sold recently. They tend to meet down by the big rocks. Okay, I know I suck, but I've got some binoculars up here and I've watched them. They're def not hooking up on the down low. I think she finds him annoying most of the time."

Something nasty rolled in his gut, but he shoved that shit down. He wasn't doing this to her again. "I'm sure there's an explanation. Kay wouldn't cheat on me."

"I didn't think she was." Jared winced. "Shit. I shouldn't have said anything."

"It's cool. I'll ask her about it." Reasonably. Calmly.

Before Jared could say another word, he turned and found himself walking out of the house, going down the stairs to find her. She was at the base of the stairs, washing her feet off in the faucet he had there.

"You know even your feet are gorgeous," he said, sitting down on one of the stairs.

Her lips curled up in the sweetest smile. "I try. I know you love a pretty foot, weirdo."

This was what he loved about them. Them. She teased him in a way no one else would, in a way he likely wouldn't tolerate from anyone else. He was self-aware enough to get that. He hoped they could joke their way through the next couple of minutes. They definitely needed to do this alone. He glanced behind him and sure enough, Shane was standing at the top of the staircase. "Could we have a couple of minutes, Shane?"

Kay grinned the bodyguard's way. "I can protect him. There's also a seal out here I cut a deal with. The two of us will take down any sea gull that tries to nest in that hair of his."

He laughed because he could actually see her trying that. Shane nodded and left them alone. Josh turned to Kay, getting serious. "Who's the guy you were talking to?"

She didn't miss a beat. There was no fluctuation on her face, no shock. "The one I was talking to just now?"

He nodded. "Jared says he's seen you talking to him a couple of times. Is he bugging you?"

See reasonable. Logical. She deserved that. She'd done not a damn thing to make him think she would cheat on him. She wasn't other women. She was Kay. She was his.

"Not at all. He's staying at an Airbnb somewhere down the beach with his boyfriend. The boyfriend isn't very nature oriented. Honestly, I don't think that relationship is going to work out. Do you want to meet him? He's nice."

He held a hand out. When she took it, he pulled her onto his lap and sighed with pleasure. "No. Sorry, baby. Jared mentioned it. I thought I would ask."

She settled against him. "It's okay. I'm an open book. How was your lunch?"

Shit. He didn't want to mess this up, but he had to. Williams had made sense. "It was enlightening. I'm not smart when it comes to reading people. I think I am. I guess everyone does, but this afternoon proved to me that I'm an idiot."

She shifted so she could look him in the eyes. "Why would you say that?"

He hated admitting how stupid he'd been. "According to the DEA guy, my friend Hector is the head of a cartel. Like a big one. I've been to dinner with the guy and he's murdered hundreds of people."

Her eyes widened. "Are you serious?"

"Have you ever heard of the Jalisco Cartel? According to Williams, he's the head of the cartel. I have to believe him. He's former DEA. If he doesn't know, who would?"

"What was his name again?"

"Tyler Williams. Seems like a good man. Definitely knows his stuff."

"Wow. I didn't expect that."

He kissed her cheek. "Neither did I. That's why I've decided to completely cut ties with the man. I won't be seeing him while I'm on the shoot in Mexico."

"Are you sure this guy is right about this?" Kay asked. Her body had gone still. "Maybe I should try to look into it. It wouldn't be the first time someone got accused of some crime he didn't commit. Up until now he's been perfectly good to you, right?"

Suspicion played along his spine. Something wasn't right here. "I saw pictures."

"Pictures can be doctored." She wiggled off his lap. "I'll get my team on it. I would hate for you to lose that contribution because some ex-DEA agent has a thing against a businessman. You know some of them are totally paranoid. I should know. I could tell you stories about crazy damn CIA agents. They spend so much time dealing with conspiracies that they start to see them everywhere."

He was surprised at her reaction. "The charity can handle it. I'll do another fundraiser and more than make up for it. I think the cautious thing to do is to believe the man who put his life on the line and stay away from Morales. I'm going to explain that my schedule has changed and I can't make it out to his place this time. I'll ignore his calls from now on and it will be fine."

One brow rose over her eyes. "You're going to ghost a drug lord?"

"I thought you weren't sure he was a drug lord." This was starting to feel like an argument, but not the one he'd expected.

"I don't know," she shot back. "That's the point. You're listening to some guy I've never even met. You're allowing him to manipulate you."

"Manipulate? I'm allowing him to make me rethink two days of my life. I'm rethinking going to a party. I don't think that's some grand manipulation. Why is this important to you?"

"I don't like someone playing you."

He shook his head. This was insane. "Baby, it's not a big deal. Here's what I'm going to do. I'm heading down to the set in two days. I'm going to get my work done as quickly as possible and I'll be home with you before you know it. You can stay here or go have a nice visit with your dads. Hell, invite them back here. I won't be gone more than a week."

"What? You're going there by yourself?"

Now this was the fight he'd expected. He'd prepared for this fight. The whole time he'd been driving home, he'd come up with a plan to make her feel better about it. "Not at all. I'll take Shane and Dec with me. If you think I need someone else, I'll hire a third guard so I'm never without two. I have no intention of doing something foolish. I have you to think about now. I want to come home whole, believe me."

She shook her head, her eyes clouded with disbelief. "You can't leave me behind. We've planned for this trip. Why would you ditch me?"

"No. I am absolutely not ditching you. I'm worried about you." He reached out for her hands, holding them between his own. "Baby, have you thought about what a man like Morales would do to you if he even caught a hint of your background? I can't risk you. Come on. Let's go upstairs and we can talk some more. I know you're freaked out that you're not going with me, but let's bring Shane and Dec in on the discussion and make some…what do you call those…protocols for me to follow. I'll do everything by the book. I don't want you worrying."

She seemed to lose color, her shoulders slumping as though something terrible went through her head. "We can't go inside and talk."

"Why? I think we'll be way happier in the kitchen than bringing those two bruisers out here. I don't even think Dec can fit on the stairs. He's a big dude." He tugged her close. "It's going to be all right. I'm not going anywhere until you're comfortable with this."

"Why? Why do you have to be reasonable now?" She pulled her hands out of his, the first sign that something was seriously wrong with this scenario.

Kay always touched him. It was one of the things he loved about her. She was so touchy-feely and he'd never realized how starved for affection he was until she'd given him some. Now he craved it, craved her hands on him even when it wasn't particularly sexual. He would have said he was a solitary being. After everything he'd gone through, he didn't like to be touched, but it was different with her. Everything was different with her. It was like she'd walked in and flipped a switch he hadn't known he had—the one where he was a good boyfriend, one where he was capable of giving and receiving affection and yes, where he was capable of love.

"I thought you wanted me reasonable." What the hell was going on? There was a little voice in the back of his head saying stop. *Don't go any further. This is where it all falls apart.* It was time to distance and save himself. He wasn't going to listen to that voice. "I'm trying to be a better Dom for you. That's stupid. We've gone far beyond the D/s boundaries. We both know I mean boyfriend looking for something more. Kay, I'm insanely crazy about you."

She bit her bottom lip and looked so forlorn, he wanted to draw her back in, cuddle her until she smiled for him again. "And I'm crazy about you, but I don't know if you're going to believe me five minutes from now. Do you know what I want to do, Joshua?"

"What?" He would do almost anything. He simply couldn't willingly put her in the line of fire.

"I want to start the day again and this time I won't let you go. I'll keep you in bed with me and everything and everyone else can go straight to hell." She turned and looked at him. "Will you get in a car with me and run away? We don't need anything. We can start driving and not look back."

Now she was scaring him. "What are you talking about? There's a hundred-million-dollar movie relying on me right now. Also, we wouldn't get far. No matter where we go someone will recognize me. You want to tell me what's going on and why you went pale? Let's go upstairs and get a drink."

"We can't go and talk in your house because it's wired for sound and the Agency is listening to every word you've said inside there." She spit the words out like she was worried if she didn't she wouldn't be able to say them at all.

He felt the world go still, everything slowing to a terrible stop as her words hit him. It was rather like watching an accident. He could see himself sitting there as though he was outside his body, watch as the words changed him. From here he looked calm, as though nothing had processed yet.

He shook his head, utterly dumbstruck. "Why would the Agency listen to me?"

"Because Hector Morales has one of their operatives and they need your access to his home in order to find out what happened to him. Or rather they need me to use your access to his home to find out what happened to him." All the words were said calmly, each one making perfect sense, and yet that wasn't what he heard.

I lied to you.

I used you.

I let the wolves into the only place you've ever felt safe.

He stayed still because he wasn't sure what would happen when he put himself in motion again.

Why had he thought she was different? Oh, he could look back and see why. She was fabulous at getting under his skin. She'd read him like a book. If she'd come in and played the perfect sub, he would have held her at arm's length, but she'd been weird and quirky and so entertaining he couldn't resist her. She'd been light to his never-ending darkness, and that had been the most brilliant play of all.

The funny thing was she'd *told* him who she was. She'd *told* him time and time again that she was a spy and an assassin, and he'd thought because she'd made the stories humorous that he was somehow exempt.

And the Oscar goes to…

"Josh?" She was standing in front of him, her gorgeous face tense. "I know this is a shock, but I need you to understand that it doesn't change anything between the two of us. Nothing."

Oh, but it changed everything. "Did you wire the place yourself?"

"What?"

"Did you do the wiring or did someone else do it? Who came into my home and turned it into an audio drama for bored agents to listen in to?"

She was quiet for a moment before she answered. "Riley did it."

That made sense. Maybe he wasn't such a bad judge of character. He'd never trusted Riley Blade. His mind worked the problem even as he ignored the howling in the pit of his gut. He wasn't going to give in to that. He would hurt her if he did. If he examined that wound for one second, he would lose control, and that couldn't happen now. Better to let it bleed without acknowledgement. He'd bled before and been forced to deal with the wound at a later date, when he was alone and safe again.

"Riley was in on it." Which brought up another point. "I suppose you tagged my phone, too. That was how you followed me last night. I knew I didn't fuck up. That plan should have worked perfectly. That's good to know."

"Let's take a walk and talk about this," she said, reaching for his hand.

He pulled it away before she could touch him. "Don't do that."

Now the tears showed up. He was sure she'd been saving them. "Please. I didn't know you when I took this assignment. I only knew that somewhere out there another agent is in trouble, maybe even dead, and I was the one who could help him. I didn't plan on falling in love with you."

Sure she didn't, but then it had been a handy way to manipulate him.

Now he could easily see every move she'd made had been to get him to a point where he would place her in the best possible position to do her job. In some ways, he even admired her for it. He could understand. Hell, his job was all he'd had until he'd met…his job was all he had, too.

"They listen to me in the playroom?"

"I'm not sure," she replied. "It's very likely."

So they would know about his proclivities. They would have heard him topping her, saying things that could be taken in the nastiest of contexts. They wouldn't be able to see his expression or how she responded. Without the aid of sight, the words themselves would be harsh, the commands of a man merely using a woman for sex. Since they'd talked openly about the club and its members, he would have to deal with that as well.

But that wasn't his only problem.

"They listen in my bedroom. Don't they? They would have heard us talking last night after your dads went to bed. Are they really your dads? They were surprisingly effective. They could be actors."

She swallowed once and then again. "Yes. Yes, they are. And I wasn't thinking about that last night. Josh, those tapes won't ever go anywhere. No one outside this operation will ever hear them."

He'd whispered his story to her because she'd been the only one on the planet he wanted to share it with. In doing so, he'd spilled his secrets to a group who dealt in them, who fed off them. His words would go into a file for the Agency higher-ups to read and they would decide what to do with the information. His sad-sack life, his blood, spread out for everyone.

He'd paid blackmail for years, but love had been the thing to bring him low.

"Please say something," she begged.

"You wouldn't like what I have to say." His heart actually ached. It thudded in his chest, squeezing and unclenching, and every beat hurt.

"I love you."

He closed his eyes because he couldn't stand to look at her. "Don't say those words. They're meaningless coming from your lips."

"Josh, I do love you. We have to talk. I know you don't want to, but I can see you're angry with me. It's okay. I would be pissed off, too. I've lied to you, but that doesn't mean I don't love you. It doesn't mean that I intended to leave you. I prayed we would get to Hector's and save the operative and you wouldn't have to know. I was going to stay with you."

He opened his eyes and looked at her. Really looked at her. She was wearing chic clothes that had designer labels all over them, her hair still shiny from the blow-out she'd had earlier. Of course she was staying. She had a taste for his lifestyle now. "I'd like you out my house in the next hour. Tell Shane and Declan they're fired as well. I think I'll stay at Jared's until I can find somewhere else."

"What?"

He stood up. It was time to put an end to whatever this was. And maybe he wouldn't go to Jared's. It was time to end that, too. He'd been better off without friends. Jared was the one who'd talked him into... Of course. What a complete idiot he was. "Jared's in on this. His brother works for you people. Naturally."

She shook her head. "No. No. Jared has no idea what's going on. He's your friend and he thought he was helping you. He wouldn't do this to you. I promise. You can trust him. But Josh, you can't kick us out. You can't fire us. I know this is all going to hell, but we need to talk."

"Talk about what?"

"Talk about why you're so cold right now."

"I'm cold because this is who I am." He was cold because if he let even the slightest hint of heat in, he would have a hand around her throat. He was cold because it was important that he stayed nice and numb. If he let a sliver of emotion in, he would hate her every bit as much as he'd ever loved her. He put a hand up. Perhaps there was another way to end this. "Look, you're making a lot of something you probably shouldn't."

She sighed, her eyes soft as though she pitied him. "Don't try to tell me this wasn't real. I won't believe you."

He had to make the attempt. Maybe if he said the words, he could believe them. "I got emotional last night. I'm sure a shrink would tell me I carried that secret around for too long and it got to me. I mistook good sex for real affection. Rookie move, but I'll get over it. You were excellent in bed and genuinely amusing. The funny girl thing works for me. I'll make a note of that when I find the next one of you."

There wouldn't be a next one. Not ever again. He'd been burned so often, but it would be this woman who finally taught him the lesson.

Again that nauseating sympathy lit her gaze. "I don't buy that for a second. I can see you creating dialogue in your head. You think I haven't learned you inside and out? I know that when the emotional shit gets too real, you go deep and find some character to play so you don't have to deal with it."

Excellent. Then she wouldn't mind if he played the massive asshole. "And when you come up against a problem, sweetheart, you spread your legs and make a whore of yourself."

He prepped for a bitch slap and was surprised when she merely took a deep breath and sighed.

"Okay, I can handle that. I can even see the point. I don't like the word, but you're feeling mean right now, and given what I took from you, I'll allow it."

"Allow it?" Did she honestly believe she was in control here? Well, he supposed that was his fault since up until now she'd happily led him around by his stupid cock.

"Yeah, call me names, babe," she encouraged. "Whore, bitch, cunt. I can handle them all as long as we keep on talking because at the end of this conversation, we're going to be okay."

"There is no *we*. There never was a *we*. There was an idiot me who let his dick do the thinking and there was a manipulative, ruthless bitch who saw an easy mark and took it." Despite his best of intentions, he was starting to heat up. "And of course you would stay, darling. What whore leaves a john who can buy her anything she wants? All you have to do is fuck me and hope I never find out all the other shit you've lied about. Who was the man on the beach, Kayla?"

Because it occurred to him that she'd been lying about everything today. Every fucking thing.

Her jaw firmed. "He's another agent."

He bet that's who he was. From the way Jared explained it, the two had been cozy. "Does he like you fucking the targets? Is that why he took off the way he did? Did you tell him he was going to lose you at the end of this op? How many of us have there been?"

"More than I like to admit," she replied quietly.

"Hey, it's cool. I was a whore, too, but then you know that and now all your buddies know it, too." They would use it against him. Something like that didn't get hidden away somewhere.

"I will get that tape. I'll make sure it doesn't exist. I swear it."

"Your lies mean nothing. Get your shit and get out. Take the assholes with you. If I ever see your lying, whore face again…"

"Hey," a deep voice said from above. "What the fuck is going on? You don't talk to her like that."

"Declan, this is between Josh and me," Kay said quickly.

Ah, finally someone he could turn a little rage on. Despite everything she'd done to him, he couldn't start a real fight with her, couldn't wrap his hands around her throat and squeeze. And she couldn't give him the physical pain he needed. But this asshole could. "Nah, this is a fucking family affair, man. You in on this? Does she fuck all of us? Is that how she keeps you two in line? I'm going to tell you, sweetheart, whatever Kegels you're doing, they're fantastic because somehow after all that cock, you're still tight as a drum. Although maybe Dec's a little light in that department."

Instead of punching him in the face, Dec looked back at Kayla. "Shit. He knows. What the fuck? I thought we were going to get through this without telling him and have a goddamn happily ever after. You knew that shit was going to fuck his brain over."

Kay put her hands on her hips. "Well, it wasn't my idea to tell him. I was planning on going to my damn grave with that one. I didn't want to hurt him that way."

"Fucking Agency," Dec spat. "They can't do anything right. Who screwed up? I'll take them out. I hate these jobs. Josh, you gotta understand that me, Shane, and Kay, we were all for knocking on your door and asking for your help. This undercover shit is not how we do business. I'm sorry."

"You're sorry?" That wasn't what he wanted to hear. Not even close. "I don't give a damn about your apologies. You can take it and shove it up your ass. I want you and Shane out of here, and take the whore with you."

Dec's eyes flared, but Kay got between them.

"Don't. It's his affectionate name for me now," she told the big bodyguard. "He's using it to get to you because he can't hurt me the way he wants to. He's in bad shape and I don't know how to fix it."

"You can fix it by leaving my house." And then he would sell the place because it was tainted now. He wouldn't be able to trust it. He would move again. This time he would find a place far outside of town and be alone. Someplace where no one could find him.

And maybe he had enough money. If he gave up his career, no one would give a crap that he'd been a child used and discarded again and again. The only reason anyone cared now was his status as a movie star. If he sacrificed that, they would leave him alone.

"We can't go," Kay was saying. "You still need protection. And we have to think about our operative. Morales is more dangerous than you know."

"Do I have to call the police?"

"The Agency will override them, man," Dec said with a long sigh.

"I'm not helping you or anyone. You can all go to hell as far as I'm concerned."

"I can get it all back for you," Kay said with a tremble to her voice. "I can promise you that tape will never see the light of day, will be utterly and completely erased, but you have to let us come with you to Mexico."

He stared at her for a long moment. "Ah, there's what I expected. A little blackmail of your own."

She shook her head. "You won't let me protect you any other

way. I have to do this job and I have to make sure you're alive at the end of it. Morales wants something from you and he won't allow you to brush him off with excuses. When you don't show up, he'll know something's gone wrong, and I think he's going to come after you."

"Why?" He didn't understand any of this.

Her jaw tensed. "I don't know."

"You're lying."

She moved into his space. "It doesn't matter now. I fucked up. I get that. You're not going to come back from this and there's no happy beach life for us at the end of this op. But you will be alive and I will handle all those problems I said I would. When this mission is over, you won't worry about blackmailers again and Morales won't darken your doorstep."

"You're going to kill him?"

Her eyes had darkened and it took all he had to stand his ground. This was the Kayla he hadn't seen, only heard about. This was the warrior goddess who enjoyed the kill, who lived for it. "Oh, yes, Joshua. I'll have his head and bring down his entire organization if it's the last thing I do on this earth."

God, she was glorious. Why did it have to be her? Why had she turned into such a liar? She could win back almost everything, but trust? That was gone and it wouldn't come again.

"We can go to the room Shane and I are in and talk about this," Dec said reasonably.

He wasn't about to do that. He wasn't going to listen to fucking reason. He stepped down a stair, coming up against Kayla. "Move out of my way."

"If you want to take a break, I can understand," she said. "But you have to take Declan."

He reached for her, unable to contain it a second longer. She was right there and he still fucking wanted her. After everything she'd done, all the lies, all the brutal manipulations of his life, what he wanted to do was carry her upstairs, strap her down to the spanking bench, and not let her up until she was properly submissive to him. He'd played around with it, but she'd still truly been in charge. The primal male inside him knew he wouldn't find another like her. That fucking caveman wanted to mark her, bind her, take her until she couldn't lie to him ever again.

Until she couldn't leave him.

His hands wound around her arms, shaking her a bit harder than he'd meant to, but then violence was bubbling up and she wouldn't let him fucking go. "You do not give me orders. You do not have me on your goddamn leash."

He felt a hard hand on the back of his neck and he was pulled away. Fuck that hurt and it lit something inside him. Declan had hold of him, the monster of a man easily hauling him off his feet.

"Go away, Kay. I need to deal with this. Send Shane down. He's going to need more than one of us." Declan eased him down.

Kay's eyes widened. "No. No, you can't hurt him."

But fuck he wanted that hurt more than he'd ever wanted anything in his life. Maybe even more than he'd wanted her. That pain would be real and visceral, and it would release the agony he was in.

She'd been nothing but an illusion.

He struggled, but Declan strong-armed him down the stairs past Kay. He maneuvered Josh into the basement, away from prying eyes.

"No ears down here," Declan said, letting him go.

He wheeled on the larger man and hit him with an uppercut to his gut. Declan didn't move. Didn't grunt. Didn't show that he'd felt anything at all.

"That's it, buddy. Take it out on me. I can handle it," he said. "Hell, sometimes I fucking crave a good fight. A few rules though."

"You can't hit his face," Kay said, looking vulnerable as she stood watching them. "Declan, please don't hurt him."

"He needs this," Declan replied. "We can do it this way or he'll find a way to hurt himself. I should know. I would do the same. He's a pressure cooker waiting to explode and destroy everyone around him, but you and I are going to let off a little steam here."

Declan pulled the T-shirt he was wearing over his head and tossed it to the side, but not before Josh saw that his back was covered with ink.

"Are those wings?"

Declan turned, a predatory look in his eyes. There was a smile on his face, but it was a feral thing. "Yeah, I'm a fucking guardian angel.

Remember that over the next couple of minutes. And remember that you can take all this out on me, but you touch her and I'll take your balls off."

"Please don't hurt him," Kayla said.

"Fuck that," Josh growled.

And went to town. That first punch he took had him seeing stars, but he was finally satisfied.

This…this was exactly what he deserved. Pain. Cleansing pain. Agony that would remind him that this was all the universe had to offer him.

* * * *

Kayla barely managed to make it up the stairs. She couldn't watch that, couldn't see what she'd done to him. Josh and Declan trading punches was nothing more than the outward symbol of how she'd just dealt him a damn death blow.

She'd watched the light die in his eyes. He'd been sitting there, holding her and being the warm, loving man she knew he was, and the next minute her words had shoved him right back into the darkness. He couldn't do anything else. He'd tried to protect himself, tried not to show how badly she'd hurt him. Not for one second did she buy the whole "you meant nothing to me" routine. She had ears. He'd been trying to leave her behind out of pure terror for her safety.

He loved her.

Had loved her.

She'd killed that love.

She stumbled on the step because she could barely see from the tears that now poured down her cheeks. The world was blurry and the steps she'd come to know so well now seemed to shake under her feet.

Probably because it sounded like someone was being thrown against the side of the house.

He was down there, taking a beating because he had no other way of letting the pain out. She'd done that to him and put the entire op in danger. What were they going to do if they couldn't convince Josh to go along? It wasn't like she could force him.

Although she'd practically blackmailed him to do it. That's exactly how he'd seen it.

"What the hell is going on?" Shane stepped out of the house. "I can feel this place shaking. Are we having an earthquake? Hey, are you crying?"

She wiped away the useless tears. They wouldn't bring him back. "Josh knows."

Shane stilled. "How?" When she was silent he cursed under his breath. "Damn it, Kay. I know you care about the guy, but this is going to get you fired. I like the guy, but he's unpredictable to say the least. Is Declan with him? Or did he take off on his own and we need to go find him?"

The stairs shook again and a low moan could be heard. That sound was all pain.

"Dec's with him," she admitted. "They are working things out the hard way. Dec asked me to get you."

Shane started down the steps, stopping on the one below her. "I suspect he took it poorly."

"I think I ruined his life, Shane. The way he looked at me…"

His head shook in the negative. "You were doing your job. You didn't lie to him about your feelings. This is why I hate the spy shit. I'll go down and make sure no one gets hurt. Well, seriously hurt. I take it Josh needed someone to take his anger out on and Dec volunteered?"

"I think Dec is giving as much as he's getting. He thinks Josh needs an outlet. Pain and violence were their selections today."

"I can see that. Though sometimes I think that big bastard enjoys the fight way too much. I'll make sure they don't kill each other."

She had something she had to do as well. "Can I use your room? I don't want to tip off the Agency until I've made the call."

Shane put a hand on her arm. "Of course you can. You know this is still your op. If you want to wait and see if we can talk Josh into being quiet. Maybe if the three of us…"

"No. Absolutely not. This is my op and I've put us all in danger. I'm not making another dumb play. I wish I could, but it's only right." She moved up the stairs, not looking back even though her whole soul ached when she heard Josh's pained shout.

He was letting his body be tortured because she'd shredded his soul.

What had he meant when he'd said he would stay at Jared's until he could find another place? She stepped into the house she'd come to love. She'd even started sneaking some color into it. He hadn't said a thing when she'd bought some blue and yellow pillows for the stark white couches. He'd merely used them while they laid on it together watching a movie. And he'd smiled as she'd hung the dachshund surfing picture she'd gotten at a local surf shop. The place was filled with peace for her and she knew what it meant to Josh.

But she'd invaded his sanctum. Would he leave it now because it would be forever tainted? Had she cost him his very home?

She forced herself to walk even though every step felt leaden. At least this would cost her, too. She was about to pay the bill for what she'd done to Josh and then she would be free to do what she needed to. After the op was over, she would hunt down Morales and anyone else who could hurt him and end all those threats with as much blood and pain as possible. She would find his blackmailer and give him back his peace.

If it was the last thing she did...

Kayla moved into the room they'd taken to calling security central. It was the one place where they could talk without the Agency listening in.

It was time to remember she was a professional and not merely some ridiculous girl in love.

Because she'd just killed that girl, too.

Joshua Hunt was the love of her life and that feeling wouldn't come around again. She would live out the rest of her days hollow on the inside because that essential piece of her would always be missing.

She picked up the phone, her hands trembling because she was about to lose another essential piece of herself.

"This is Knight," the familiar voice said.

If he was pissed she'd woken him, she couldn't hear it in his voice. Damon was steady as a rock. Damon would never be in this position. He would have figured another way out. He would have made this call a critical twenty minutes earlier. "It's Kay, Damon."

There was a momentary pause as though he'd heard something in her voice, and then his own softened. "Tell me what's happened."

"I fucked everything up." The tears began again as she started the story that would end her career.

It didn't matter. She'd ended everything important to her when she'd killed the light in Josh's eyes. There was only the op left now.

And after that revenge.

Chapter Fifteen

An hour later, Kayla sat on the steps again, but the brutal sounds of Declan and Josh beating on each other had ground down to whispers and the occasional groan.

She felt like she'd aged on that step. Like she'd gone down to the beach one woman and come back someone older, harder than before.

Declan stepped out from the room at the base of the house, tugging his shirt over his head. She could easily see where Josh had gotten some good jabs in, but it appeared they'd both left each other's faces alone. "Your boy's pretty vicious. If I hadn't been fairly quick, he would've pile drived my junk in there."

A low laugh got cut off by a moan of obvious pain. "Fuck you, Burke. I wasn't as fast. You got to teach me that move. After my balls inflate again. Hopefully they'll do that."

She gasped and stood up. "I told you not to hurt him."

Declan held a hand up as though warding her off. "He needed that pain and I did as you asked. Look at this. His face is fucking perfect."

"But my kidney is not," Josh said, though he appeared slightly lighter than before. "I think I felt it go back there."

"Do you need to go to the hospital?" Kay asked. He looked like hell despite the fact that no one had hit his face.

"No." He stared through her. "I just need you to go away. I've agreed to keep Dec and Shane on until after the shoot. It's too soon to find and train new guards. I'll let the Agency send in someone else. Not you."

He was willing to deal with everyone but her. Yeah, that made sense. Unfortunately, it couldn't happen. "The Agency isn't going to barter with you. They'll still want me to go. If you think it's too late to bring a couple of bodyguards up to speed, how do you think the Agency feels about their operative? Also, Morales is expecting me. I assume you've sent him my name as your companion."

"I'll tell him I got tired of banging you and found a younger model," he said with a smirk.

Dec turned. "Hey, what was part of our deal?"

"I didn't call her what I wanted to call her," Josh said, his hand on his ribs.

Shane appeared, leaning against the doorjamb. "Just try to be civil, man. I told you she's hurting, too."

"We'll have to agree to disagree on that," Josh replied. "Now, if there's nothing else, I'm going to take a long shower."

"You can't leave me behind, and I don't think it's a good idea to tell the Agency that you know what's going on." She had to be reasonable here. "If they know, it might occur to them to use what they know about you to ensure your silence. I have a better plan."

"I'm sure you do. Can we talk about it over Scotch?" He started toward the stairs. "I know we can't talk openly in my home, but at least we could do this in the secure room. Dec said you didn't wire up that part of the house. Let's hear this brilliant plan of yours."

"I'm not the one who's going to sell you. Tomorrow, someone from McKay-Taggart is coming out to set up a plan. He'll explain what you get from us if you help. I think you'll like the plan. It fixes most of what I screwed up."

"Most?"

"I don't think Big Tag can make you believe I love you, Josh."

He rolled his eyes and started up the stairs. "Keep that shit to yourself. I don't want to hear it."

"I'm not going to not say it because you don't want to hear it." She followed him, a little afraid he might fall back. "If you'll meet with my boss, I think you'll find he can help you out. We can't meet here. I've arranged a meeting at The Reef in the morning. Riley will have everything ready."

He kept moving, not looking back at her. "Naturally your plant will have things ready in my club. It's good. I can leave my resignation letter there."

"Resignation? Why would you do that?"

"Because unlike you I have some personal honor. I let the wolves in. I didn't know I was letting the wolves in, but they got in because of me. I won't put people I care about in danger. They could lose their jobs, their privacy, and all because of me. I don't know why I thought it would work in the first place." He looked back at Dec and Shane. "You think I should hear what this guy has to say?"

Awesome. The guys had bonded and it looked like she was the one left out.

"Yes." Shane didn't hesitate. "If he's coming here, then he's serious and he's got something to offer you. He's not like the Agency."

"But that means we're playing this our way," Dec said. "And it means the Agency can't know that you know. They can't know Kayla gave you classified information."

"Ah," Josh said with a sigh. "The company is protecting its own. That I understand. I can work with that. What you're saying is we can't talk about this upstairs and we have to pretend everything is normal. That's going to be fun for me. All right. I'll talk to this guy but only because I would like to get my fucking life back and I'm not a monster. I would have helped out if someone had asked. Hell, I would have done it just for the experience. I would have used it to play a spy somewhere down the line. I don't like getting cast in roles I didn't fucking audition for and 'pathetic idiot who gets taken down by a warm pussy' is the kind of role my agent tells me to turn down."

"I was hot," she corrected. "If you're going to insult me at least get it right. I was the hottest pussy you've ever had, babe."

"If you say so." He turned and started back up the stairs.

"Kay, can you handle him tonight? Because I think maybe he's still in a mood to tear you up," Shane said. "We can make an excuse about you having to go see one of your dads or something."

271

She shook her head even as she prayed Josh managed to make it up the stairs. He wobbled once, but held on to the railing.

He cursed and bent over. "I still feel that kick to my gut, asshole. If I do stay around, one of my demands is that you teach me how you move like that."

"He can't teach you what's built into his DNA," Shane replied. "No one moves like Dec. But we can both teach you a lot about how to fight. We'll start daily training sessions when you're ready."

Without glancing back, Josh nodded. "I'll look forward to it."

He kept moving until he hit the landing and shuffled on.

She rounded on the bodyguards. "I do not understand men. He's friends with you two now?"

Dec sent her a grim look. "I wouldn't say friends, but he does need us. He gets that. He can't go down there on his own. And quite frankly, he's going to need someone to beat on for the next couple of weeks. It's a male thing."

"Is it? You think because I don't have a dick I don't want to punch something right now? Because you would be wrong." She wanted to kill someone and his name was Tyler Williams. "What do we know about the DEA agent who busted our op?"

"We know he was a DEA agent. He passed our trace," Shane explained. "You can't go after the guy for doing his job."

"He's retired," she pointed out, frustration welling.

"Yeah, well, I think we all have that case we would come out of retirement to deal with," Dec continued. "I know I've got a couple. And the DEA guy has no idea the Agency's got its nose up Morales's butt. He's trying to protect Josh the same way we are. When we get down to Mexico, I'll see if I can talk to him, maybe get a feel for the guy."

"I want to meet him." She didn't trust that this was coincidence.

Shane's mouth turned down. "I don't know that he's going to change his mind about letting you go."

"I'm the only one who can go. Any change at this point will likely make Morales suspicious. You could go with Josh, but you won't have the same freedom I will. You're a bodyguard. You'll be expected to stay close to Josh. I can move around and get lost and act like a ditzy chick and no one will question it."

"I get that, but Josh is angry and he's not being reasonable," Dec pointed out. "You need to get up there and make sure he doesn't say anything that will bring the Agency down on all our heads. I assume we're not calling Green or Fain to let them know we've told the target that he's actually the target?"

"That could put Josh in a bad position," Kay said. She'd thought of nothing but how to handle this since that terrible moment she'd blown the op wide open. "Right now I don't know who all has listened to the tape from last night. Josh told me some things he wouldn't want out in the world."

"Riley's listening in," Shane replied. "The whole twenty-four seven listening thing takes up a lot of man hours. For some reason Green wants contractors on this one so Riley's listening and summarizing for him every few days. Mostly Riley is listening for information about Hunt's movements and to see if he mentions Morales at all."

Then they might have a chance. "Call him and ask him to redact my conversation with Josh in the bedroom last night. He'll know what I'm talking about. If that conversation ever got out in public...well, I think it simply makes Josh more heroic, but he would find it embarrassing. He's spent years and millions of dollars to protect his past."

"That bad, huh?" Shane asked.

"Nothing that was his fault. He's overcome a lot," she replied. "He deserves some peace. There's something I didn't tell him. I think Morales might be the man behind what was done to him as a child."

Dec whistled. "Don't tell him unless you want a half-cocked, walking bomb to go off down there. You've got to deal with that yourself. I don't know how he would handle killing someone in cold blood. For some people that's an edge you can't come back from."

She knew Josh had already killed, but that had been pure self-defense. This would be vengeance and it was different. That was her world and she didn't want Josh tainted with her sins. It was the one gift she could still give him. "I'm going up to make sure he doesn't do something stupid."

She'd done enough of that for both of them. She should have regrouped and taken the problem to Damon, but she'd lost it. For the first time in years, she'd panicked.

"Hey, everything's okay with base?" Shane asked.

It was a nice way of asking if the inevitable had happened. "Damon and Ian agree I need to be the one to go in. After that, Damon said we would have a very thorough debrief where I will likely be fired. My words, not his. I'm sure he'll try to put me on probation or something, but I'm going to hand in my resignation at the end of this op."

"That's a little overdramatic," Dec said. "Unless you have plans that you can't follow through on while in the employ of a company with a good reputation. You going to take out Morales for Hunt?"

"I'm going to take out everyone I can find who ever hurt that man," she vowed.

"Going after Morales alone is a suicide mission," Shane argued.

"Yeah, I don't think she cares about that right now." Dec sighed. "Come on. Let's go get Riley on the phone. We've still got time to turn this around, but we've got to keep the Agency out of it. No knock-down, drag-outs with your boy. If they get a hint of discord between the two of you, Green is likely to swoop down, and we can't trust that Riley's the only one who's listening in. Green is a slippery sucker. I prefer Fain. At least he's honest with his underlings. I get the feeling Green likes playing chess with us as his pawns."

She watched as they walked upstairs and then followed. She walked into the home that seemed so perfect for her up until this point. Now she could practically hear the way silence invaded and filled up the space.

She walked up the stairs, hearing the shower going in the master. She turned the handle, surprised to find it unlocked.

Josh was standing in the middle of the room, stripped down to his boxers. She could already see the bruises and contusions from the session with Declan. Damn, idiot men.

"Let me look at those," she insisted.

"Did I tell you you could touch me, sub?" His voice went hard.

She widened her eyes to silently question him.

"New play, baby," he growled her way. "New protocols. You know I like to mix it up. Don't touch me unless you're given leave to. I think I might like some silence, too. Unless you're going to safe word out on me. You always have that choice."

Asshole. "So I don't speak unless spoken to and I don't touch you. Where would you like me? Would you like your sub to stay in her room until you're ready to take her out and play with her?"

Maybe that was the best for both of them. There were only twelve hours before they met with Big Tag at The Reef. A cooling down period could do them both good. She could sit in her room and think about what happened to operatives who chose their targets over their missions. She could study up on Hector Morales. Yes, that would be good.

"Get in the shower."

She stopped and then remembered she wasn't supposed to speak. She stared at him for a moment.

He dropped his boxers and tossed them aside. He was standing there in his full glory. The last few weeks had toned him further as he'd gone into training mode for his shoot. Every single muscle was defined and ripped. He looked lean and hungry, like he could eat up the world and still want more.

His anger was still there, simmering now, but he'd found another way he could burn it off. He could use her.

Her body softened, ready for some of that stress relief. She could do that. Her soul flinched at the thought of treating what had been even momentarily sacred as a transactional exchange of bodies.

"Did you not hear me, sub? I told you to get in the shower. Take off your clothes and get in the shower. Your Master fell while jogging and needs your help to get the freaking sand out of everywhere. But I shouldn't have to explain what I need from you. I give you the order and you either follow it or choose to leave. I thought you understood D/s better than this."

He was going to be a hardass to the end. He was standing there challenging her. What was more important, those cold eyes of his asked—her pride or the mission? Would she let him use her?

Pride was overrated and she won absolutely nothing if she got out of the game. Five minutes before she would have sworn Josh would never even look at her again. Now he was ordering her into the shower, commanding that she take her clothes off for him.

Was he doing it merely to humiliate her? That's not what his cock was telling her. The man had taken a beatdown and his cock was twitching as he looked at her.

She pulled the T-shirt over her head. No bra for her so her breasts were immediately on display and that cock stopped twitching. His erection swelled, drawing his balls up tight against his body.

Not mere humiliation. He still wanted her. Oh, she had no doubt what was going through that male brain of his. He was telling himself he could still use her, probably should, that it would be foolish to not fuck the woman who'd betrayed him. Hell, she owed it to him.

But those were all excuses. She shimmied out of her shorts, tossing them aside, too. His brain was coming up with a million reasons he could still have her, but there was one he wouldn't acknowledge. There was only one reason he could still want her.

He still cared deep down. Josh was the type of man who could easily turn off his emotions. She'd watched him do it. Why hadn't he been able to do it with her?

If there was even a spark of feeling for her left in his soul, she had a chance. She could use sex to bind him, to keep that little flame alive so it could grow again.

But she wouldn't do that by fighting him. No. She had to play this his way. "I'll be waiting for my Master. Waiting to give you comfort in any way you need."

She started to move past him, but one hand came out, tangling in her hair and tugging her close. Her belly brushed against his cock and his eyes closed briefly.

"Anything?" The word was a challenge.

Now she could see him for what he was. An angry, wounded predator who couldn't quite eat his prey. He couldn't make himself let go. This was the only way he could have her. But wounds could heal and they had some time. "Anything."

He leaned in. "What does that make you?"

She was sure there were a ton of nasty words going through his head in answer to that question. Whore. Slut. Skank. Prostitute. But there was only one word for her. "Yours, Joshua. It makes me yours."

He didn't seem to have a pithy comeback for that and released her. "Go clean yourself up. I'll be there in a minute. I mean it, Kay. Anything I want."

"Anything."

As she walked into the gorgeous bathroom, she was feeling better. Her lion was roaring and she wasn't going to come out of this without some wounds of her own, but she healed fast. And he wasn't throwing her out.

She still had a shot and she was going to take it.

* * * *

What the hell was he doing? He hated her. It sat in his belly like a sickening anchor, weighing him down. He hated her and his cock still hardened at the mere thought of her. He hadn't locked the door because he'd known damn well she would come looking for him. He fucking wanted her to find him, to see him without a stitch on, and then he was going to order her to her own room where she could fuck herself.

And the instant he'd caught sight of her, her eyes red from crying—fucking crocodile tears—he'd known he wasn't about to let her off that easy. She owed him. That was it. She'd signed a contract and she owed him obedience and sex. He'd gotten a bunch of anger out sparring with Declan, but it was rushing back in and he could let it fester or find another way to cope.

His cock knew exactly what it wanted.

He would still throw her out. He would still get rid of her because she was a liar and a manipulator and the worst kind of woman, but as long as she was here, why not use her for what she was good for?

Every muscle ached, but nothing worse than his...god, he couldn't even think that word. Couldn't give her that much control over him. He'd been stupid. He'd known she was too good to be true and guess what?

But some of what Declan and Shane said had pierced through his rage. There was an agent out there who had likely been killed in action, and Josh's connections were the only way to get to the truth. He might hate the way the CIA had gone about it, but could he really not try to help?

They'd also talked about getting his privacy back, ensuring no one ever heard that tape. He was in the same position with the Agency as he was with his blackmailer. They had him by the balls.

But Kayla needed him and he fully intended to use that to his advantage.

He would use her for what he'd brought her in for in the first place. Sex and submission.

He stalked into the shower. It was a monstrosity of a shower with natural rock and an open entrance. He stopped as the marble of the floor gave way to the tile of the shower. Despite the fact that she'd ripped his world apart with those well-manicured hands of hers, his breath caught because she was the single most beautiful woman he'd ever seen. She was graceful and slender, her long raven-black hair falling to brush against the cheeks of her ass. Her face was turned up to the hot water as though it could wash away her sins.

Nothing could, but he could damn well do some sinning of his own.

Her eyes came up, big and guileless. She'd been built to do what she did, to seduce men into giving her their secrets, to manipulate powerful people into doing what she wanted. So sweet and innocent. No one would believe she could do what she was capable of.

"Please don't look at me like I'm a monster," she said quietly.

Wasn't she? A gorgeous, sleek and deadly predator. She certainly managed to mangle him with her delicate claws. "I thought you didn't want our listening audience to know there was anything wrong."

"There's no device in here," she replied. "And it's too big to let the one in your room pick up our conversation. They can't hear us on the balcony either. They tried, but the ambient sound is too much."

The surf was quite overpowering at certain times of the day. "So I can say what I like in here?"

"Sure. Light me up, Josh. I still won't leave you."

He'd called her enough nasty names for the day. "I thought I would go over the new rules. I was indulgent with you before."

"I thought we'd gotten those out of the way," she replied. If it bothered her to be nude in front of him, she didn't show it. But then again her body was her greatest weapon. It was certainly working against him. His cock was aching for her. "I'm to obey you in all things if I want to stay around. I told you. Anything you want, Joshua."

"Except if I want you gone."

"Except that." She stepped close to him, her chin tilting up. "I'll be gone soon enough if that's what you want. I'll be gone the minute the op is over, but you should understand that won't be what I want. I want to stay with you."

"Yes, I can see you've gotten used to the lifestyle."

"I've gotten used to loving you."

"My first rule," he ground out between clenched teeth, "is that you never use that word around me again."

"Just because I don't say it doesn't mean it isn't true." Her eyes closed and she dropped down in front of him. Her slender, luscious body found her submissive position. On her knees, legs splayed, head down. "I submit to my Master. I give him the control he needs and I trust him not to hurt me."

"Then you're a fool." He would hurt her. He would hurt her in every way and enjoy each moment of her pain. But not before he'd had his pleasure. "You're honestly telling me you'll still fuck me?"

Her head didn't come up. "Yes, Joshua. I still want you."

Damn if he didn't want her, too. "You will get nothing from this. Nothing but incidental pleasure because from this moment on you mean nothing to me. You are nothing but a lovely body for me to use. Do you understand?"

"Yes."

Why the fuck wasn't she running? Why wasn't she slapping the fool out of him and telling him to keep his cock to himself? "Tell me something, Kay. Did it bother you to have to fuck me? Did you clean yourself up after I came inside you?"

Now that head came up, her eyes confused. "What?"

"I'm filthy." He stroked his cock as if he needed that evidence to make his case. "Do you have any idea where this has been? How dirty I am?"

She stood up and her hand came out, smacking the shit out of him. "Don't you ever say that about yourself. Never again. I'll take a lot of crap from you, but not that. Never that."

He didn't understand her, couldn't comprehend what kind of game she was playing, but he couldn't seem to stop taking his turn. He should walk away. His whole body ached, but all he could do was push her further. "Suck it, sub. Get back down on your knees and prove it. Suck my cock like it means something to you."

Why had he said that? He didn't fucking care if it meant a thing. He didn't care about her at all. This was about getting back some of his own.

So why did something settle deep inside when she dropped to her knees and rubbed her cheek against his cock? That wasn't what he'd asked for. He'd told her to suck it and expected her to immediately drag his cock into that hot mouth of hers, to show off all her skills so he would keep her around another day.

She didn't jump on the porn star performance. No, not Kay. She had to be different, had to be weird. She rubbed her cheek against his dick and then breathed him in like she couldn't get enough of how he smelled. She ran her nose over him, reveling in him before starting in on the butterfly kisses.

It was pure torture and it was right there on the tip of his tongue to command her again. He could reach out and wrap his hands in all that hair of hers, tangling it in his fingers and taking control of her. He could force his dick into her mouth and throat fuck her until he came hard, never letting up until she'd swallowed him dry. Then he would wash himself and tell her to get out. If she wanted to get clean, she could do it in her shower. He'd tell her he was done with her and go to bed early, avoiding her the rest of the day.

Except he simply stared down at her, watching as she worshipped his cock, lavishing him not with some lusty manipulation, but with sweet affection. She pressed kisses along his stalk as her small hand reached up and cupped his balls. After she kissed his length, her tongue finally made an appearance and he groaned at the feel. Heat pulsed through his system. He stared down, watching as she took that first pass, her tongue lapping up the weeping arousal on the tip of his dick. She sighed as though she loved the taste.

Good. She was incredibly good at pulling him in, at making him believe she meant everything she said and did. He could almost believe she loved this, loved his cock, and everything she was offering him was truth.

Then she sucked him behind her lips and he didn't give a fuck. Her tongue whirled around his cockhead, sucking lightly, and he couldn't breathe. She'd barely started and he could feel the need to come pounding at him.

Her hands grazed up his legs as she held his cock deep in her mouth. This was what fucking Kayla was like. It was like she couldn't get enough of him. She gave and gave until he rolled her over and pinned her down, forcing her to take her pleasure, too. His sexuality was complex and stained with what had happened, but he forgot everything when he was with her.

Why couldn't she have been real?

His hands found her hair, but she was drawing all the anger out of him and leaving him with nothing but pleasure and this aching wish in his soul that today hadn't happened, that this was some bad dream and he would wake up beside her and this time he wouldn't go meet Tyler Williams. He would choose again. He would go to brunch and laugh with Jared and get lectured by her dads and he would eat carbs and kiss her madly even when everyone was looking.

He petted her hair as she sucked him, her mouth working him over. Somehow even as she took his cock deep, there was a sweetness to the act that had been absent with every woman before, a sense that this wasn't some simple exchange, that this was connection.

A connection he would have to cut. A connection that had only ever gone one way.

He pulled on her hair because if she kept it up, he would come straight down her throat. That had been the plan, but then all his plans got blown up. He was an idiot and he had so little time left with her. He would give her up at the end. He would send her away, but not tonight. Not tonight.

"Get up."

She sucked him one last time. "Josh, let me finish. I want to."

She needed to learn to listen to him now that she was primarily his submissive. "And I told you to get up. The only reason I'm not spanking you is that I don't trust myself not to hurt you. Turn around and put your hands on the tile and spread your legs."

Her eyes flared. "Really?" She shook her head, beginning to turn. "I mean, yes. Yes, Joshua."

She placed her hands flat on the tile and offered up her delicious body.

He was too hungry to play, too needy to tease. He moved in behind her, letting his dick play through her pussy. Wet. The woman always got so fucking wet for him. They'd tossed out the condoms when their blood work had come back clean. She was on long-term birth control.

Or she could be lying about that, too. She could try to keep her lifestyle that way, get him to knock her up. He should get a condom, but his cock was already thrusting inside.

If he did get her pregnant, he wouldn't be able to kick her out. He would be caught.

He thrust deep inside, forgetting about everything but how tight she was around him, how silky smooth the glide was as she accommodated him. He held her hips as he moved in and out. Every muscle ached, but he didn't care. All that mattered was where they connected, his hands on her hips, his cock deep inside. He was alive there. The rest could rot for all he cared. This was where he lived.

He reached around and found her slick clitoris, pressing down and starting a slow slide. He was too tuned up. The emotion of the day pressed in and shot his control, but he would be damned if he would go over without her. All thoughts of causing her pain had fled, replaced with the idea of making her hurt as much as he was. She would miss this, miss him. She would never find another lover who could do this to her.

Yeah, he could do that. He could take these last days and fuck her so long and hard and true that she could never find another man to satisfy her.

"Josh. Please, Josh." Her throaty cries filled the shower and he wished everyone on the planet could hear that.

He knew what she wanted and pressed down hard while he thrust in as far as he could, let loose with his release. He pounded into her as she clenched him tight, milking every drop he had inside him. Fuck fighting. He'd needed this.

"Josh." She said his name like a benediction.

He held her against him, his cock slipping out, but still warm against her. "It doesn't mean anything."

She sighed, but let her head come back, resting against his chest as he fondled her breasts. "Then let me clean you up, Master. If it doesn't mean anything, then it's all right to let me do it."

He was still as she grabbed the soap and started moving her hands over his body, washing him clean.

It didn't mean anything, he told himself. He closed his eyes against the sight of her serving him.

It didn't mean a fucking thing.

Chapter Sixteen

The next day as he sat in The Reef's small conference room, Josh had to admit the big guy had presence. The smaller guy in the suit had style. The other guy was half asleep.

These were Kayla's coworkers and it was exactly like he'd thought. Her delicate beauty didn't fit with these hulking, massive men.

"I'm Ian Taggart," the biggest of the men said as he settled into a chair opposite Josh. "Yolo McSwaggins here is named Adam Miles, and Sleeping Beauty is my business partner, Alex McKay. Don't mind Alex. He recently adopted a second child and then his sperm totally went on a hyper salmon run and his wife turns up pregnant. They went from no kids to looking at having three under the age of five. Welcome to my world, buddy. I'm pretty sure he's here because he thought he could get some sleep."

Alex McKay's middle finger made an appearance and he sat up and stretched. "I'm here because I don't trust you to not piss off the dude who could sue us. This is going to require some subtlety."

The third man smiled, a smooth expression. "And I'm here because I'm the brains. Adam Miles, head of Miles-Dean, Weston and Murdoch Investigative Services." He turned to Taggart. "Yolo McSwaggins? Where the fuck do you get this shit? Do you troll

Urban Dictionary?" He obviously didn't need an answer as he immediately turned back to Josh. "Mr. Hunt, I'm happy to meet you. I'm a big fan."

Wow. It was weird. He knew these dudes even though he hadn't met these dudes. It was like watching a movie but the faces had changed from the actors playing the roles to the real live people. He couldn't help it, but he had to look to Kayla. He'd meant to ignore her completely. After the shower incident the previous night, he'd ignored her the rest of the evening. Well, until it had been time to go to bed. Then he'd shown up at her door and practically fallen on top of her when she opened her arms. While they'd been fucking—he wasn't going to call it by the other term—he'd been content. The minute he'd rolled off her, he'd wanted to go to sleep, her small body wrapped up in his like some super-sexy teddy bear he clung to to keep the bad dreams away. He'd forced himself to get up and walk back to his own bed where he'd sat and watched the ceiling most of the night.

But he couldn't ignore her now because she had answers. He caught her eye. "Pierce Craig?"

He'd totally seen this movie. The big Viking who was made of sarcasm was obviously Pierce Craig from the movie *Love After Death*. Jared had almost played that role. Josh had been the one to sit by as Jared had dissected everything the actor who'd gotten the role after him had done wrong. Funny, it was hard to see his soft-hearted friend playing the massive ex-Special Forces soldier.

Kayla's lips curled up, though he noted the smile didn't reach her eyes. "Yes, and Axel and Zan. I think they're shooting Zan and Ava's movie in a couple of months."

"I am not Zan." McKay yawned discreetly behind his hand and frowned Miles's way. "Couldn't Serena come up with a more manly name? I sound like I should be in a sci-fi movie. You know if I'd known she was going to turn around and write a freaking book about my life, I would never have told her that story."

Miles shrugged. "Yeah, she was there. How quickly they forget. She kind of saved your ass, so you owed her."

The big guy frowned. "Wait. Are you trying to tell me I'm actually Pierce Craig?" His face went still. "Holy shit. She did. That's my story. Huh. At least they got a handsome bastard to play me.

Adam, I'm going to need a cut of that."

Now Miles's middle finger showed up. "Not happening. You're lucky I'm even willing to help you out at all. You're the asshole brother I never, ever wanted and would like to give back."

Taggart's smile proved the man could have been on the big screen if he'd wanted to be. "Ah, you say the sweetest things. What's this hellhole? I like it. Reminds me of real clubs. My wife needed Sanctum to look like a combination high-tech torture palace/five-star hotel. This place is real. I bet you don't even have much of an electricity bill."

Alex moaned. "I will pay the fucking bill if you will stop complaining about it. Dear god, you're a multimillionaire and you complain about one high utility bill."

"How do you think I stay a multimillionaire? It sure ain't by giving TXU my paycheck. I grew up poor, Moneybags. I can't pay out because a couple of Doms wanted to see if they could keep the hamster wheel going for a solid week."

"It was for charity," McKay shot back. "And I grew up next to you. Literally in the house next to yours. Could we get on with this? There's a hotel room with my name on it."

"No, there's not," Miles said with a sigh. "We're scheduled to go back as soon as this meeting's over. We can't afford for the Agency boys to figure out we're here. But Big Tag didn't tell you that."

McKay stood up. "You suck, Ian. I'm going to find some coffee. It's going to be a long day."

He sort of stumbled back toward the kitchen where the bodyguards, along with Riley, were waiting.

Big Tag pulled out a bunch of paperwork. "Don't look at me like that, Kay. We came in on the small 4L jet. It's got a bedroom because Drew Lawless is freaky that way. Even now the flight attendant is making sure Alex has lavender-scented sheets and a white-noise player that will only switch to baby screams twenty minutes before we land. See, I'm not a complete asshole. Now how about we get down to business. I hear a little birdy's been giving out classified intel."

Kay stiffened beside him. "Yes, sir. I laid out the plan to Mr. Hunt after it became obvious there was no other way to keep the op going."

"None? You can't think of a single other option opened to you? Because I can," Taggart asked, one brow climbing up. That was one judgmental brow. The rest of the man's face hadn't changed at all, but there was such power in his expression.

It would look good on film. He could try it later in the mirror. He filed the expression away and tried not reach for Kayla's hand.

"I should have called in and gotten advice." Kay's voice was tight, her usual happiness dimmed to the point that she seemed lethargic. It was hard to see her that way because she was always bright and full of life. "I should have put the choice in Damon's and your hands. I didn't call in until I'd already screwed up. I'm sorry."

"I am, too," Taggart replied without a hint of sympathy in his arctic tone. "You put this company in a tricky position. We're contractors here. If the Agency finds out how you've jeopardized this op and its position, not only will our government contracts get shut down, we'll likely be brought up on criminal charges. And Hunt here can sue the shit out of us."

Criminal charges? He shook his head, trying to process what that meant. "I don't understand. What do you mean they could arrest her? For telling me the truth?"

Yolo...what was his name again...Miles leaned in. "In this case, telling you the truth could be considered anything from leaking classified intelligence to straight up espionage."

"Or otherwise known as treason when it's an American citizen committing the crime against an American intelligence agency," Taggart pointed out. "She's looking at anything from ten years to life, though the more realistic outcome would be to quietly move her to a federal facility where she wouldn't be heard from again."

His heart threatened to stop in his chest. "Just for telling me something I should have known? I had the right to know."

"Not according to the United States government, you didn't," Miles said, not without sympathy. "They take security seriously, especially when it comes to embedded agents. Do you think the Mexican government knows we have an operative working in Jalisco? I assure you they do not."

Alex McKay walked back into the room, a coffee mug in his

hand. "We've got a lawyer on it back in Dallas in case it comes out. We're here to make sure it doesn't. None of us wants this information out in the public. We're here to offer Mr. Hunt a few...gifts in exchange for the greatest gift of all. Silence."

"I thought you said your wife was the greatest gift," Taggart said with a shit-eating grin.

"That was before we had kids," McKay replied. "Now it's definitely silence."

How could they joke when Kayla could go to jail? "I'm not going to talk. I'll do the job and then we'll go our separate ways."

"Really? Well, that was easy." Taggart started to get up.

"Ian, please," Kay said quietly.

Taggart frowned and sat his ass back down. He flipped the file folder around. "First, we're willing to offer you bodyguard services for half the going rate."

"Ian," Kay said, fire in her eyes.

"Fuck me hard. A year's worth of bodyguard service for...for...for fucking free. In that time we'll train two people of your choice and at the end you'll keep them on." It was obvious the offer had taken a lot out of him. Taggart sank back as though utterly exhausted. "In addition, Riley has already discovered that the tape from two nights ago has a terrible defect. Something went wrong for approximately twenty-three minutes. It was late and that was why he didn't catch it."

McKay slid across a thumb drive. "This is the original and the only copy. No one here has listened to it with the exception of Riley Blade, and he's signed a nondisclosure agreement. It's going to be forwarded to your attorney, but understand we're very vague about the hows and whys that tape came into existence."

Josh shook his head. "Send it to me. I don't trust anyone with it. I'll keep the NDA in case I need it." Could he trust these men? Kayla did, but then he didn't trust her at all. Except that maybe she'd been willing to go to jail...*whoa, hold your horses there, dumbass. That wasn't about you. That was about the mission.* Still, it was obvious these men had something to lose if it all came out. "Thank you for the tape. I appreciate it not getting out."

Taggart moved on briskly. "In addition, Adam has the file you wanted, Kayla. He found her."

"Her?" Josh asked. "Her who?"

Miles passed him a folder. "Kayla asked me to locate a woman named Hannah Lovell. I didn't have much to go on. She couldn't give me more than name, approximate age, and the fact that she'd been in the foster care system in the Wichita area. She went missing as a young child from a foster home that was later found to be committing fraud."

His heart damn near seized. He'd been sure she was dead. "You found Hannah?"

"I asked Adam to find her. I got her records last night. Adam is pretty brilliant at finding missing persons," she replied. "Consider it a peace offering. Although you might not like where she is."

"I located her in a prison in Cleveland. She's doing time for possession and multiple counts of solicitation. I don't know who this woman is to you, but she's had a hard life," Adam was saying. "She's scheduled to come up for parole in six months, but she's also got a public defender."

One thing he could do. One good fucking thing. "I'll pay for her lawyer. Could you find me someone, the best someone? She was a good friend. We were in..." Hell... "Foster care together. I always wondered what happened to her. I...thank you for finding her."

It might be too late. She might be too far gone, but he could help out. He'd thought he was too far gone, but Tina had offered him something different. What if he could do the same?

What if he could do the same for a lot of people who'd spent time in Hell? Nothing could fix the hole inside him.

Had he tried? Had he attempted in any way to fill that hole or had he determined he was broken beyond repair and given up and given in to hopelessness, to believing the only way to live was to pretend to be someone else, always denying what had happened to him.

"We'll keep it quiet about who's paying the legal fees," McKay was saying.

He found himself nodding, but he wanted to see Hannah. He couldn't, of course. That would bring up too many questions. It would put him too close to the truth.

"I want to visit her."

That brow of Taggart's rose again, though this time it seemed more curious than judgmental. "You know someone is going to want to know why you would visit a drug addict and a prostitute in jail. It will get out."

"Fuck 'em," Josh said. He wanted to see her. It probably wouldn't go well, but he had to try. Even if only to apologize to her. For not saving them both. For not being able to protect her.

"That's the first smart thing you've said," Taggart replied. "We'll make that happen too. Now can you promise me you're going to be a good boy and do your job? Wait, let me be clear about what your job is. You will go to the party at Morales's place. You will get Kayla in. You will get her out. You will keep your mouth closed and maybe we can save this operative's life. If not, at least we can figure out what happened and how he became compromised."

"I can do that," Josh said, holding on to the folder Miles had given him. Hannah was in that file. Her picture showed a hardened woman, aged before her time.

Did she have to stay that way? Was the damage permanent or could her pain be eased with a friendly hand reaching out, a compatriot in the horror who wanted to help her find some kind of light? Did her life have to be over?

Did his? Did his heart have to harden because one woman had lied to him? The problem was he was fairly certain it had only softened because of her in the first place.

The only way to beat the darkness is to drag it all into the light, Josh.

Sometimes he wondered if he'd exchanged one prison for another. One had been dark, the other gilded, but in neither could he be himself, could he have true control over who he was. One had been a fight to exist, the other a constant battle to hide his history. He'd found a career where he didn't have to be himself, where it was of the utmost importance that he almost never be himself.

Who was he? The scared child? The unrepentant and violent teen? The man who shut everything down so he didn't self-destruct?

"Do we have a deal?"

From the tone of Taggart's question, Josh figured it might have been asked more than once. "Yes, we have a deal."

"Excellent." Taggart closed the folder in front of him and turned Kay's way. "Could you go and have Riley call the pilot and tell him we'll be ready to leave early?"

"Wait," Adam said, a frown on his face. "Doesn't anyone want to know about how I found her so fast? You see I wrote this software that searches all known databases for…"

Taggart groaned. "No one cares, nerd. We all know you're a genius. You have my investment. Don't ask for my damn attention unless you're a bottle of Scotch or a lemon pie. Are you either of those things?"

"I'll text Riley," Kayla said, pulling out her phone.

"I didn't ask you to text him," Taggart said, his voice going low. "Please, go and ask him in person. And maybe get yourself a cup of coffee."

Kayla frowned, looking from man to man to man as though trying to figure out exactly what they were going to do. "I don't think that's a good idea."

"It's an excellent idea." McKay sat up, looking a little more awake. "Go on. I'll make sure the beast stays on the leash."

Kay got to her feet. "I don't know why the beast needs to be here at all. This is my problem, Alex. I need to handle it. I don't need the brotherhood rushing in to save me like I'm some delicate princess."

McKay shrugged. "Did you not see the delicate princess clause in your contract? The brotherhood doesn't care that you're competent and capable of handling things yourself. The brotherhood cares that you're a woman we care about. Now go. You're on thin ice. Let us do what we need to."

She sighed. "Fine. But I'll be right back."

And he was left alone with them. Was he about to get some kind of warning?

"Mr. Hunt, would you care to tell me why the sunniest woman of my acquaintance looks like death warmed over?" McKay asked. "I've seen that girl with the flu and she still smiles like she's at Disney World."

That was interesting. "I don't know. You'll have to ask her."

"Oh, but we're asking you." Miles was suddenly side by side with Taggart, their bickering tossed aside in favor of putting forth a united front.

Against him.

"Yes, and the answer to that question will let me know a whole lot about you," Taggart said.

Jeez, when the guy wanted to look psychotic, he could turn that shit on. "I suspect she's upset that I didn't take her deception well."

"You didn't take it well as in you got angry and hurt and wouldn't talk to her, or you tried to hurt her?" Miles asked.

"I beat the shit out of your bodyguard." He sort of lied. He'd hit the guy. It wasn't his fault Declan Burke seemed to be made out of granite. "But I sure as hell didn't physically hurt Kayla. You can't expect me to be happy that she lied to me. She used me on every level. I have to say she's excellent at her job. She knows exactly how to make a man give it all up. I wouldn't fire her if I were you. A good one is hard to find."

"A good what?" McKay asked. "Choose the next word you say with some caution. I told Kay I would keep the beast on a leash, but one wrong word out of your mouth and I won't be able to hold him. You see, Big Tag and Kay understand each other. They know what it means to sacrifice for their country. They know how to make the hard calls, the ones that haunt a person for the rest of his or her life, and they know what it means to care about the very person they're supposed to be targeting. It can be hard."

Miles took over. "Someone like Kay doesn't make mistakes. Never. She's the solid one, the one we send in when everyone else has fucked up. She knows protocol and that it's there for a reason. There's only one possible conclusion I can draw as to why she fucked up here. Of all the intricate and complex cases she's handled, she's only let her emotions lead her in one and that's yours. So please, clarify your last statement because I need to know if I should call in a cleanup crew. A good *what* is hard to find?"

Shit. He was sitting in a room with three men who'd killed, and likely multiple times. They'd done it in service of their country, but it looked like they would also do it in service of a friend. "Operative. Agent. Whatever terminology you would use."

"Sure. That's what was going on in your head. The last time a woman I loved fucked me over hard, I didn't think of her as an 'operative.' You're smarter than me. Keep it up, kid." Taggart looked at the other two men. "Why don't you give me a minute alone with our new friend?"

McKay sighed. "Just remember that you hate paying for stuff and cleaners are expensive."

Miles shrugged. "I'll go halfsies for this one. Good luck, Hunt."

They filed out of the room.

Taggart stared at him for a moment.

Hunt stared back. What was the guy going to do? Murder him right here? "If you're going to beat the shit out of me, get going, asshole. You won't be doing a damn thing that hasn't already been done and by people who were bigger and meaner than you."

Another lie, but he'd been so much smaller then that proportionally he was probably correct. It was good that he could use math to compare beatings. A gift from playing a numbers savant once. He needed to play a boxer next.

"I can only imagine what you've been through."

He stiffened. "I thought you didn't listen to the tape."

"I don't have to listen to a tape to know that you disappeared from the time you were twelve until adulthood. And that woman you had us search for, she had a history of...well, her records are what nightmares are made of. I have three children, Mr. Hunt. I would never want them to experience a tenth of what you must have. But that's neither here nor there. Your secrets are your own, though I've found keeping secrets is a good way to be miserable. There's something shitty about the human psyche that punishes us for burying the bad stuff. There's something freeing about the truth. I'm going to impart some truth on you, Joshua Hunt."

"Hit me." It wouldn't change anything. This stranger knew nothing about him.

"That woman who hurt you could only hurt you because you cared about her."

He shrugged. "I'll admit I fell under her spell. She's excellent at sizing a man up and figuring out what he needs. I didn't even know I was attracted to weird chicks."

Taggart's lips curled in a way that let Josh know the man genuinely liked Kay. "What did she do? Talk to plants? She likes to do that. Says they grow even faster if you sing to them. She does a mean Pink."

"Dolphins. She talked to dolphins," he corrected. "And a seal."

Taggart chuckled and then got serious again. "I'm going to tell you a story. Well, maybe you've heard it. It's the one about this bright-eyed college kid who found out she had a twin sister trapped in a terrible life as a spy for a foreign country."

He knew she'd gone in young, but she hadn't mentioned a sibling. "Kayla had a sister?"

"Oh, yes. One of the nastiest female operatives I ever went up against. I mean that on a couple of levels. Nasty in a good way that would get me in trouble with my wife if she knew I talked about it, and nasty in a way that would likely make my wife high-five her because my Charlie is a chick who doesn't mind a bit of castration, if you know what I mean. Not that Kun managed it with me, but she did try. When I met Kay, I couldn't quite believe they were twins because Kayla was like sunshine and her sister was dark. I don't mind dark, but Jiang Kun was a bottomless pit of it."

"How did Kayla end up in the States?" He didn't want to be fascinated by that woman. He wanted the cold he'd felt yesterday, to be able to easily wave this guy off because he didn't care to know anything more about her.

"She was born when China had the one child rule. Her mother discovered she was having twins and found an underground that helped out women in her condition. She delivered the twins in a small rural hospital where they doctored the records, and then she kept Kun and sent Kay to an orphanage. Again, not something you can truly understand until you've held your own kid in your hand. The sacrifice her mother made was incredible."

"And then Kay was adopted by Fred and Jim and came to California," he finished. What a miracle for her. Not a miracle. Her mother had made that happen.

"Yes, and then years later, her sister reached out. Kun had been recruited by Chinese intelligence. At a young age, she showed a propensity for moral flexibility, physical prowess, and high intelligence combined with a lack of compassion."

"She was a sociopath." All that psych came in handy from time to time.

"Yes, but we don't tell Kay that," Taggart said, his voice deep. "She thinks her sister was a victim of circumstance, and for the most part she was. But she was twisted. Whether that happened as a circumstance of birth or what MSS did to her, she became quite good at torture and killing. But Kun was excellent at pretending to be an actual human being. She would have made a fine actress. She took what she knew from her mother and managed to find her sister. She reached out to the Agency, saying she wanted to connect to the sister she'd never met. Naturally, the Agency got right on that. Kun wrote to her, started a conversation, and then went in for the kill."

There had been two Kaylas. It was hard to imagine. Did she miss her sister? Even though she hadn't known her, sometimes twins felt the loss as something missing deep inside them. Did Kayla feel incomplete without her twin? "She wanted to come to the US?"

"Oh, yes. And that's when the Agency came up with the plan," Taggart explained. "I wasn't a part of this, but I knew the two men who handled Kayla. I was recruited into the CIA by a man named Ten Smith, but for the majority of my time there both Ten and I worked under John Bishop. Bishop decided to use Kayla to bring Kun in. It was a good plan because Jiang Kun was one of China's best agents and she had the highest security clearance. She was a gold mine of information and all she wanted was what her sister had—freedom. We got the clearance to bring her in, but we had to do it all quietly. Naturally everything went sideways and Kun was killed. Bishop had a choice. He could lose it all or he could plant his own spy."

"Kayla." One minute she'd been ready to meet her sister and the next, she'd *been* her sister, taking over her life as a spy for the enemy. What kind of courage had that required?

"She went from crying over the body of the sister she barely knew to walking into the mouth of the beast. And she was magnificent. I owe her my life more than once. So understand when I tell you a woman like that doesn't fuck up for any reason other than the one none of us can avoid. She's in love with you. You can take that love or you can leave it, but at least acknowledge the fact that she was attempting to do a service for her country, that she never meant to hurt you, that in the face of losing the only thing she really knows now, she chose you."

"You're wrong. Don't romanticize this. She chose the mission," he argued. "Like I said, she's a good operative."

But what had Taggart ragged her about? Protocol? The op's parameters had changed after his talk with Tyler and she was supposed to have called back to her boss and figured out another plan. Instead, she'd panicked and blown the whole thing wide open.

Why? Because she was desperate to save that operative who was likely already dead? Or because she didn't want her lover walking into something he couldn't understand?

Taggart sat back. "Well, I can't fix stupid. All right, then. That's all. Don't get my agent killed by doing something dumb. You know your role. Escort her in. Let her do her job. Escort her back out. And then what happens is up to you. We'll send a plane for her. You're dismissed."

Like he was a soldier. "I'm not your employee."

Taggart was on his phone, texting someone. He didn't bother to look up. "No, you are not. I wouldn't hire you."

"And this is not your club." Being dismissed rankled.

Arctic blue eyes came up. "I heard it wasn't yours either. Aren't you quitting?"

Someone had been talking, but then he couldn't simply blame Kayla for this one. He'd talked about it with Declan as they'd traded punches. Shane had heard him, too. He'd gone over everything Kay had cost him. God, even thinking about the things he'd called her made him wince. And why? He had every right to call her all the nasty names he wanted to. She'd done this to him, not the other way around. Everyone kept forgetting that he was the victim here. "Yeah, I'm going to leave the club. I can't stay here. From what I understand you have your own club, so you should understand. These people depend on everyone here to keep things private, and I've proven I can't do that."

"What's gotten out? Did Riley finally give up the game and sell photos to the tabloids? I thought I saw him eyeing a pair of sneakers he can't afford the other day. I always suspected that was why he took the job," Taggart said with a sad shake of his head. "Fucker."

Some woman somewhere put up with this guy's shit? "No,

obviously, but it could have happened. That's the point. I'm not staying around and waiting until something bad happens because I made a poor judgment call."

"And no one in this club ever brought in someone who could have done something bad? Dear god, Jared Johns is a member of this club. He brought a serial killer in and no one kicked him out. Did you have a trial and put him on suspension or something? Make him work his way back in, because I think serial killer trumps bringing in bodyguards who behaved poorly."

Wow. He hadn't thought of it that way. No one had been pissed at Jared. There certainly hadn't been a meeting where they discussed getting rid of him. He was one of them. The club had closed ranks around him and supported him. "This is different."

"Yes, because it's about you and you're very hard on yourself, aren't you, Joshua? You know my wife tells me holding myself to a far higher standard than anyone else is a sign of egomania. I think I'm just better than everyone else, right?"

"No. I don't fucking think that, asshole."

"Yet, you don't deserve a do-over, huh?" Taggart shook his head ruefully. "Dude, sorry. It's none of my business if you want to leave a place where you could relax. Hell, you probably have a million of them. You probably belong to a bunch of clubs."

"No, I don't. I had two places in the whole world where I felt safe enough to relax and I have to give them both up now. They're both tainted because I was too stupid to protect them. I have to give up my house because I'll never be able to trust it again." He would always be able to see her in that house. Years of memories and peace wiped out because anytime he opened the door, he looked for her now. His eyes would immediately go to the balcony to see if she was standing there, or to the kitchen where she often made snacks for the guys and he would say no and then sneak one anyway.

"What did the house do to you? Is it haunted?"

Why was he even talking to this asshole? And yes, it was haunted. She would be the ghost he could never get rid of, but he wasn't about to admit that to Taggart. "It's bugged. It was invaded by a bunch of people I don't know. I was safe there and now I'm not."

"Yeah, you know we can get rid of the bugs after the Agency is gone," Taggart said as though he was talking to a four-year-old. "Easy peasy. We can even teach you how to check for bugs so you can chill on the paranoia. And in case you weren't aware, other places can get bugged, too. When you think about it you're not safe anywhere."

He was preaching to the choir. Josh was getting antsy, ready for another fight. Or another session with the woman he shouldn't ever touch again. "Yeah, I fucking get that. Believe me I know that nowhere is safe."

"Then you should know that none of what went down in the last couple of days was your fault, man, and go easier on yourself." Taggart stood up and stuffed his phone in the laptop bag he'd brought with him. "And it's cool that you can't forgive Kayla. I get that now. It's hard to forgive anyone when you can't ever forgive yourself."

"Myself? What the fuck do I have to forgive myself for?"

Taggart nodded as he started for the door. "That's a damn good question, kid. Answer that one and maybe the rest of your life can fall in line." He paused at the door. "She won't stop after the op. She'll keep going until you're safe. She'll handle all of it so you'll be safer here than you were in the first place. I think some lucky blackmailer is going to be getting a visit from our Kayla soon. I hope she videotapes that. Fun times. Good to meet you."

She was going to what? He found himself staring at the spot where Taggart had sat. It was obvious the man lived to fuck with people. Kayla wouldn't go after his blackmailer alone. That would be ridiculous. She'd said that in order to get closer to him, but after the op was over, she would be done with him. He'd made himself plain.

Only a woman who really loved a man would still want to put herself at risk.

He didn't understand her, didn't understand any of this.

He sat and thought about everything they'd said, but that guy was wrong about him. He didn't have anything to forgive.

And he would never forget.

Still, when the time came to leave, he kept the letter he'd written to the club members in his pocket along with his keys. Maybe he should think about that.

Maybe.

* * * *

Kayla looked up as Big Tag walked out. She'd tried going back in to protect Josh from him, but Adam and Alex had blatantly waylaid her with a bunch of bullshit questions about the op.

"What did you do to him?" With Big Tag it could be anything from a simple but obnoxious talking to right up to brutal murder she would likely be left to clean up after.

Taggart gave her a smooth smile that was probably meant to put her at ease, but the man always reminded her of a satisfied predator when his lips curved up like that. Like he'd eaten someone he shouldn't and his belly was happily full. "Not a thing. Just wanted to make sure we were all on the same page. We are. So I can get back to my regularly scheduled programming of riding around in a billionaire's jet, drinking his Scotch, and changing all his playlists to classic rock. Can you believe Drew Lawless has a playlist titled Team TayTay for Taylor Swift's greatest hits? I'm taking his man card and ripping it up right in front of his wife's face. Hair metal. It's the only manly thing to listen to."

Somehow she doubted that was really Lawless's playlist. She looked up at the man who'd hired her when she'd needed a job. He could joke all he liked, but she was the reason his whole week had been upended. He'd been far closer and that was why he'd come out to California in Damon's stead. She was the reason he'd had to hustle to ensure his business didn't get ripped apart by lawsuits and potential criminal inquiries. "I'm sorry, Ian."

He frowned and shoved sunglasses over his eyes. "Come on. We should talk before I go. Adam, Alex seems to have fallen asleep on that spanking bench over there. You know what to do."

Adam grinned and held up his phone. "I'm documenting this for humanity and so I can photoshop in some crazy shit later. I'm going to miss this when I'm the boss."

Big Tag walked to the outer portion of the club. Sun streamed in from the overhead skylight but they were still out of the way of prying eyes. Riley had gone to pull the car around and they would be behind tinted windows in seconds, their identities protected from reporters and the Agency alike. "The idea of Adam being in charge scares me.

He'll spend all his profits on fancy shoes. At least he's got a good team around him. Too bad it's my damn team. I hate hiring people. You know, your boy is a hardass."

"He's been hurt. A lot." She couldn't even imagine what Josh had gone through.

"That kind of hurt doesn't go away on its own. Oh, you can try to self-medicate with Scotch and good music, but in the end you have to reopen that wound and let the toxins out or they'll kill you."

"I think I'm the first person he's ever told his story to." And then she'd betrayed him. She was starting to understand that he couldn't come back from that. She'd slipped into something that for most people would be the exact thing couples' therapy was made for, but in Josh's case it was quicksand, and the more she struggled to make him understand, the deeper she went with him. He wasn't going to up and get it. He wasn't going to forgive her. Ever.

When the op was over, he would shut the door on their relationship and move on. If there was one thing she'd learned about him, he was good at compartmentalizing. He would put their relationship in a room in his brain and lock the door and never think about her again.

And it didn't matter. She still loved him. She would still do what she needed to do. It was so odd to finally fall truly, deeply in love only to understand how painful it could be and that it was also the thing that could make her stronger than she'd ever been.

Loving Josh made her happy. The fact that he couldn't love her back might end up being the tragedy of her life, but at least she'd known what it meant to love.

"Well, you shouldn't be the last one. That kid needs some therapy. He's obviously got the weight of the world on his shoulders. The good news is I don't think he's going to sue us," Tag said. "There's bad news, of course."

Yep. This was the part where she got fired. "I'll resign."

Taggart's brows came together. "That's between you and Damon. I'm not going to mess with his personnel policies. He runs the London office and it's up to him whether or not you remain employed. I'm talking about the fact that this op of yours has a million moving pieces and I'm worried that Levi Green and Ezra are about to have a knock-down, drag-out, and only one of them will come out of this with his job. I think Green is making a play to get rid of Fain and I don't know why. I'm trying to figure it out. Normally I would get Chelsea on it, but she's buried under the startup. Given that I recommended the startup to my investor group, I'm caught between curiosity and making money. Charlie wants another kid and they eat cash, so I'm stuck with Hutch. I love that idiot, but he hasn't got Chelsea's ability to put a puzzle together. He can hack into anything, but I need someone who can see shit coming from a mile away. I would get Li working on it, but he's on freaking paternity leave. Charlie did this to me. She's got weird ideas on how to run a business."

Avery had recently had a baby girl. Daisy O'Donnell. She'd seen the baby over Facetime when Liam had called into the London office to let them know mother and daughter were doing fine.

God, she would miss them all. Miss all the babies and the way they were a family. She probably wouldn't get that at her next job.

"Ezra said he was called back to Langley," she told him, trying to stay professional. "I thought that was odd. Why have two handlers and then ditch one?"

"I don't know about that either, but I would have been more comfortable with Fain taking the lead. Which could be the point." Tag paced, his long legs eating up the space before turning and striding again, a lion in a cage. "If they thought you were the only operative who could do this op, they would need to make me and Damon comfortable, and having Fain in the mix would do the trick. I don't think I'd let you do this if Green had come to me himself. Now we're down to the nitty gritty and they dump Fain."

"They might have dumped him, but he claims he's not going anywhere."

Tag nodded. "Yeah, we've talked. Hutch is going to cover for him. He's got everything set up so it looks like he's being a good boy, but that plane we're on is going to pick him up and quietly take him down to Mexico City. It's the only reason I haven't pulled you off this op."

"I would go anyway." She couldn't leave Josh on his own.

He stopped, his lips curling up faintly. "Yeah, I suspect you would. Josh Hunt, huh? Don't tell him, but he's pretty badass in those car movies. That's what the world needs more of. Fast cars and very little plot line. I can follow that shit even though I fall asleep two or three times per film. I like to call them dad movies."

"I won't tell him that at all." But she smiled at the thought. Not that he would care what she said. "Is this ache going to be with me forever?"

He was quiet for a moment and she'd forgotten that men didn't like to talk about the relationship stuff.

"If it's real love, yeah," Tag said quietly. "If it's real then there will be this hollow place inside you that won't go away. The good news? I have never met anyone with as much love to give as you, Kayla. If he won't accept it, move on. It'll take you a little time, but you'll be able to try this again eventually. Hey, I got a son who'll be ready for you in about twenty years if you like 'em young."

It was about the biggest compliment he could give her, and it took everything she had not to cry.

"Would it help if I told you I think he'll come around?" Tag asked.

She took a deep breath, banishing the tears. "I don't see how."

"I've done this a time or two and he's already questioning himself. Push him over the next couple of days. Not to forgive you. Just remind him how nice it is to have you around. I think it'll work. And if it doesn't, well, I've got a couple of projects we need to work on."

"If Damon doesn't accept my resignation," she replied grimly. "I blew up an entire operation because I fell in love with a guy."

"If Damon does fire you, well, I didn't fire that crazy-ass Irishman when he did the same thing. Hell, if I fired everyone for doing stupid shit, I wouldn't have a team." He got serious again. "When this is done, I want to go find Bishop. Holy shit. I'm still trying to process the fact that he's alive. I don't care what Ezra thinks. Ezra doesn't know Bishop. He would never turn."

That was one thing she could get on board with. "Yes, I think we should. I think we should head to that little town and figure out what the hell's going on."

"I've heard they have a nudist resort," Tag said. "And a shit ton of ex-law enforcement. Ezra makes it sound like it could be some secret base for bad guys, but I can't see it. Bishop was the single best operative I've ever worked with. Ten agrees with me, so when you get back, we're hunting his ass down and getting some answers."

"Agreed." But she did have something else to do. "I might need a few days before we head to Colorado."

"In order to assassinate Hector Morales, who probably ran a ring that trafficked children throughout the US? Yeah, I thought you would say that. I suspect you'll be hunting down a blackmailer, too."

Her stomach tightened because he might be the only person in the world who could stop her. "I need this, Tag."

"I'm not going to stop you," he replied, his voice sure. "Just won't let you go alone. Take Boomer and do it from afar. I know you would rather gut the fucker, but he's surrounded by killers. His death will have to be justice enough. Boomer can handle it from a mile away and we can pay him in hot dogs. Forgive me. You'll be in Mexico. Tacos. Lots of tacos."

She should have known he would understand. "You're pretty cool, Ian Taggart."

"Yeah, that's what all the girls say." He glanced down as his phone buzzed. "Adam, carry our sleeping princess out. We gotta go. Car's here."

Alex yawned as he stepped out. "That bench you got is pretty comfy. Eve always complains about ours."

"Well, Eve is usually in another position on it," Adam argued. "I don't think you would find it so comfy if you had a large plug up your butt and someone was spanking you."

"Let's find out," Ian said as the door opened. "Five hundred says Alex gives up before the plug even comes out of the package."

"I'll take that," Adam replied. "I think he's tougher than he looks."

"Fuck you both," Alex said, striding out to the car.

And they were off. She loved Josh, but she also missed the easy camaraderie of her coworkers.

"Can we go home now?" Josh walked through the doors that led to the main part of the club.

Remind him how nice it is to have you around.

"Sure," she said. "Unless you want to play for a while. I only got to come here once."

He stopped, his whole body stilling. "You won't win me back."

She had to keep this casual. Push him physically but not emotionally. That would come because he wouldn't be able to stop it. "Then there's no problem with enjoying each other until we can't anymore."

His face had flushed and there was no way to miss how his jeans tented. "It won't mean anything."

"Will it mean an orgasm? Because I've had a shitty morning and I could use one. I'll just take care of myself when we get home." She shrugged it off like it didn't matter even though her heart ached. "When is our plane tomorrow?"

He was suddenly behind her, his hand on her shoulder. "You are not allowed to masturbate unless I say so. How quickly you forget. You're under contract until the job is over. Take off your clothes and find your place in the main dungeon. We'll see if I can spank the rules into you."

She was smiling as she began to strip.

Chapter Seventeen

Seven days later, Josh grimaced as he stared at the tux he would have to stuff himself into. He looked at himself in the ornate mirror and wished this fucking party hadn't been black tie.

"I find it interesting that this Tyler asshole didn't bother to show up for work," Kayla complained from the bathroom.

"According to the director, he said he couldn't leave the US right now. It's cool. I got everything I needed out of him," he replied.

She looked out the door, her body wrapped in a robe. Her hair was pinned up as though she was about to get into the shower he could hear running. "I would love to have talked to the man."

"I'm sure you would have." He could bet she would have been polite and pleasant and found a way to make her point. He was kind of glad Tyler Williams had decided to stay stateside. Kayla was highly suspicious of the dude. Earlier today, he'd caught her looking the man's name up on her laptop. He suspected she wasn't merely attempting to put him on her Christmas card list. "Did you enjoy the tour of the grounds?"

He had to be careful what he said because almost immediately after they'd been shown to their suite of rooms in the west wing of the massive compound at the edge of the jungle, Riley had run some kind of device over the walls and shaken his head at Kayla.

Bugs, bugs, and more bugs. Soon his life would be bug free and he was fucking keeping it that way. He'd cleared his schedule, pulling out of two films and pushing back another. He needed time and space to sit and think.

He needed to figure out how to be without her.

A solid week they'd spent on set. He'd worked fourteen-hour days and somehow she'd still managed to put her stamp on each and every one. The first day on set, she'd brought pastries in for the crew, making them all laugh and fall madly in love with her. Even the director, who pretty much hated everyone, had told Josh that one was a "keeper."

The second day, he'd twisted the same damn ankle he'd hurt in the canyon and she'd sat in the small medical facility with him, bringing him coffee and taking his mind off the pain.

Every single frame of this film would remind him of her.

It would be better when she was physically away from him. The trouble was they were still thrown together and had to make everything look good for the people who were watching them.

Kayla stepped out of the bathroom. "Hector was a pleasant companion. You were right. He's an incredibly generous man and this place is spectacular."

Every word they said had to be measured. First because the Agency had been listening in, and now because Hector Morales apparently liked to spy on his guests, but then given that the man was head of a major drug cartel, it was likely an occupational necessity.

"He has his own zoo," she was saying. "It's pretty tricked out. This place is huge."

"Yeah, I suspect we would need a map to get around," he replied. He prayed her Agency contact had gotten her one.

She winked his way. "Nah, I'm only really interested in the ballroom. I'm playing princess tonight. Want to be Prince Charming? Because you worked out earlier and my Prince Charming isn't stinky."

He hadn't, but the shower was the only place they could talk. And do other things. God, he'd had that woman every way he could think of and his cock surged the minute he realized he could have her one more time. For the last three days he'd promised himself every time was the last and every time she smiled his way, his dick overrode all of his good intentions.

This might be the last time. The very last time.

The party was tonight and they'd decided it was the perfect time for her to slip away and download Morales's computer. There would be a hundred people milling about the mansion, many wanting to meet Hector's special guest—Josh. Security would be tight, but Kayla assured him she could deal with them.

He pulled his T-shirt over his head and tossed it away. If she got what she needed tonight, Riley Blade would take the intel and hand it off to someone called Mr. Green and they would be done. They would wake up tomorrow, have breakfast with the drug kingpin, and head back into the city. He would go back to work and Kayla was scheduled for a flight to London tomorrow night.

And they would never see each other again.

He shoved out of his jeans and those joined the T-shirt along with his boxers. "I wouldn't want your Prince Charming to be anything less than perfect. Is this your first ball?"

He would go back to his life. Or maybe not. He would take some time and decide what he wanted. He could apply for hermitship. Or maybe become a hobo.

God, she was in his head. He couldn't even brood properly anymore. No. Every time he started to go seriously dark she was there making fun of him, teasing him out of his dark places.

Why had she been a lie?

He entered the bathroom naked, his cock fully erect. "Take off the robe."

It hit the ground in an instant. She was completely obedient when it came to sex, seemed to need and crave his dominance. Unfortunately, outside the bedroom, she was an utter mystery to him.

Wouldn't it be nice to spend the next fifty years figuring her out? Learning all her secrets. She hadn't once spoken of her sister. Did she miss Jiang Kun? Did she sometimes miss *being* Jiang Kun? All questions he'd wanted to ask and stubbornly had kept silent about because he'd told himself none of it mattered.

She stepped into the shower. Morales's mansion was done up like a palace. Versailles in the New World as he'd called it the first time

Josh had been here. The floor beneath their feet was marble, the bathroom designed like it was made for French royalty. He followed her in, his hands already on her skin. He couldn't fucking help himself. If he hadn't forced himself to sleep on the couch of the hotel suite they'd been sharing, he would have ended up wrapped around her, cuddling her close and fucking her every time he woke.

He had no idea what would happen tonight. The hotel suite had been safe, Kay had assured him. Well, just audio. No video. They couldn't be sure about these rooms so they had to assume Morales could see as well as hear.

"Calm down, babe," she said, her voice low. "Everything is going great. Morales is perfectly charming. He speaks highly of you and can't wait to show you off to his guests tonight. That was all he talked about this afternoon, how proud he was to have such a big star in his home. All you have to do is perform tonight and no one is going to notice me slipping away."

He leaned over, breathing in her scent, the heat from the shower making his body relax for the first time today. Every second she'd been with Morales had seemed like hours, but he'd been stuck talking to some of Hector's relatives and he couldn't think of an excuse for her to not go with him. He traced the scar under her right clavicle with his thumb. Even her scars were pretty. He loved this one in particular because they joked about it. Little Miss Muffett.

No spider would frighten his girl away. "I hated watching you walk off with him."

"I know," she replied, letting him touch her, look at her. She would stay there until he'd looked and touched to his heart's content. She would stand there until the water got cold and they needed to go because that was simply who she was as a lover.

Giving. Never faltering. He traced a line down to her nipple. "Do you know where his office is?"

"Yes, and it's a bit tricky because it's in an opposite wing of the house, but my handler sent me the blueprints. The good news is Hector mentioned that he would have the pool and the gardens open tonight. I'm just going to get a little lost when I need some fresh air. Riley assures me he can cut into the security feed. He'll put it on a loop and we'll be out of there before you know it. I'll come back here and we can dance the night away."

He traced a finger around and around that pretty nipple, watching it peak for him. "And Riley will take the intel to your handler?"

She nodded. "Yep, so even if they suspect me of something, I won't have anything on me. Touch me. Everywhere. I don't want this to end."

Then she should have thought about turning into a liar who stole his last bit of privacy. He took a step back because he was doing it again. "I'm sorry. I can't trust you, but god, Kay, I do want this from you. I wish I could lie and hurt you like you've hurt me. I wish I could tell you this thing between us wasn't the most electric I've ever felt, but it's true. I'll miss it, but I know how to survive. I learned it a long time ago. Lesson number one. Never make the same mistake twice."

"We could make totally new ones," she said but with a sad smile, as though she knew what the answer would be.

He reached around and pulled her close. "I *am* going to let you get on that plane. I *am* going to say good-bye to you. I'm going to do it to save me, and maybe that makes me a coward, but I can't do this with you. It couldn't work now. Honestly, it wouldn't have worked even before. I would always be waiting for the other shoe to fall."

Her head came up, tears shining in her eyes. "I'm going to miss you until the day I die, Joshua Hunt. Maybe longer. Someday you're going to love a woman and she will be the luckiest woman on earth, and I need you to understand that I genuinely want that for you."

He shook his head. She didn't understand the full extent of his agony. "That won't happen because I love you."

She stepped back, taking a deep inhale and obviously trying to get herself under control. "No, you don't. If you loved me you wouldn't be able to leave me. A smart dude taught me that. It's okay. We don't get to pick who we fall in love with."

It was perverse, but he hated the fact that she didn't believe him. "I told you I love you. I've never said that to anyone."

"Sure you have," she replied. "You say it at the end of every movie, babe. You're good at it."

He knew she was trying to lighten the mood, but he didn't want it lightened. He wanted to be acknowledged. "Don't blow me off,

Kayla. I said it and I meant it."

Her eyes were soft on him as she spoke. "But you don't. If you loved me, that shoe you're waiting on wouldn't mean anything. People in love are brave. I'm not saying you aren't. Please understand that. I think you're one of the bravest human beings I've ever met."

"I am not." He was fairly certain he was the worst kind of coward.

"Sometimes bravery isn't about slaying a dragon. Sometimes bravery is about getting out of bed every morning and going to work even when the pain is so bad you can't stand the thought of going on. I think you're very brave, and one day you're going to find a woman you can't live without. I want that for you because you deserve it, and if she's ever a bitch to you, send her my way."

"You'll take care of her, huh?"

She nodded solemnly.

"Like you're planning on taking care of the woman who's blackmailing me."

She was silent for a moment and then she nodded again. "And Morales. I'm going to kill him too, and then he can't put you in a bad position ever again."

Crazy-ass bitch. She was a true psycho chick and she was going to get herself killed. She was going up against one of the most dangerous men in the world. "You can't do that."

"I assure you, I can." She turned and started to reach for the soap.

Why? Why the fuck would she do that?

He gripped her arm and turned her back toward him. She made him crazy. She confused him. She made him fucking feel alive.

He leaned over and kissed her. Days of not kissing her had left him desperate for her mouth. He dominated her, needing to feel that moment when she softened against him, submitting to him. Her whole body seemed to lean into him, giving over, and in that moment he was a fucking king.

In that moment, it didn't matter what she'd said or done because she was his and he would handle it. If it was a simple mistake, they would get through it. If she was the fucking baddest of bad guys, he would tie her down and discipline her until she never lied to him again. He could chain her to his side and make sure she never stepped out of line again.

No more assassinations. No more letting the CIA use her sweet beauty to play their wicked games. She would be his and only his, and anyone who tried to come between them would fucking find out how badass he could be when he wanted to. She would work for him and him alone, and only when he wanted her to. She would spend the rest of her life following him around the world and making animal friends and doing weird shit that made him laugh and fucking him. She would spend the rest of her life fucking him.

He crowded her, shoving her back against the wall and lifting her up. Her legs went around his hips while he never once let go of her mouth. That gorgeous mouth he dreamed of at night. She was the only woman he'd ever willfully kissed, the only one who'd ever felt the slow slide of his tongue. God, she was the only woman he'd ever willingly gone down on.

Only her. For the rest of his life. If he never saw her again after tomorrow, he would go to his grave with the taste of her on his lips.

"I do love you." He whispered the words against her flesh.

He flexed his hips and his cock found its home. It was like the damn thing knew exactly where to go. He thrust inside because she was already wet and ready for him. No woman in the world had ever responded the way she did, as though she'd been built specifically for him.

Was he willing to let that go? For any fucking reason?

"I love you, Joshua. I love you so much." Her arms wound around his neck. She held him like she would never let him go.

He pumped into her, his whole being focused on their connection. When he was inside her, he didn't think about what she'd done, how they didn't work. When he was inside her all that mattered was the here and now, and it was perfect.

He thrust and thrust, his mouth finding hers again and taking over. His lips moved over hers, tongue delving deep inside, imitating the hard moves of his cock. He wanted to penetrate her in every way, to connect them as physically as they could possibly be connected. This was it. This was the final moment of his time with her and he wanted to make it last.

Because he *would* give her up.

Wouldn't he?

The idea of a crazy-bitch warrior goddess who would love him and be with him and fucking protect him for the rest of his life—that was the wish of his childhood self. The adult, the man he'd become long before his childhood should have ended, knew she was a lie the universe told. She was another trick. Another falsehood. Another beautiful dream he would wake up from.

Long before he wanted to give up, she tightened around him, all those seemingly delicate muscles deep inside her milking him for all they were worth. He couldn't fight her. That was the truth of his existence. He was weak when he should be strong.

He was hard when it would be smarter to be soft.

He was stubborn when he should yield.

Josh let the orgasm wash over him, even as something deeper worked on his soul. She would be with him always. There was no way to wash her away or cleanse himself. And to even seek it was stupid. She was the clean part of him. She was the part that believed he'd never been dirtied at all.

"I love you." He said the words as though he couldn't keep them from coming out of his mouth. He said them as his insistent cock faded and all that was left was the emotion he wanted badly to dam up and hide. Like that Edgar Allan Poe short. He wanted to take his heart and put it underground, but it kept beating for her. It kept insisting and begging and prodding until he couldn't hear anything but the beat, that fucking rhythm it had taken the moment she walked into his life.

"I love you," she replied. "I'll always love you. I'll always want you. I'll always be waiting for you to come home to me, Josh. After this is done, I think I'm going to retire. After one last job, I'm going back to Santa Barbara and I'm going to find that stupid girl I was and see what happens, but know the woman I am will always be waiting. Even when I'm old and gray. There will only ever be you for me."

She wrapped her arms around him, her affection something he'd come to rely on. Such easy affection, as though her soul had known his without effort or cause. As if she'd simply loved him from the beginning, no restrictions or clauses.

As if the universe had known what he'd lost, had never had, and formed this perfection of love meant only for him, to lift him up, a prize he'd won simply because he'd survived the worst. Love at its purest. At its rarest.

But how could he trust it?

She kissed him and left the shower, leaving him alone.

As he'd always been. As he would be if he couldn't be the brave man she thought he was.

He stood under the shower, praying for strength.

* * * *

He was the single most beautiful man she'd ever seen and her heart was oddly peaceful. Josh stood across the room from her, looking perfectly cast as the Hollywood star in his tailored tuxedo. His hair was slicked back, showing off his perfectly chiseled features and those swoon-worthy eyes. Every woman in the room had eyes on him. A whole lot of the men, too.

It was going to be okay. Something had settled between them after that moment in the shower. She'd made her play, told him how she felt. If she lost him anyway, she would take her love and put it into something else because she knew there was only one man for her.

There was something comforting about acceptance.

"You look beautiful. *Mujer hermosa*," Hector said as he approached her. "Josh must be proud to have you at his side."

But she wasn't at his side. He was across the room, talking to some lovely woman who would likely be donating a ton of money to his charity. He smiled at the lady, though Kay knew that was his rich-donor smile and not the one he used when he was truly happy.

He was going to let her go. He was going to stand back and let them break, and there was nothing she could do. She wasn't his love. It hurt her. It fucking broke her, but she wasn't the woman who would heal Joshua Hunt. She was somewhere out there. Kayla prayed she was because Josh deserved her. That was love. Wanting more for someone even when she couldn't be the one to give it.

Oh, how she wanted her dads. She wasn't going to be stoic this time. That London flight was taking a big old stop in Santa Barbara, where she intended to cry on her dads' shoulders and let them take

313

care of her. Her dad would talk to her about love and life and try to give her sage advice. Her papa would make never-ending rounds of comfort food and swear to put the whammy on Josh the next time he went to see Miss Maybelle, his psychic. The dog would growl and try to lick her mouth. She would revel in their love. She would let them help her plan a future without Josh because they were her fathers and that was their job.

"Thank you for saying so." She smiled Hector's way, letting the grief she felt sink back into her subconscious. She had a job to do. There was time to pine for what she couldn't have later. "I'm simply happy to be here. It was kind of you to open your home to us."

To me, especially, because I'm bringing your house of cards down all around you, asshole.

Hector Morales was a stout man. With a barrel chest and strong limbs, he was somewhere between dad bod and fit, that odd place a lot of vain, almost middle-aged men fell. He took care of himself somewhat, but she could also tell he likely sampled his own product from time to time. There was something about his florid face that spoke of hard nights. "I adore Joshua. Such an amazing young man. I have admired him for years. I love the survivors."

"Survivors?"

His skin flushed, but he didn't miss a beat. "You know, Hollywood is a rough business and Josh rather grew up on screen. That's not an easy task. He wasn't as good in the beginning, but now he is the foremost of all the actors in America. I'm very proud of him."

Awesome. He was proud the kid he'd forced into prostitution had made something of himself. It was funny, but when she looked at Hector, she could already see the bullet hole in between his brows. Boomer was getting so many tacos. "I am, too. You know I forgot to ask earlier, but exactly how did you meet Josh?"

A secret smile flashed on Morales's face and then was gone in an instant. "I was always a fan, but then I was in Los Angeles and met his agent. Not the one he has now, but the one who got him his start in the business. I might have strong-armed my way into one of Joshua's charity receptions. He had just started his children's foundation. We met and struck up a friendship. We both have strong feelings about children. They must be protected. They are the future."

He'd certainly built a business on their suffering. "I'm surprised you don't have any children of your own."

He waved that off. "I've spent the last several years working on building my business. I have only a few more professional issues to get out of the way and then I'll be announcing my plans to marry."

She'd heard nothing about a girlfriend. "Very nice. I'm sure you'll throw an incredible wedding. Is your future fiancée here tonight?"

"She's around, but she can be a bit shy," he admitted. "She's very involved in my business, you see. You would like her. I think you would find you have a lot in common. Perhaps I'll introduce you if all goes well and I can tempt her out."

More information for the Agency. "I would love to meet her."

Morales nodded as the band started playing. "Excuse me, dear. I have a full dance card. Please enjoy yourself."

She thanked him and watched as he walked up to a woman she thought she recognized from a telenovela. The woman was lovely and older than she would have suspected Hector liked his women, but then she wouldn't have thought he would marry a business associate either.

The man had secrets and it was time for her to steal a few of them.

Across the room Josh caught her eye.

She gave him a smile.

Don't go.

It was easy to read his expression because he looked plainly panicked.

She tried to make sure her smile this time was a thing of great confidence. *It's going to be okay.*

His jaw tightened and then someone touched his arm and he was right back to playing the gracious on-screen god, mingling with the mortals.

Kayla slipped out the back of the ballroom and into the gardens. She would give it to Morales. The man knew how to throw a party. He knew how to live, too. The mansion was dazzling and intricately designed. She glanced up at the security camera and watched the red

315

light switch off.

Riley had done his job. Her stepping in front of that first camera was his signal to start the loop. They'd taken the footage the night before. With all the dancing, no one would suspect there was a reason the gardens were empty. There was a grand ball going on, the likes of which many of these modern, successful people had likely never experienced. It was a scene right out of a historical film where the king welcomed his courtiers into his palace.

Her role for the night? Thief and spy. Luckily it was a role she was well used to playing. Some might even say she'd become typecast.

"You have a guard coming up on your left as you reenter the building," a voice said in her ear. She was wearing a small comm device that allowed her to hear Riley as he steered her around the house. He had the full range of security cameras while the guards in the house would see what he wanted them to see.

That was the key to a proper operation. Illusion. Deception. Control. These people wouldn't even know there was a show going on around them. To them, it was exactly what it looked like—a party, and no one would notice the woman sneaking away.

If for some reason they did, she had her excuse. If they didn't believe that, then she had a small semiautomatic in her clutch and a couple of knives strapped to her thighs.

"Give him a second. He's not good at staying still. He paces. You'll have about ten seconds to get back into the house, but from what I can tell, the doors aren't locked."

Morales had said he wanted his guests to enjoy the gardens, but there had been a forecast for rain this evening. The guard would likely send anyone caught in a storm back toward the ballroom. Unfortunately, she was going another way.

"Go now."

She didn't hesitate, moving across the cobblestoned garden path and back into the house. To her left she could see the armed guard walking away from her. Out that way were some buildings and cottages where security and personnel lived. She'd marked the small guesthouse where Shane was staying. Declan was waiting to pick up Riley once the handoff had been made. He would drive Riley back into the city where they would meet up with Levi Green or one of his operatives at a café in the morning.

Shane was staying behind to drive she and Josh back to the set tomorrow afternoon.

She slipped into the darkened part of the house, the music faint from here. Moonlight illuminated the center of the hall so she clung to the sides. The floor here was parquet, the walls done up in pretty white wainscoting and sporting painting after painting.

Kayla breathed in and slipped out of her heels. No matter how silently she moved, they would click on that wood. Once free of the five-inch Louboutins, she waited, her back to the wall as the guard took his place again in front of the door. He seemed to peer inside as though he knew something had happened but he wasn't sure what.

Calm. She stayed perfectly calm and still and after a moment, the guard started pacing again.

"Go, Kay," Riley said in her ear. "You've got someone at the base of the stairs but he's a friendly. Tell Ezra hi for me. Damn, he's good. This is the first time I've seen him."

She sprinted down the hallway and turned right.

Ezra Fain peeled away from the shadows, his body in all black. There was even a balaclava covering his head so he could pull it down and blend in with the darkness. He nodded her way.

"Where did you come in from?" She had to ask because somehow it was hard to see him hiring on as part of the catering staff.

His lips curled up a bit. "Walked in from the jungle. I do not recommend it though. Next assignment I want to be infiltrating a spa or golf course or something without massive bugs. Everything gone all right?"

"It's gone perfectly," she replied. "I'm afraid you hung out with the bugs for no reason."

His eyes told her he didn't agree. "I don't trust perfect. Let's get this over with. Maybe I can hide out and hitch a ride back with you two in the morning."

They moved in time, going up the stairs to the second floor where Morales's private office was kept.

"At least we caught one break," Riley was saying in her ear. "I'm close to you. I'm in Shane's cottage and I can easily get under the window. You won't have to leave the house to get the package to me. You're clear on the second floor. He's got all his guards on the outer periphery. Declan is going to drive me out with the excuse that he's got to pick up Mr. Hunt's prescription in town. They've been told to give Josh anything he wants. They won't check the trunk. It would be insulting."

Poor Riley. She wondered how he'd drawn that duty. Despite the fact that the limo had a nice-sized trunk, she doubted it would be comfy for him.

She stopped, some instinct deep inside her telling her she wasn't alone.

Ezra paused beside her and suddenly there was a Ruger in his hand. "Where is it?"

"I can't tell," she replied quietly.

"You okay? I'm not picking anyone up," Riley assured her.

She couldn't help it. Perhaps she was too emotional, too close to the heart of the op. She was sensing things that weren't there.

"Let's get into the office," Ezra urged. "We're in the open out here. Come on."

She followed him up the stairs. He was right. They needed to get this done and she would feel better. She would meet up with Josh and they would have one last night together.

It was five minutes and then she would be done and she could get on with the rest of her life.

She used the security card she'd lifted off Morales earlier at dinner and the door clicked open. Thanks to her boys, the guards wouldn't get that notification either.

"All right, Kay. I'm coming to you. Be there in roughly three minutes."

The line went dead and she was on her own.

She glanced over at Ezra. "Riley's on his way. We're making the drop via...well, drop. I'm dropping it out the window."

He nodded, glancing around the wood-paneled office before holding out a drive of his own. "Make me a copy?"

He really didn't trust Levi if he wanted his own copy. She plugged in the drive to the computer's USB port and let the program it uploaded start to work.

Her heart rate was up. Damn, maybe she was right to get out of the business. Lately all she'd been doing were corporate jobs and bodyguard assignments. She was off her game.

She wanted out of the game. She greatly preferred hanging with Tucker and the Lost Boys to risking her life. In the beginning she'd found her inner adrenaline junkie, but over the years she wanted peace more than some thrill.

Josh would think Tucker and the boys were a hoot. It would have been fun to introduce him to her world. Josh was like a sponge. Perhaps it was all the years of going without learning, only surviving from day to day, but Josh was so vibrant when he was learning something new. He soaked up every experience.

Huh, funny. That was what they had in common, a thirst for life, for new experiences, for stories untold and people they hadn't met yet. He was quieter about it, as though he didn't trust he would get the experience if he wanted it too much.

Could it be that he wanted her too much and he didn't trust the world to let him have her?

"Are you going to be okay? I heard Josh didn't handle the truth well." Ezra moved to the front of the desk.

Big Tag was such a gossip. "I'm fine. Well, not fine. I ache. I hate this part of the love thing. This part sucks, but I knew he wouldn't be able to handle it if I told him. I made the choice. I couldn't send him in here alone even if it meant losing him."

"And this DEA agent who tipped him off about Morales? You know anything about him?"

"I'm working up a file on him, but he seems legit. I mean he's DEA, shouldn't he know who the drug lords are? If I were in Tyler Williams's shoes, I would have told him, too."

The device Levi had given her pinged and she changed it out for Ezra's.

A few minutes more and they would be done.

"Why don't you head out with Riley?" She didn't like the idea that he could be found. The point of Riley taking the drive was so if she got caught, no one could connect her. There wouldn't be any evidence that she'd taken a thing.

"Because I'm not leaving you here without backup."

"Everything is fine. Riley's got the cameras on a timer. I'll have five minutes to get back. I only need two. If I get caught, I was looking at the paintings and didn't realize how far I'd gotten from the ballroom. I'm good, Ez." She turned to the window. The glass was beautifully paned and like everything in the mansion had a certain European flair. Many of the windows downstairs had been left open so the scent of the night-blooming jasmine could fill the ballroom. It appeared it was all on one security system. She opened the window and there was Riley, standing on the ground under it.

"I'm staying on," Ezra replied. "I'm at least getting you to the ballroom. I'll hike back through the jungle if you're worried about getting caught with me in the car."

Overprotective men. "Suit yourself."

Not that she would actually let him hike back through the jungle in the dark. She would have to sneak him into Shane's room.

"Rapunzel, Rapunzel let down your thumb drive," Riley said with a cocky grin.

Somehow it didn't have the same impact. She dropped it down and he caught it with one hand. "Go. Get out of here as quick as you can. Tell Levi I'll meet him at the airport tomorrow."

Riley gave her a salute and then his long legs were taking him and the prize across the grounds and toward the place where Declan was waiting.

Ezra's device pinged and she detached it, handing it over. "See. Job well done. Let's get back to the ball."

Back to Josh for the last time.

She opened the door and stopped in her tracks, realizing that perhaps she'd been the one to see only what she'd wanted to see. Because when things seemed too easy, they usually were exactly that—too easy. Too good to be true.

Levi Green was standing in the doorway with three armed men. Before she could take a breath, he lifted his gun and shot Ezra Fain straight through the heart.

Kayla watched him fall, Ezra's eyes shocked as he hit his knees, hand going to his chest.

Levi put a second one in his back. "For good measure, asshole. Bye, Fain. Gentlemen, don't get blood on that dress. We're going to need it. Hello, Kay. You ready to have some fun?"

She started to fight, but someone shoved a needle in her arm. What was happening? The world went foggy and she couldn't make her muscles work.

Ezra was dead on the floor. Ezra...she'd gotten Ezra killed. Levi was here and that was a bad thing.

Josh. Where was Josh?

And then her eyes went wide because she saw someone she knew she would never see again. Someone she couldn't see.

That was the moment Kay knew she was dying, too.

Chapter Eighteen

Josh breathed a sigh of relief as he watched Kay walk back in the room. A few minutes later than he'd expected, but there she was whole and stunningly beautiful.

He should have known she would pull it off.

Somewhere deep down he realized he'd hoped she wouldn't. Not that she would get in serious trouble, but that the op wouldn't go off and they would need to try again.

He wanted more time with her.

"She is beautiful," Hector said, passing him a glass of Scotch. "You're a lucky man, Josh."

Kayla smiled at the man talking to her, snagging a glass of champagne. Now that she was done with the job, she would likely not be without a glass in her hand for the rest of the evening. Not that it would affect her. His girl could take down most men in a drinking contest.

Not his.

"I am indeed." He wasn't going to get into his relationship status with a drug lord. He took the glass, but he wasn't going to drink it. It was a prop, nothing else. "I heard someone say you're involved. I didn't think you had a significant other."

There had been tons of rumors about Morales, and now that he was in on the secret he could see how all these people talked around the truth. It had been there, but he wasn't very smart. How Hector must have laughed behind his back.

He quelled the anger because Kayla was walking his way wearing that damn dress.

He couldn't forget the last time he'd taken that dress off her. It had been the day they'd gone shopping and he'd received the blackmail instructions and damn near killed that photographer. That was when he'd found out nothing on earth quelled his rage like dominating his sub.

Kay gave him a bright smile. She walked right up to him, curling her free arm around his waist and leaning in. "Hello, Hector. This is an amazing party."

Her voice had gone low and husky, her flirty voice. It rankled a bit that she was using it on Hector. It reminded him of how good she was at her job. Had they flirted earlier in the day? Had Hector showed her around and thought about making a play for her?

"Well, I have amazing company," Hector practically crooned back at her. "I hope you're enjoying yourself."

"I am. It's been a truly fascinating party. The only thing that could make it better would be masks. A masked ball would be entertaining. You would never know exactly who you're dancing with," Kayla replied. "It's fun to pretend to be someone you're not. Isn't that right, Josh?"

This evening couldn't get over fast enough. "I don't know. I do it for a living so it's kind of nice to just be me."

He was more him with her than he'd ever been in his life. Was he really going to be able to stand there as she got on a plane?

"I suspect your boyfriend needs time off," Hector replied. "I'm sure pretending can get tedious."

"Not when the role is right," she said. "Not when it's a role you've been waiting to play your whole life. I mean, I'm sure that's how it is. Josh was telling me about how different it is to take a role for cash and one because you know it's right."

He'd talked about it with her one morning over breakfast. He'd been contemplating whether he should take a small role for scale that he loved or the multimillion-dollar offer to play a superhero. She'd passionately advocated for the small role. It was funny because now there was something odd about her. She was saying all the right things, but there was something aloof in her tone, something that made him wonder if she wasn't making fun of him. Not in the sweetly teasing way she normally did.

Perhaps she finally realized they were over and she didn't have to be sweet anymore.

"When the role is right, it fits like a glove. It's kind of like you're not even acting," he explained.

"Well, I'll have to leave it at that." Hector reached for his phone and frowned. "I'm afraid business calls. You two have a lovely time. I'll see you for breakfast in the morning. And Joshua, I think you'll like the checks my friends will be writing to the foundation tonight. We shall have to do this again and soon. Enjoy the rest of your evening."

Josh watched as he stepped away. "I wonder what part of his business he has to take care of in the middle of a party."

Kay smiled up at him. "Probably torturing young ladies. He looks like the type."

Or murdering his competitors. But it didn't matter because she was here now and she was safe. He couldn't help it. He dragged her into his arms. "I was worried about you."

She chuckled and looked up at him. "I was only spending a little time in the ladies' room. Nothing to get worked up about."

He frowned, confused. "Did you get it done?"

She laughed and managed to look a bit taken aback. "Seriously, Josh? I don't think a lady talks about that kind of thing. I'm good. I wanted to clean up my makeup a bit. Now I'm ready to dance the night away." She went up on her toes. "Unless you would rather take this back to the bedroom. I know how insatiable you are."

She was merely being careful. It was a good thing and he needed to let it go. They still had eyes on them. She wouldn't be relaxed if she hadn't finished the job. If something had gone awry, she would be pushing him to leave, not offering to dance or teasing him about sex.

Of course, he'd also expected her to be a bit more grim. She'd had an air of grief around her all day, as though some part of her had already let him go and was moving on to mourning him.

Because she loved him. Because she'd meant what she'd said.

But now she was so…content. Perhaps it was because the job was done. She had to be relieved she hadn't gotten caught.

"Let's dance a while." The faster they went to bed, the sooner the morning would come and with it all his decisions. Hard decisions.

She took his hand and let him lead her to the dance floor.

For a while at least there was nothing to worry about.

* * * *

Kayla came to, sputtering to breathe. She struggled but couldn't do more than manage to make her body squirm. Water. When had she gone underwater? And when had the world gotten so damn cold? She'd been warm and in bed with Josh just minutes ago. He'd held her and cuddled her and tickled her because he thought it was funny to make her snort laugh. He would do it until she couldn't breathe and threatened dire retribution.

Cold water sluiced down her skin and she realized that had been a mere dream, a memory of something lovely, and this was reality. Her arms were over her head and she was dangling, held by some kind of hard point in the ceiling. But this wasn't fun bondage. This was meant to hurt, to break down, to damage. Already she could feel her shoulders going numb.

Someone had been thorough. Her ankles were tied, too. She was a wriggling worm caught on a hook, waiting to be devoured.

God, Ezra was dead. The image of him hitting the floor and blood beginning to flow struck her forcibly. She didn't know what they'd done with Josh. If they'd done anything with Josh. Had Riley gotten away? Fuck. Panic started to threaten because it didn't matter if Riley and Declan had gotten away, they were literally walking into the arms of the enemy. They were meeting Levi Green in the morning and Levi Green had been the one to kill Ezra.

There was something else. Something she couldn't remember. Something important.

"Ah, sleeping beauty awakens." Levi approached her. "Thought I'd given you way too much for a minute there. Can't lose my best girl, now can I? You know I was always upset that you got out of the game before I could be paired with you. I think we would have made an incredible team. You, the deadly quirky nerd girl, and me, the dashing handler."

She let her eyes take him in. He was actually dressed in a suit, a Cuban-collared shirt making the whole ensemble look on trend. He'd dressed up for her torture. And she could smell Acqua Di Gio. Asshole. Fucking metro douchebag asswipe.

He shrugged and then she realized she'd said the words out loud. "I'm fine with the name calling. You see, I'm perfectly confident in my sexuality. It's a trait among us younger men. Men like your old handlers needed to show the world they were straight. They did it by dressing poorly. You know it wasn't always like that. Back in the olden days, men took fashion seriously. I blame democracy. When the blue-collar shits took over they tried to make it so you weren't a man if you knew a little bit about how to dress. Not a man's man anyway. I don't care that people question my sexuality. I like to leave a little mystery. And hey, I rock these Gucci loafers, sweetheart."

"You'll rock them from your anus when I'm done with you," she managed to spit.

"*Tsk, tsk,* now dear. You're showing your hand far too soon, and yes, I am completely interested in all your perversions. So many women hide them. Not our Kayla. You just let that freak flag fly high, baby girl. I'll love it." Levi moved in, taking in her body with a leer. She was wearing a thin white T-shirt, the kind men wore under dress shirts. It was soaking wet and her nipples were stiff against the fabric. "Damn, but you're pretty like this. It makes me understand why you're interested in all that pervert shit. It looks good on you, Summers."

"Touch me and I'll kill you, Levi. I swear I will."

His lips curled in a malicious grin. "Somehow I think I've got the upper hand here. You know for years I've heard about you. The whole time I was coming up in the Agency. How smart you are. How amazing Ten and John Bishop were to see your potential. I wish they could see you like this. I wish they could see the look on your face when you realize what they did to you. Well, Bishop at least. I kind of think Ten is nothing but a massive himbo who couldn't come up with an evil plan to save his life. But Bishop, oh, there was an evil genius."

Every moment she kept him talking, he wasn't murdering her. "You aren't going to convince me Bishop is working with you."

Levi laughed. "Oh, god no. I would rather slit the man's throat than work with him. I only work with people I understand, people I know how to motivate. Bishop is an enigma. Besides, he's got something else going on now and I can't quite figure out what the game is. I think he's somehow managed to get an entire team of ex-agents on his side. From what I can tell he's working with a couple of ex-DEA agents, three ex-FBI, a former member of the *Bratva*, and a guy whose file is so top secret not even my boss can get into it. Trust Bishop to be the one to finally convince a bunch of intra-agency guys to work together, likely for their common and lucrative good."

Why was he wasting time talking about Bishop if he wasn't in this particular game? "Where's Josh?"

"Well, of course you need to know where your sweetie pie is. Tell me something, did you take the job because you wanted to sleep with him?" Green paced, making sure to keep those Gucci loafers away from the puddle of water under her feet.

"I thought it would be fun."

"You owe me a hundred, Morales. I told you she took the job because we dangled that piece of man meat in front of her. Like the gorgeous sexual predator she is, she sank her teeth right in. Lucky boy should have paid me for the privilege." He threw the words behind him, but Kayla couldn't see anyone except Green. There was a light in her eyes, blinding her to anyone behind him.

"Well, you knew what a whore she was," a dark voice said. "It wasn't a fair bet."

Green's eyes narrowed. "She isn't a whore any more than I am. She's open minded, and thank god for that. I don't understand your generation, Morales. You try to judge people on a morality that makes no sense. Sex is pleasurable. There's nothing wrong with using your body for exactly what it was made for. You know for someone who makes his money off what most people would call sin, you're quite judgmental."

Now Morales moved into her line of vision. "That's because it takes a devil to know what true sin is. Are you simply going to talk to the bitch or are we going to get down to business? I don't care. I've been paid handsomely. I'd just as soon slit her throat and bury her in the backyard."

"There's the real man." She looked at Morales, all his charm gone and replaced with a coldness she'd seen only on the most seasoned of sociopaths. They could act like humans for small periods of time, but they always came back to this place, the one where they were a mere shell without a true soul to illuminate them. "Tell me something. Do you sample your own product?"

"On occasion. I am proud of my product. I stay away from the opioids. Those are for you pathetic Americans, but I'll have a line of cocaine from time to time. You should try it. Perhaps if you're a good girl, we'll let you forget the pain for a bit."

"I meant the little boys you peddle, you sick piece of shit," she shot back.

Her head snapped around at the force of his hand.

Green was laughing. "I told you she was smart. Or maybe it was Ezra, but I knew one of the two would figure it out eventually. By the way, Kay, thank you for bringing him back out here. I was worried I would have to find a way to have him assassinated in the field. This way is way messier, and I don't simply mean what he did to that rug in Hector's office." He moved in close. "But it was far more fun than letting someone else do it. Thank you, sweetheart. I forgot how good it feels to pull that trigger when the man on the other side of the bullet deserves it so richly. They teach us not to make things personal because they don't want us to know how good it fucking feels. I'm seriously jacked up after offing that motherfucker."

She spit right in his face, right on his lips.

He stared at her for a moment and then his tongue came out, taking everything she'd given him. "That won't be the only taste I get of you tonight, sweetheart. By the time I'm done with you, you'll leave here with me and you'll be happy to do it."

"You're fucking insane."

"Again, the name calling doesn't work on someone who truly knows himself."

She was genuinely at a loss. "What the hell is this about, Levi? Are you really so desperate to cover up Hector killing one of our operatives?"

He moved around her and she realized she was in some kind of bathroom. Now that her eyes had adjusted she could see the mirror behind that horrible light they were shining in her face. There was a dual sink and a massive ornate mirror that showed her Levi walking around her, his eyes on her half-naked body.

"My dear, I killed that operative myself when I realized what I needed to do. You see when Bishop resurfaced, I knew we could be in trouble. If he'd stayed dead like a good boy, I would have taken a bit more time. Not much because I see vultures circling around my prize and I'm not going to let some indie contractor steal it out from under me."

"What prize? I don't work for the Agency anymore. I know absolutely..." But she did know something. She knew something a lot of people would love to know.

What a fool she'd been. She'd seen what he wanted her to see— the mission he'd laid out. It had made sense, and he'd baited his trap with a gorgeous piece of man knowing she wouldn't pass up the opportunity.

He smiled at her. "There's my smart girl. Tell me what I'm after. I want to hear it from you."

He was one sick fuck. "I don't know where the Lost Boys are."

It was the only explanation. In fact, he'd practically declared himself that day outside the café when he'd told her what would happen if the Agency didn't claim Hope McDonald's research before someone else did. It was precisely why Big Tag and Damon had hidden the soldiers she'd done her work on. Their bodies were valuable to anyone who wanted to continue her studies.

A finger slithered down her spine. "Very good. I knew you would figure it out if you were properly motivated. Yes, I want them. One will do, though I'd like a full set, but the only one who's out in the open...well, I'm not about to piss off Ian Taggart by stealing his brother. Even I'm not arrogant enough to do that."

"You don't think he's going to get pissed off when he realizes you stole his employee. Big Tag might be sarcastic, but he takes his role as overlord pretty seriously. He will come after me."

"Only if he realized you were gone. You see, love, there was a reason you were the only person in the entire world who could do this job," he said. He moved in front of her again, his eyes serious on her as though this was some sacred moment between them. "You're the only one in the whole world who can get me into The Garden. That's where those boys are."

He knew way too much, but she wasn't going to confirm it for him. "I don't know where they are. And I'm not ever taking you to The Garden."

"You will. You just don't know it yet. You will walk into The Garden and smile that breathtaking smile of yours and convince one of them to go for a walk with you. According to your phone, you're close to someone named Tucker. I happen to know that was one of the names she gave to her 'boys,' as she called them. Did you know the sick bitch had them call her *Mother*? Weird and creepy. I'll be a much better big brother to them. I'll show them the world and all they'll have to do is a few routine medical exams. After the first one, maybe we won't even have to vivisect the rest of them. I don't know. I'm leaving that up to smarter minds than mine. I'm simply going to accept the paycheck and then do the next job my boss has for me."

She started to deny the fact that she would ever do his bidding. It was right there on the tip of her tongue to tell him to fuck himself because she wouldn't betray her friends. But that was a really good way to get a bitch killed, and he already had a shit ton of intel. "How much are you getting paid?"

His eyes lit slightly. "There's a bonus with this particular job. I'm an Agency man as long as they pay me and don't figure out my outside projects, like the one with Hector here. Hector feeds me intelligence on certain elements down here."

"Fucking narcoterrorists," Hector spat. "They're trying to take over my territory. They'll tear everything apart if they can."

Levi nodded his way. "Hector's a realist. In exchange for information that makes me look like the golden boy of the CIA, I help facilitate his business and take a little percentage for me and my partner. It was her idea, actually. She's got a brilliant brain on her."

She would love to meet his partner. When she met the partner, Kay would take her apart. "I would want a percentage."

"I thought you said she was smart," Hector said.

"She'll catch on," Levi replied. "Sweetheart, you're not getting a cut. I'm not foolish, though I will keep you around as long as you're a good girl. There are still things we need from you. What's the protocol for getting into The Garden?"

"You don't need to know. I told you I'll do it for the right cash." She would happily walk into The Garden and come back out guns blazing.

He leaned in, his hand coming out to touch her hair. "There's no amount of cash that would get my sweet Kayla to betray her friends. I told you it's odd, but that sweetness and sunshine is precisely why I'm a bit obsessed with you and your friends. I have a little fantasy about you and Ariel Adisa that would make you blush. Maybe once you're on the inside, you can make that happen for me. Perhaps you'll bring Ariel with you and Tucker and I can have all three of you."

He was confusing her. She wasn't going to lure Tucker or any of the Lost Boys out of their hidey-hole. It wasn't going to happen, so why was he talking like it was a sure thing?

"So, I need to know the protocol for getting into The Garden," Levi insisted.

What had Ezra said? Five years. Everything had changed five years before. What had happened five years before? John Bishop died. Now Levi Green was afraid of Bishop. If John Bishop wasn't a part of this collusion, then how did he fit in?

Levi stared at her. "Tell me something. Do you wonder how you managed to come out of your time with MSS and still have that smile? She doesn't smile like you. Oh, she can fake it, but I know the difference."

Tears pierced her eyes. John Bishop. It all came back to him. Her handler. Her mentor. Sometimes he'd been the only person she talked to in a year who knew who she was. Could he really have done that to her? Could he have lied and manipulated her for years?

"I think she's going to need persuading." Hector sighed and nodded. Two big men came from behind him.

"Tell me what I need to know," Levi whispered. "I don't want to do this to you, sweetheart. I would rather our relationship be one of a different nature. Give us what we need and I'll promise to be gentle."

When he raped her. Nice.

Through the ache of betrayal, she realized nothing she did would spare her the pain that was to come. Her feet were tied, but she could still use them. She brought her knees up, catching Levi in the gut. Not where she'd been aiming. "I'll cut your balls off, Levi. You watch me. Before this is done, I'll avenge Ezra and you'll know which sister you should really be afraid of."

Levi turned. "Do it. Don't kill her."

One of the big men pulled her off the hook and that was when she realized what was behind her—a lovely marble tub, and someone had been kind enough to fill it with water.

Fun times were coming.

She took a deep breath as she hit the water and two men held her under. Calm. She had to remain calm and pray Josh figured out that the woman in his bed wasn't the woman he loved.

Because now she remembered what she'd seen right before she'd gone lights out.

Her own face.

As the torture began she prayed Josh would survive the night.

Chapter Nineteen

Josh couldn't put his finger on it, but something was wrong. Maybe it was post-mission letdown, but Kayla seemed weird. Not her usual weird. She seemed happy, perfectly happy. She'd laughed and danced with a bunch of people as though she had nothing to worry about at all.

She'd played him again. Would he ever learn?

He pulled the tie off and tossed it aside.

Kayla was staring at herself in the dresser mirror, smoothing down her hair. "I love this dress."

"God knows you earned it." He couldn't quite keep the bitterness from his voice.

"I did, didn't I? I definitely earned it." She turned, leaning against the dresser so there was no way he missed the hint of her breasts on the edges of the deep *V* in the bodice. "Tell me something. Do you like it?"

"You know I like it." He had incredibly fond memories of that dress. "Considering what you were doing the last time you wore it."

A smile crossed her face. "Of course. You like getting me out of it."

He pulled his tuxedo coat off and moved to the closet to hang it up. He hit the desk with his toe and groaned. He'd lost all grace this evening, but then it kind of fit the way his life was going. The laptop Kayla had been using earlier flickered back from sleep mode.

When he turned back around, she was gone, but he heard her

moving about in the bathroom.

Did she honestly expect him to fuck her tonight? Probably. Hell, he'd proven he was the biggest fucking fool in the world when it came to her. She'd lied to him and he'd fallen on top of her three or four hours later. His dick didn't care that she was a manipulator of the highest order.

He glanced down at her screen. She was probably plotting her next mission now that she'd fucked him over so thoroughly. All that talk about going after his enemies had been nothing but dialogue written to keep him off balance.

Tyler Williams was the subject line of the email she had open on the screen. It seemed to have come from someone called CandyMan#1.

Hey, girl! Here's the skinny on your DEA agent. Hit me up next time you're in Dallas and bring back some of those sponge candy things from Trader Joe's. Can't get 'em here. Hutch.

She'd been looking into his advisor?

He clicked on the report and it came up, filling the screen with information on Tyler Williams.

Except the man in the picture wasn't Tyler Williams. The man staring from his government issued ID was blond, a bit younger, and grimmer-looking than the real Tyler Williams.

Who might not be the real Tyler Williams.

What the fuck was going on?

Something was off and had been all night. Even Hector had seemed smug and self-satisfied, as though he'd known something the rest of them didn't.

He flipped the laptop screen shut. Why would she be looking into his advisor? Maybe there was a different Tyler Williams. The Kayla who loved him would look into Williams because she would do that about anyone who got close to him. The one who'd laughed and partied all night, ignoring him for the most part until it was time to go to bed, why would that Kayla care at all? The op was done.

Wasn't it?

"Hey, I thought you might like this better. Wanna play?" She stepped out of the bathroom wearing nothing but a smile, her hair falling like a waterfall around her shoulders.

She was one gorgeous woman, and sure enough his dick throbbed to life. He stood up, unsure how to deal with her. "Has Riley texted you?"

"Riley?" She shook her head suddenly. "Of course. He said everything's perfectly fine at the club, if that's what you're worried about."

That was when he noticed it. He stepped in closer. The words that came out of her mouth confused him, but the sight of her scar made his heart pound.

"Josh? Are you all right?"

They were alone. The job was over. All she had to say was yes or no. Even if someone was listening in, it wouldn't have mattered because they wouldn't have known who Riley was. Why mention the club unless the woman in front of him thought that's where he was? He could have overlooked that but his eyes weren't lying.

Such a small thing to miss. He put his hands on her shoulders, his eyes on that scar above her right breast. He loved her scars, loved lavishing them with affection the way she did his. She would kiss them and rub her cheek there as though thanking the scar for saving the man. He'd been a good pupil, learning from her easy affection. He'd kissed that candy cane shaped scar a hundred times.

"Josh?" This time he could hear the edge of anxiety in her voice.

If she was who he thought she was, he needed to keep her calm. "You know I can't resist this body, baby. I love it when you get naked for me."

His Kayla would have waited for him to ask her to take her clothes off if play was what she wanted.

He traced the scar with his finger. Of course his Kayla's scar curved to the left, not the right. Whoever had carved this scar into this woman's skin must have been looking at a photograph. How well had she rehearsed this role? Would she be able to properly improvise when needed? "My Little Miss Muffett."

The woman who was calling herself Kay laughed, a sound that was off to his ears. "That's me. I know which tuffet I'm sitting on tonight."

Not the right answer. His stomach threatened to roll. His Kay insisted the staff-like scar was a scythe because she was never less than a badass. His Kay would never be this aggressive when she was naked and asking to play. His Kay would soften and go sweetly submissive.

Where the hell was *his* Kay?

Who was standing here in front of him?

She turned her face up, looking him in the eyes as though she'd caught on that something was wrong with him. "You're acting weird."

What would she do? He was acting out a scene and no one had bothered to give him the script, so he had no idea what happened if she thought he was about to catch on. If she figured out he knew she wasn't the woman he loved, what would she do? Where was Kayla? Because she wouldn't have done this to him. He knew that deep in his soul. This ghost was here and something had gone terribly wrong with the mission his Kay had promised would be a breeze.

His Kay wouldn't have concealed her sister and sent her twin in to deal with him. It struck him forcibly that he believed her. Kayla had lied about the mission but nothing else. Everything else had been true. When she'd said she loved him, she'd meant it. It had been there in her eyes, the grief she'd felt when she thought she was losing him. That had been real.

If her love was real, it was the best thing that ever happened to him and he would never, ever doubt it again. He would cling to that woman like the life raft she was, like the gift she was. She was his prize for surviving.

He had to put on an Academy Award winning performance. Luckily, he was pretty good at pretending. He looked down at the ghost in his arms, curling his lips up. "I'm acting weird? I should spank you for that, baby. You know better than to push me when we're playing. I get to look at you as long as I want."

Her smile was back. Funny, he hadn't noticed earlier that it didn't meet her eyes. Those remained cold and calculating. This was not a woman who talked to dolphins. "I'm sorry, Josh. Of course, you do. You're the Master, after all."

He put his hands on her hips, forcing himself to touch her. She was a gorgeous snake and he had to be careful she didn't show her fangs. How did he get out of this? He wasn't fucking sleeping with her. No way. If she was who he thought she was, she could kill him in a heartbeat. He needed out of this room and without making her suspicious.

He winced. "Baby, you're going to kill me, but I need to run out to Shane's. We used our last condom. Remember? I forgot to ask him about it earlier."

Her eyes widened. She couldn't possibly know they didn't use them. The conversation about going without had taken place while they were walking on the beach, and it wasn't like they'd mentioned it since. Or he was about to get gutted by a ghost.

"Damn it. Maybe we should go to bed and sleep instead."

He forced himself to drag her close. "No fucking way. I fully intend to rock your world. Stay here. He's right across the garden. That man is always prepared. I'll be right back. Find your position. You better be waiting for me or we'll start with discipline."

If she knew anything about playing the Kayla role, she would have practiced at least some D/s. She sank down to her knees and placed her palms on her thighs. Not turned up like her sister would have. She was hampered by the fact that they hadn't had a video feed.

She'd only been able to listen in. But the CIA had been the ones to bug his house.

Shit. Who did he turn to?

He placed a hand on her head. "I'll be right back."

He forced himself to walk out of the bedroom door, but the minute it closed, he sprinted for the back of the mansion. He was taking a risk. Was Shane in on it? Had this been some elaborate plan to switch out the twins again? Where was Kay? Where the fuck was Kay? If Shane was in on it, at least maybe he would get to go where Kay had gone.

The mansion was deadly quiet. He could hear his breath, his feet pounding on the floor.

He needed a gun. Shane would have one. If Shane didn't immediately shoot and kill him.

Cell phone. He'd left that fucker behind, too. What had he been thinking? He was running on pure adrenaline.

337

He slowed as he reached the end of the hallway. A shadow walked across the closed curtains, making Josh pull up. Fuck. He hadn't thought about the fact that Hector would have guards all over the place.

Would Hector care that the Agency was using him to play deep games? Was Hector in on it? It wouldn't be the first time the CIA had used drug dealers for their own ends.

And then he felt something cold press to the back of his neck and knew he'd made a fatal mistake.

"Don't move and maybe I won't blow your head off," a deep voice said.

He wasn't going to back down now. He'd gotten caught. All right, at least he could get one question answered. "I want to know where my girlfriend is because that bitch you sent back to me isn't her. Where is my Kayla?"

A long, relieved sigh hit his ears and that pressure at the base of his skull disappeared. "Joshua? Fuck, man, I thought you were one of Morales's goons. Thank god. So Jiang Kun is already in play?"

He turned and faced the man who had called himself Tyler Williams. He was dressed in all black, but it couldn't hide the smear of blood that crossed his jawline. "You're not Tyler Williams."

"My name is John Bishop. Tyler Williams is a friend of a friend. I used his identity because I had to get myself into this game somehow. I'd like to point out that if you had taken my advice, we wouldn't be in this situation. I would be quietly taking this obnoxious threesome out. But instead of listening to my excellent advice, now I have to deal with saving a bunch of people. Help me get my new friend out of here and I'll get Kay back for you. Help him while I take out the guards." He didn't wait for Josh to answer. The man simply started for the door.

That was when Josh realized he still wasn't alone. A man leaned against a chair in the grand living room where just the day before, Josh had sat with Kayla as they sipped cocktails.

"She's alive," the man said. "I was the expendable one. They'll need her to give up Knight's protocols if they want to get Jiang Kun into The Garden in one piece."

"Why would she need to get...that's where Kay works." She'd

338

talked about The Garden. That was where her London team was based. And this man looked familiar, though when he'd seen him before he'd seemed far healthier.

"Yeah, I think we can safely say I was right about this one. Doesn't make getting shot at point-blank range any better," the man said. "Fucking tactical vest spared me the worst. I pretended to be dead, but Morales sent two of his guards to bury me and they quickly figured out I wasn't as deceased as I appeared. During that fight, one of those fuckers managed to get a wild shot between the plates when I tried to get away. They're both dead, but I can't fucking breathe in this thing."

"You're Kayla's handler. You're Ezra. She said you were going to back her up." Josh finally saw enough of his face to ID him as the man who met Kay on the beach from time to time. "What the hell is going on here?"

"Fuck if I know," Ezra replied. "I think our new friend is going to have to explain. He's not as bad as I thought he was. You know how to shoot?"

"Yes, but I've only ever shot at a gun range," he admitted.

"Better than nothing. Reach down and take the spare out of my boot. Bishop's coming back."

Sure enough, the door opened as Josh reached down and came up with a small semiautomatic. The weight felt good in his hand. "Bishop?"

The only Bishop he'd heard of was dead.

The man he'd known as Tyler Williams strode back into the hall. "John Bishop is a ghost I hoped I could leave behind. John Bishop is someone I'm not proud of right now, and he's the one who has to clean this mess up so I can go back to being Henry Flanders."

"I'm confused about the names and the whole death thing," Josh admitted. "It doesn't matter. Could you just tell me if you're going to help me find my Kayla?"

"Getting Kayla Summers out of here alive is my highest priority. Help me get Fain out to the guesthouse and I'll tell you the whole story," the dude with a shit ton of names said.

"Yeah, I'd like to hear it, too," Ezra said.

"Help him," Bishop ordered. "I'll take point. And be careful of the bodies. Wouldn't want you to trip and fall."

Ezra groaned as he tried to straighten up. Josh put a shoulder under Ezra's arm, giving him some balance as they began to follow Bishop.

That was a lot of bodies. As they followed the mysterious Bishop through the garden, he counted at least five men down. He hadn't heard a single shot, and there was a surprising lack of blood. The guards looked as though they'd simply dropped where they stood, one every couple of hundred feet or so. Like a nasty treat trail leading them where they needed to go.

"Did you leave anyone alive?" Ezra complained. "You know sometimes it can be helpful to interrogate people. It's hard to do when you internally decapitate them."

"I couldn't risk putting them out," Bishop replied. "I don't know how long they would stay out. Besides, you have no idea what these men have done. Every single one of them. I worked inside a group like this for years. You don't get this close to the boss without proving how far you'll go."

"Oh, I know." Ezra groaned a little but managed to keep up. "The question is what have you been doing for the last five years? Where have you been since you faked your death and ditched your responsibilities?"

"I found more important responsibilities," Bishop shot back and then seemed to take control of his temper. "As to what I've been doing, would you believe growing a sensationally non-lucrative but cruelty free business selling crafts and organic vegan baked goods while my wife supports us with money she makes writing naughty books? Don't call them porn. She gets upset at that term. Her books are about love. And sex. Lots of filthy sex, but mostly the love thing." He stopped and listened for a second before waving them on to the small outer building Shane was staying in.

"No, I wouldn't believe it," Ezra shot back. "The idea of you wearing Birkenstocks and eating tofu while selling homemade dream catchers is ridiculous."

"And yet that's how I spent last summer, but my present isn't the problem," Bishop returned. "My past is back with a fucking vengeance. You hate me for leaving the Agency the way I did. I get that. But don't think for a second I'm not paying for it right now. I faked my death because I wasn't sure the Agency would let me leave, and even if they did I would have had enemies coming after me for the rest of my life. And I lied to my wife about my past. I should have been honest, but I didn't think my Nell would be able to handle the truth. Now she has to face it and the fact that the very reason I faked my own death is coming back for me. I should be at home protecting my pregnant wife, and yet I'm here for one reason and one reason alone—because I owe Kayla Summers."

"Is this because of what happened with her sister?" Josh asked. Despite what the Ezra guy said, he'd actually watched Bishop eat tofu. He'd developed a taste for the stuff, and nothing about his demeanor this evening made Josh think he was lying.

"Yes," Bishop replied as he got to the door. "Joshua, let Shane see your face. I'm afraid he doesn't know me."

Josh handed Ezra over and knocked on the door.

Shane opened it. "Hey, what's…holy shit. Ezra?"

"Bad night, man. Op didn't go the way we thought it would," Ezra said as Bishop got him through the door. "Shane Landon, this is John Bishop. He's a dead man and we're going to join him if we don't find Kay and get the fuck out of here."

Shane had pulled out his phone, not bothering to ask another question. He was on the phone to his headquarters the minute he realized things had gone awry. "Boss, sorry to call late, but this thing has gone to shit. Ezra's shot. I don't know how bad it is yet. Kay's been taken by god knows who. I've got Hunt, but Riley and Declan are on their way back to the city. And there's someone here named John Bishop."

He stepped away, but Josh noted he didn't turn his back on Bishop.

"If that's Taggart, tell him Green's gone rogue and he needs to pull his men out of that drop tomorrow," Bishop said. "It's meaningless at best, could be deadly at worst."

Shane started talking to his boss, relaying the message.

Bishop was busy trying to get a look at Ezra's wound. Whatever he saw there made him frown.

"Can you get me out of this fucking vest?" Ezra asked. "I can barely breathe. I took one to the back. It didn't get all the way through, but it hurts like hell. I do thank you for saving me from the assholes who came to bury me."

"You're welcome," he replied. "I was in the shadows. There were too many for me to stop them from taking Kay, but if they're planning what I think they're planning, they need her alive for a little while. Eventually they'll figure out she won't talk, but for now Levi will try to finesse his way out of this. And no, I can't get you out of the vest. It's literally the only thing stopping the bleeding from your chest cavity. I pull this off you anywhere but an OR and you bleed out."

"Fucking awesome." Ezra turned a nice shade of pale. "I'm going to kill Levi Green."

"Not if I get to him first, brother," Bishop swore.

Josh looked down at the gun in his hand. Could he pull the trigger? Fuck, yeah if it meant saving Kay. Actually, he was thinking about pulling the trigger just to let those assholes know they couldn't take his sub. A protective instinct like nothing he'd ever known welled up inside him. How fucking dare anyone take her from him.

"Yes, sir. I understand." Shane hung up, shoving the phone in his pocket and staring at Bishop like he was some mythical creature. "Who the hell are you? My boss told me to do anything you asked of me. He told me you were in charge and if he found out I'd done anything but follow your orders to the letter, he'd…well, he likes to talk about entrails a lot."

Bishop's lips curled up. "Young Taggart. He's made something special of himself and that company of his. He was one of my trainees back in the old days. When I joined the Agency, I was recruited by a man named Franklin Grant. After I became proficient, Grant let me train some of his special recruits, including his adopted son, Tennessee Smith. Ten recruited Taggart and I took him with me on some of his first missions." Bishop looked back at Josh. "Where is Jiang Kun?"

Shane's eyes widened. "Kayla's sister?"

Ezra was looking firmly at Bishop, his eyes practically blazing. "Jiang Kun is dead. She was killed during…you son of a bitch."

"She's back in my room. They switched them out and expected I wouldn't notice the difference." Josh didn't care who was a son of a bitch or what Bishop had done in the past. All that mattered was Kayla in the here and now and what they were doing to her. The thought of her alone and in pain gutted him. This was what it felt like to really fucking love someone. He would change places with her in a heartbeat. "She thinks I'm getting condoms."

"I want to know what happened," Ezra said. "Big Tag might give you a pass, but I won't."

"You want to take me out after this is over, come and find me in Colorado," Bishop replied, his jaw tight. "You won't be the only one gunning my way. And what I did with Jiang Kun and Kayla Summers was done with the full approval of the director of the CIA and the president of the United States. Everything I did at the Agency with the exception of how I left was with the support of command. Believe me, they were more than happy to hear this particular plan."

"What was the plan?" Josh asked.

"When Jiang Kun reached out to the Agency and asked about her twin, I quickly realized the opportunity we had. I put her in touch with Kayla. After Kayla had been properly vetted, of course. Tennessee Smith wanted to bring Kun in immediately, to turn her, but the truth is the minute she came over to our side, her usefulness gets cut in half, hell, maybe more."

"Because if MSS knew she'd defected, they would change everything," Ezra explained. "They would change their protocols, scrap any plans she knew about. You needed to switch them out so MSS never realized it lost an agent."

"Yes, and I was under orders to do it in a way that Summers and Smith never knew what had happened. They worried Summers would balk because she wanted to be with her sister. It was the point of it all for her. But she showed a propensity not only for deep loyalty but also for revenge. It was why I had Kun write those letters to her, to build a loyalty to family. All the while, I was turning Kayla into a weapon. She tested off the charts and she spoke perfect Mandarin. It was the kind of setup every spymaster dreams of. And it worked perfectly, right down to Ten Smith taking out an operative the South Koreans had been trying to deal with for years. And no one knew we had Kun. I dealt with Kun and soon discovered she's a sociopath. Whether it was what the Chinese did to her during training or she was born that way, the woman is bad. She gave us what we needed, but it was obvious to me that she was going to cause trouble. We tried giving her what she said she wanted, a nice American life. She robbed a bank. We couldn't let her go into the penal system. Too many secrets. I took her with me on a few assignments hoping to…I don't know…Dexter her or something. She liked killing. I gave her bad guys to kill, but at some point in time she made contact with Hector Morales and set up her business, which included blackmailing famous people."

Josh felt his stomach turn. "She's my blackmailer?"

Ezra groaned as Bishop kept poking and prodding him.

"Yes, and she got that intel from Hector, whose organization kept up with their products. From what I can tell, he recognized you from certain private films his people had you make when you were a teen. Stay calm or I'll put you out myself." Bishop's words hit him, but it took a minute for him to truly understand them.

Hector had those terrible tapes because Hector had run the business.

All those years of torture and pain and it had been to line Hector Morales's pockets. His pain. Hannah's. The horror everyone he'd grown up with had faced had all been about making one evil man's life better.

"He has Kayla." Rage was replaced with pure panic.

Bishop stared at him as though willing him to stay calm. "And I'll handle it. This is my mess. I made it when I decided to walk away. I thought…hell, I was so in love, I didn't think at all. I just knew I wanted a better life for myself, for Nell. The Agency would go on, I told myself. And it did. Jiang Kun was given a new handler after my unfortunate demise. Levi Green. I don't know if she turned him or he was already willing to walk on the bad side, but I believe the two of them have been working with Hector."

"How do you know this?" Ezra asked.

"I've stayed away for years," Bishop explained. "I hid in plain sight. I enjoyed my life and my town. I was normal for once. A few months ago, someone figured out I wasn't as dead as I'm supposed to be. That was when one of the cartel's I took down showed up in my quiet little town. So now the Agency knows and I need to find out how and who's coming after me next. I have a friend who is very likely the best hacker on the planet. He got me the data I needed and I put the pieces together. I still don't know who figured out I wasn't dead and gave me up, but I saw the pattern that emerged with Green and Kun. I started investigating and discovered the Morales connection. When I realized they'd drawn McKay-Taggart into this 'op' of theirs and specifically Kayla, I knew what they would do. They want to pull off the same switch I did except in reverse, and it's all about getting to Hope McDonald's research projects," Bishop said. "If they can get one of the men McDonald experimented on, they can either be heroes with the Agency or potentially sell the man to any number of interested parties."

"This is about research?" Josh couldn't quite put things together in his head.

"Hope McDonald developed a drug that makes it possible to experience time in a different way," Ezra explained. "It's miles ahead of anything anyone else has. One of the side effects of later iterations of the drug was memory loss and the subject becoming very susceptible to suggestion in the early days. The men she experimented on were typically soldiers and they retained muscle memory, could fight and do things like put together a complex rifle with no trouble. But they had no memory of their pasts and were eager to please."

"Super soldiers," Josh said. "That's how Kay explained it. They would be like ducklings, desperate to imprint on anyone who could make the world make sense. Ducklings who came out of the shell knowing how to kill."

"Kayla is close to them. She can walk in and any one of those men would walk out with her, never understanding she's leading them to slaughter," Shane said. "They love her. She's been in charge of them since Big Tag shipped them to London."

Bishop nodded. "Yes, I believe that's what they're counting on. Once she's got them on the outside, she can either say she lost them and try to stay on, or Damon Knight will believe she turned. What other explanation would there be? No one else knows Jiang Kun's alive. She'll take her sister's place and McKay-Taggart won't go after Green for vengeance because it'll be Kay's fault, not his."

"You said he won't kill her right away." Josh had been a pawn, a means to an end. It had always been Kayla they were after.

"It would be easier if they had the protocols to get into The Garden," Ezra explained. "But if she won't give them up, they could still have some uses for her. They could use her to draw Damon Knight out. He wouldn't understand that he wasn't getting the right agent back. They would show him the real Kayla being tortured, offer her up for a certain amount of cash, then switch her out for her sister at the last minute. Jiang Kun would be welcomed back into the arms of her 'family' and then she would go to work. Any memory lapses could be attributed to PTSD. And then she would get one of the Lost Boys. Hell, maybe more than one." He looked at Bishop, his eyes narrowed. "Look me in the eyes and tell me you're not playing some angle."

Bishop stared at the CIA agent. "I am here because I want to be a man of honor. I left the Agency because I'd lost mine. I came back because I can't let them get away with this. Because it's the right thing to do and that is all the skin I have in this game. I will save Kayla and then I will go home and try to rebuild my life there if the Agency will let me. If the world will let me."

Slowly Ezra shook his head. "All right. I believe you."

Bishop stood up. "Shane, you got a car here?"

"Yes, I'm driving Hunt and Kayla back to the city in the morning," Shane replied.

"Not now. Now you're taking Agent Fain to a hospital," Bishop explained. "Get Hunt out of here, too."

"I'm not leaving without Kayla." He wasn't a fucking agent, but he wasn't some wimp either. He could do things. He could take a bullet if he needed to, if it meant her getting out alive. All he knew was he wasn't getting in a car and leaving her behind.

There was a knock on the door and Bishop went still.

"Take Ezra out the back," Bishop ordered, his voice a mere whisper. "Hunt, looks like you get your wish. Don't say I didn't warn you. Stall her as long as possible. If she takes you to wherever Kayla is, tell them all this."

He leaned over and whispered in Josh's ear. Josh nodded. It was a good bit of dialogue. If Bishop ever wanted to give up the vegan-bread-selling game, Josh would let the man work on some of his scripts.

Shane had Ezra, hauling him out as silently as possible. Bishop nodded and then disappeared, too.

Fuck. It was just a role. Another part to play. He went to open the door. *Don't be her. Don't be her. Don't be her. Don't be her.*

The gun. He had the gun in his pocket. Would she check him there?

"Josh?"

He leaned down and shoved the small gun into his dress sock. He was wearing traditional black dress socks and the tuxedo pants were straight cut. It was possible they wouldn't check. It was also possible he was going to shoot off his own foot, but he needed to give them the best chance he possibly could.

He was back on his feet when the door flew open.

Jiang Kun stood in the doorway, and she wasn't alone. Three large men with guns flanked her. She said something to them and then two of the men started to run around toward the back of the house, but not before Josh heard the sound of a car peeling away. There were some gunshots, but that car was gone.

Good for Shane.

Maybe Declan and Riley would come back. Maybe. Maybe John Bishop would do everything he said.

Jiang Kun had changed into jeans and a black shirt, one he recognized from Kayla's closet. "What gave me away?"

She stalked in, her guards following behind.

"A man knows the woman he loves," he replied. "And I sure as hell don't love you."

Kun's lips curved into a malicious smirk. Her hand touched his chest. "Too bad. I'll admit getting to fuck the hell out of a man with your prodigious experience was one of the reasons I was going to enjoy this assignment. Your loss. Mine, too. I was going to tape it all and send it to little sis. Guess I can torture you in front of her instead. Boys, let's take Mr. Hunt to see his one true love. Be careful with him. He's used to VIP treatment now."

The two guards took him by the arms and started to haul him out.

At least he would see Kayla.

One last time.

Chapter Twenty

Kayla couldn't stop shaking. How many times had they put her in that freezing cold water? A hundred? It fucking felt like it. Her lungs hurt from how many times she'd had to cough up water from them.

It had happened over and over. Morales would ask her the same questions. She would tell him to fuck off and they would put her under. She would watch for a moment, seeing the oddly monstrous face distorted by the water, and then the burn would begin. Her lungs would ache and panic would set in as she began to drown. They would haul her out and she would shiver and shake on the cold marble.

She was going to die here. They would hold her under one too many times and she wouldn't come back.

Would her sister kill Josh? Or would she simply walk away and Josh would be left thinking she didn't love him, that she'd been everything he'd feared she was. Cold. Manipulative. Unloving.

It was funny. That was what hurt most. Josh wouldn't know she loved him with all her heart. She would be buried somewhere in a shallow grave and he wouldn't know she'd gone there loving him, wishing things had been different, praying he one day found someone he could love the way she loved him.

"Hey, sweetheart." A hand swept her wet hair back.

Warm. She finally had some hope of warmth, and in that moment, she could feel Joshua's arms around her, his big body sheltering her. Had he found her? Had he brought Shane and called Declan and Riley back? Had they stormed the mansion and saved her, and now she was safe and warm?

So weak. That last session had been a doozy. They typically dropped her on the hard floor when they were done with their torture for the moment, but now she was being held tenderly. She cuddled closer, trying to get that feeling of safety Josh always gave her. Maybe all wasn't lost.

"That's right," a voice that wasn't Joshua's said. "Stay close to me. I'll take care of you."

She winced when she realized where she was. She was wrapped in a big fluffy towel, the warmth starting to penetrate her skin, and there were masculine arms around her, but they weren't her lover's arms.

"It's all right. The bad man is taking a little break so we're going to rest for a bit," a deep voice promised her. She was sitting on his lap, her hands still bound. Levi Green might have been a good-looking man if he wasn't such a righteous dung heap of a human. He was practically cooing at her like she was some baby bird he was trying to draw back to life. "Sweetheart, stop being stubborn. No one wants to hurt you. Well, *I* don't want to hurt you. If I'd had my way, this would have gone differently. I vastly prefer seduction to strong-arm tactics. Let's get you some hot chocolate and warm you up and you and I can talk. Give me what I want and you don't have to get back in that tub."

Such sweet words.

She pulled away from him. It would be smarter to play into his obviously obsessive fantasies about her, but she hated him too much to even pretend. They were going to kill her. Levi might think he would get to keep her as a pet, but she knew the truth. If they got the information they wanted out of her, she would be dead two minutes later. They couldn't risk her getting out, and she suspected only Levi was certain of the extent of his sexual prowess when it came to getting women to talk.

Still, she wasn't above using him to try to figure a few things out.

"My sister's alive? How is that possible when I saw her die? I was there."

He looked down at her and then back up as though trying to figure out who would be listening in. "You saw a carefully crafted drama played out by a master. That scene was set up just for you. You understand what Bishop did to you?"

He'd betrayed her utterly. He'd tricked her, and the spy in her understood why he'd done it. It didn't make her heart hurt less, but on an intellectual level she could see why he'd played it the way he did. "He wanted MSS to keep their plans on track. Couldn't do that if they thought the Agency was on to them. Besides, with me on the inside, he got a twofer."

"He should have told you." Levi took a deep breath, cradling her close. "I would have told you."

Sure he would have. "So when Bishop died...left the Agency...you became my sister's handler?"

"I did, and we found we were better suited than she and Bishop. Bishop attempted to keep her more violent tendencies in check. He thought he could let her assassinate the odd dictator once a year or so and that would feed her. I knew what she needed. Bishop's faked death also had the added effect of setting off a war between the cartels. Jalisco came out on top and Hector, Kun, and I formed our partnership. Hector thinks Kun is going to marry him, but I'm fairly certain at some point she'll take his head off and start running the cartel herself. She likes to come up with new ways to make money."

"Is my sister the one blackmailing Josh?" It wasn't a huge leap. Hector had the information. If her sister thought she could use it, apparently she would. All that crap about wanting a sister had been about wanting out. Her sister had found MSS too constrictive, and she hadn't minded sending baby sis in to take over her unwanted life.

"Yes, though Josh isn't the only one," he admitted. "We've got dirt on a bunch of people. Hollywood stars, a couple of athletes, a few politicians. I find giving Kun something to do keeps her out of trouble. Well, something criminal to do. Your sister isn't like you. She lives to hurt other people. And she hates you most of all."

Her sister hated her? She was starting to understand that, but it made no sense. They'd never spent real time together. They'd only known each other through letters, and Kay had been over the moon to get to write to her sister. "Why?"

The door opened and there she was. Her sister.

"Aww, what a tender scene," her sister said with a nasty twist to her lips. "You don't want to miss this, Hunt. Look at the almighty spy cuddling with the enemy."

Her heart nearly stopped as Josh was hauled in.

"Get your fucking hands off her," he snarled. His hair was mussed, a trickle of blood on his lower lip. He'd obviously taken some persuasion to get here.

Josh, who'd gone through so much. Josh was going to be tortured yet again. She didn't know if she could watch it happen, but she might have to. God, she was going to be sick.

Levi's arms tightened slightly around her. "You want to explain what happened? You're supposed to be fucking him not beating the shit out of him."

"He figured it out," her sister admitted. "It didn't take him long either. Turns out I'm not good at being little miss sunshine. Bring her into the bedroom. This is a massive clusterfuck but maybe we can still get something out of it."

Josh looked at the tub and the water on the floor, his eyes going wide as his mind likely made all the correct connections.

She had to calm him down. They needed time because someone would figure out the op had gone wrong. She wasn't sure who that someone was since Ezra was dead, Riley and Declan were halfway to Mexico City, and Shane was likely getting some sleep before they left in the morning. But she had to hold out some hope because she couldn't watch Josh die. "It was just a little bath, babe. It's okay. I'm still here and kicking. Well, I'm going to kick this asshole's ass when I get my energy back. How did you know it wasn't me?"

"She doesn't glow the way you do," he replied even as Morales's men started to haul him back. "When she smiles I don't feel it in my soul. I knew she wasn't you very quickly, pet. All that shit I said earlier, god, I didn't mean a bit of it. I love you, Kayla. I won't give you up."

Ah, such sweet words, but there was a problem. They were probably going to die and soon. "Josh, I love you, too."

351

Levi stood up, his face going cold. If her weight bothered him, he didn't show it at all. "You're not playing the game as well as I thought you would. Of course, your sister didn't play it at all. Three hours? You managed to get through three whole hours of being Kayla? You fucked up, Kun." He followed her sister and Josh out into the large bedroom where someone had nicely laid out a tarp and two chairs. "You know she managed years as you. Years pretending to be you in a nest of spies and people who know how to size a woman up. You couldn't even fool some dumbass who gets by on his looks."

Oh, but they were wrong. Josh was smart, too. He could pick things up very quickly.

Morales stood near the large bay windows, his arms over his chest and a fierce frown on his face. If she remembered correctly they were on the third floor and those windows separated them from a big balcony that overlooked Morales's zoo. He'd pointed out to her that he liked to be able to look down into his tiger's pen and know he was the king of his own personal jungle.

Kun shot Levi a look that could freeze fire. "You might want to rethink your worship of my baby sister. She got lucky. I'm the one who's worked with you for years. I'm the one who's made you money and kept up your appearances as the Agency's golden boy. She's weak. I'm shocked you haven't gotten what we needed yet, but then I'm also not since you seem to think you can stroke her into telling you what we need."

"I'm not some animal who thinks the only way to win is to slit everyone's throat," Levi shot back. "You watch yourself. Just because I don't like to get my hands bloody doesn't mean I won't. You would be nothing without me."

Kay liked the violent vibe happening between her sister and Levi. That could definitely work in their favor. Hers and Josh's.

Was there any way to get out? She needed to get some strength back. Where was Shane? Was he sleeping, not knowing what was happening? Would he wake up in the morning and realize Ezra was dead and she and Josh captured? Or had her sister already put a bullet in him?

"I think I should take over baby sister's interrogation," her sister said. "Bring Hunt over here. I think fucking around with her boyfriend could yield some positive results. What do you say, sis? If I pull off a couple of Joshua's pretty fingers, do you think you would tell me what I need to know?"

The thought sent her into a near panic. She looked at Josh as they dragged him back, and his eyes were steady on her.

"Don't you give them a thing," he said. "I didn't like my fingers anyway. Anything they cut off, we'll just make that part of me bionic."

"Oh, but I think little sister would miss parts of you a whole lot," Kun crooned. "You're an amazing kisser, Josh. Do you like how he kisses, little sis? Do you like the way he uses that skilled tongue of his?"

"Is that how you knew, babe?" Kayla asked. "You knew because her kiss left you cold. You see, I'm the only one outside of his work that Josh has kissed in a long time. You'll have to do better, big sis. You can't pull mean-girl tricks on me. You can't make me feel bad about myself."

"We'll see how you feel when he starts bleeding," Kun promised.

Levi set her in a chair across from Josh. She noted that both chairs were well within the tarp. Yep, one of the first things Bishop had taught her was when there was tarp underfoot, that was a bad sign.

She needed to keep her sister talking. Every minute Kun's mouth was working, she wasn't hacking off parts of Joshua's body. And honestly, she wanted some answers. "Why the hell do you hate me? What did I do to you?"

"What did you do?" Her sister moved in front of her, locking eyes with her, and she could see what Josh had likely seen. Yes, her sister looked exactly like her, but there was a deadness to her eyes, a coldness that wouldn't be banished with a simple smile. "You took my life. It should have been me."

Was she serious? "Our mother chose you. She kept you."

"And she sent you to fucking paradise. Do you have any idea what my childhood was like?"

"I know you had a mother who loved you," Kay replied.

"Love?" Kun scoffed at the word. "She loved me enough to keep me like some fucking doll she needed to hold on to. She couldn't feed me. She couldn't clothe me in anything but rags. She finally found a man who would take us in and he beat the shit out of her and then me. I guess he prepped me for the spy life, eh, sis?"

Kayla shook her head, unwilling to take on that particular guilt. "That wasn't my fault. If I hadn't been born, it could have turned out the same way."

Her sister's eyes rolled. "But you were born. She told me she decided to keep me because it was fate. Her firstborn. She gave up the second. You were one too many and yet you were the one who got all the treats. Imagine my surprise when I realized you were still alive and happy and healthy. You were a smart girl. I got your testing scores. Near genius level, and you'd been a gymnastics prodigy until you wimped out."

Another time her fathers had saved her. "My dads pulled me out when they realized how unhealthy an obsession it was for me. I was starving myself. I listened to coaches who told me I was only worth the medals I could bring in. My dads taught me differently."

"You were a quitter," Kun said with a triumphant smirk.

"Oh, baby, is that how you do that thing with your thighs?" Josh asked. "I know it must have been rough as a child, but you are still so fucking limber it makes me crazy."

She knew what he was doing. He was using humor to tell her that he was here with her. Always here with her. This was what they did when it got bad. They found the humor because they knew it would be okay in the end. He accepted her weirdness and she eased him out of his natural broodiness, and if they managed to not get murdered they were going to be such an awesome team.

"I love you a lot, Joshua Hunt," she said.

"You're going to love his corpse in a minute, sister." Kun let Kayla get a good look at the gun in her hand.

"You want to explain how we're going to deal with the dead body of a Hollywood star?" Morales asked, biting off his words. "I only agreed to this because you said we wouldn't have to kill anyone but the girl, and no one would realize she was dead."

"What was I supposed to do?" Her sister paced. "He figured it out. He was going to tell the bodyguard and we'd have even more trouble. Because that fucking bodyguard killed a bunch of your guards and he took off in his car. He's gotta be calling the authorities."

"Shane Landon ran?" Levi asked, his eyes narrowing.

"Like a scared baby," Kun replied. "I'm not worried about the local authorities. We own them, but the minute he calls Taggart in we're all fucked. I don't know how much Landon knows. Also, where did you stash the Agency asshole? Levi's got to get his story in before Taggart does."

"My men are dealing with it," Morales explained. "No one will find Fain's body."

"Landon wouldn't run," Levi was saying. He stood in front of Josh. "He knows something, but leave Taggart to me. Ezra won't be a problem. He wasn't supposed to be down here. I might be able to pin a lot of this on him now that I think about it. Someone get me something I can tie this asshole down with. We need to know everything he knows and what he told Landon."

"You don't have to tie me down. I'm not going anywhere without her," Josh replied, his shoulders straight.

"You'll forgive me if I don't believe you," Levi shot back. One of the guards held out a set of handcuffs, but Levi ignored him. He pulled a nasty-looking knife out of his pocket. "Who was in that car?"

"Shane Landon and Ezra Fain," Josh replied, his voice as calm as if he was talking about the weather.

Levi's hand tangled in Josh's hair and pulled his head back, the knife straining at Josh's throat. "I want the truth."

Josh smiled fiercely, the skin of his throat taut and vulnerable. "As one of my favorite movies will tell you, you can't handle the truth."

Oh, god. She could already see a hint of blood. Panic threatened. She couldn't lose Josh. This was it. She had to get out of this game because she suddenly had way too much to lose. This was why Big Tag and Damon didn't do undercover anymore. Their lives, seemingly easy to trade before, were suddenly precious because of the years they could spend with the person they loved. The idea of having a family slammed into her brain. Josh, walking the beach with a small hand in his. Her dads spoiling their grandbabies rotten. Her friends coming out with their own children to visit. None of it would happen if they died here. Her normal calm was utterly blown by the need to protect their future.

"Please, Levi. Please don't kill him. I'll be a good girl. I'll do whatever you want. Let Josh go. You've got more than enough on him to keep him from talking. Hector's right. You can't explain Josh's death or disappearance. Well, Hector can't. The heat will come down on him hard. You wouldn't treat your partner that way."

She had to get Morales to see that killing Josh would be on him. Hurting Josh would be on him. Her sister and Levi would go back to the shadows, but everyone knew where Josh had been and if he wasn't seen again, the heat would come down squarely on Morales.

"There is nothing you have on me that will make me back down," Josh vowed. "You hurt her again and I'll tell everyone in the fucking world. Or I'll let my corpse do the talking."

Levi's face was set in ferocious lines as he held that knife against Josh's jugular. "You ready to die for her? Because don't think I won't do this. I already killed her friend right in front of her face."

"Ezra Fain was wearing a vest. Go check on those guards of yours," Josh replied. "They're the dead ones."

Morales looked at his men and nodded, sending two of them out.

Ezra was alive? Or was that Josh's play to get those men out of here so they would have a better chance. Josh wasn't bad at this. She managed to sit up a little straighter. He'd gotten two of them out of the way. They were down to Levi, her sister, Hector, and the men on the door.

She needed out of these damn bindings.

"Levi, please don't do this," she pleaded. "Let's go. If Josh is right, Shane won't call in the locals, he'll call in the feds, and more importantly, Ian Taggart will be down here with a group of men the likes of which you haven't dealt with, and they won't stop. Take me with you. Let Josh go. He won't talk because you'll hold me over his head."

"Are you trying to make this hard on me," Josh complained.

"I'm trying to get the knife off your throat," she shot back. And closer to her, so he might cut her free and she could walk out with him. "I would do anything to get that knife off your throat, baby."

He chuckled, the knife cutting into him slightly.

"I swear Levi, if you don't put that knife away I won't do a thing to help you," she promised.

The knife came away and Levi cursed. "We need to move out." He got to his knees and sure enough, he cut through the bindings on her feet before he stood up. He made no move to get her hands out. "I'll take Kayla with me. You take Hunt and we'll figure out what to do with them later. Go down to the safe house and I'll meet you there. Hector can handle law enforcement. He's got plenty of practice."

Hector didn't look happy with that prospect, but he nodded anyway. "I'll have my men make it look like Hunt left earlier."

"I'll drive and smile for the security cameras," Kun said. "Having my sister's face comes in handy sometimes. But I think we should all go together. We can dump baby sis in the trunk."

"No," Levi replied. "I'm taking her separately. We need to talk and you're upsetting her. She can be reasonable. I'm going to outline all the ways this makes money and sense for her."

Kun frowned her way. "Nice. You'll take baby sister with you and then you have the one prize that will satisfy Taggart."

"You shouldn't worry about Taggart, you crazy bitch," Josh said with a grin as he glanced toward the balcony. "He's not the one you should be worried about. There's a ghost coming for you. Do you remember what he told you all those years ago about betraying him? What did he promise you? He's here tonight and he will bring hell down on your head."

Her sister paled. "Bishop? Bishop's here. Oh, shit. Landon didn't kill all those guards. It was Bishop."

"Bishop is somewhere in Colorado," Levi said, his voice a bit shaky as if he'd just realized the boogeyman was here and looking for him.

John was here?

Josh glanced toward the balcony before looking back at her. "Kayla, he has a message for you. Remember Jakarta."

Jakarta. She'd been captured by a group of Indonesian extremists. MSS chose to leave her behind, but Bishop and Ten had come for her. They'd stormed the warehouse she'd been at, spraying the place with bullets after she was safely on the ground. Jakarta taught her to do one thing.

"Duck!"

She threw herself to the carpet as the glass from the balcony exploded and rained down in a hail of bullets. The world above her seemed to explode.

Josh threw his body over hers.

She looked up and watched as those bullets took out one of the guards, but she saw Levi on the floor, crawling toward the door that would lead him out of the big bedroom.

Then she couldn't see a damn thing because Josh was covering her head, keeping her down.

"He's getting away," she complained.

"Let him," Josh said, not moving an inch. "We'll take care of him later."

She had to tell him. If she let the chance to kill the man who'd hurt Josh get away, she would never forgive herself. "Josh, you have to let me up. I need to make sure Hector is dead."

He whispered in her ear. "Not on your life, and I know what he did to me. You're more important than revenge. You're more important than anything in the world to me."

"Roll us behind the bed and cut through the bindings on my hands. I need them free." She needed a gun, but she was completely helpless without her hands.

He didn't hesitate. He tightened his arms around her and then the world was spinning as he maneuvered them to the relative safety of the bed. She caught a glimpse of John Bishop coming through the ruined windows. He held a gun in both hands, and his eyes were grim as he pulled the triggers.

Josh immediately went to work on her hands, deftly untying the knots. "I played a ship captain once. I'll have you out of these in no time at all. Kay, there's a gun in my right sock. I think if one of us is going to be armed, it should be you. I'll follow you and I'll listen to orders, but don't think I'm going to leave you."

"I wish you would." But she knew it was futile. "Stay behind me. I have to see if I can find Levi or my sister. They're dangerous."

She crawled to the edge of the bed and watched as her sister tried to get a shot off at Bishop.

Kayla immediately took the shot, but Kun was on the move and it went wide. She saw her sister's eyes go round as she realized Kay was there on the ground.

Time to move. Kun raised her gun.

"To the left, Josh." She rolled as the bullet breezed by her head. Even rolling, she took another shot, trying to give them some cover.

She watched as one of Bishop's bullets took out the guard nearest to the hall. Her sister swiveled and took her own shot and then sprinted for the door. Bishop had taken cover and Kun was gone.

That couldn't happen. Levi she might be able to deal with. She might be able to convince the Agency to handle him, but Kun would be back. She'd seen it right there in her sister's eyes—pure hatred. If Jiang Kun got away, she and Josh would never be safe again. The blackmail would start up and they would always be looking over their shoulders.

Her sister. Time seemed to slow as she got to her feet and braced herself. Kun's gun was coming up, too, and it would be a matter of who was faster. An Old West gunfight, but in that moment she remembered how she'd felt to know that she had a sister, someone who shared her blood and DNA. All her life she'd been the weird one, the adopted kid who couldn't even pretend her parents were her real parents.

Except they were. Her dads loved her beyond blood and DNA. Beyond the simple circumstances of birth. They'd chosen her. Her mother had loved her enough to risk everything so she could live. And her sister…her sisters had nothing to do with blood. Her sisters were Ariel and Penny. Her brothers were Damon and Nick and Brody and the Lost Boys.

She pulled the trigger, letting go of that dream. That shot was true. She knew it the moment she took it, but her sister's mirrored her own. They would hit each other squarely in the chest. Identical heart shots.

Except Josh tackled her, shoving her out of the way. She watched as her sister's shirt bloomed with blood, her eyes going wide and startled.

Kayla hit the floor with a thud, Josh landing on top of her.

The room was suddenly silent, eerily quiet after the hail of bullets.

She took her first deep breath in hours. "Are you okay?"

"No, baby," he said, keeping his body over hers. "Don't hurt her, Hector."

She glanced up as much as she could and Hector was standing over them, his gun pointed their way.

What had happened? Where was John Bishop?

"What do I get if I don't hurt her, Joshua?" Hector's voice was silky-smooth evil. "You might not ask me for mercy if you knew some of the things I've done."

"I know exactly what you've done," Josh replied, his whole body covering hers as if he could magically form some cone of protection around her. "I know what you did to me. I know your group was behind it all. Think of what you could get for the tape of me now, Hector. Let her go and I'll do anything you want. You know how good I am at it, right? You remember."

"Josh," she said, her whole soul aching. He could barely talk about what happened to him as a child, much less give himself back to the monster who'd profited off all of it.

"Don't," Josh said quietly. "I realized I would go through it all again if it brought me here to you. All of it, Kay. I've been half a man, walking around like a ghost, but you are worth the pain. I love you and I'm going to get you out of this. I owe you everything."

Hector chuckled. "I might enjoy seeing how you handle one of my brothels. Tell me, Josh, do you miss the drugs? Do you miss the…"

Hector's head kind of exploded. Josh covered her again, shoving her down and tensing over her. He was ready to do it. He was ready to take a bullet for her. Probably many.

"I owe Kay, too," a familiar voice said. "Come on. Let's get you two up. Joshua, we're going to have to patch up your arm. Sorry, I got hit and fell back on the balcony. Luckily my vest held up better than Fain's. I have to thank Stef for that. I borrowed it from the Bliss County Sheriff, but Stef paid for it. Nothing but the best."

Bishop. She had no idea who he was talking about, but he was here and she was alive and Josh was alive. Josh got to his knees, helping her up. There was blood on his left arm and he winced when he moved it.

"He saved you from your sister," Bishop said quietly. "I saw it happen. It was incredible. You moved like mirror images. Those shots would have been perfect."

But she'd had a man who loved her enough to risk himself for her. Her sister's hate had been nothing compared to Joshua Hunt's love.

She cupped his precious face. That face had graced a thousand movie screens, but no one on the earth got to see him as open and vulnerable as he was now. No one but her. "I love you, Josh."

"Good, because I'm never letting you go," he said. "You get into trouble, pet. I think you need to stay with me."

She hugged him. Staying with him was right where she wanted to be.

Epilogue

Mexico City
Eighteen hours later

"What do you mean he got away?" Kayla stared at Big Tag. Even in the confines of Josh's massive, super-pimped-out million-plus trailer, Big Tag made everything look small. "How the hell did Levi Green manage to get out? We called the authorities. We called the Agency."

Big Tag had hustled down to Mexico. Even as he'd been shooting his way out of the compound, Shane had called and updated Ian. Ian had gotten on a plane as quickly as he could, showing up this morning with Tennessee Smith at his side.

They were all sitting in Josh's trailer. The shoot was going on outside, but Josh was taking the day off due to having a bullet cut out of his left bicep. He looked over at the former CIA agents. "How could the Agency let a rogue operative slip away like that? Are they looking for him?"

"They don't have to," Ten said, his mouth a tight frown. "They can walk into his office at Langley if they want to know where he is."

"Are you fucking kidding me?" Declan asked, a cup of coffee in his hand. "He just walked back into the office after shooting Fain?

They don't give a crap about him attempting to murder another agent?"

Declan and Riley had turned around and gotten back in time to get her and Josh out of Morales's compound before the police showed up.

But not John Bishop. He'd faded into the shadows and disappeared again before she'd even had a chance to tell him off the way she'd wanted to. Or given him a hug and a thank you for saving them all.

She moved closer to Josh, his arm immediately coming out and wrapping around her. He didn't hide his affection at all now. Something deep had broken inside Josh the night before, some seal that had kept much of his emotion buried. After they'd had his arm looked at, he'd wrapped himself around her and held her for the longest time, telling her all the things being in a room with Hector Morales brought back, all the horrors. Somehow in telling them, in letting it all loose, in holding her while she cried for the child he'd been, a new Josh had been born. A warm and loving man. A man who knew he was worthy of being loved, too.

But this afternoon he was going to get a lesson in how shitty life in the intelligence community could be sometimes. She cuddled close to him but looked up at Big Tag and Ten. "They're taking Levi's side, aren't they?"

She hated to think about what that meant for them all.

Big Tag nodded. "I don't have the whole story, but I've already got Case and Theo picking up Ezra from the hospital. I know he shouldn't be moved yet, but I can't risk leaving him in a hospital bed when they could come and arrest him at any moment. Luckily Faith was in town with Ten. She's going to oversee him all the way home and then we'll let him recover at a safe house."

It was good to have a doc on call. The Dallas team had Faith Smith and London had just gotten their own in Stephanie Carter.

She was going to miss her team, but her heart was always going to be in California. Or wherever Josh was.

"Arrest the dude who nearly got killed trying to save us?" Josh asked. "That's insane. I'll testify for him."

There was a knock on the trailer door.

"There won't be a trial for Fain," Ten said grimly. "The Agency is going to choose the story that best fits the narrative they want. The Jiang Kun mission will remain top secret, potentially scrubbed from the files. Fain will be attached to Morales. Levi Green will be the good guy, the one who tried to find out what happened to the agent there."

Josh held up his hand. "I know. Levi Green killed him. I do not get this. This is a poorly written script because the bad guy is getting away."

"Yeah, that's how it works sometimes," a quiet voice said as he stepped up the stairs and into the trailer. "That's one of the reasons I got out, though not the most important one."

Everyone stopped, all eyes on the newcomer. He looked so different. The Bishop she'd known had worn mostly black. His hair had been longer, his eyes flat much of the time. Every now and then she would coax a smile from him, but there had always been a darkness about John Bishop that she'd been sure nothing could banish.

The man in front of her wore a T-shirt that proudly stated that life was better in Bliss, Colorado. He had a touristy Cuban-style shirt over the *T* and khaki shorts that her dads might pick out and say were sporty. They weren't. Nor were the Birkenstocks on his feet or the Tilley hat covering his trimmed brown and gold hair.

He stood back as though afraid of his welcome.

Ian Taggart's face actually went soft. "Sir, it's a pleasure to see you again. Never thought I would."

"Ian." Bishop held a hand out.

"Hell," Big Tag said before pulling the smaller man in for a bear hug. "We thought you were dead, Henry."

When Bishop pulled back there was surprise in his eyes. "You called me Henry."

Big Tag looked deeply pleased with himself. "You're Henry Flanders now. That's what all this was about. You're Henry and you're Nell's husband, and that's the truth. That's why you did everything you did. You did it so you could be the kind of man your wife would be proud of. Why is everyone looking at me like that? I'm fucking sensitive, too. I can figure things out."

Ten rolled his eyes. "I told him all that on the plane ride here. Henry, it's nice to meet you, man. And thank you for letting my old friend Bishop come out to play this time. I think we would have lost a lot had you not."

"I had to come," Henry said, his eyes finding Kay's. "I owed it to you. Kayla, I did what I did…"

She gave him her middle finger. "You suck, Bishop."

His face flushed.

He really was a different person. A happy person. Josh could be that with the right love. Her love. She bounced up off the couch to her feet and crossed the space between them. "But this Henry guy seems awfully lovable. It's good to see you."

She threw her arms around her old mentor, forgiving him in that moment. He'd done his job and known when to take that off-ramp he talked about. He'd found his and now she had hers. Forgiveness wasn't hard when he'd been the one to save Joshua.

His arms wrapped around her. "You, too. Do you have any idea how proud I am of everything you did? Including saving these two numbskulls a couple of times. Just because I've been dead doesn't mean I haven't kept up with my people. Well, a friend of mine who's quite good at hacking a system got your mission files for me. I was happy to hear Ian got out when he did. I worried about him, especially after his wife died. I was thrilled to hear she's back. I'm not the only one to pull the old 'I'm dead' routine. Ten, though, I always knew would find a nice woman and settle down."

"Glad you knew," Ten shot back. "Someone might have mentioned that to me. I always thought I was a broody son of a bitch no one would ever love."

"I need more punches," Tag said. "When he says shit like that I need more punches."

Ten's eyes narrowed and he pointed at Tag. "Don't you dare. You used up your last punch."

Tag turned to Henry. "Did those reports tell you about the time that asshole stormed my building with a full Special Forces team? My building. I have a daycare there."

Ten shook his head. "Are you seriously tattling on me like a damn four-year-old?"

Henry's smile was brilliant as he put a hand on both the badass ex-operatives. "Boys, let's go grab a beer and you can tell me all about it. I was kind of hoping I could catch a ride back to the States. After all, we have more to talk about. I need you to fill me in on what's left of Hope McDonald's experiments. I think it's all about those boys."

"Yeah, we know about that." Ten looked back at the three bodyguards. "Come on, then. Let's leave the lovebirds. We've got a plane to catch in a few hours."

They would be going home, but she was staying here with Josh. They would need bodyguards, but she would find some who lived in the area and not in her house. She could handle his protection when they were alone.

But she would miss her boys.

Tag stayed for a moment while the men filed out. He stared at Josh. "You take care of her or you'll deal with two mad dads and me. Not sure which is worse."

Tears misted her eyes. "Thank you for everything, Ian. And don't think I'm gone. We got word this morning that the studio is looking for someone to play Tex Jones in the new Soldiers and Doms movie. I'm going to convince Josh. He would definitely have to do his research."

"No, he wouldn't if he's playing Ten. He just has to talk real slow and pretend he's got a brain in his head. Well, he shouldn't pretend too hard." Tag smiled. "Seriously, don't be a stranger. Either one of you. And if you see anything suspicious, call. You might not be on the payroll any longer, but you're both family now."

He strode out the door.

"Your family is scary," Josh said, standing up and closing the space between them. "I like them."

She went up on her toes, wrapping her arms around him. "I think they like you, too. And I know I love you."

He kissed her, a sweet brushing of his lips. "I love you, too. Does that mean you'll marry me? You know after I sufficiently wow you with a spectacular proposal?"

Her whole soul felt light and happy. "I think as long as the proposal is suitably extravagant, the answer will probably, absolutely be a yes. But you should know my dads are going to want a hell of a wedding."

"Jared is trying to train the dolphins even as we speak. I thought they would make excellent bridesmaids," he teased and then got sober. "Baby, I'm going to tell my story to the press. To everyone."

Her jaw nearly dropped. "You don't have to now. There's no more blackmail."

"But I do have to. I have to tell it for every kid who's in danger. I have to tell it for everyone who went through it. I have to tell it for Hannah. I have to tell it for me because I'm done being ashamed. I was a victim then and now I'm a survivor. If I can help one person, then all the flack I'll get will be worth it."

Now she was crying for another reason. Because she was proud of him. "You are the strongest man I know. And I'll be by your side the whole time. Anyone says shit and I'll assassinate him."

His smile took her breath away. "My own personal bodyguard."

"You better believe it."

She would protect him for the rest of their lives. Hey, a girl couldn't ask for more.

She kissed him again and looked forward to the rest of her own personal happily ever after.

* * * *

London, England
Two Weeks Later

Ezra Fain stood outside the door, looking straight up into the camera. It was the first time in weeks he'd wanted someone to see his face. After a second the door clicked open.

It was time.

It had been two weeks since he'd woken up in a hospital in Mexico City, barely hours out of surgery and knowing damn straight he wasn't going to lie in that room and recover like a normal person. Oh, no. He'd known from the grim look on Case and Theo's faces that his rest period was over.

Burned. Disavowed.

A decade of his life he'd given to the Agency and they had chosen Levi Green over him without even giving him a trial. It seemed that the powers that be at the Agency were more interested in what Green had promised them than in what was right or moral. It had been naïve of him to think it would be different.

His chest still ached where he'd pulled out the tube. Luckily, Faith Smith had been waiting on the plane with her husband, Tennessee. Faith had stabilized him again while Ten and Ian and Bishop talked about what to do now.

After a week recovering in Dallas, his chest had hurt for another reason. Mia had come to see him. She'd been sweet and kind and everything he would never have. She'd promised she would look into the story and try to clear his name. Of course, her massive husband had stood behind her, promising to keep her safe while she looked into the Agency.

It was better she'd picked Case Taggart. Ezra was cursed and he knew it.

Still, even a cursed man could do some good, and he was about to prove it.

If the Agency wanted a war, McKay-Taggart would give them one. And Ezra Fain would play his part. He had a new team now.

He strode into the lobby and past the pretty blonde who waved him through. He moved through The Garden, to the back of the club where he'd been told his new job awaited him.

There they were—six men who'd had their memories wiped, their whole worlds taken from them so Hope McDonald could prove she could. Now their bodies held secrets every intelligence agency in the world would kill to get hold of.

"I thought I was only taking five." He settled his duffel bag over one shoulder. Everything he owned in the world was in that bag, the rest left behind because like these men, life as he knew it before was gone.

Damon Knight stood amid what looked like his whole team. His wife, Penelope, was dabbing at her eyes, her small son on her hip as she moved around the men they'd come to affectionately call the Lost Boys.

But he'd thought Owen Shaw was staying here in London.

They'd made the call because Owen was different. He'd had his memory wiped, but he knew his real name, had all the documentation he needed to be safe. The Agency wasn't going to swoop in and take Owen. He had too many ties. Like Theo Taggart.

Unlike the rest of the men who didn't even know their real names.

Yet, Owen had a backpack on. "This is my family. You're not leaving me behind. If we're going to ground, I'm going, too. Robert can't leave me behind like he's leaving her."

More than one face frowned Robert's way. Robert was the oldest of them, well, in Lost Boys' years. He'd been around the longest. He'd been in the first group. Only he and Theo Taggart had survived that first round of experiments.

"It's better that she stay here," Robert said, his eyes staring straight ahead and not back at the gorgeous woman named Ariel Adisa.

Damon stepped in, his voice going low so only Ezra could hear him. "Ariel wanted to come along. Robert won't allow it. It had to be a unanimous thing or you would be dealing with disharmony where you need peace, brother."

"I take it the others wanted to bring the good doc along?" Ezra looked at her, her face strained and tight in a way she normally wasn't. Ariel was the group's psych expert.

She was also firmly in Levi Green's line of fire, according to Kayla. Well, and Levi himself.

Damon sighed. "Yes, they disagree with how to deal with the threat against her. Levi Green called her last week. Bold as brass, that one. He asked if she wouldn't mind forwarding the files on the lads. Of course she said she had no idea who he meant. He asked if they could discuss it over dinner, said he would be in London soon and would love to see her."

Bastard. "We can take her along, but it might be smarter to keep her here. Green is trying to provoke a response. Does Robert have a thing for her?"

"Robert is hopelessly, madly in love with her," Damon replied. "Not that he's done anything about it. They've kept it professional up to this point. He's panicked and not thinking straight. Give him some time. We might be shipping her out to you soon. In the meantime, she's left you profiles of all her boys, as she calls them. We'll keep her safe."

"Do that," Ezra replied. "I don't trust Green. He'll do anything to win."

Damon held a hand out. "Everything is set. The plane is waiting. Good luck to you all."

Ezra looked at his new team. "Men, I know it sucks to leave home, but we're going to make it through this. We keep our heads down and let the men and women of McKay-Taggart figure a way out of this for us. We'll go to ground, but not to hide. We'll do our best along the way to earn our keep, to use our talents for the betterment of those around us. Up until now very little has been asked of you, but that changes today. We're on our own in a few short hours. We're going into a war where you are the prize."

"Have you seen my abs?" That had to be Tucker. He pulled up his shirt and slapped his cut stomach. "I've been told they are a prize in and of themselves."

"Stop talking about yer abs, ye bastard," Owen said, his thick Scottish accent coming out. "You painted those things on."

"I did not," Tucker shot back.

"I could shoot you both and put us all out of misery," a Hungarian-accented voice said. "This would be good fun, no?"

They were bickering like siblings.

Damon slapped him on the back. "Good luck, brother."

Luck had nothing to do with it. There was a plan in place. An audacious plan that only McKay-Taggart could have come up with. It was time to hide in plain sight. "Let's go, boys. We've got to get to our new home. I think you're going to like it."

"Where are we going?" Jax asked. "Because I was thinking someplace tropical. Girls in bikinis."

Well, there would be naked people. "Colorado. We're going to spend some time with a friend."

Then they were off debating and fighting and arguing over where they should be going and who got the window seat.

Ezra took it all in. This was his army and they were going to war.

It was a war he intended to win.

The Lost Boys will return in the exciting spinoff to Masters and Mercenaries—Masters and Mercenaries: The Forgotten. Coming to all retailers August 2018.

Close Cover

A Masters and Mercenaries Crossover Event
By Lexi Blake
Now Available

Remy Guidry doesn't do relationships. He tried the marriage thing once, back in Louisiana, and learned the hard way that all he really needs in life is a cold beer, some good friends, and the occasional hookup. His job as a bodyguard with McKay-Taggart gives him purpose and lovely perks, like access to Sanctum. The last thing he needs in his life is a woman with stars in her eyes and babies in her future.

Lisa Daley's life is finally going in the right direction. She has finally graduated from college after years of putting herself through school. She's got a new job at an accounting firm and she's finished her Sanctum training. Finally on her own and having fun, her life seems pretty perfect. Except she's lonely and the one man she wants won't give her a second look.

There is one other little glitch. Apparently, her new firm is really a front for the mob and now they want her dead. Assassins can really ruin a fun girls' night out. Suddenly strapped to the very same six-foot-five-inch hunk of a bodyguard who makes her heart pound, Lisa can't decide if this situation is a blessing or a curse.

As the mob closes in, Remy takes his tempting new charge back to the safest place he knows—his home on the bayou. Surrounded by his past, he can't help wondering if Lisa is his future. To answer that question, he just has to keep her alive.

* * * *

"The Daleys are perfect examples of what a family can do when they band together, work hard, and help lift each other up. I'm the only failure."

Remy sat back as though considering how to handle her. "You have an MBA, Lisa. That's not a failure. The job market isn't great right now. That's not your fault."

Of course, he didn't know the whole story. "I got a job easily enough. Two weeks out of school and I was making seventy *K*. Then I blew the whistle on my employer. Apparently that gets around."

He frowned, the expression doing nothing to make him less gorgeous. "Blew the whistle?"

"I work in accounting. My boss runs the biggest valet service in DFW. Lots of cash," she began.

His eyes widened. "Cash? He was laundering money?"

Well, no one could accuse him of not understanding how the world worked. She hadn't even considered it. She'd walked into that job like fucking Snow White, with birds singing on her shoulders. Everything was happy and shiny in her eyes. "See, that's what Bridget said the minute I mentioned he offered valet services. She told me I had to be careful because cash intensive businesses are magnets for the mafia and drug dealers and…how did she put it…douche canoes with dirty money. Have you ever met a crazed, paranoid person who turns out to always be right? It's annoying. Something happens or we meet someone new, Bridget comes up with some crazed theory and we all laugh and bam, a month later the guy who sent Lila flowers for saving his life in the ER is taken away on a seventy-two-hour psych hold after trying to break into her house."

Remy shook his head. "Your sister had a stalker?"

Lisa sighed. "Yeah. And he seemed so nice."

"Maybe you should listen to Bridget more."

Bridget thought she should be in a safe house. The idea sent a shiver through her. "Anyway, I found the doctored books, went to the cops, and now my old boss got off on a technicality and I'm left without a job or any way to get a job because I have zero references and oddly enough, no one wants to hire the whistle-blower."

Remy had sat back up, his spine going straight and that hawkish look he got when he was hyper aware coming into his eyes. "Whoa, are you telling me the man you tried to send to jail is out and you were walking around this afternoon without any protection?"

Did everyone think she was an idiot? "Of course not. I have

373

pepper spray."

"Pepper spray isn't going to stop the damn mafia."

"Well, neither did the truth, so I don't see why they would come after me now." This wasn't the conversation she wanted to have with him. Of course she wasn't sure what she wanted from him.

Except sex. Except comfort. Except one night where she didn't sit up and worry about what was going to happen to her.

He was leaving soon. Not just leaving the apartment building. He was leaving town and he wouldn't be back. That actually made it way easier. Was she brave enough to ask him again? He'd said he was scared of her, but if she promised she wasn't looking for anything but a couple of hot nights from him, would that change his mind?

Or had it all been bullshit? Had he been attempting to be kinder to her than he'd been before?

"Lisa? Are you listening to me?"

Nope. "Yes, of course."

He stared at her like he knew she hadn't. "I was saying you need to take this seriously. You're in a dangerous position."

"Jimmy isn't violent. He's a jerk but he's not violent." Suddenly she wasn't so hungry. The whole day had been one long mistake. Did she need to cap it by making one more? "You know what? I'm really tried. I think I'm going to go to bed."

"So I hit on a touchy subject and you punish me by sending me away?"

"No, I'm tired and I had a shitty day and I want to go to bed."

"I want to go to bed, too."

The moment seemed to stop, his words right out there in the open, his eyes intent on her. There was heat in those eyes.

"Ask me again, Lisa. Give me another chance."

All the reasons she shouldn't fell away because damn it, she was an optimist and at some point in time her luck had to change. She didn't want to miss that because she was too scared to try. "Would you like to go to bed with me, Sir?"

"Tell me why you left the club."

Damn it. That wasn't an answer. "Because I gave up my car and I didn't want to admit it to my family because they're nosy as hell. Because I've been too depressed to play. Because I couldn't play with the man I wanted to play with."

His hand came out and he tugged her up, maneuvering her until she was sitting on his lap.

And what a comfy lap it was. She fit easily, her butt on his big thigh, his muscular arm around her waist making her feel dainty and feminine.

"I'm going home soon and I likely won't be back," he explained.

She nodded. "It's okay. I wasn't looking to get married. I'll be honest. When I asked you six months ago, I was looking for a Dom, but not now. Now I just want someone to help me get through the night."

"I don't want to hurt you, *ma crevette*," he whispered in her ear. His cheek rubbed lightly against hers, letting her feel that masculine scruff he always seemed to have. "But I have to go home and it's not a place you would be happy."

"I have a home, Remy." God, how had she gone from bone tired to every cell in her body awake and alive with anticipation. "I don't need some man to come in and save me. Well, except from how long the nights are lately. I could use a rescue from that. I'm not asking you to be my knight in shining armor. I'm just asking if you want to spend tonight with me."

"No."

She stiffened and started to get off his lap, but his arms were a cage around her.

"Hush," he admonished. "We're talking and we're negotiating. I'm not about to lie to you again. I will want more than one night with you. I won't be able to hop into your bed and hop back out again and pretend like it never happened. I've wanted you for far too long for that to happen. Can we make a deal? A contract?"

A contract with her dream Dom? It was likely one more bad idea in a long line of them, but she found herself nodding. Why would she say no? Her pride? Her pride hadn't gotten her anything good lately. Because she was worried about being hurt? She'd been numb for so long that being hurt seemed like a halfway decent trade-off for feeling anything at all. He was being upfront with her. "Yes."

His hands moved on her waist, brushing up toward her breasts. "God, chère, this is where I'm supposed to set you across from me and we talk about what we want and need out of this contract."

"I want an orgasm, Remy," she stated plainly. "Can we forego the negotiations tonight and agree that we're going to get into bed and not leave again until you've made me come a couple of times?"

"Oh, I like how you negotiate," he whispered.

Lexi Blake Crossover Collection
Now Available

Justify Me: A Stark International/Masters and Mercenaries Novella
by J. Kenner

McKay-Taggart operative Riley Blade has no intention of returning to Los Angeles after his brief stint as a consultant on mega-star Lyle Tarpin's latest action flick. Not even for Natasha Black, Tarpin's sexy personal assistant who'd gotten under his skin. Why would he, when Tasha made it absolutely clear that—attraction or not—she wasn't interested in a fling, much less a relationship.

But when Riley learns that someone is stalking her, he races to her side. Determined to not only protect her, but to convince her that—no matter what has hurt her in the past—he's not only going to fight for her, he's going to win her heart. Forever.

* * * *

His to Protect: A Bachelor Bad Boys/Masters and Mercenaries Novella
by Carly Phillips

Talia Shaw has spent her adult life working as a scientist for a big pharmaceutical company. She's focused on saving lives, not living life. When her lab is broken into and it's clear someone is after the top secret formula she's working on, she turns to the one man she can trust. The same irresistible man she turned away years earlier because she was too young and naive to believe a sexy guy like Shane Landon could want her.

Shane Landon's bodyguard work for McKay-Taggart is the one thing that brings him satisfaction in his life. Relationships come in second to the job. Always. Then little brainiac Talia Shaw shows up in his backyard, frightened and on the run, and his world is turned upside down. And not just because she's found him naked in his outdoor shower, either.

With Talia's life in danger, Shane has to get her out of town and to her eccentric, hermit mentor who has the final piece of the formula she's been working on, while keeping her safe from the men who are after her. Guarding Talia's body certainly isn't any hardship, but he never expects to fall hard and fast for his best friend's little sister and the only woman who's ever really gotten under his skin.

* * * *

Say You Won't Let Go: A Return to Me/Masters and Mercenaries Novella
by Corinne Michaels

I've had two goals my entire life:
1. Make it big in country music.
2. Get the hell out of Bell Buckle.
I was doing it. I was on my way, until Cooper Townsend landed backstage at my show in Dallas.
This gorgeous, rugged, man of few words was one cowboy I couldn't afford to let distract me. But with his slow smile and rough hands, I just couldn't keep away.
Now, there are outside forces conspiring against us. Maybe we should've known better? Maybe not. All I know is that I want to hold on, but I know the right thing to do is to let go...

* * * *

Rescuing Sadie: A Delta Force Heroes/Masters and Mercenaries Novella
by Susan Stoker

Sadie Jennings was used to being protected. As the niece of Sean Taggart, and the receptionist at McKay-Taggart Group, she was constantly surrounded by Alpha men more than capable, and willing, to lay down their life for her. But when she learns about a friend in trouble, she doesn't hesitate to leave town without a word to her uncle to help. After several harrowing weeks, her friend is now safe, but the repercussions of her rash act linger on.

Chase Jackson, no stranger to dangerous situations as a captain in the US Army, has volunteered himself as Sadie's bodyguard. He fell head over heels for the beautiful woman the first time he laid eyes on her. With a Delta Force team at his back, he reassures the Taggart's that Sadie will be safe. But when her past catches up with her, Chase has to use everything he's learned over his career to keep his promise...and to keep Sadie alive long enough to officially make her his.

* * * *

Her Guardian Angel: A Demonica Underworld/Masters and Mercenaries Novella
by Larissa Ione

After a difficult childhood and a turbulent stint in the military, Declan Burke finally got his act together. Now he's a battle-hardened professional bodyguard who takes his job at McKay-Taggart seriously and his playtime – and his playmates – just as seriously. One thing he never does, however, is mix business with pleasure. But when the mysterious, gorgeous Suzanne D'Angelo needs his protection from a stalker, his desire for her burns out of control, tempting him to break all the rules...even as he's drawn into a dark, dangerous world he didn't know existed.

Suzanne is an earthbound angel on her critical first mission: protecting Declan from an emerging supernatural threat at all costs. To keep him close, she hires him as her bodyguard. It doesn't take long for her to realize that she's in over her head, defenseless against this devastatingly sexy human who makes her crave his forbidden touch.

Together they'll have to draw on every ounce of their collective training to resist each other as the enemy closes in, but soon it becomes apparent that nothing could have prepared them for the menace to their lives...or their hearts.

Kayla recommends...

As you might have noticed, our Kay loves her romance books.
Here are a couple of her favorites...

Vampire's Faith

A Return to the Dark Protectors
By Rebecca Zanetti
Now Available

Vampire King Ronan Kayrs wasn't supposed to survive the savage sacrifice he willingly endured to rid the world of the ultimate evil. He wasn't supposed to emerge in this time and place, and he sure as hell wasn't supposed to finally touch the woman who's haunted his dreams for centuries. Yet here he is, in an era where vampires are hidden, the enemy has grown stronger, and his mate has no idea of the power she holds.

Dr. Faith Cooper is flummoxed by irrefutable proof that not only do vampires exist... they're hot blooded, able to walk in sunlight, and shockingly sexy. Faith has always depended on science, but the restlessness she feels around this predatory male defies reason. Especially when it grows into a hunger only he can satisfy—that is if they can survive the evil hunting them both.

* * * *

CHAPTER 1

Dr. Faith Cooper scanned through the medical chart on her tablet while keeping a brisk pace in her dark boots through the hospital hallway, trying to ignore the chill in the air. "The brain scan was normal. What about the respiratory pattern?" she asked, reading the next page.

"Normal. We can't find any neurological damage," Dr. Barclay said, matching his long-legged stride easily to hers. His brown hair was swept back from an angled face with intelligent blue eyes. "The patient is in a coma with no brain activity, but his body is... well..."

"Perfectly healthy," Faith said, scanning the nurse's notes, wondering if Barclay was single. "The lumbar puncture was normal, and there's no evidence of a stroke."

"No. The patient presents as healthy except for the coma. It's an anomaly," Barclay replied, his voice rising.

Interesting. "Any history of drugs?" Sometimes drugs could cause a coma.

"No," Barclay said. "No evidence that we've found."

Lights flickered along the corridor as she passed through the doorway to the intensive- care unit. "What's wrong with the lights?" Faith asked, her attention jerking from the medical notes.

"It's been happening on and off for the last two days. The maintenance department is working on it, as well as on the temperature fluctuations." Barclay swept his hand out. No ring. Might not be married. "This morning we moved all the other patients to the new ICU in the western addition that was completed last week."

That explained the vacant hall and nearly deserted nurses' station. Only one woman monitored the screens spread across the desk. She nodded as Faith and Dr. Barclay passed by, her gaze lingering on the cute man.

The cold was getting worse. It was early April, raining and a little chilly. Not freezing.

Faith shivered. "Why wasn't this patient moved with the others?"

"Your instructions were to leave him exactly in place until you arrived," Barclay said, his face so cleanly shaven he looked like a cologne model. "We'll relocate him after your examination."

Goose bumps rose on her arms. She breathed out, and her breath misted in the air. This was weird. It'd never happen in the hospital across town where she worked. Her hospital was on the other side of Denver, but her expertise with coma patients was often requested across the world. She glanced back down at the tablet. "Where's his Glasgow Coma Scale score?"

"He's at a three," Barclay said grimly.

A three? That was the worst score for a coma patient. Basically, no brain function.

Barclay stopped her. "Dr. Cooper. I just want to say thank you for coming right away." He smiled and twin dimples appeared. The nurses probably loved this guy. "I heard about the little girl in Seattle. You haven't slept in—what? Thirty hours?"

It felt like it. She'd put on a clean shirt, but it was already wrinkled beneath her white lab coat. Faith patted his arm, finding very nice muscle tone. When was the last time she'd been on a date? "I'm fine. The important part is that the girl woke up." It had taken Faith seven hours of doing what she shouldn't be able to do: Communicate somehow with coma patients. This one she'd been able to save, and now a six-year-old girl was eating ice cream with her family in the hospital. Soon she'd go home. "Thank you for calling me."

He nodded, and she noticed his chin had a small divot—Cary Grant style. "Of course. You're legendary. Some say you're magic."

Faith forced a laugh. "Magic. That's funny." Straightening her shoulders, she walked into the ICU and stopped moving, forgetting all about the chart and the doctor's dimples. "What in the world?" she murmured.

Only one standard bed remained in the sprawling room. A massive man overwhelmed it, his shoulders too wide to fit on the mattress. He was at least six-foot-six, his bare feet hanging off the end of the bed. The blankets had been pushed to his waist to make room for the myriad of electrodes set across his broad and muscular chest. Very muscular. "Why is his gown open?"

"It shouldn't be," Barclay said, looking around. "I'll ask the nurse after you do a quick examination. I don't mind admitting that I'm stymied here."

A man who could ask for help. Yep. Barclay was checking all the boxes. "Is this the correct patient?" Faith studied his healthy coloring and phenomenal physique. "There's no way this man has been in a coma for longer than a couple of days."

Barclay came to a halt, his gaze narrowing. He slid a shaking hand through his thick hair. "I understand, but according to the fire marshal, this patient was buried under piles of rocks and cement from the tunnel cave-in below the Third Street bridge that happened nearly seven years ago."

Faith moved closer to the patient, noting the thick dark hair that swept back from a chiseled face. A warrior's face. She blinked. Where the hell had that thought come from? "That's impossible." She straightened. "Anybody caught in that collapse would've died instantly, or shortly thereafter. He's not even bruised."

"What if he was frozen?" Barclay asked, balancing on sneakers.

Faith checked over the still-healthy tone of the patient's skin. "Not a chance." She reached for his wrist to check his pulse.

Electricity zipped up her arm and she coughed. What the heck was *that*? His skin was warm and supple, the strength beneath it obvious. She turned her wrist so her watch face was visible and then started counting. Curiosity swept her as she counted the beats. "When was he brought in?" She'd been called just three hours ago to consult on the case and hadn't had a chance to review the complete file.

"A week ago," Barclay said, relaxing by the door.

Amusement hit Faith full force. Thank goodness. For a moment, with the flickering lights, freezing air, and static electricity, she'd almost traveled to an imaginary and fanciful place. She smiled and released the man's wrist. "All right. Somebody is messing with me." She'd just been named the head of neurology at Northwest Boulder Hospital. Her colleagues must have gone to a lot of trouble—tons, really—to pull this prank. "Did Simons put you up to this?"

Barclay blinked, truly looking bewildered. He was cute. Very much so. Just the type who'd appeal to Faith's best friend, Louise. And he had an excellent reputation. Was this Louise's new beau? "Honestly, Dr. Cooper. This is no joke." He motioned toward the monitor screen that displayed the patient's heart rate, breathing, blood pressure, and intracranial pressure.

It had to be. Faith looked closer at the bandage covering the guy's head and the ICP monitor that was probably just taped beneath the bandage. "I always pay back jokes, Dr. Barclay." It was fair to give warning.

Barclay shook his head. "No joke. After a week of tests, we should see something here that explains his condition, but we have nothing. If he was injured somehow in the caved-in area, there'd be evidence of such. But... nothing." Barclay sighed. "That's why we requested your help."

None of this made any sense. The only logical conclusion was that this was a joke. She leaned over the patient to check the head bandage and look under it.

The screen blipped.

She paused.

Barclay gasped and moved a little closer to her. "What was that?"

Man, this was quite the ruse. She was so going to repay Simons for this. Dr. Louise Simons was always finding the perfect jokes, and it was time for some payback. Playing along, Faith leaned over the patient again.

BLEEP

This close, her fingers tingled with the need to touch the hard angles of this guy's face. Was he some sort of model? Bodybuilder? His muscles were sleek and smooth—natural like a wild animal's. So probably not a bodybuilder. There was something just so male about him that he made Barclay fade into the *meh* zone. Her friends had chosen well. This guy was sexy on a sexy stick of pure melted sexiness. "I'm going to kill Simons," she murmured, not sure if she meant it. As jokes went, this was impressive. This guy wasn't a patient and he wasn't in a coma. So, she indulged herself and smoothed his hair back from his wide forehead.

BLEEP
BLEEP
BLEEP

His skin was warm, although the room was freezing. "This is amazing," she whispered, truly touched. The planning that had to have gone into it. "How long did this take to set up?"

Barclay coughed, no longer appearing quite so perfect or masculine compared to the patient. "Stroke him again."

Well, all righty then. Who wouldn't want to caress a guy like this? Going with the prank, Faith flattened her hand in the middle of the guy's thorax, feeling a very strong heartbeat. "You can stop acting now," she murmured, leaning toward his face. "You've done a terrific job." Would it be totally inappropriate to ask him out for a drink after he stopped pretending to be unconscious? He wasn't really a patient, and man, he was something. Sinewed strength and incredibly long lines. "How about we get you out of here?" Her mouth was just over his.

His eyelids flipped open.

Barclay yelped and windmilled back, hitting an orange guest chair and landing on his butt on the floor.

The patient grabbed Faith's arm in an iron-strong grip. "Faith."

She blinked and then warmth slid through her. "Yeah. That's

me." Man, he was hot. All right. The coming out of a coma and saying her name was kind of cool. But it was time to get to the truth. "Who are you?"

He shook his head. *"Gde, chert voz'mi, ya?"*

She blinked. Wow.

Rough Ride

A Chaos Novella
By Kristen Ashley
Now Available

Rosalie Holloway put it all on the line for the Chaos Motorcycle Club.

Informing to Chaos on their rival club—her man's club, Bounty—Rosalie knows the stakes. And she pays them when her man, who she was hoping to scare straight, finds out she's betrayed him and he delivers her to his brothers to mete out their form of justice.

But really, Rosie has long been denying that, as she drifted away from her Bounty, she's been falling in love with Everett "Snapper" Kavanagh, a Chaos brother. Snap is the biker-boy-next door with the snowy blue eyes, quiet confidence and sweet disposition who was supposed to keep her safe…and fell down on that job.

For Snapper, it's always been Rosalie, from the first time he saw her at the Chaos Compound. He's just been waiting for a clear shot. But he didn't want to get it after his Rosie was left bleeding, beat down and broken by Bounty on a cement warehouse floor.

With Rosalie a casualty of an ongoing war, Snapper has to guide her to trust him, take a shot with him, build a them…

And fold his woman firmly in the family that is Chaos.

* * * *

He spit on me.

I felt it land on the side of my chin and slide down.

I didn't move to wipe it away.

I couldn't.

Lying on my side, curled into a ball, the pain screamed through me. All of it—and there was a lot of it—demanding attention, I couldn't concentrate, couldn't think, couldn't move in case it got worse. I couldn't do anything but lie there and pray that it was over.

It wasn't.

He bent over me, grabbed my hair, yanked it back, and I felt his hot breath hit my face.

"See if he wants you now, you stupid bitch," he hissed.

He let my hair go and I felt him retreat, but he still wasn't done.

He kicked me so hard with his foot in its heavy motorcycle boot, my body slid across the cement.

I was too far gone even to grunt.

I felt something bounce off my hip, clatter to the floor, and then his voice came back, this time from further away.

"There you go, baby," he drawled. "Your line to Chaos. We're done with you. *I'm* done with you. Now they can have you."

I heard boots on cement, more than just his, his Bounty brothers in the club. I sustained a couple more kicks as they passed. One of them grabbed the underside of my jaw and shoved my head back into the cement, also spitting, his hitting my neck.

And then they were gone.

I lay there, my focus on breathing and continuing to do it even though each breath was not only an effort but an agony. The fear I'd felt early when he took me, how he'd taken me, the way he'd handled me and I knew he'd figured it out, had dissipated as pain took its place. Now, the fear was returning that they'd come back and dish out more.

He'd come back.

Throttle.

No, to me he was Beck. My boyfriend. Gerard Beck. He hated the first name Gerard so everyone called him Beck. All his life. Or since he could demand that happen and not allow anything but that. Even his mother called him Beck.

Until he got his club name, Throttle. All his brothers called him that. When I was with him when he was with his brothers, I also called him that.

But when we were alone, at home, he was Beck.

My Beck.

My man. My lover. My protector. My future.

The man who'd just spit on me and kicked me.

But he'd done more before that.

He'd grabbed me from work and delivered me right to them, right to where I was right then. Even starting it, choking me until I thought I'd blank out, then clocking me in the temple, then on the jaw, then on my cheekbone.

Throttle.

That name was given to him for a reason but not the reason he'd now become Throttle to me.

I shut my eyes tight, opened them, reached to the phone he'd tossed at me and endured the immense pain that scoured through me, leaving me feeling even more raw, which if my brain had room to process anything further, I would have thought unimaginable.

My fingers closed around the phone and I huffed out little breaths, which were hard to take since each one sent fire through my midsection. So I tried deep breaths, and those were worse because the fire lasted even longer.

Dread intermingled with all the rest as I tried to focus on moving my thumb to open the phone, but I saw the black creeping in at the sides of my eyes.

I couldn't pass out.

I had to call for help.

I had to get out of there.

My body had different ideas, sending the message to my brain that this was too much, it couldn't take more.

So I passed out.

* * * * *

I came to woozy and disoriented.

The pain, the stench of the room, the feel of the cement beneath me brought it all slamming back, along with the panic.

389

Having no idea how long I was out, feeling the phone resting in my hand, I actually grunted with the effort of sliding it up, wrapping my fingers around it, using my thumb to flip it open.

An old-style flip phone.

A burner.

We'd joked about it, Snap and me. He'd called me Scully. He had a burner too, so there'd be no caller ID when he phoned me. So I'd called him Mulder.

I was going to call him.

Not because I was working for Chaos anymore. I wasn't. That officially ended on that cement. Definitely not because I was protecting Bounty. I'd tell the police. Absolutely, I'd tell the police my boyfriend's motorcycle club beat the snot out of me. It didn't matter that I broke the code, and knew it. It didn't matter that I'd betrayed my man, and done it deliberately.

I was trying to save him. Save his brothers. Save his club. Save everyone.

I closed my eyes tight, my thumb moving over the phone from memory, knowing the way on its own, I called him so often. That was why I was calling him now rather than 911. I knew how to get to him. To Snapper. And the effort would be less. I could dial the digits to get him up on speed dial in my sleep, so I could do it lying on a cement floor, beat to hell and practically unable to move.

I couldn't lift the phone to my ear so I just shoved it across the floor closer to my face, listening to it ring.

"Rosie?" Snap answered.

I closed my eyes tighter as understanding hit me with a blow almost as brutal as every strike I'd just taken.

God.

I hadn't done it to save Beck. To save his brothers, his club…everybody.

At first, I'd done it to make Beck into Shy.

And then I'd done it to make him be Snapper.

And last, I'd done it to make his club Chaos.

"Rosie?" Snap's Eddie Vedder baritone got sharper.

Oh no.

No.

The black was creeping in again.
"Sss…" was all I could get out.
"Rosalie," he bit out, curt, alert, *alarmed.*
"Hurt," I whispered.
And then, again, I blacked out.

Justice for Milena
Badge of Honor, Texas Heroes Book 10
By Susan Stoker
Now Available

It's been years since Milena Reinhardt has seen TJ "Rock" Rockwell. The last time, he was nearly a shell of a man…but he was her man…and he tore her heart out of her chest. Circumstances unbeknownst to TJ have ensured Milena's never fully recovered.

TJ left his sniper days behind—for the most part—when he left the Army and become a respected Texas Highway Patrolman. He also left behind Milena. He's convinced it was the right thing to do at the time, but that doesn't mean he's ever forgotten the woman who loved him in his greatest time of need…or has stopped thinking of her since.

Neither thought they'd see each other again, until a pedophile's operation is taken down and the evil man sets his vengeful sights on Milena. This could be their second chance, even though TJ and Milena have enough secrets and trust issues to end any relationship before it starts. But when the bad guy closes in, they'll have to set aside their fears and trust in each other, to save the one thing that means the world to them both.

** Justice for Milena is the 10th book in the Badge of Honor: Texas Heroes Series. Each book is a stand-alone, with no cliffhanger endings.

* * * *

Sadie sat cross-legged on Milena's bed later that night. The room was lit only by a lamp on the bedside table.

"He flat-out said he loves you?" Sadie asked, her eyebrows drawn down in disbelief.

"Yeah. Just threw it out there like I was supposed to fall at his feet or something," Milena said caustically. She knew she was being unfair, but she felt off kilter.

The years had been good to him. When they'd been together three years ago, he was still healing from the wounds he'd gotten overseas. But since then, he'd healed completely and had filled out. His arms were thick and muscular, and she had a feeling if she ever saw him without a shirt, she'd see that he was even more chiseled than he'd been in the past. His brown hair was shorter than when they'd been together before, and he seemed to have a perpetual five o'clock shadow now, which was sexy as all get out.

But it wasn't just his looks that were slightly different. He seemed even more intense than he'd been back then…if that was possible. His brown eyes were penetrating. Whereas before, he frequently looked away from her when he was talking, as if he felt guilty about something, now he had no problem holding eye contact. All that attention on her made Milena feel as if whatever she was saying was the most important thing he'd ever heard. It was a little discomfiting, but also made her feel all squishy inside.

"And did you?" Sadie asked.

"Did I what?" Milena repeated, not sure what they were talking about as she'd gotten lost in memories of TJ.

"Fall at his feet?"

"Of course not!" Milena said quickly—maybe a bit *too* quickly.

"But you want to." It wasn't a question.

"No, I don't." The look of skepticism was easy to read on Sadie's face. "Look, he's just here because he feels guilty or something. And he might be assigned to look after me until Jeremiah and Jonathan are found."

Sadie shook her head. "I'm sure he does feel some guilt, and he should. He was a dick. But, Milena, he doesn't have to protect you. The Feds can assign someone else to you. There are thousands of law enforcement officers in this city. Any one of them can protect you."

Milena blocked out the common sense her friend was using. "He's arrogant to the nth degree. He strode into the house and practically told me I was his…like a caveman or something. He thinks that throwing money at me and putting me on his insurance will fix everything."

Sadie shifted until she was lying on her side and her head was propped up by a hand. She was about as different from Milena as she could get. Her dark auburn hair fell messily around her shoulders and her green eyes were piercing in their intensity. She was almost five inches taller than Milena, and slender in a way Milena would never be.

"Let me tell you something about dominant men...once they decide they want something, they're gonna get it one way or another."

Milena shook her head. "That's not how things work."

"It is," Sadie insisted. "Let me guess, he told you he left for your own good, right?"

"Yeah, pretty much."

"Men like TJ have crazy high standards for themselves. It's ridiculous, really. They think they have to be perfect. I'm guessing he was really good at what he did in the Army..." Sadie's voice trailed off, as if she was asking a question without coming out and actually voicing it.

Milena nodded. "Yeah, I got that impression. He was a sniper."

"Oh Christ," Sadie murmured, and turned to flop onto her back. "Yeah, so he was probably *very* good at his job. He got hurt and was sent home...to him, I'm sure that felt like a massive failure. He was frustrated he wasn't over there still fighting, and then he was chaptered out of the service altogether. When he had healed enough, he lived with you, right?"

"He didn't have anywhere else to go," Milena told her friend defensively.

"Don't you get it?" Sadie asked. "There he was, still healing, no home, no job, he probably felt like he'd let his friends and country down. He was lost. I'm frankly surprised he stayed as long as he did."

Milena couldn't help but flinch. That hurt.

"Oh sweetie," Sadie said, and leaned over and put her hand on Milena's knee. "I didn't mean that in a bad way. What I meant was that he *had* to have loved you to have stayed for as long as he did. He left because he didn't feel like he was man enough for you. He was trying to be noble. Men like him don't like to feel vulnerable. At all."

"I didn't judge him, Sadie. Not for one second. I would've been there by his side as he worked through whatever he had to, but he didn't give me the chance."

Sadie turned back over and stared at the ceiling once more. "You have to be sneaky with men like him," she informed her friend. "They need your support, but you have to do it in such a way that they don't really realize what you're doing. He's got a group of close friends, right?"

"I have no idea."

"He does," Sadie said with conviction. "His tribe. And I'll bet those friends have women of their own. You need to get to know them. Get close to them. They'll be your source of support when it comes to your man because TJ isn't going to come home and tell you when he's had a bad day. You'll be able to sense it, but he won't tell you why. And that's okay, but you can talk to the other women to help yourself deal with how he is. You can set up guys' nights out. Let him blow off some steam. Cook him dinner. Initiate sex. Let him take you how he wants and needs. *That's* how you help a man like TJ."

"How do you know all this? You're single!"

Sadie smiled up at the ceiling. "I'm a good observer. My aunt married a man just like TJ. Well, maybe not *just* like him, but close enough. You know I was the administrative assistant for McKay-Taggart. Everyone who works there is just like your man. Alpha, obsessive, insanely jealous, and when they fall for someone, they fall *hard*. And it might look like the men are in charge, but ultimately, it's the women who hold most of the power. I've seen my uncle leave in the middle of an important meeting because my aunt called and needed something. He's big, and sometimes scary, but my aunt and his kids mean the world to him."

Milena sighed. She wanted to believe her friend, but it was so hard. "He let me down, Sadie. Big time. I don't know that I'll ever be able to trust him again."

"You will," Sadie said with conviction.

About Lexi Blake

Lexi Blake lives in North Texas with her husband, three kids, and the laziest rescue dog in the world. She began writing at a young age, concentrating on plays and journalism. It wasn't until she started writing romance that she found success. She likes to find humor in the strangest places. Lexi believes in happy endings no matter how odd the couple, threesome or foursome may seem. She also writes contemporary Western ménage as Sophie Oak.

Connect with Lexi online:

Facebook: Lexi Blake
Twitter: authorlexiblake
Website: www.LexiBlake.net

CPSIA information can be obtained
at www.ICGtesting.com
Printed in the USA
LVHW101134211222
735680LV00001B/48